Gems from World Literature

Gems from World Literature

The Greatest German Classics

Edited by

J.A. Hammerton

CREST PUBLISHING HOUSE
G-2, 16 Ansari Road,
Darya Ganj, New Delhi-110 002

Published by Crest Publishing House
G-2, 16 Ansari Road
Darya Ganj, New Delhi - 110 002

The Greatest German Classics
ISBN 81-242-0488-8

First Crest Impression : 2004

Printed by Saurabh Printers Pvt Ltd
A-16, Sector IV, NOIDA 201 301

Editorial Board

Editorial Note

A SHORT story may be a mere anecdote of three hundred words or a work of ten or fifteen thousand. In content it may be anything from a glimpse of character, an incident, to a highly finished picture of life. But it should be a complete work of imagination, its effect achieved with a minimum of personages and events.

To select the best thousand examples was a task that could be achieved only on arbitrary lines. As to length, three thousand words was the ideal average, but this excluded some of the finest stories, so exceptions had to be allowed. National characteristics also had consideration. Another test was the value of a story as illustrating the development of the art.

PROBLEMS of arrangement were not entirely solved by classification according to the country of each writer's origin. This puts Richard Steele into the Irish volume and separates those ideal literary partners Agnes and Egerton Castle. But it is the best possible arrangement for the work, and the index makes reference easy. The inclusion of a series of stories of the War became possible when the War itself ruled out all modern German work.

A WORD as to the method of selection. The general editor prepared a trial list of titles, which was submitted to all the members of the Editorial Board, who rejected and added according to their individual tastes and knowledge, These individual lists were then collated and the final list evolved. The thousand stories selected are therefore representative of the combined opinion of the whole group of editors. A very few modifications of the final list were made necessary by difficulties of copyright and considerations of Anglo-Saxon taste in certain translations from foreign literatures.

MOST of the foreign stories have been specially translated, and all copyrights, in both stories and translations, the use of which authors and publishers have courteously permitted, are duly credited at the end of each volume.

J.A. HAMMERTON

Contents

CONTENTS

Old German Story-Tellers

WITH two short stories by Augustus Friedrich Langbein (1757–1835) this volume of the older German story-tellers appropriately begins. Appropriately, because in the first, "The Irreconcileable Man," the note of horror is tragically sounded, with full accompaniment of sentiment, and in the second, "The Lady's Palfrey," a whimsical light-heartedness predominates. And in the main it will be seen that the tragical-sentimental and the fanciful-grotesque are the prevailing notes in the short story of old Germany. Langbein himself, a Saxon, is remembered rather as a writer of light verse than as a prose writer, and his easy touch and pronounced attachment to witty and frivolous themes produced considerable entertainment for the reader. "The Lady's Palfrey" is a characteristic specimen of Langbein's talent, and with the triumphant absurdity of its climax displays his gifts to ready advantage. "The Irreconcileable Man" has none of its author's best-known qualities. It is the tragedy of temperament, the temperament of hate, told briefly, and only at the very end is the gloom lightened by an outburst of sentiment that promises in death the reconciliation denied in life.

Langbein

JOHANN FRIEDRICH VON SCHILLER (1759–1805) is of the world's immortals, and with Goethe is the crowned of all German imaginative writers for all time. But the varied and high genius of neither Goethe nor Schiller is directed to the short story, and only in "The Sport of Destiny" can the latter be represented in this volume. Humour must not be expected in Schiller, great as his genius is seen. Possibly those six years of youth in the Duke of Würtemberg's school at Stuttgart, where the system of education was so efficiently maintained on the principles of the parade-ground, and the stiff formality of military drill governed the methods of the teacher and the conduct of the pupil, choked that fine sense of the incongruous in life we call humour. Perhaps from the first Schiller, with his natural reserve, his solitary habits, his calm detachment from the life around him, his want of human passion, his indifference to social affection, was disinclined from the cultivation of humour. Of a truth it is clear the author of "Wallenstein" and "William Tell,"

Schiller

of " The Robbers " and " The Song of the Bell," had no mind for any mere play of exaggerated fancy on common elemental things, no relish for violent jokes, no taste for the unexpected eruptive sallies that set people laughing. " The Sport of Destiny " is a masterpiece in its way; a character study wrought with rare simplicity of style, a story of ambition and its fall, on the old text of the fickleness of princes' favours. Only when the end is reached and the tale finished does the reader wake up to the fact that the author allows no place for love-making or marriage in " The Sport of Destiny."

Jean Paul and others

TO pass from Schiller to Jean Paul Friedrich Richter (1763–1825) is to leave a well-ordered, stately garden for the gloriously flowering meadow of the pageant of summer. Jean Paul, for so he signed his earlier work, teems with a humour irrepressible. He is a romanticist to whom form is nothing. The whimsical and the profound jostle and crowd his pages, and his riotous conceptions are often seen to bring forth much sound philosophy. With Jean Paul boisterous absurdity will serve as well as any other vehicle for the expression of some fine original thought, and the farcical disguise a parable for those who can discern. Thus Richter's " Van der Kabel's Last Will and Testament " must be read. It is wildly extravagant satire; by no means to be counted as nonsense because the author refuses to prefer the method of solemnity for dealing with human foibles, and chooses rather to poke fun at his neighbours in his own vastly more entertaining way.

Three writers who lacked the genius of Jean Paul, but yet were justly accounted meritorious in their day, follow Richter. M. E. Engel (1764–1836), whose observant art, displayed in " Toby Wilt " and " Lady Elizabeth Hill," is concerned whimsically with the manners of provincial life in Swabia; J. F. Kind (1768–1843), who in " The Beggar's Marriage Gift " allows the moralist to hold the stage, and gives full play to the sentimental vein of the German story-teller; and August Gottlob Eberhardt (1769–1845), whose tale of " The Bet " is an admirable specimen of humour flavoured with sentiment. The two bishops, kindly in their cups, and yet for all their good-nature keenly alive to the main chance and the prospect of winning the bet, are excellent, while Conrad's problem and its solution happily provide sufficient sentiment.

Zschokke

FROM all the prolific literary output of J. Heinrich D. Zschokke (1771–1848) it is not easy to choose the best short stories, but the two here given, " The Broken Cup " and " How the Vicar Came Round," have, we think, been well and wisely selected. Time has proved the enduring qualities of these capital stories. Their vivacity, imagination, and playful humour are abundant, and they are thoroughly typical of their author's style. Zschokke, who early migrated from Magdeburg, his native city, to reside in Switzerland, achieved an even greater popularity with his devotional poetry (" Stunden der Andacht ") than he did with his famous " Bilder aus der Schwiez," or with that widely-read book, "Das Goldmacherdorf." But it is as a writer of fiction, and of fiction modelled admittedly on the Waverley Novels, Zschokke is remembered to-day, and by the short stories here included we may judge his excellence.

In "The Unlucky Miser," by Caspar Friedrich Gottschalck (c. 1772), a writer whom fame has long forsaken, and in "The Elves," by Ludwig Tieck (1773–1853), foremost leader of the German romantic school, we have reached a change of form in the short story, and are face to face with the popular legend and folk-tale as the basis of the writer's art. "The Unlucky Miser" combines simplicity with the moral purpose so commonly found in popular legends, while "The Elves" (Carlyle's translation is the version here given), with its charm, its delicacy, and its pathos, gives us Ludwig Tieck at his best in the short story. Tieck, who never makes an excessive use of the supernatural in his romantic tales, manages in "The Elves" to invest with human feeling the Little People who belong not to this our world, but to the realms of fancy.

Gottschalck and Tieck

IT is into the realm of the uncanny, however, that we are led by E. T. W. Hoffmann (1776–1822). This celebrated writer sat for many years as a judge of the Criminal Court in Berlin, and his stories are a peculiar blend of the ghostly, the chimerical, and the gruesome. Edgar Allan Poe, who was certainly influenced by Hoffmann, surpasses him at times in the creation of an atmosphere of horror; but Hoffmann's genius, on the other hand, can, with a touch of realism, a humorous illustration, a homely phrase, bring a wonderful vitality to the uncanny figures in his tales, and carry conviction to the reader that in spite of horrors the story may be true. Hoffmann's "The Cremona Violin" is at once wildly fantastic and horribly tragic. It brings out its author's wide musical knowledge, and is not devoid of a certain grim humour. The amazing triumph of the story is the effect of fidelity to life; an effect maintained throughout all the queer happenings, and in spite of stark tragedy surpassing the common woe of mortals.

Hoffmann

"THE Field of Terror," by De la Motte Fouqué (1777–1843), is a fine example of the work of the author of "Undine." Fouqué relies on the supernatural, here as elsewhere, but he had the gift of endowing miraculous incidents with a peculiarly innocent charm, and of blending the natural and supernatural in a degree greater and more convincing than many of his German contemporaries. He outlived the reputation won by "Undine" by some twenty years, and in addition to that classic tale, "The Field of Terror" and a few other stories alone remain to testify to his genius.

De la Motte Fouqué

ALL the world knows "Grimm's Fairy Tales" (published 1812), that marvellous collection of folk-tales, gathered with patient industry from countless sources. Here we include five gems from the treasury of the Brothers Grimm (Jakob, 1785–1863; Wilhelm, 1786–

1859): "Tom Thumb," "The Turnip," "The Twelve Dancing Princesses," "Pee-Wit," and "The Golden Goose." If in childhood we sought and found our pleasure in these tales, it is certain that age will also enjoy their rediscovery. For "Time cannot wither, nor custom stale the infinite variety" of "Grimm's Fairy Tales." The simplicity of style, the ingenious discomfitures of folly (as in "The Turnip"), the victory of wit and cunning over a thousand foes (as in "Tom Thumb" and "Pee-Wit"), render such tales as are here selected a joy for ever. These are not moral tales—certainly "Pee-Wit" is not—for their origins predate the Christian morality. Only in "The Golden Goose" is mere kindness of heart rewarded by a happy marriage with a king's daughter. "Pee-Wit" may be studied as an early contribution to the doctrine of superman. By sheer brain power Pee-Wit brings ruin and death to all who stand in his way, and with a lying wit not only escapes the violent death allotted to him, and provides a substitute, but turns that very substitute's death to his own account.

Brothers Grimm

Karl Gottlieb Praetzel (1785–1861) and the writer whom we know under the *nom de plume* "Lothar" (eighteenth century) have hardly survived contemporary fame. Yet Praetzel's "A Father's Authority" is capital comedy, excellent in its characterisation, and Lothar's "The Arch Rogue" and "Castle Christburg" are romantic tales of a high order; in the former the hero performs his tricks unaided by outside forces, while in the latter we are in the under-world of supernatural things.

Praetzel and "Lothar"

THE authorship of "Married or not Married?" "The Senator of Bremen," "Uncle's Will," and "Who could have believed it?" remains unclaimed to this day. They are widely different—these four stories—in both style and subject-matter, and "The Senator of Bremen"—an old eighteenth-century tradition of that city—stands quite apart from the rest. Ingenious are these anonymous tales in their conception and motive. Close observation of manners reveals a secret marriage in the first. Marriage happily accomplished, and unhampered by conditions imposed by an uncle's will, the irksome conditions being cunningly outwitted, is the theme of the third. While in the last story a young Vienna noble falls in love with his own wife—"to such a dreadful extent may a man be led by one thoughtless step"!—to the mutual happiness of both.

Anonymous Tales

A voluminous writer was the short-lived Franz von Gaudy (1800–1840), and while much of his work is necessarily forgotten, his story of "Antonello the Gondolier," pure fantasy with a queer semblance of reality, well deserves a lasting and honourable place in the library of imaginative fiction. Wilhelm Hauff (1802–1827), a Swabian, like Zschokke, looked to Sir Walter Scott as his master, but the influence of Hoffmann is equally marked in his admirable stories. Hauff's undoubted genius for fiction never ripened to maturity; we see the possibilities in such a story as "The Severed

Gaudy and Hauff

Hand." The writer has a story to tell, and tells it lucidly and in singularly attractive style.

In "The Blue Apron," by Johann Gabriel Seidl (1804–1875), and still more in Fritz Reuter's work, we can note the influence of Dickens. If "The Blue Apron" has none of the uproarious fun that the genius of Dickens revelled in, it has, brief as it is, all that tenderness for sorrow and affliction, that charity that thinketh no evil, and that sympathy with patient suffering and with the innocence of youth that we recognise in the art of the creator of Little Nell and her Grandfather. "His Serenity and the Thunderstorm," by Fritz Reuter (1810–1874), strikes the more humorous note; the lively contrast between the characters of the stout-hearted, God-fearing old Konrektor and his Serene Highness the Duke, and the nonsensical panic of the latter in the presence of the thunderstorm, provide a most diverting entertainment. Reuter, for all his long imprisonment, when a student, at the hands of the Prussian Government, an imprisonment that ruined his life, never lost the saving gift of humour, and retains, deservedly, a high popularity for his descriptive stories of his native province of Mecklenburg.

Seidl and Reuter

A GENUINE realist, knowing the country-side through and through, Berthold Auerbach (1812–1882) is unrivalled in his studies of peasant life on the Swabian side of the Black Forest. He made his name in 1843 with a volume of village stories—"Schwarzwälder Dorfgeschichten." Both "Tonele" and "Clumsy" are stories of broken love and disappointed passion, not unworthy of our own Thomas Hardy. "Tonele," indeed, is sheer tragedy, and if the ending of "Clumsy" is less mournful, its pathos is keener. The test of time has proved the real talent of Berthold Auerbach, and his peasant characters are as alive in their ill-fortune to-day as they were in the middle of the nineteenth century.

Auerbach

The art of what has been called the Swabian school of German fiction is well maintained by Hermann Kurz (1813–1873), whose tale of "My Grandfather's Wedding" is perhaps the happiest of the author's many short stories. The amazement of the villagers at the sight of the heroine's parrot, and their efforts to remove what they imagined was an artificial colouring, till the unfortunate bird succumbed to the various hot and cold washings with soap and soda inflicted on it, make but an incident in the story of the wooing of the lively Salome, but it is an uncommonly funny incident, sorrow as we may for the parrot's sufferings. Kurz was not in the main a writer of fiction, though two historical romances from his pen were popular in their day; to the translation of other men's work—notably "Orlando Furioso"—most of his literary life was given. Nevertheless his talent for short-story writing is not to be denied.

Hermann Kurz

PRIMARILY a poet of nature and still life, Theodor W. Storm (1817–1888) was in fiction a romanticist. Nowhere is the prose of Storm more delicately shaped than in this sketch of old-fashioned family life "In the Great Hall." The sentiment of the grandmother's story of her childhood and courtship has, as it were, an aroma of lavender, as of some well-preserved raiment that has long lain in seclusion to be brought forth on high occasion; and brought forth it is found as beautiful and dainty as ever. The charm of the story is in its setting no less than in its telling; and it is the charm of a day that is past, reminiscent of love's young dream and of far-off things. No hint of coming stress or trouble clouds the picture of family happiness. No intrusion of realism is allowed to mar the gaiety of the scene. "Happily and contentedly" the grandmother has come to old age, and her one prayer is that her grand-daughter may enjoy a like happiness and contentment.

Theodor Storm

To pass from Storm to his contemporary Theodor Fontane (1819–1898) is to leave the quiet of a well-ordered country house for the cheerful bustle of the city. Fontane is the novelist of Berlin life, the pioneer of the modern German novel, a typical late nineteenth-century Berlin man of letters. His literary method changed with the years. It was only step by step he moved from historical romance to realism, and not till 1895, when his masterpiece, "Effi Briest," was published, was it seen how fully Fontane had been influenced by the French school of realists. Slight as are the two sketches here included, "Whither?" and "The Barrowman of Griffelsbrunn," they are sufficient examples of Fontane's lighter touch, his humour, observation, and mastery of character. The humour is spontaneous, the conversation bubbles up in natural fashion, and flows on without let or hindrance. The characters are alive, people to be met every day, and Fontane makes us see how amusing every-day life is to the observer, and how good the play that is daily enacted before our eyes.

Fontane

ACCOUNTED a poet of no mean ability in his day, Hermann Lingg (1820–1905) produced a very limited amount of prose work. His fiction was of the romantic-historical order, and his style may well be judged from this tale of "Nikisa," where the rich vein of sentiment, the Eastern colouring, the dramatic episodes, and the appropriate ending are all used by the author in his accustomed way. Lingg in his "Novellen" proved himself a story-teller, and left it at that.

Lingg

An historical novelist of vastly different style from Lingg is Wilhelm Heinrich von Riehl (1823–1897). A native of South Germany, and by far the most brilliant writer of short stories in the Munich circle of his day, Riehl has a mastery of character and humour. His "Wooing the Gallows"—a short story of the sixteenth century—is as full of wit as it is of humanity, and is a joyful satire on the cruelty and folly of petty provincial rulers.

Riehl

ONLY one woman writer of short stories has a place in this volume—Marie von Ebner-Eschenbach (b. 1830), whose sketches of Austrian high life (notably "Die Freiherren von Gemperlein," 1881, and "Zwei Contessen," 1885) were immensely popular in their time, and may still be enjoyed by the reader. With the publication of "Ein Spatgeborener" in 1875, Marie von Ebner-Eschenbach established her fame, and the originality of her wit and satire were at once applauded. "An Original," the story here presented, has strength and reality, and its pathos is entirely genuine and sincere. As a character study, Gabriel Teufenberg, the subject of the story, is a remarkable piece of work, shaded and completed with wonderful skill. The awakening from a life preoccupied and indifferent to surroundings, the sudden tragedy and the relapse, with "the old chill light in his eyes" and the extinguishing of "the flame that illumined and warmed him," are set out with a power as rare as it is excellent, and make "An Original" a short story curiously impressive.

Ebner-Eschenbach

"The Sad Tale of Seven Kisses," by Richard Volkmann (1830–1891), belongs to the realms of fancy, where imagination plays queer tricks, and all sorts of quaint and unexpected things happen. The tale is short, and may be read as allegory or fable; the moral being that lovers' wishes must not be lightly granted. The quaintness of the idea and the delicacy of the treatment give high value to "The Sad Tale."

Volkmann

PAUL VON HEYSE (1830–1914) may, on the whole, be called the most versatile German writer of the nineteenth century. Both in prose and verse he maintained a high standard, and he is to be seen at his best in some of his short novels, and in especial in the writing descriptive of Italian life, where the "beauty and poetry of conquering passion" are displayed by Heyse with all an artist's cunning. In such a story as "The Fury"—or "L' Arrabiata"—(the first of the three chosen specimens of Heyse's art) we have the Italian scenery and the burning "conquering passion" of youth in love, passion consummated in triumphant happiness. In the second story, "The Hungarian Countess," passion triumphs temporarily, and ends in tragedy. In notable contrast are these two tales, save for the common note of passion. The one is all warmth and sunshine, the other gloom and winter. The third tale, that of "The Huntsman," illustrates the diversity of the author's gifts: it is an incident in a deerstalker's day in the German Alps, told with an engaging simplicity rare in Von Heyse, and the element of human passion is conspicuously absent.

Von Heyse

Contemporary with Von Heyse, and manifesting the same deep sympathy with rustic life and the humblest actors in the world's great tragi-comedy, was Ferdinand von Saar (1833–1906), the eminent Austrian novelist and poet. "The Toilers of the Rocks" is the best example of his work in the short-story vein. It opens with a fine feeling of tragic gloom, and develops with the inevitableness of great drama, providing a wonderfully vivid picture of a little-known phase of labouring life, and ending on the note of joy.

Von Saar

Sacher-Masoch

Leopold von Sacher-Masoch (1835-1895), the last of our German story-tellers, was born at Lemberg, the capital of Galicia, and the best of his tales are studies and sketches of Galician life, illuminated by a kindly, tolerant humour and a wide sympathy. "Thou shalt not Kill" is concerned with two Jewish admirers of a certain Croatian Countess, who are only restrained from fighting a duel by the urgent and humane appeal of the Rabbi. The point of the story is that the insult that provoked the challenge was the one calling the other a Jew! Sacher-Masoch, a man of notable learning, and in his longer fictions strangely decadent, almost to perversion, held a professorship at Lemberg. He was by birth a "Little Russian," and it is pleasant to note that he cannot help poking fun at the egregious but malevolent German historian, Treitschke, in this delightful little story—a story that well writes *Finis* to the older German fiction.

It will be observed, and surely approved, that none of the German writers whose work is characteristic of the Prussianised or Hunnish era have been admitted to the company of this volume.

J. C.

AUGUSTUS FRIEDRICH LANGBEIN
1757–1835

THE IRRECONCILEABLE MAN

Away with insults, hate, oppression;
Reach me still the friendly hand;
Soon we part unreconciled,
Travellers to a distant land.
Feel we not life's bridge beneath us,
Trembling 'mid the o'erwhelming tide?
See how fast it rushes over!
Say we loved before we died.

WITH these words the unfortunate Councillor Lambert despatched an appealing letter to President Dornfeld, one who had been formerly his inseparable friend and companion, but who had become estranged, and was now even one of his bitterest foes. Their acquaintance had commenced at college; amidst study or amusement they were ever at each other's side; and it was only the self-willed and somewhat overbearing disposition of Dornfeld that had, at any time, interrupted their mutual regard; but they were always reconciled in a few hours. And it was Lambert's gentle and noble feelings which usually led to this reconciliation; he recovered his friend's affection and esteem without humbling himself to his whims.

Their friendship followed them into the affairs of life, and, what is more, continued during the space of ten years after they left college. Although greatly inferior to his friend, both in knowledge and in talent, Dornfeld had the advantage in point of wealth and influence, and by such a lever quickly assumed a situation in life somewhat higher than the former. This, however, was assigned to its real cause, and pronounced unjust; but Lambert was rejoiced at his friend's good fortune, and it only served to increase their attachment.

They had severally attained to the age of thirty-five, connected together in all their pursuits; but a dark cloud hung over them, and love it was that threw the apple of discord across their path. On the same day, and in the same hour, they beheld the beautiful Amelia, and both left the house where they had seen her with a burning secret in their breasts.

It was the first they had kept from each other, for both were deeply smitten, and it was long that night before they could close their eyes. They had leisure enough to think of the lovely lady ; they had never seen any so attractive and beautiful ; and their whole thoughts were occupied with the means of again seeing her, and if possible of engaging her affections. Each proceeded in his own way, without a word confided to the other, to accomplish the end he had in view.

Dornfeld, whose busy influence had already raised him to the level of nobility, considered wealth and rank as possessing the most irresistible attractions for the female heart. He imagined that a man of his vast consequence must be the object of admiration and of the secret wishes of all young unmarried ladies whom he knew. Under this impression, his attentions to Amelia betrayed anything but diffidence and doubt ; he appeared to make quite sure of success from the first, while his manner expressed all the confidence and triumph which he really felt. His proposal assumed the air of condescension, and he could not conceal his astonishment on receiving a refusal. He left her highly offended ; his admiration was converted into a feeling of hatred and desire for revenge.

Amelia's heart was already won by the more gentle and modest assiduities of his friend. He had displayed little or nothing, indeed, of those shining qualities so highly valued by the vain ; but his every word and action were the evidence of a gentle and noble mind, which drew its source from the purest and best feelings of our nature. It was thus their mutual esteem ripened into love ; their thoughts and feelings knit in unison together ; and Amelia's parents approved her choice.

Delighted beyond his hopes, Lambert hastened to acquaint his friend, entreating his attendance at their marriage in quality of bridegroom's man. Imagine the chagrin and astonishment of the new President (for he was just made President of Council) on hearing this request. He leapt from his chair, and loudly inveighed against Amelia's character.

In a fit of scorn and passion, he likewise betrayed his own secret, until then unknown even to his friend, and concluded by beseeching him, as he valued their long friendship, not to prosecute his suit ; to abandon one scornful woman out of pity to the agony of his feelings ; and that everything he had in the world he might consider as his own.

" Ah, you require too much, my dear Dornfeld," replied his friend.

"Do not refuse me possession of a blessing which Fortune has denied you; think how many others you possess—as I would have done were she about to become yours."

"Nay, do not imagine I am going to hang myself," cried Dornfeld with a bitter laugh; "it is not that, but the scornful simpleton ought to be well punished for her airs; and you, my noble friend, can do it. Let us be revenged upon her heartless pride: for my sake, draw back, and let her die an old maid!"

Lambert, while he expressed his surprise and sorrow at such words, attempted to inspire him with nobler feelings, and to dissuade him from all idea of taking revenge where no injury had been intended. Yet he could not in the least soften him. Dornfeld insisted upon revenge; and spoke as if he were extorting it from a slave. Lambert then directly declared that he was free, and should please himself, without binding himself down to the consent of any one.

"Do it at your risk," thundered Dornfeld, while scorn and rage shot from his eyes. Without deigning a reply, Lambert turned his back upon him, and walked away.

Not long after this separation followed the nuptials of Lambert and the lovely Amelia. Out of respect, the name of President Dornfeld was never omitted from their cards of invitation to their friends; but he never came.

This scornful conduct served the President as a declaration of hostility. He even broke off all communication with his old friend; and when Lambert once called to inquire after his health, the President being unwell, Dornfeld's servant was told to order him from the door.

Nor was he content with this; he opposed him in public, and in all his affairs, crossing him on every side, and dogging his steps, like an evil spirit, resolved to embitter his whole existence. This he was, likewise, enabled to do, owing to their respective situations in the Council. The most heavy and laborious share fell to the lot of Councillor Lambert. A sort of conspiracy was at work against him; yet he cheerfully persevered in his duties, though he had hardly an hour's relaxation that he could call his own. He was employed in writing incessantly, often whole nights as well as days. It hurt him, however, to find that his best exertions were not appreciated, that they were even reviled, and rejected in favour of those of known inferior worth.

Yet the President's opposition and aversion did not stop here. He spoke ill of the Councillor in all societies where he could venture to do so ; and on one occasion, when it was expected that Lambert would be raised to a higher rank in the Legislature, and one of greater profit, such were the representations made to the Prince that another was elected, and all his just hopes of promotion disappointed.

Until this occurrence, he had borne all the insults that had been heaped upon him with patience. But he was now the father of a family, and he began to find his means inadequate to their support. He had never wished to become the enemy of the President ; he had never retaliated ; and now more than ever he wished to become reconciled for the sake of his family, as he found that Dornfeld had both power and inclination to injure him.

So he resolved to come to an open explanation with his bitter and unrelenting foe, and wrote the letter mentioned at the commencement of this account. He sent it, but received no answer, while he still continued to receive the same harsh and ungenerous usage at his persecutor's hands. He had then recourse to other methods of resisting or of softening Dornfeld's hostility ; but they proved equally abortive. Here was only a fresh source of triumph to the President, who loudly boasted of it among his friends and dependents.

" Councillor Lambert had humbled himself before his rival ; he had resisted, and he was now in disgrace." And there, he had the unfeeling malice to add, he would leave him, as a punishment for venturing to become his rival—would leave him, without giving him a helping hand, though he lay there until the day of judgment !

About the same time, Lambert was sitting one evening engaged as usual at his desk ; suddenly, one of his most intimate college friends, Councillor Von Buhren, entered his apartment. His manner was hurried, and his features bore traces of strong emotion.

" My best friend," he cried, half out of breath, " I am in one of the most awkward predicaments you can imagine ; to you only I look for support. I am just now in want of five hundred dollars ; my life and honour are both at stake ; save me, I beseech you."

Lambert expressed his astonishment ; for Buhren did not stand first in the list of his friends. On the contrary, he was extremely intimate with the President ; and, till this moment, had either slighted or given him proofs of the ill-will of the latter. Yet the weakness of Lambert's heart was not able to resist the appeal of one apparently in distress ; and he did not even reproach him. He sought to console him in the most friendly manner, declaring he would have been glad to assist him had it been in his power ; but for a truth he did not possess the tenth part of that sum just then.

This was the simple fact, though he had cash in his possession to a much higher amount, some of which he was employed in counting. Now Buhren, though aware that it was public property, still persisted in his lamentations and prayers, beseeching that possession of the money would save him from despair.

" No ; excuse me," said Lambert ; " I would myself prefer dying of hunger to touching the least portion of any property entrusted to my hands."

Notwithstanding this honourable avowal, the other persisted in his entreaties, taking a most solemn oath that he would restore the sum without fail, within eight days, threatening at the same time to despatch himself, if Lambert did not consent.

The kind-hearted Lambert was greatly distressed between his feelings of duty and compassion. The last at length obtained the victory, and he tried to reconcile it to his conscience, by thinking that Buhren was one of the President's chief favourites, and would be able to smooth the way, more than any one else he knew, to a final reconciliation with Dornfeld. Full of this hope, he opened the iron chest with a trembling hand, and took out a bag of five hundred dollars.

" Behold, then," he cried, " I am now doing that for you which nothing on earth would induce me to think of doing for myself. Breathe it not to any one, but keep your word, and restore me the money, or you will assuredly ruin me."

Buhren embraced him in the excess of his gratitude, and hastened home with the money.

Overwhelmed with business, Lambert had no time to indulge in reflections upon the possible consequences of what he had done. He again sat down to his desk, and wrote without interruption until midnight. At length, however, uneasy feelings began to prey upon his mind ; and the thought of having disposed of property entrusted to his hands now filled him with alarm and remorse. He could not sleep, for, when he closed his eyes, unpleasant dreams haunted his rest, and he fancied he beheld himself in chains and wasting in a dungeon. He rose at the break of day, like some wretch released from the rack. In his anxiety, he could remain in no one place ; he went out to find one of his most faithful friends, and to him he communicated the cause of his unhappiness, and entreated his advice.

" Bad, very bad," said his friend, shaking his head ; " you have permitted your goodness of heart to blind your understanding. We can do nothing but provide, as soon as possible, against the worst that can happen, and replace instantly the amount you have advanced."

" There is the difficulty—I have no means, " replied Lambert.

" Then I will tell you how," continued his friend ; " I am barely master of five hundred at this moment ; but in two hours they shall be at your disposal. So give yourself no further anxiety about it. I will send the money to your house ; go home."

Lambert thanked him, and went away. It was hardly eight o'clock when he returned. On entering the room, he found two state officers of rank with his Amelia, waiting for him. He was startled at the sight ; and they requested to speak with him alone. They then submitted to his inspection an order from the Government for an examination of the amount of cash entrusted to his care. It met his eyes like a thunderbolt, and he had nearly fainted in his chair. It was only the consciousness of having committed no premeditated villainy that supported him. He opened the coffers, and acquainted the officers with the sum of money that was wanting—(concealing the name of Buhren) and besought them not to make the affair public, as it was certain of being replaced within a very few hours.

They only shrugged their shoulders by way of answer, took particulars of all the other sums, put the royal seal upon the coffers, and went their way, without committing themselves by any promise.

Two hours afterwards, Lambert's friend sent him the five hundred according to agreement. But at the same moment entered an officer of police, who handed him the order for his arrest, and a sentinel was placed before his door. It was now made evident that the President was in the plot, and directed every movement. Lambert instantly wrote to him in an indignant tone :

" I know you, my Lord President !—you are the sole author of all my misfortunes. You plotted the vile conspiracy of which I am made the victim, by means of your creature, Councillor Buhren. My intention, much injured as I have been, was to hold out to you once more the right hand of fellowship, and I hoped I was conferring a favour upon you by assisting your favourite Buhren in his misfortunes. *You* have rewarded me by disgrace and imprisonment. When will your revenge be satisfied? Surely you are not quite lost to humanity. Free me from the net in which you have entangled me! You can do it; you can stem the flood of ruin before I am engulfed. Think that I only disposed of the money, during a few hours, and to serve a friend of yours."

No answer was returned, though it was intended, on the ensuing day, to remove the sentinel from his door, serving an order at the same time upon the prisoner, to forbid his entrance into the Council chamber, and removing him from the office he enjoyed. The affair quickly took wind, and Lambert was everywhere held up as an unprincipled man, unworthy of the confidence of Government, all which greatly surprised the people.

When he had been submitted to this species of moral torture for about a month, he received the following letter from one of his few faithful friends:

"I am this moment informed that your destiny is decided. The prosecution against you will be dropped; but you will be deprived of your rank and offices. Yet President Dornfeld has it in his power to rescue you from this last degrading punishment, if you apply to him; there is not a moment to be lost. To-morrow it will be too late."

Lambert was no longer proof against such a blow, it fell too heavily upon him, and he felt that he could never survive it. He had no hope in appealing to the stony heart of the President, yet it was his last resource; his family were on the edge of ruin; so he sat down once more in the bitterness of his soul, wrote, and despatched his letter by a trusty messenger whom he not only entreated to put it into the President's own hand, but to beseech him to read it, for that it was a matter of life or death.

Dornfeld was that day engaged in celebrating his birthday with a party of friends. It was already evening, and the Lord President was seated at the card-table when the messenger arrived. He took the letter and put it unopened into his pocket, notwithstanding the earnest entreaties of Lambert's bearer to consult the contents upon the spot. "There will be time enough," he answered, and gave it not a second thought.

About eleven o'clock the party left the cards and went to supper. Among the costly drinking vessels which decorated the tables was a grand crystal vase that had been presented to the President many years ago by Lambert on his birthday. What is more, the names of the donor and the receiver were to be seen in gold characters, apparent to every eye: it had never before been permitted to appear; and strange that it should be thus exposed, strange, thought every one, that the President's feelings could sustain such a sight.

An uneasy and indescribable kind of emotion was felt by all present, which they sought to banish by forced gaiety, and, as the clock tolled twelve, the host, according to an old German custom, filled the vase with wine, to be passed round from guest to guest.

Just as the Lord President was going to drink a health to his friends, and touched the edge of the crystal with his lips, a sharp, shrill sound struck his ear, and rung with a tremulous tone round the glass. It was heard by all the guests with an exclamation of surprise; the vase was examined by the lights, and a flaw was visible in it, running through the part where Lambert's name appeared upon the crystal.

The letter now occurred to Dornfeld's memory, and he shuddered; he had already had it for more than six hours in his pocket. He rose from the table, and went into another room to peruse it. He broke the seal and read:

" I stand upon the brink of a precipice, between life and death. The tidings I have just heard, that I am to-morrow, without trial, to be deprived of my means of livelihood, and overwhelmed with disgrace, to be ranked only in the list of beggars, has brought me to the close of my career, and I am resolved to free myself from my sufferings by one resolute effort. This, Dornfeld, is your work; but there is yet time to snatch me from inevitable fate; and you will, you must, do it, Dornfeld, if a drop of human blood yet courses in your veins. Send me, then, as a token of your goodwill, one word subscribed with your name, and let it be '*Yes!*' I will wait most patiently for this single word of comfort until midnight. Yet do not delay it longer, as you would not in future wish to associate your birthday with the day of my death. For the morning will never shine upon *me* which is to hold me up as an adjudged criminal to the world."

Now, for the first time, Dornfeld felt the pangs of conscience; he looked at his watch: it was past midnight, and he dreaded the worst. In an agony of remorse, terrific as it was sudden, he rushed out, in order to prevent a deed which seemed to threaten to stamp his forehead, like that of Cain, with the indelible mark of murderous shame.

He was too late: that deed was already done. Before Lambert's residence he found assembled a crowd of neighbouring people, who had been drawn thither by the report of a pistol. With his hands over his face, Dornfeld, without asking a single question, made his way through the crowd.

Loud and bitter lamentations smote his ear as he entered: guided only by such sounds, he found his way to the fatal chamber; and, with the impulse of agony and despair, he opened the door. The body of Lambert, bathed in blood, was the first object that met his sight: Amelia, his wife, was kneeling, convulsed with heart-breaking sobs and moans, before the couch on which he lay. She heard some one approaching; she looked round, as if expecting to behold a spirit, and there upon the threshold stood the deadly enemy of the deceased. He drew nigh, but she motioned him wildly away, for she could not speak; yet he came nearer, and then she made an effort: "I beseech you to be gone! —the blood of my husband is crying out for vengeance to Heaven: save yourself—fly!"

He felt as if the voice of the Omnipotent were addressing him; and trembling, he obeyed. He hastened back to his own house, but he had not courage to take leave of his guests. He sent word to them that he had been taken suddenly unwell; and concealed himself from every eye as if he had been convicted and shunned by all.

The fate of Lambert was universally commiserated; the real cause of his afflicting end remained no secret. Every humane and honest man avoided the President's society. His rank protected him, indeed, from open punishment; but a more terrific species of justice took possession of his breast, and condemned him never more to experience peace upon earth. Sorrow and remorse consumed him; and only insanity came to his relief.

At length he imagined he was incessantly pursued by the angry spirit of his friend. Often was he heard wildly conversing with it aloud, and always in a beseeching tone, stretching out his hands in supplication; and then he would break out into the ravings of despair, and beat his head against the walls of his cell, crying out that he would never, never be reconciled!

Years did he continue in this state; and often his keepers were compelled to have him chained down to his bed, until the powers of nature being at length exhausted, he was suddenly restored to perfect reason for a few moments, uttered a prayer, and feebly adding, "He is reconciled!" he died.

THE LADY'S PALFREY

AUGUSTUS FRIEDRICH LANGBEIN

THERE was once a young good-natured monarch who never so much as dreamed of vexing the least of his subjects; and yet he did not please them. He was too easy in the exercise of his royal prerogative, and treated them rather like spoiled children than hirelings and apprentices, until they began to think of assembling in parliament, like the frogs, and of petitioning Jupiter to grant them a proper king.

The truth is, that State business boasted less attractions than a very handsome young lady of the Court, named Adelaide, who had made herself complete mistress of the young King's heart, as well as of his time. Such was her influence over him, that some of the old Privy Councillors began to take alarm, and tried every courtly means of enticing him out of the paradise which he seemed to enjoy in her society; for it was not without a good deal of difficulty that they could prevail with him even to take the trouble of signing his name to a sentence of execution.

To most State ministers, perhaps, this bitter aversion to business might have been highly agreeable, and they would have turned his delegated authority to very good account. But these belonged to that more rare class of statesmen who have rather a dislike to office, and who discharge its functions purely for the benefit of the people. They were only ambitious of rousing the royal young lover from his trance and inspiring him with a sense of his dignity—to wield his sceptre with becoming majesty and power, so as to convince his subjects that they had a king.

They assembled, therefore, and laid their heads together in a cabinet council, the result of which was to delegate one of the oldest and wisest of their sapient body to bear their grievances and remonstrances to the ear of their enchanted young Prince. Now, Privy Councillor Alphonso, the ambassador on this occasion, was no sneaking, soft-tongued old courtier, who would hardly venture to call his soul his own; but bold, blunt, stiff, and unbending as a poker, he marched forthwith to seek an audience, and roundly stated the object of his visit. He declared in the most earnest manner, with due commendations on the virtues of princes who never neglected their royal duties, that both the capital and the country were beginning to feel very much dissatisfied with his style of governing, or rather of not governing at all.

They thought it odd enough, he continued, that his attachment to a single girl should absorb that due to all his people, for whom he did not seem to care a jot. Indeed, it was thought that he would not give his little finger to save all his subjects from eternal damnation; such was the perfect indifference he displayed towards them, as well as to his own royal dignity, to the power and splendour of a crown.

The Prince seemed quite dumbfounded at these serious charges, and it was clear that his conscience was at work, for he had not a word to say in interruption. He listened earnestly to the whole sermon, which insisted greatly on the necessity of industry, temperance, self-control, and other great and princely virtues of that kind. "Very true, my good Alphonso," replied the good-natured monarch, "only I fear you have never been in love."

The old minister, with a shrug of his shoulders, confessed that he had never yet found time to fall in love. At the same time, having delivered his sermon, he took his leave, shaking his head as if he entertained no great hope of reaping any harvest from the good seed which he had just sown.

For once, however, the wise old counsellor was mistaken; the Prince awoke, as it were, out of a dream, became sensible of his royal duties, and never went near his beloved during the next three days. Meanwhile it would be impossible to form an idea of the number of tears shed by Adelaide as she sat in her lonely chamber. She was the living picture of grief, until about the fourth day, finding it began to border upon despair, she conceived that it would be the most prudent course, before she made a noose of her garter, to pay the young monarch a visit. He uttered an exclamation of surprise on beholding her in his royal presence, and at his feet, before he had a suspicion of her approach, softly inquiring *how* she could have offended him.

Touched to the very soul at her words, the Prince pressed the weeping beauty to his breast.

"Adelaide, my own Adelaide," he cried, "pray be calm. You are an excellent girl, and you have not vexed me at all. I love you as much as ever, and shall never cease to love you ; only I must not, I dare not, see you any more."

This was at once delight and torture to Adelaide's heart ; his first words were balsam, but his last were daggers. A flood of tears was her only reply, for her grief was too great for utterance. At length, with an abundance of broken sighs, she sobbed out :

" You would see me no more ! and yet assure me of your love !—would you hand me a bowl of poison garnished with roses ? Away with such flowers for sorrow, and tell me frankly that you hate me, and that our parting is dictated by a frigid heart ! Alas ! it must be so, for who would be found bold enough to check the ardour of a monarch's soul ? "

The good King now found himself in a very perplexing situation, for he was ashamed to confess that he had been tutored by an old moralising minister, and sought every means of disguising from her the real truth. But her sighs and tears again appealed so powerfully to his feelings that he could not refrain from relating the whole history of his short-lived efforts to vanquish his love.

This confession removed a load from Adelaide's heart. With the joyful consciousness that her affairs were not quite in so hopeless a state as she had pictured them, she recovered all her usual animation and good-humour. This charming vivacity was as formidable as her tears.

" Stop a bit, you sulky old pedant," she cried, laughing through her tears, " and I will reward you well for the three days' anguish you inflicted upon me ! With your royal permission, I will play off a trick upon the grudging old churl, which shall save him in future the trouble of preaching his prosy sermons in your Majesty's ear. No, he shall never indulge the least inclination to moralise any more. I have hit upon it already—a most excellent plan. If your Majesty will please to slip into the castle gardens about sunrise to-morrow, and conceal yourself near the pavilion, which this old notorious peacebreaker has converted into his summer residence, you shall see a sight which I think cannot fail to amuse you heartily. If my plan succeeds, you shall have the pleasure of seeing this most sage and philosophical greybeard play such pranks before high Heaven that you may easily repay him, with interest, all the fine speeches and reproaches which he has so philosophically bestowed upon you."

The King, much amused, seemed to approve of the idea, with the single condition that the joke should not be carried too far. Adelaide promised, and ran joyfully home.

Early the ensuing morning, while the Court lay buried in repose, the malicious lady, intent upon revenge, took her way towards the castle gardens with the speed of a young roe. She was attired in a charming morning dress, whose exquisite whiteness might have shamed the snow. Her raven hair floated loose upon the breeze, or wantoned over her swan-like neck, while her bosom itself was but lightly veiled from the eye of the young god of day.

Thus cruelly armed with the weapons of seductive destruction, the lovely nymph began to wander round the immaculate minister's abode. He was already seated at his official desk, and from time to time cast longing glances at the delicious gardens, which seemed to invite him down. To entice him to the window, Adelaide began to sing a song, sweet as the nightingale's:

> I was a little lively thing—
> To school each morn upon the wing:
> Yet loved I something better
> Than sugar bread for alphabet,
> And learnt no words that I was set
> Save that of Love—Love-letter.
> And fain I would my wit apply,
> If some loved one would love as I,
> And wear with me love's fetter.

The first notes of the decoy bird attracted the old courtier's attention. He laid his pen down, elevated his wig a little above his right ear, and listened.

"Who in all the world can be singing so prettily?" thought he, as he rose from his desk.

He crept softly to the window, peeped behind the curtain into the garden below, and was not a little surprised to observe the very young lady whom he had served so ill a turn only a few days before.

At first he turned once more to his desk; but his curiosity being piqued, he again rose, he peeped, he gazed; he admired, he longed, he lost himself. Love pinned him to the spot, or at least he was only able to turn one eye to his seat—the other was in the garden.

"You old fool!" at length he began, half laughing to himself; "I fear thou art bewitched with a girl young enough to be thy granddaughter. But zounds, she looks so desperately beautiful, old father Nestor himself might well fall in love with her. Zounds, I never envied my royal master so much in my life as I do now. How happy he must be! What wonder that in her society he should forget that he wears a crown, or that he has any subjects except herself in the kingdom!"

During this monologue the wicked Adelaide had contrived to fix her basilisk eyes upon him through the window, and played the part of a love-sick damsel to admiration. She plucked roses and forget-me-nots, which she made into a wreath—and sighed. Added to such artifices, she kept drawing nearer, and sang again:

Here, here I was captured
By Love's mighty power,
And wander enraptured
Till life's latest hour.
I would thou might'st feel, Love,
What I suffer now;
I would I might steal, Love,
To offer my vow.

The old courtier was enraptured too; and his head turned so giddy with the delicious song that he could no longer distinguish sense from nonsense, but took the compliment as he should do. He grew merry and wanton as a young colt, felt quite feverish, and his long-ossified old heart began to grow tender and melted away like wax. More greedily than a fish takes the bait, his eye fastened on the lady's charms; and, like some fierce pike, he was caught with the hook sticking in his gullet.

He threw his morning gown aside, seized his best Court suit; yet recollecting, just as he began to decorate himself, that she might perhaps retire, he resumed his morning gown, and ran to the mirror to adjust his wig. Alas! he was shocked at his own figure; never had his cheeks looked so flat and fallen, nor so deeply ploughed by the hand of years. Indeed, they resembled shrivelled parchment so much that the voice of reason exclaimed:

"Thou art playing the fool, old greybeard! What! in the winter of thy days to think of making love to a blooming flower of spring! Down to thy desk again! where for years thou hast sat turning the rudder of the State, and heed not the song of any siren that attempts to bring the vessel of thy fame upon the rocks."

So argued reason, and would have said more; but the nightingale again trilled her tender song from the garden, and three times sweeter than before sang her third song:

Fonder than the fondest dove,
Once within a leafy grove,
  Sat a maiden fresh and fair,
Watching for her one beloved:
Yet ere from that spot she moved,
  Came woe and death to end her care.

This was too much for the sage statesman's prudence, and it turned his head. His passion escaped quite beyond the bounds of reason; he lost both rudder and compass, and ran like a horse broken loose down the steps into the garden, and never stopped until he dropped at Adelaide's feet. She had purposely averted her face, and started, as if suddenly taken by surprise, as her unwieldy lover plumped down before her.

"For Heaven's sake," she cried, at the same time taking the old courtier by the shoulders as if to raise him up, "what is the matter?"

"Nay, most lovely lady," he exclaimed, in the most tender accents, and gazing on her with melting looks, "suffer me to remain where I am, kneeling in the dust, until I obtain your full forgiveness, your smiles, your love."

"You surprise, you distress me greatly," replied the artful Adelaide, biting her lips to avoid bursting into a fit of laughter; "but rise, I entreat you to rise, for I must first learn whether you be jesting or in earnest."

"In earnest, upon my soul! Doubt not the truth and fervour of my passion! It would be an insult upon that divine—that exquisite—that angelic beauty which compels all men to adore you. Even I, I who have ever boasted perfect freedom, must now submit myself a happy slave and prisoner, ready to wear your chains."

"Truly, I feel proud of such a conquest: yet I cannot consent to deprive you of your freedom—I dare not."

"But you must," replied the enraptured lover, "you cannot avoid it; for death only can rid me of your chains. This, too, he will shortly do if you should not quickly take compassion on me, and consent that you will be mine."

"Such a formal declaration," replied Adelaide, "from your lips almost makes me imagine I am in a dream, a delightful dream. Leave me, pray, before I awake; for, alas! I fear you are very far from being indifferent to me. Must I then confess it! I have long sighed for this hour; and besides, I have been haunted this some time past by the strangest emotion, the oddest wish you can imagine, the gratification of which depends wholly upon you."

"Name it, I entreat you; only name it, my adored Adelaide."

"Indeed, I feel some diffidence—I do, indeed, in mentioning it; you will think it so very singular; yet I feel I cannot be happy unless you consent to indulge me in it. So I think I had better tell you."

"Oh, yes! give yourself no anxiety, not a moment's hesitation. Only state your wish, and have it: bid me mount the scaffold—the funeral pile—or the top of the town hall—and I will do it. I would march through fire and flood to reach you;—'sdeath, but I would."

"Would you really? Then I will mention it boldly; for I require no such terrible proofs of your affection. Freely and frankly, therefore, I have a most inexpressible desire, were it only for a few minutes, to take a short ride round these fine gravel walks."

"Whimsical girl! what can have put this into your head? However, there is nothing shall prevent it; you shall have a pad to carry you round the walks instantly."

"No, there is no occasion for that: it would most gratify me to be borne upon your own Right Honourable shoulders; it is that I long for; that must be the price of my affections; if you would only go down upon your hands and knees."

"Cruel, cruel girl! surely you are jesting. You mean to make a fool of me. Ask any other favour in the world; only spare my feelings; I know you would not wish to make me a laughing-post: consider my dignity—my official character—I am a minister."

"So, then," cried Adelaide, "you would permit these cold, haughty maxims of yours to stand in the way of true passion and devotedness to the object of your love: how can it make you ridiculous when there is no one to see you? I vow eternal silence on the subject, as you may well believe; and the pretty birds and squirrels in the trees above us will surely tell no tales."

The poor lover stood in great perplexity some time, till, at length, the violence of his passion mounting into the sublime quite overpowered his sense of the ridiculous, and he bent down upon his hands and knees with all the grace and agility of an octogenarian, though he was little more than sixty. The lady then took a silk sash, and bitted him very dexterously; and next seizing the reins, she lightly sprang upon his back, almost convulsed with laughter, so that she had much difficulty in keeping her seat.

Scarcely, however, had he crawled at a snail-like pace a few yards, when suddenly the King sprang from his ambush among the shrubs and confronted his old minister upon his servile career.

" Ah, ah ! " quoth he, " such scenes are worth my whole treasury in gold ! To see such a philosopher and avowed enemy of the fair sex converted into an old hobby-horse. It is too much—too much," and he held his sides for laughter.

The old Privy Councillor gave a shriek of horror, just as if the sky had fallen, at his sight. Yet, after a long struggle, he tried to force a smile, and exclaimed, in a tone of mingled chagrin and good-humour :

" I know I am ridiculous enough, but I never before knew the enchanting power of love. I see now that if the little imp spares us in our youthful days, it is only to make a greater fool of us in old age. So jest and laugh, my Prince, to your heart's content ; you must find some other Court preacher in future : I have done ; I have surrendered without discretion to love—that ' mighty conqueror of hearts.' "

J. C. FRIEDRICH VON SCHILLER
1759–1805

THE SPORT OF DESTINY

ALOYSIUS VON G—— was the son of a commoner of some note in the —— Company's service, and the germs of his naturally happy genius were early unfolded by a liberal education. While yet young, but well grounded in the principles of knowledge, he entered into the military service under his native Prince, to whom he soon made himself known as a young man of great merit and still greater expectations. G—— was now in the full glow of youth, and the Prince about the same age G—— was rash and enterprising; while the Prince, of a similar disposition, was fondly attached to such characters. Endued with a rich vein of wit, as well as information, which gave a zest to their intercourse, G—— became an agreeable addition to every circle in which he moved, from the evenness of his good-humour, and the charm and spirit which he infused into every subject. The Prince had, likewise, good sense enough to appreciate his virtues; virtues which he himself possessed in no ordinary degree. Indeed, all he attempted, even his recreations, bore a lofty character: difficulties deterred him not, and no disappointment could vanquish his spirit of perseverance. The value of this last quality was heightened by a very pleasing figure; an appearance of blooming health and Herculean power, animated by the eloquent play of a spirit which shone in his eye, in his carriage, and even in a natural dignity, relieved by a due share of modesty of manner. If the Prince was charmed with the spirit of his new associate, his seductive exterior appealed no less powerfully to his approbation and his taste. Similarity of age, of inclination, and of character shortly led to a degree of intimacy, which to all the warmth of friendship added all the fervour and sympathy of early youth. G—— stepped from one promotion to another, although these proofs of favour still appeared in the eyes of the Prince to leave him far behind what his deserts entitled him to. His good fortune rapidly advanced, for the author of it was his greatest admirer and his warmest friend. Not yet twenty-two years of age, he already saw himself placed upon an eminence formerly attained only by the most fortunate at the close of their career. But his active spirit was incapable of reposing long in the lap of ease and idle vanity, or contenting itself with the glittering trappings of a large fortune, for the application of which, however, as well as its enjoyment, he by no means wanted either inclination or power. Often when the Prince was engaged in parties of pleasure, his young favourite would seek the calm oak or beechen shade, and devote himself with unwearied assiduity to affairs, in which he at length became so skilful and judicious, that no opportunity of employing him was omitted in which the talent of a single individual was required. From the mere companion of his pleasures, he soon became first counsellor and minister, and finally the director of his Prince. In a short time there was no way to obtain the royal favour but through him. He had the disposal of all rank and offices; all rewards and remunerations were received through his hands.

Still G—— was far too young and inexperienced, and had risen by too rapid strides, to enjoy his vast influence with moderation. The height on which he contemplated himself made his ambition giddy, and all modesty forsook him when he achieved the last honours which he had in view. The respectful humility and attentions shown him by the first nobles of the land, by all who, in birth, fortune, and reputation, among the oldest and most experienced of their age, so far surpassed him, excited the slumbering embers of pride and tyranny, while his unlimited power produced an evident hardness of character, which thenceforth, throughout all the variations of his fortune, remained. There was no service, however painful or great, which his friends might not venture to solicit; but woe be to his enemies! for, in proportion as his favours exceeded all due limits, his revenge was bitter and fatal. He was less solicitous to enrich himself than a number of his creatures, such as were most eager to do him fealty, and obey him as the author of their fortunes, while sheer whim, not justice, dictated his choice of them. Yet, by exacting too much, by the haughtiness of his commands and whole demeanour, he soon weaned from him the hearts even of those who were most bounden to him; while his rivals, and secret enviers of his power, were quickly converted into his deadliest enemies.

Among others who kept the most jealous eye upon all his motions, and with the quick, steady hand of hate were collecting the materials for his future accusation, and slowly undermining the pillars of his greatness, was a Piedmontese count, named Joseph Martinenzo, belonging to the Prince's suite. G—— himself had promoted him, as a poor, harmless, obedient creature, to his present post—that of supplying his own place in attending upon the pleasures of his princely master—which he began to find too irksome, and which he willingly exchanged for some more important occupation.

Viewing this man merely as the work of his own hands, which he might, at any period he best pleased, again consign to its original nothingness, he felt assured, from equal motives of fear and gratitude, of the fidelity of his creature. He thus fell into the same error as was committed by Richelieu, in entrusting Louis XIII. to the care of the young Le Grand, as one of his playthings. Without Richelieu's ability, also, of repairing so great a mistake, he had, moreover, to deal with a far bitterer enemy than the French minister had to encounter. Instead of boasting of his good fortune, or allowing his patron to feel that he could venture to dispense with his further patronage, Martinenzo was only the more cautious to maintain the show of dependence, and to bind himself with affected humility in closer alliance with his benefactor. Meanwhile, he did not omit to avail himself of the advantage afforded him by his office, to ingratiate himself by every means in his power personally with the Prince; until, from being useful, he became indispensable to him. In a very short period he made himself master of the Prince's mind—he discovered all the avenues to his confidence and favour, in both which he then gradually usurped a place. All those arts which pride, and a natural elevation of character, had taught the minister to hold in contempt, were brought into play by the Italian, who was not in any way scrupulous, in the attainment of his object, about the means employed, however vile and despicable. He was well aware that mankind never stand so much in need of a guide and companion as in the career of vice, and that nothing so much conduces to unreserved confidence as participation in common foibles. With this knowledge he proceeded to play upon the Prince, to excite passions which had hitherto lain dormant, and direct them, as his confidential adviser and accomplice, to the worst of purposes. By a train of the most seductive arts he plunged him into excesses which admitted of no participation and no witness; and thus finally became master of secrets which were to be entrusted to no third person. Upon the progressive degradation of the Prince's character, he now began to lay the foundation of his own fortunes; the secrets which rendered him so formidable soon obtained for him complete dominion over the Prince's feelings, before G—— even suspected that he had a rival.

It may appear strange that so important a change should escape the minister's sagacity; but he had, unluckily, too high an opinion of his own worth, to suspect that a man like Martinenzo would venture to start up as an opponent; while the latter was himself too cautious to commit the least error which might tend to rouse him from his proud security. The same overweening confidence which had caused the downfall of so many of his predecessors from the slippery summit of royal favour was fast preparing the minister's ruin. The confidential terms upon which he saw his own creature Martinenzo with his master gave him no uneasiness; he was glad to resign a species of favour which he despised, and which had never offered itself to him as the goal of his ambition: it was only as it smoothed his path to power that he had ever valued the Prince's friendship, and having ascended the summit of his wishes, he inconsiderately threw down the ladder by which he had risen.

Martinenzo was not the man to play a subordinate part. At each step in the Prince's favour, his hopes, too, rose higher, and his ambition, in so friendly a soil, began to strike deeper and stronger roots. His artful game of humility towards his benefactor became daily more hateful to him, in proportion as the growth of his reputation excited haughtier feelings. The minister's deportment towards him, on the other hand, so far from becoming more delicate with his rapid rise in the Prince's favour, evidently aimed at humbling his growing pride, by wholesome admonitions reminding him of his dependence—a species of tyranny which finally grew so intolerable, that he eagerly laid a plot to end it at a single blow, and aimed boldly at the destruction of his rival. Under an impenetrable veil of dissimulation he brought his plan to full maturity. Still he did not venture to enter into open competition with his rival: although the first glow of the minister's favour was at an end, it had commenced too early, and spread too deep roots, to be torn rudely from the bosom of the Prince. The slightest circumstance might restore it to all its former vigour—a truth which convinced the Italian that the blow which he was about to strike must either fail or prove fatal. The ground which the minister had lost in the Prince's affections was perhaps compensated by the degree of respect and awe acquired in its place with which he held both his mind and counsels in control; a control arising out of his political skill and fidelity, not easily shaken off. Dear as he had once been to his master as a friend, he was now equally powerful as a minister.

By what means the Italian actually succeeded in his object remains a secret with the few who aided him in directing and in striking the blow. It was reported that he had detected a secret correspondence of a treacherous nature carried on by the minister with a neighbouring Court; but whether his proposals had been listened to or rejected remained matter of doubt. Whatever degree of truth there might be in the accusation, it fully answered the end proposed. The Prince viewed G—— in the light of one of the most ungrateful and treacherous of mankind, whose delinquencies were fully proved, and only awaited their due punishment. This was arranged secretly between the new favourite and his master; G—— was unconscious of the gathering storm, and continued wrapt in this fatal security, until the last startling and terrific moment, which precipitated him from the summit of princely honours—the envy and the gaze of all eyes—into the lowest depths of obloquy and contempt.

On the appointed day G—— appeared as usual upon the parade, no longer an ensign, as he had commenced not many years before, but as an officer of distinguished rank. Even this was only meant as a modest veil for the exercise of his political power, which, in fact, placed him above the foremost of the land. The parade was his favourite place of indulging all the pride of patronage, of receiving the obsequious attentions of his creatures, and thus rewarding himself for the laborious exertions of the day. His chief dependents, all men of rank, were seen gathering round him, eager to offer their obeisance, yet evidently anxious as to the kind of reception they might meet with. The Prince himself, as he passed by, beheld his chief minister with a relenting eye; he felt how much more dangerous it would be to dispense with the services of such a man than with the friendship of his rival. Yet this was the spot, where he was flattered and almost adored like a god, which had just been cruelly selected for the revolting scene of his disgrace; but the Prince rejoined the Italian, and the affair was suffered to proceed. G—— mingled carelessly in the well-known circle, quite as unsuspicious of the bursting storm as their honoured patron, offering their distant and most flattering respects, and awaiting his commands. Shortly appeared Martinenzo, accompanied by some State officers, no longer the same meek, cringing, smiling courtling; the presumption and insolence of a lackey suddenly elevated into a master were visible in his quick, haughty step and his fiery eye. He marched straight up to the prime minister, and confronted him, with his hat on, for some moments, without uttering a word; then, in the Prince's name, he required his sword. This was handed to him with a look of silent, terrific emotion; and, thrusting the naked point into the ground, he split it into shivers with his foot; the fragments lay at G——'s feet. At this signal, the two adjutants likewise seized him; one strove to tear the order of the cross from his breast; the other pulled off the shoulder-knots, the facings of his uniform, and even the plume of feathers from his hat. During this cruel and unmanly proceeding, which passed almost in an instant, not a single voice was raised; a breathless silence reigned throughout the immense throng. Yet more than five hundred persons of rank were present; but all, with pale cheek and beating heart, stood motionless around him, the most painful expression of surprise visible in every quivering lip and every muscle of their face. At this trying juncture, while thus bereaving him of his honours, G—— presented a singular but no despicable picture to the eye; he laughed, but with difficulty could conquer his surprise: it was a laugh, such as can only be heard at the gallows tree, in spite of nature and of death. Thousands in his place would have sunk powerless to the earth; his firmer nerves, his unflinching spirit, bore him through, and supported him, while he drained the cup of poison to the dregs.

When this procedure ended, he was conducted, through rows of numberless spectators, to the very extremity of the parade, where a covered carriage was in waiting for him. He was motioned to ascend; an escort of hussars being ready mounted to attend him. Meanwhile, the report of this transaction was spread on all sides: windows were opened, the streets were filled with throngs of curious people pursuing the carriage, and whose mingled cries of triumph, of scorn, or of indignation, at what had passed, were echoed far and wide—all connected with his name.

At length, however, he escaped the hideous din, though a no less fearful trial now awaited him. The carriage turned out of the high-road into a narrow, unfrequented by-way, towards the place of judgment, whither, by command of the Prince, he was borne along at a slow pace. Here, after he had suffered all the torture of anticipated execution, tenfold embittered by its manner, the carriage turned off into a more public path. Exposed to the sultry summer heat, without hearing any accusation, without attendance or consolation, he passed seven heavy and afflicting hours before he arrived at his place of destination. Late in the evening the carriage stopped, when, deprived of all consciousness, his gigantic strength having at length yielded to twelve hours' fast and consuming thirst, G—— was dragged like a felon from his seat. On again returning to life, he found himself consigned to a subterranean dungeon, dimly lighted by the rising moon, which cast its sickly rays from a height of nineteen fathoms through a few grated openings, admitting also the cold air from above. Near him he found a portion of coarse bread, with a vessel of water, and a heap of straw for his couch. He endured this situation without any interruption until noon the ensuing day, when he heard a sash of one of the iron windows in the centre of the tower drawn aside; two hands were visible, lowering down a basket, like that which he found containing his food the day before. For the first time since the frightful revolution of his affairs, he felt some inclination to inquire into the cause, and into the nature of his future destiny. But he received no answer from above; the hands disappeared; and the sash was closed. Thus, without beholding the face or hearing the voice of a fellow-creature; without the least light thrown upon his destiny; left in utter ignorance as to both the future and the past; never feeling the warmth of the sun nor the freshness of the air; remote from human aid and human compassion; he numbered in this frightful abode four hundred and ninety long and heavy days, sustained upon a small allowance of coarse bread. The last, too, was provided with that sorrowful monotony on the noon of each day, which, while it sustains life, only renders it more sensible of its utter wretchedness. Yet this was not enough. He one day made a discovery which filled up the measure of his calamity. He recognised the place; it was the same which, in his rage of vengeance against a worthy officer, who had had the misfortune to displease him, he himself ordered to be constructed only a few months before, and had even suggested the manner in which it might be rendered more revolting and terrific. He had likewise visited the place only shortly before, in order to witness its completion. What added the last bitter sting to his punishment was, that the same officer who had been destined to occupy it, an aged and meritorious colonel, had just succeeded the late commander of the fortress, and, by a sort of retributive justice, was made the master of his enemy's destiny. He was deprived, as it were, of the last poor comfort, the right of compassionating himself.

He knew he did not deserve it; he was to himself an object of disgust and the bitterest self-contempt—a feeling of all others the hardest to support by a haughty mind—to depend wholly upon the magnanimity of a foe to whom he had shown none.

His gaoler was, fortunately for him, a man of noble feelings, who scorned to take a mean revenge. He felt sorry at the idea of fulfilling the part assigned him; yet, as a faithful subject and an old soldier, he did not think himself justified in departing from the usual rules; and he feared to swerve from his instructions. Still he pitied him, and pointed him out to a benevolent assistant, the preacher of the prison, who, having been able to ascertain nothing beyond mere report against the prisoner, resolved, as far as possible, to mitigate his sufferings. This excellent man, whose name I unwillingly suppress, believed he could in no way better fulfil his pious charge than by bestowing his spiritual support and consolations upon a being deprived of all other hopes of mercy.

As he could not obtain permission from the commandant himself to visit the prisoner, he cheerfully proceeded to the capital, in order to solicit personally the Prince's consent. He fell at his feet, appealing for some mitigation of the poor captive's sufferings: destitute of the aids of religion, never denied to the worst of felons; pining in solitude, and perhaps on the brink of madness or despair. With perfect confidence and sincerity, he then insisted, in the name of his pious calling, on free admittance to the prisoner, whom he claimed as a penitent, and for whose soul he was responsible. His subject made him eloquent; and he already began to make some impression upon the Prince, who at first had refused his request. Nor did the pious man relinquish his efforts until he had extorted full permission to visit the wretched prisoner and administer to his spiritual wants.

The first human face G—— saw, after a lapse of sixteen months, was that of his new benefactor. He was eloquent in his gratitude, for he was the only friend he had in the world: in all his prosperity he had never boasted one. The good pastor's was like an angel's visit: it would be impossible to describe his feelings; but from this day forth his tears flowed more freely; he had found a being who sympathised with and compassionated him.

The pastor was filled with horror and astonishment on entering the frightful vault. His eyes sought a human form, and beheld, creeping towards him from one corner, a white and wild-looking living skeleton, his couch resembling rather the den of a beast of prey than a human resting-place. All vital signs seemed fled from his countenance; grief and despair had traced deep furrows there; his beard and nails were grown to a frightful length; his raiment had fallen from about him in tatters; and, for want of water and all means of cleanliness, the air was contaminated around. In this state he found the favourite of fortune; his iron frame had stood proof against the severity of his trial. Almost terrified at the sight, the pastor soon hastened back to the governor, in order to solicit a second alleviation of his sufferings, without which the first would prove of little avail.

This, however, being in opposition to the strict letter of the governor's instructions, the noble-minded being resolved on a second journey to the capital, in the hope of obtaining some further concessions from the Prince. He declared that he could not, without violating the sacred character of the Sacrament, administer it to a wretch who had been deprived of the exterior resemblance of a human being. In this object, too, the good man succeeded; and, from that day forth, for the first time, the prisoner might be said to enjoy a new existence.

For many years, however, G—— was condemned to languish in captivity, though of a less revolting character than that he had previously suffered, more especially after the short summer of the new favourite's reign was passed, and others succeeded in his place, who either possessed more humanity, or had no motive for revenge. Yet ten years expired before the hour of his delivery approached, without any judicial investigation, or any formal acquittal. He was presented with his freedom as a sort of princely gift, being, at the same time, requested to banish himself for ever from his native country. But here the oral traditions, which I have been able to collect respecting his history, begin to fail; and I find myself compelled to omit an intervening period of about twenty years. During the interval, he entered upon his military career afresh, in foreign service; which at last brought him, by combined industry and skill, to a pitch of greatness equal to that he had formerly attained in his native land. Time, likewise, finally a friend to the unfortunate, which ever makes slow but sure approaches to decrees of justice, took some retributive acts upon itself. The Prince's days of passion and of pleasure were over; humanity gradually resumed its sway over him; and, when his hair became blanched and he trembled over the brink of the grave, the friend of his early youth appeared to him, and constantly haunted his rest. In order to repair, as far as he yet could, the injuries which he had heaped upon him, the Prince, with friendly expressions, invited the banished man to revisit his native land, which, for some time past, he had eagerly longed to do. The meeting was extremely trying, though apparently warm and cordial, as if they had only separated a few days before. The Prince looked earnestly, as if trying to recall features so well known, and yet so strange to him ; he appeared as if numbering the deep furrows which he had himself so cruelly traced there. But nowhere, in that aged, grief-worn countenance, could he recognise the features of his early companion and friend. The welcome and the look of mutual confidence were evidently forced on both sides ; mutual shame and dread had virtually separated their hearts—to meet no more. A single look, which brought back to the Prince's soul the full sense of his guilty precipitancy and violence, hurt the Prince ; while G—— felt that he could no longer entertain any regard for the author of his misfortunes.

Yet, in a short time, G—— was reinstated in all his ancient honours and authority, the Prince attempting to salve his conscience by vanquishing his dislike, and showering upon him the most splendid favours, as some remuneration for what had passed. Never, however, could he win back the sincere goodwill and attachment which had once distinguished his former favourite ; the man's heart was closed to all the enjoyments of life. Could he restore to him the years of hope and happiness of which he had deprived him, or bestow the shadow of pleasure on old age, which only seemed to mock the real energies and delights of life, which he had formerly extinguished ?

G—— continued in possession of this clear, unruffled evening of his days during nineteen years : neither fate nor time had quenched the fire of passion, nor wholly obscured the lively humour and spirit of his character. In his seventieth year he was still in pursuit of the shadow of a blessing which he really possessed when he was only twenty. He at length died, being then Governor of a fortress for the confinement of State prisoners. One would have naturally expected that he would have conducted himself with humanity, the value of which he had so sensibly experienced, towards his unfortunate fellow-creatures. Nothing of the kind ! he treated them with harshness and ill-temper ; so much so, that in his eightieth year, a sudden fit of passion, into which he threw himself, against one of his prisoners, deprived him of his existence.

JEAN PAUL RICHTER
1763–1825

VAN DER KABEL'S LAST WILL AND TESTAMENT

EVER since Haslan had been a duke's residence there was no record of anything having been looked forward to with such curiosity—excepting the birth of a hereditary prince—as the opening of Van der Kabel's last will and testament. Van der Kabel might have been called the Crœsus of Háslan, and his life a comedy of coins.

Seven distant relatives of seven deceased distant relatives of Kabel's indulged in some little hope of a place in the testament, the Crœsus having sworn to remember them there ; but the hope was a faint one, as he seemed not greatly to be trusted, not only because he was in the habit of managing his affairs in a grimly moral and unselfish manner—in matters of morality the seven relatives were but beginners—but also because he handled things in so cynical a spirit and with a heart so full of traps and snares that there was no depending upon him. The continuous smile about his temples and thick lips, and his shrill sneering voice, impaired the good impression which his nobly-formed features and a pair of large hands, dropping New Year's gifts and benefits every day, might have made ; therefore the swarms of birds declared this man, this living fruit-tree, which furnished them with food and nests, to be a secret snare, and would not see the visible berries for invisible nooses.

Between two strokes of paralysis he had dictated his testament, and entrusted it to the magistrate. When in a half-dying state he handed the receipt of deposit to the seven heirs-presumptive, he said, in his old tone, that he should greatly deplore it if this sign of his approaching decease would strike down sensible men, whom he liked to picture as laughing heirs rather than as weeping ones.

In due time the seven heirs put in an appearance at the Rathhaus with their receipt of deposit. There were the Right Reverend Glanz, the Police-inspector, the Court-agent Neupeter, the Court-attorney Knoll, the Police-inspector Harprecht, the Bookseller Pasvogel, the

Preacher Flachs, and Flitte from Alsace. They urged the magistrate to produce the *charte* of the deceased Kabel, and open the will with all the formalities of the law. The high executor of the same was the ruling burgomaster in person; the low executors were the town councillors. Without delay the *charte* and testament were fetched out of the private closet and deposited in the court-room, passed around to the senators and heirs, that they might gaze upon the printed town-seal. The directions written upon the outside of the *charte* were read in a loud voice by the town-scribent to the seven heirs, who were therewith informed that the deceased had in truth deposited the said *charte* with the magistrate, and entrusted it to the same *scrinio rei publicæ,* and that on the day when he had thus deposited it he had been in his right mind; last, the seven seals which he himself had placed thereon were examined and found intact. After the town-scribent had entered a registry of all these proceedings, the testament was opened in God's name, and read aloud by the ruling burgomaster as follows:

"I, Van der Kabel, herewith declare my last will and testament this 7th day of May 179—, here in my house in Haslan in the Hund-gasse, without many millions of words, though I was once a German Notary Public and a Dutch dominé. But I believe I am still sufficiently conversant with the art of a notary to be enabled to act the part of a testator and bequeather in a proper and becoming manner.

"As for charitable legacies, so far as they are any concern of the lawyer's, I declare that the poor of this town, 3000 in number, shall receive as many light florins, for which they may celebrate the anniversary day of my death next year by pitching a camp upon the public common, make a merry day of it, and then take the tents to make clothes out of them. To all schoolmasters of our dukedom I bequeath a Louis d'or apiece; and to the Jews of the place I bequeath my pew in church. As I desire to have my testament subdivided into paragraphs, this may be considered as the first.

"*Paragraph* 2.—Declarations of inheritance and disinheritance are universally counted among the essentials of a testament. I therefore bequeath to the Right Reverend Glanz, the Court-attorney Knoll, the Court-agent Peter Neupeter, the Police-inspector Harprecht, the Preacher Flachs, the Bookseller Pasvogel, and Herr Flitte, nothing for the present, not so much because the most distant relatives can lay no claim to a *Trebellianica,* nor because most of them have enough to pass on to future generations as it is, but mainly because I know from their own assurance that they esteem my humble person more than my large fortune, of which I must therefore dispose otherwise."

Seven elongated faces here started up. Especially did the Right Reverend Glanz, a young man noted throughout Germany for his spoken and printed sermons, feel himself keenly injured by such sneers. Flitte, from Alsace, permitted a whispered oath to escape his lips; and as for Flachs, the preacher, his chin grew longer and longer, and threatened to grow into a beard. Many a whispered ejaculation was overheard by the magistrate, addressing the late Herr Kabel by such appellatives as scoundrel, fool, antichrist. But the ruling burgomaster waved his hand, the court-attorney and the bookseller set all the elastic springs in their faces as in a trap once more, and the burgomaster continued reading, albeit with affected seriousness:

"*Paragraph* 3.—Excepting my present residence in the Hundgasse, which, according to this third paragraph, I will leave, with all that pertains thereto, to that one of the afore-mentioned seven gentlemen who, in one half-hour (counting from the reading of the paragraph), shall outdo his six rivals by being the first to shed a tear over me, his deceased relative, before an honourable magistrate, who shall register the fact. Should there be a drought at the end of that time, then the property must accrue to my heir-general, whom I shall forthwith name."

Here the burgomaster shut the will, remarking the conditions to be unusual, but not illegal, and in accordance therewith the court would now proceed to award the house to the first that wept; laid his watch, which pointed to half-past eleven, upon the table, and sat down silently to note, together with the lawyers, in his office of chief executor, who would first shed the required tears.

That so long as this world has existed there has ever been a sadder and more ruffled assembly than this of seven dry provinces united as it were to weep, cannot fairly be assumed. At first precious moments were lost in dismay and smiling surprise; it was no easy matter to be transported so abruptly from cursing to weeping. Emotion pure and simple was not to be thought of, that was quite evident; but in twenty-six minutes something might be done by way of enforcing an April shower.

The merchant Neupeter asked if that was not a confounded affair and fool's comedy for a respectable man to be concerned in, and would have nothing to do with it; but at the same time the thought that a house might be washed into his purse on the bosom of a tear strangely moved his lachrymal glands.

The Court-attorney Knoll screwed up his face like a poor workman getting shaved and scratched by an apprentice on Saturday night by the light of a murky little lamp ; he was greatly enraged at the misuse of testaments, and was not far removed from shedding tears of wrath.

The sly bookseller at once proceeded to apply himself assiduously to the matter in hand, and sent his memory on a stroll through all the sentimental subjects he was publishing or taking on commission ; he looked much like a dog slowly licking off the emetic which the Paris doctor, Demet, had spread on his nose ; some time must necessarily elapse before it could take effect.

Flitte, from Alsace, danced about the Session-room, looked at all the mourners with laughing eyes, and swore, though he was not the richest among them, he could not for the whole of Strassburg and Alsace weep when there was such a joke abroad.

At last the Police-inspector Harprecht looked at him very significantly and remarked that if Monsieur hoped to extract the required drops from the well-known glands by means of laughter, and fraudulently profit thereby, he begged to remind him that he would gain as little as if he were to blow his nose, for it was well known that the *ductus nasalis* caused as many tears to take that direction as flow into a pew under the most affecting funeral sermon. But the Alsatian assured him that he was only laughing for fun without any serious intentions. The inspector on his part tried to bring something appropriate to the occasion into his eyes by opening them very wide and looking fixedly at one spot.

The preacher Flachs looked like a beggar on horseback, whose nag is running away with him ; like the sun shining on a dismal day, his heart, which was piled about with the most suitable clouds of hardships at home and in church, might easily have drawn water on the spot, but unfortunately the house swimming in on the high tide proved too pleasant a sight, and repeatedly served as a dam.

The Right Reverend Glanz, who knew his nature from his experience in New Years' and funeral sermons, and who was quite certain that he would be able to work upon his own feelings if only he were granted an opportunity of addressing himself in touching language to others, now arose and said with dignity that he was sure every one who had read his printed works would feel convinced that he had a heart in his bosom, and that it was rather to be expected of him to suppress such sacred symbols as tears, so as to deprive no human brother, than to extract them by force. "This heart has overflowed ere now, but it was in secret, for Kabel was my friend," he said, and looked about him.

With satisfaction he saw that they were all sitting there as dry as so many sticks. As things stood now, crocodiles, stags, elephants, and witches could have wept more easily than the heirs, irritated and enraged by Glanz as they were. Only Flachs had a turn of good luck. He thought of Kabel's good deeds and of the shabby dresses and grey locks of his congregation at early service, then in haste he gave a thought to Lazarus and his dogs and to his own lengthy coffin, then to all the people who have been beheaded at one time or other, the "Sorrows of Werther," a battlefield; and last he gave a pitiful thought to himself, how young he was, and how he was working and slaving for a miserable paragraph in a testament. Another good heave with his pump-handle and it would fetch him water and a house.

"Oh, Kabel, my Kabel," continued Glanz, almost weeping at the glad prospect of mournful tears, "when on some future day, beside thy precious bosom now covered with dust, my own lies mouldering——"

"I believe, gentlemen," said Flachs, getting up sadly and overflowing with tears, "I am weeping." Thereupon he sat down again and allowed them to run cheerfully down his cheeks; he was high and dry now; he had successfully angled the house away from Glanz, who was very much put out by his efforts, because he had talked away his appetite all to no purpose. Flachs's emotion was duly registered, and the house in the Hundgasse was legally assigned to him. The burgomaster was gratified that the poor devil should have it. It was the first time in the dukedom of Haslan that the tears of a teacher and preacher, like those of the goddess Freya, had changed into gold. Glanz was profuse in his congratulations, and jocosely reminded Flachs that he himself had perhaps been instrumental in bringing about this happy consummation.

M. E. ENGEL
1764–1836

TOBY WILT

ONE of the chief ornaments of a little provincial town, his native place, flourished Mr. Toby Wilt. At no period had he evinced a desire to travel, and never, on any occasion, exceeded his prescribed limits round the adjacent hamlets.

In spite of this, however, he knew more of the world than many who had travelled a great deal farther, and some who had expended the best part of their fortune on a fashionable trip to Paris or Italy. He was possessed of a rich fund of little anecdotes of the most useful class, which he had obtained by observation, and retailed for his own and his friends' edification. And though these showed no great stretch of genius or invention, they possessed considerable practical merit, and were, for the most part, remarkable for coming before company, coupled together, always two and two.

Among his acquaintance was a careful young gentleman of the name of Till, a great admirer of Mr. Toby Wilt for his known prudence and stock of observations. On one occasion he ventured to express his high opinion of them, to which his old friend replied in his stuttering style, "Ha! hem?—what, do you indeed think me such a wiseacre, then?"

"Why, all the world says so, Mr. Wilt; and I should be glad to become your pupil."

"Would you so, young man? Nothing more easy. If you really wish to become a prudent youth, in fact, you have only to study the conduct and deportment of fools."

"In what manner do you mean?"

"What manner! by trying to act differently, to be sure."

"May I beg an anecdote, by way of illustration?"

"I believe I can accommodate you with one, Mr. Till. When I was a young man, there resided in this town a Mr. Veit, an old mathematician, rather a meagre and morose sort of personage. I used often to see him walking about, muttering to himself as he went along, and never stopping to salute any of his neighbours and acquaintance; much less would he look them in the face and converse with them; being always too earnestly engaged in solving the problem of his own perfections. Now what do you suppose, Mr. Till, that people were in the habit of saying of him ? "

" Most probably that he was a very shrewd, wise old gentleman," said Mr. Till.

" No ; you are somewhat on the wrong side ; they called him an old fool. So, so ! I used to think within myself—for this sort of title, however general, was not at all to my taste—I must take care how I imitate my old friend Mr. Veit. I see that will never do ; one must not appear to be too full of oneself. Perhaps it is not well-bred, at all events, to go muttering with oneself ; I see we must be more sociable, and talk a little to our neighbours. Let me hear your notion on the subject, Mr. Till ; did I judge rightly ? "

" Oh, indisputably ; I think you were in the right."

" Nay, I am not so sure of that ; not exactly so, as you will find. For we had another genius, a finical kind of personage, and a dancing-master, the very converse of the old postulating mathematician ; and yet he did not please ; though he used to stare in everybody's face as he skipped along. He was glad to talk to every one who would listen to him, as long as their patience lasted. Well, Mr. Till, and what do you suppose people used to say of *him* ? "

" Most likely they would call him a wild, merry sort of fellow ; somewhat of a bore withal."

" There you are not so very wide of the mark, Mr. Till ; for they called him a fool. You see he won the same title by a very opposite kind of merit. Here's for us ! I thought to myself ; this is odd enough. What must one do ? how in the world must one contrive to win the reputation of a wise man ? It is plain one must take neither Mr. Veit nor Mr. Slight for our model. No, first of all, Mr. Till, you must look persons full in the face and salute them like the dancing-master, and then you must have your eyes upon yourself, and reflect seriously ; talk with your neighbours, like Mr. Slight, and think of your own affairs afterwards, like Mr. Veit. That was my mode of arguing, Mr. Till. I compounded the gentlemen, sir : people called me a prudent, long-headed fellow ; and this is the whole of the mystery."

On another occasion, our prudent citizen received a visit from a young merchant of the name of Flau. He, too, came to consult ; and, after making some wry faces, he began to lament the extent of his losses and misfortunes. " Well," replied old Wilt, giving him a tap on the shoulder, " and what does all this amount to ?

" You must be on the alert, sir, and pursue fortune more diligently. She is a shy bird ; and you must be on the look-out, like a sportsman."

" So I have been, sir, this long time past, but all to no purpose. One unlucky blow followed another, till I was fairly tripped up by the heels. For the future, I shall fold my arms, and rest quietly at home."

" In that you are wrong again, young gentleman ; you must be on the look-out, I tell you ; you need only to have a care how you carry your head."

" How I carry my head ! What do you mean by that ? "

" Only what I say ; you must have a care how you carry your head, and the rest will follow of course. Let me explain how. When my left-hand neighbour was employed in building his new house, the whole street was paved with bricks and beams and rubbish, not very pleasant to pass over. Now one day, who should happen to be going that way but our worthy mayor, Mr. Trick, then a young fashionable alderman. He always carried his head high, and thus he came skipping along, with his arms dangling by his side, and his nose elevated towards the clouds ; yet the next moment he found himself sprawling upon the ground ; he had contrived to trip up his own heels, to break one of his legs, and obtain the advantage of limping to the end of his days, as you may often see. Do you take ? do you comprehend me, Mr. Flau ? "

" Perhaps you allude to the old proverb, ' Take heed not to carry your head too high.' "

" To be sure, but you must likewise contrive not to carry it too low ; faults on both sides ! If you have borne it too high, don't bear it now too low ; you comprehend me ? and you will do yet.

" Not long afterwards, Mr. Schale, the poet, was passing the same dangerous way, Mr. Flau. He was, perhaps, spouting verses, or brooding over his *res angusta domi*—I know not which ; but he came jogging forwards with a woeful aspect, ' eyes bent on earth,' and a stooping, slouching gait, as if he would be glad to lower himself into the ground, sir. Well ! he walked over one of the ropes ; smack it went, and one of the great beams came tumbling about his ears from the scaffolding above. But he was too miserable a dog to be killed : he unluckily escaped ; but was so terrified and nervous, poor devil, with the shock, that he fainted away, fell sick, and was confined to his garret for several weeks. Do you comprehend my meaning yet, Mr. Flau ? How would you carry your head when you passed ? "

" I ! I would keep it in just equilibrium, to be sure."

"True; we must not cast our eye too ambitiously towards the clouds, nor fix it too demurely upon the ground. Whether we look above, around, or before us, Mr. Flau, let us do it in a calm, becoming sort of manner, and then we shall get on in the world, and no accidents will be likely to befall us. Let us preserve our equanimity: you comprehend me? Good-morning, Mr. Flau."

On a third occasion, a certain Mr. Wills waited upon his friend, Mr. Wilt, for the purpose of borrowing a sum of money to complete some little speculation he had in hand. "It is quite a prudent step; very sure," he said to old Mr. Wilt, "though I am sensible it is not one of your lucrative speculations; but, as it happens to come very *apropos*, I should like to turn it to account, and make the most of it."

Old Wilt did not much relish this style of salutation, and seeing whither it would lead: "Pray, my dear Mr. Wills," inquired he, "how much money, do you think, will serve your turn?"

"It is nothing much of a sum, a mere trifle; a hundred dollars will suffice."

"So! if it be no more, I will directly comply with your request. Indeed, to show how much I have your interest at heart, I will also present you with something else, which, between ourselves, is worth more than a thousand dollars."

"Ah! pray explain yourself, my dear Mr. Wilt."

"Nay! it is only a short story; but it will serve our turn. In my younger days I had rather an eccentric kind of man for my neighbour, a Mr. Grell. He had continually a certain cant phrase at his tongue's end, which at last proved his ruin."

"You surprise me! I should like to know it."

"You shall. When any of his acquaintance used casually to accost him, observing, 'Well, Grell, how does business go on; how much did you clear by your last bargain?' 'Pshaw!' he would say, 'a mere trifle—some fifty dollars or so, but what of that?' Then again when he was asked: 'Well, Grell, how much are you minus by the last bankruptcy?' 'Pshaw!' he would answer, 'it is not worth speaking of; a mere trifle, some five per cent.' Now, though Grell was a lively fellow in his day, I can assure you, this foolish phrase of his brought him to ruin. He was at length compelled to decamp, sir, bag and baggage.

"What was the sum, Mr. Wills, which you stated?"

"I think I requested the loan of one hundred dollars."

"Exactly so; but my memory is growing treacherous. Well, Mr.

Wills, but I had another neighbour, one Mr. Tomms, a corn-dealer. By means of another saying, did that man build the fine mansion you see yonder, with all its offices and warehouses to boot, sir. What say you?"

"I say it is very strange, indeed, Mr. Wilt: I have a great curiosity to hear this second phrase."

"You shall, Mr. Wills. Why, when his friends accosted him, 'Well, Mr. Tomms, how does business proceed? what cleared you by your last concern?' 'A good round sum, a hundred, that I did!' was his invariable answer, at the same time you might see that he was in high glee. When they perceived on the other hand that he was low, very low in spirits, they would inquire: 'What is the matter, Mr. Tomms? how much have you lost?' 'No joke indeed! a good round sum; some fifty dollars, I assure you.' Now this man began his career with a very small capital; but, as I told you before, he has built that large house with all its offices, I say, and warehouses round it. Now, Mr. Wills, which of these phrases seems best suited to your taste?"

"Why, the last of them, Mr. Wilt, of course."

"Yet," replied old Wilt, "this Mr. Tomms does not quite suit me. He had the knack of saying a good round sum, to be sure, even when he was paying his poor-rates or his taxes. Then, I think, he ought to have employed, like a humane and loyal man, the saying of my other neighbour—'a mere trifle, nothing worth speaking of.' The truth is, Mr. Wills, that as they were both my near neighbours, I carefully preserved both their phrases, and apply them according to the circumstances of time and place; sometimes speaking like Mr. Grell, and at others like Mr. Tomms."

"Not so with me," cried Mr. Wills; "I admire Mr. Tomms' phrase; I do from my soul, sir."

"What was your demand—the sum you need, Mr. Wills?"

"A good round sum of money—one hundred dollars: no trifle, my dear Mr. Wilt!"

"There you talk like a man of sense—a very prudent man, Mr. Wills: you have really learned your moneyed catechism very well. Your answer was quite correct. Had you come to request really only a small trifle, I might perhaps have listened to you; but, as you observe it is a good round sum, allow me to pause. I wish you a good morning, Mr. Wills." But, having thus amused himself, old Mr. Wilt lent him the sum of money

LADY ELIZABETH HILL

M. E. Engel

THERE was formerly a wealthy young widow, who formed the chief attraction of a small provincial town in Swabia, where she had lately taken up her residence, to the no slight perplexity of the inhabitants ; for she puzzled them exceedingly in gaining a knowledge of her character. She was never what she appeared to be ; she was constantly playing a double game, or suddenly assuming some new shape or some fresh pursuit.

During the period that a certain aulic councillor had resided at the same place, being a man of taste and letters, her ladyship was occupied from morning till night in reading novels and romances ; but the moment he took himself off, she bestowed her whole admiration upon one of the medical faculty, a great frequenter of all kinds of routs, assemblies, and festivals ; her books were all thrown aside, and she had not a moment to spare from dancing, visiting and dress.

Shortly afterwards came a pious dignitary of the Church, appointed to the post of superintendent by the reigning Prince himself ; so that the town had never before been honoured by so very reverend a personage. In a day or two her young ladyship was observed modestly attired in a sober suit of mourning ; no more music and dancing was heard in *her* house, and it became the blessed resort of all kinds of saintly characters.

The change was this time so very remarkable, that all the professional gentlemen in the place were struck with it ; they were at a loss to account for so sudden a revolution, and canvassed the subject at some length. There was a great diversity of opinions : First, the school rector (a man of wit and very good parts, which he displayed in one of the literary journals) was positive that her ladyship had no character at all ; that she was fit neither for a poet nor a novelist, and that she was as little adapted to the stage ; in fact, from a literary point of view, she was good for nothing.

Secondly, the superintendent, with his spiritual friends, hazarded more speculations upon the subject : the theatre and the novels forming no part of their lucubrations, they doubted not but that Lady Elizabeth had, at one time, been carnally minded; devoted to the perusal of ungodly books, and to other pomps and vanities of the world, she was thus betrayed into open acts of impiety, having been seen at public dances and festivals, the very gayest of the gay. At length she felt the grace of God, which she had been too wise to resist, and they doubted not her conversion was sincere.

But it was now the doctor's turn; and fixing his eyes upon the animal system of her ladyship, leaving the concerns of her soul quite out of the question, as he presumed, he said, to the office of neither critic nor divine, his opinion was, that Lady Elizabeth had, in the first place, hurt her constitution by hard reading and studying romances in the day; and secondly, by dissipation and revelling at night. He added that a course of bleeding and frequent use of mineral waters in the spring might be of great service to her.

These gentlemen had thus adopted their own peculiar systems, much in the same manner as if they had provided themselves with false glasses, which prevented them from seeing any object clearly, but reflected it only in one light and colour. Nor was this all; for the rest of the citizens, conscious of the weakness of their own organs, were accustomed to repose implicit confidence in those of their superiors. Each contented himself with embracing one or other of the previous opinions, as he happened to be more or less swayed by motives of private interest.

Thus, the bookbinder, who had cleared a good sum by equipping for her ladyship a library of religious works, quartos and folios, all in a superb dress, at once declared himself in favour of the clergy, and very sincerely congratulated the lady upon her conversion.

But the linen-draper, whose profits were formerly very considerable, finding his custom dwindled almost to nothing, declared for the doctor's more uncivil hypothesis, and magnified a slight fit of religious melancholy into downright insanity.

Next came the shoemaker; and he, having lost only about one half of his former earnings since her ladyship had ceased dancing, embraced the more moderate opinion of the rector, lamenting only that so excellent a lady as her ladyship should be so very changeable in her plans, and not so much as know her own mind.

There was only one man in the whole place, and that was the tailor, who, having never injured the natural strength of his optics by the use of glasses, and having had no dealings with her ladyship, as she was accustomed to wear Dutch linen, showed more sagacity than all the rest of the politicians put together.

He saw the matter in a clear light ; and one Sunday evening, when these worthy citizens of the second class were assembled at a tavern, their usual place of resort after service, the bookbinder broke out into this pious exclamation :

" The grace of God is said to have wrought miracles upon good Lady Hill."

The tailor positively contradicted such an assertion, declaring that there was no kind of grace at all concerned in the business. This brought as flat a denial again from the bookbinder ; while the other retorted that she had plainly lost her senses, to which the shoemaker agreed, adding, that she did not so much as know her own mind.

" The lady," continued the tailor, " knows very well what she is doing ; and if you had all of you the proper use of your eyes, you might perceive what she is aiming at, as well as she does, or as well as I do.

" When the late aulic councillor was here, who do you suppose was the most important personage in the place ? Why, the aulic councillor to be sure.

" Now, upon his departure, when the doctor came to reside here, who then, pray, was the person before whose face one and all of us were accustomed to bow and take off our hats ? Why, the doctor to be sure ! And again, when our good Prince was pleased to appoint a superintendent to visit us, who then was the person who took place of the doctor, and topped all that had come before him in dignity and grace ? This is the superintendent himself ; and only let us seriously reflect upon all these circumstances, and we shall presently find, my friends, a key to the whole of the mystery."

The others laughed at the tailor's joke, and they were all of opinion that the little fellow was much more shrewd and long-headed than they had credited him with being. Their open admiration gave him no little satisfaction, as he was always mightily pleased to find himself in the right.

" Gentlemen," he continued, striking the table with his fist, and in a more assured tone ; " gentlemen ! I say, that if the good superintendent should happen to die, and no one should be appointed in his place, I'll wager my life upon it we shall see her ladyship taking the side of the doctor again."

This, however, did not exactly come to pass, luckily for the superintendent ; though a fresh revolution took place. The Prince, being a truly godly Prince, recalled the superintendent to his own Court, in order to make him his confessor. Instead of him, however, he quartered a regiment upon the town, the command of which was entrusted to a major, a fine bold-looking fellow of his cloth.

In the course of a month the major was invited to dine with Lady Hill, and her ladyship soon began to dine with other company at the major's. Now the major's own lady was much admired for her elegant appearance, especially when on horseback. Lady Hill, sensible of her own charms, took airings on horseback, joined the major's lady, and was dressed in a green habit richly decorated with gold lace.

" That lady has no character, assuredly," cried the rector, as she was riding past his school.

" Say, she is no longer under the influence of grace," said a clergyman, just then returning from visiting the sick.

" The lady now adopts a proper regimen, and takes exercise," cried the doctor, as he smoked his cigar. " No fear but she will at last recover her health."

Thus did each of these self-complacent gentlemen try to justify his particular system, in such a way that the very incidents which went to refute it were employed to confirm it. The tailor was more fortunate, and meeting Lady Hill upon the bleaching-green returning from her ride, he shook his head, and said, " Behold what Vanity can do ! "

The reader may perhaps be inclined to laugh at the trivial character of my story, but it has at least the merit of being true ; and if he be an attentive observer, he will not want occasions on which to apply some of the foregoing remarks.

J. FRIEDRICH KIND
1768–1843

THE BEGGAR'S MARRIAGE GIFT

OTTO VON D——, after an absence of several years, two of which he had spent in the luxurious capital of France, was recalled to his native Germany by the unexpected death of his father. He found the family estate involved in difficulties, chiefly occasioned by extravagance and mismanagement, which would have appeared inextricable to a mind possessing less energy than his own; but by at once adopting a system of curtailment and method he soon succeeded in bringing matters into such a train as not only enabled him to discharge the accumulated arrears of interest, but also gradually to reduce the principal debt with which his property had been improvidently burdened.

It was not until his mind was relieved of this first care, and he could uninterruptedly form his plans for the future, that Otto thought of choosing a companion who might share with him the sweets of life, and assist him in combating its toils. He had left Adelaide, the youngest daughter of his neighbour Von Z——, an interesting girl of fourteen; on his return he found her blooming in all the charms of youthful innocence; and he was not slow in observing, as well in the hearty welcome of her parents as in the tell-tale blush of the maiden herself, that his addresses would not be unacceptable.

He therefore embraced an early opportunity to declare his sentiments; and, after the preliminaries usual on such occasions, the happy day was fixed, arrived, and was observed with all those ceremonies which the country people in some parts of Germany still religiously keep up, according to the good old custom of their forefathers.

First came the wedding guests, conducting the bride, modestly clad in white, with a veil covering her face, and who were met on the lawn by the peasantry, preceded by the village musicians. The married women brought their offering of a cradle and fine baby linen, spun by themselves; the lads presented a handsome plough and harness; the maidens a snow-white lamb; and the children doves and flowers. Adelaide gave her hand to all in silence; Otto spoke few but impressive words, and, on concluding, invited the whole party, in the name of the bride's father, to a collation and dance on the green, for which preparations had already been made.

The lamps were now lighted up, and fiddle and pipe were sounding merrily under the sweet-scented linden-trees, when a foreign livery-servant, whose coat was rather the worse for wear, made his appearance on the dancing place. His singular tones and strange gesticulations soon collected around him a troop of laughing villagers; but it was not without considerable difficulty gathered from the broken German of the orator (whose hands and feet were equally eloquent with his tongue), that his master's carriage had been overturned in the neighbourhood, and that a wheel was broken to pieces, which he was anxious to have put to rights, in order that he might prosecute his journey.

"Who talks of mending wheels, or going farther to-day?" hiccuped the bride's father, whose satisfaction at his daughter's good fortune had displayed itself at table in copious libations.

"To-day," added he, patting his ample sides, "let all wheels go in shivers; no man shall pass this house to-day; you may tell your master so; but stay, you may as well take me to him."

So saying, and attended by a crowd of followers, he proceeded to the highway, where they soon perceived a small waxcloth-covered carriage lying upset on the road, one of its hinder-wheels being as effectually demolished as if an axe had been used in the operation. A tall thin figure, dressed in a plain blue frock-coat, having his right arm in a sling, a patch over his left eye, and whose woebegone looks imparted to his general appearance no distant resemblance to the Knight of the Rueful Countenance, stood near the vehicle, holding a jaded Rosinante by the bridle.

No sooner did he perceive the party approaching than, hastening towards them, he addressed their leader in French, with much politeness of manner and fluency of utterance. Unfortunately, however, old Z——'s Court language had lain too long rusty, and the state of his ideas was too muddled to enable him to brush it up at the moment, so that he was obliged to make the stranger understand, more by signs than words, that he must not think of continuing his journey that day at least, but must remain with them as a wedding guest.

The invitation was accepted with many thanks; and the stranger, having caused his Sancho to wipe the dust from his hat and boots, put his collar to rights, and opened his surtout, under which a sort of uniform modestly peeped out. Thus prepared, he set himself in motion, by the help of a stout crutch-stick; and it then further appeared that his left foot was also disabled, though there was something not ungraceful in its hobble. On reaching the linden-place he requested to be introduced to the young couple, and after wishing the bridegroom joy, he kissed the bride's hand, with the air of an old beau, and whispered many flattering things to her in his own language.

When this matter was settled, all hastened again to dance and play. Otto soon removed his bride to another quarter; and it seemed quite natural that the stiff and wearied old man should choose his seat on a bench apart from persons who could no more understand him than he could understand them.

On supper being announced, the stranger accompanied the rest to the eating apartment, where he planted himself, with considerable adroitness, between two of the rosiest and plumpest lasses in the room, to the no small mortification of a young lieutenant, who had fixed on this place for himself. Hilarity and mirth now presided over the happy party: the good-humoured joke was bandied about, and the hearty laugh echoed round the room, when one of the servants entered with a packet, which a messenger had just delivered, with directions that it should be given into the bridegroom's own hands. The curiosity of all was excited, and Otto was induced by their solicitations to open the packet immediately; and, after removing almost innumerable covers, he at length produced a plain wooden drinking-cup, with a silver rim, on which was engraved, "*Present de noces du Gueux.*"

"Jaques!" cried Otto, kissing the cup with emotion. Adelaide cast an inquiring eye at her lover, and lifted up the cup to examine it more nearly; but she had scarcely raised it from the table when its unexpected weight occasioning her to replace it rather smartly, the bottom fell out, and discovered a rose-coloured case, containing a pair of bracelets, set in brilliants of the purest water and newest fashion: the words "*a la belle épouse de mon ami*" were embroidered on the satin.

The surprise and curiosity on all sides may be easily conceived. All the guests rose from their seats, except the stranger, who remained sitting with the most perfect indifference, and an expression of countenance that almost appeared to indicate contempt for what was going forward. Otto, whose growing dislike to the stranger was not lessened by this conduct, measured him with an eye of indignation, and allowed himself the more readily to be persuaded, by his bride and the other guests, to satisfy their inquiries.

"Yes!" he began, a fine glow suffusing his manly cheeks; "yes! I am not ashamed to own it: a beggar—Jaques is the worthy man's name—is my dearest friend; is, to express all to you in a few words, the preserver of my life and honour. However painful it may be to me, on an occasion like the present, to accuse myself of a youthful indiscretion, yet I shall not hesitate to do so, as I cannot otherwise, perhaps, do justice to the noble-minded Jaques, whose marriage present shall ever be dear to my heart, and the most valued ornament of my Adelaide."

"Then let me wear it to-day," said the lovely girl, with tremulous voice; and the bracelets were quickly transferred from their rose-coloured covering to the white satin of her arms. Otto resumed, after a short pause:

"During my residence in Paris I was almost daily in the habit of passing along the Pont Neuf. At one end of the bridge, and generally about the same spot, there sat a beggar, who, although he seemed scarcely more than fifty, had frequented the place upwards of thirty years, and was commonly known by the name of 'old Jaques.' Not out of any feeling of compassion, but merely because his general appearance rather interested me, I threw a sou into his hat as often as I chanced to pass near him. This became at length so habitual to me that whenever I approached his station I put my hand involuntarily into my pocket.

"He always wished me every possible good—chatted with me, when I was at leisure, about the news of the day—even warned me now and then against the dangers of the town; in short, in the course of half a year we stood together on the footing of acquaintances, who, though of different rank, are yet mutually pleased with each other.

"My time in Paris was spent very agreeably, and I may flatter myself not altogether without advantage. I lived as decently as my means permitted, but never extravagantly, till, a short time before my departure, my evil stars brought me acquainted with some young men who were addicted to gambling, and who, by little and little, led me on to stake, first small, and then large sums at play. The consequence of this was as may be supposed: but it was not until I had lost all my own money, and had become deeply indebted to my *soi-disant* friends, that I began seriously to reflect on my situation.

"I immediately formed the resolution to pause ere it was too late, and quit the capital for ever, after discharging the debt which I had contracted. I therefore wrote to my father, requesting such a remittance as might be necessary for this purpose; but that letter, and several which I sent subsequently, remained unanswered. My bills meanwhile became due. I was forced to have recourse to the assistance of usurers, and ruin stared me in the face.

"Disheartened, gloomy, and silent, I now passed Jaques without noticing him; his fixed and earnest gaze became intolerable, and I avoided the place where he stood. At length I received the long-looked-for letters from home; but instead of the remittances with which I had hoped to silence the most clamorous of my creditors, they brought me the intelligence of my father's death, after a short illness, and announced the impossibility of sending me more money than would barely suffice for my travelling expenses.

"Nursed in the lap of affluence, and unused to privation of any sort, it may easily be supposed that I was but little prepared for such news. The death of my good father filled me with sorrow. The involved situation of his affairs, which I now learned for the first time, deprived me of all hope for the future. The idea of having debts which I could not discharge, and the prospect of prison in a foreign land, threw me into despair. The longer I considered, the more did my situation appear utterly hopeless, till at length, in a state of mind bordering on frenzy, and with a determination which such a state only could inspire, I walked out after a sleepless night, and bent my course towards the river. I was already within a few paces of the Pont Neuf, when Jaques threw himself, with greater importunity than usual, in my way. I *would* not see him.

"'One word, sir,' said he, in a tone of entreaty, and taking hold of the skirt of my coat. 'Leave me, old man,' said I, with forced composure; 'to-day I have given *all* away.' He guessed my meaning better than I intended he should.

"'By all that's sacred, my dear young master,' said he solemnly, 'confide in me. What has happened?'

"'What is that to thee?' I replied; 'thou canst not help me.'

"'Who knows? Only speak, sir! I cannot rest until I learn what has so changed you. Tell me the cause of your dejection.'

"'Why, only a paltry thousand louis!' said I, with a shrug.

"'And *is* that all? Good! I will lend them to you.'

"'You, Jaques! Good old man, you have been drinking too freely this morning.'

"'Well, only take the trouble of coming to me to-night; and till then, I conjure you, do nothing rashly.'

"The earnestness of his manner, the firmness with which he spoke, and the reflection that I could at any time carry my intention into effect, brought my thoughts into another channel, and induced me to yield to his request. Jaques gave me his address, in a remote suburb, and I pledged my word of honour to meet him there the same evening.

"Urged by curiosity more than by hope, I appeared at the appointed time and place, and found Jaques in a small but extremely clean apartment, plain but neatly furnished; he now wore a decent coat, and came forward to meet me with a friendly look.

"'Consider all that you see here as your own,' said he. 'I have neither child nor relation, and what I daily receive from the benevolent suffices for my own and my housekeeper's wants.'

"Little as I had calculated on the old man's assistance, yet this address appeared too ridiculous; and I was hesitating whether I should consider him a fool or a madman, when he at once put an end to my doubts; for, requesting me to partake of the refreshments which he had provided, he raised a part of the floor, and brought from underneath a heavy wooden vessel, which he placed with difficulty on the table. On removing the lid, you may figure my astonishment when I saw that it was filled to the brim with gold pieces.

"'Help yourself, sir,' said he, smiling; 'here are about twelve hundred louis. It is all I have by me in ready cash, but I can soon procure more. Do not mistake me,' continued my honest Jaques, 'I am no common beggar, driving the trade from love of idleness, and cheating the needy of the charitable gifts of the compassionate. I am of noble, though poor birth. Having lost my parents early, I entered the army in my sixteenth year, served under the great Saxe, and if worthy of such a leader, let this testify': a cross of St. Louis lay on the heap of gold.

"'In my twentieth year a cannon shot carried away my right arm. I received my discharge, and was thrown on the world destitute and hopeless. Ignorant of any trade by which I could gain a livelihood, and rendered incapable of labour by the loss of my arm, I abandoned myself to a profound melancholy, which threw me into a long and severe illness. When I recovered, my disappointed prospects, and a sort of spite at the world, made me a beggar. My youth and infirmities gained me more compassion than I had expected; and I soon earned not only my daily subsistence, but became enabled to lay by a trifle daily, which by little and little amounted to a considerable sum. Out of this I assisted such of my companions in misery as had been less fortunate than myself in this calling, and thereby acquired a sort of consideration amongst them, but no disinterested attachment. This vexed me. I adopted a foundling as my own child, and began to live even more sparingly than before, in order to make provision for him. I had him carefully brought up and educated till his sixteenth year, when a councillor was pleased with the lad, and took him into his service. This very boy—O François, François, how many tears have I shed on thy account!—soon began to consider it beneath him to be on terms of intimacy with a beggar; and on the same day that you first gave me an alms, he had the cruelty to pass as if he did not know me. He was ashamed of me—of *me,* who at that moment was begging to make him independent. "He heeds me not," said I, and his unnatural conduct drove all the blood to my heart. "Thou all-powerful Being! give me then another son." Scarcely had I uttered the prayer when you approached, and threw, with a compassionate look, a gift into my hat.'"

Otto was moved even to tears, and was forced to make a pause. "'*You* will not be ashamed of me,' continued Jaques. 'You are now unfortunate: make the old beggar happy by accepting his assistance.'

"You may easily imagine how I felt at this moment. The wonderful intervention of Providence to prevent the commission of a crime at which I shudder; the noble, I may say the heavenly look of the good old man; but, above all, my own dreadful situation, crowded into my thoughts, and I did not hesitate to avail myself of his generous offer. My intention of disclosing to him the cause of my embarrassments was needless, for he had already informed himself of every particular. I allowed him to count out one thousand louis, and then requested pen and ink, in order to give him an acknowledgment for the amount; but my benefactor would not hear a word of this. 'Take,' said he, 'as much as you require: and if you die,' added he, 'you can pay me yonder! I want but little here. *You* are sent to me as a son, whether you will or no; and you, at least, cannot deprive me of the secret satisfaction of being your father.'

"'Yes, father! preserver and father,' cried I, falling on his bosom.

'Nature gave me one, and when I lost him Heaven replaced him in you.' I did not leave Jaques' cottage till a late hour, when I returned home with a lightened heart, and refreshing sleep once more visited my eyelids. Early on the following day I paid off every creditor, had another *tête-à-tête* with Jaques, and prepared immediately to quit France. My first care, on arriving here, would most certainly have been to discharge this, which I could truly call a debt of honour; but as he had expressly required me at parting not to think of this till after the end of a year at soonest, to give him, as he said, a proof of confidence, I deferred doing so till very lately, when, on repaying him his loan, I had the satisfaction of acquainting him with my approaching union."

"And he shall be *my* father also," said Adelaide, pressing his hand; then rising, and filling the goblet with wine, "Let us drink to the health of my worthy fathers—John von Z—— and Jaques the beggar."

Every one present pledged the toast with enthusiasm, except the old stranger, who, still evincing the most cutting indifference, pushed his chair back, and hastily rose up, with a countenance on which was written, in pretty legible characters, "What a fuss about a beggar!"

"Sir, you abuse the rights of hospitality!" cried Otto angrily, and going up to the Frenchman with the determination of making him quit the apartment.

"Mon ami, ah, mon fils!" replied the old man, with the tenderest expression, and removing at the same time the bandage from his left eye, "now indeed I am satisfied that my choice has not been misplaced. You have not been ashamed to acknowledge the old beggar; your lovely bride, too, has called me father. For this alone have I undertaken a long journey, and caused my carriage to be overturned at your gate." He was now in his turn overcome; all the guests crowded round him with praises and caresses, and the grateful Otto, kissing his Adelaide, called this the happiest day of his life.

"Only allow me to pass my few remaining years with you," added Jaques, as he drew from his bosom a packet with his left hand, it being now remarked by all that the right was skilfully formed in wax. "There, my son, are your papers back. I will never be a burden to you. I have twelve hundred livres yearly of rent, and all I request is a small apartment in your house, or wheresoever else an honest beggar may patiently await his end."

Otto tenderly embraced his adopted father, and the wooden cup was frequently replenished in the course of the evening.

AUGUST GOTTLOB EBERHARDT
1769–1845

THE BET

IT happened that the Reverend Father in God, Henry, Bishop of Halberstadt, who flourished about the end of the sixteenth century, had once the pleasure of a visit from another Reverend Father of equal rank, which continued for several months. He was received in the most hospitable manner; and one summer evening, as both host and guest were chatting familiarly together, the large round well-filled wine-cups, all fine silver, standing before them, they seemed inclined to drink more than usual. For the cups, they said, were but small, and the wine that day was very good.

From the moment they sat down to dinner until now, nine in the evening, they had been chiefly entertained from the same large favourite wine vault, bequeathed years ago to the host by a celebrated bishop, whose diocese also lay near the Rhine.

Both now agreed in opinion that it behoved every spiritual prince who had a just regard for his honour to follow so laudable an example, and build his cellar on the scale of the deceased prelate; and they proceeded to discuss how best such an undertaking might be executed. While minutely inquiring into all the bearings of such a building, the wine kept pace with the subject; but as the two together produce a soporific effect, our good bishops had something to do to keep their eyes open.

They yawned, and sipped, and rubbed their eyes; but they had almost exhausted their topic, which they could not renew as easily as their bottle; the dialogue became still more dull, and was just on the point of coming to a standstill, when the host bishop's shepherd, Conrad, appeared, driving his master's flock, a well-washed, well-fed, and numerous flock of sheep, as usual, past the bishop's window.

Now the good bishop was himself in the habit of reviewing his flock every evening. As Conrad drew nearer to the spot, and he heard the bleating and the tinkling of the bells with which some of them were adorned, he could not resist his old practice of going to meet them, and he took his guest along with him into the courtyard. As he passed by, Conrad, the shepherd, respectfully doffed his cap to his master with his customary salute of " God save the Lord Bishop ! "

" Good e'en to you, Conrad," was the reply ; and then followed the old inquiry : " And where is the tame ram ? Where is Harne ? "

Conrad stuck his two fingers in his mouth and gave a whistle, so loud and shrill that the stranger bishop, not expecting such a cracking sound quite so near him, put both his hands to his ears as if to save their drums. After this whistle there came bounding along a large, handsome, clean-washed ram, who ran first to the shepherd, and next presented himself to the bishop. The latter stroked and offered him some pieces of bread, which he always put into his pocket for the purpose after dinner. Then, after saying a few more words to the shepherd, he concluded with the question : " Are you making preparation yet for your marriage ? " Conrad only shrugged his shoulders, and drove along his flock in perfect silence.

" Is not that an extraordinarily fine sheep of mine ? " said Bishop Henry to his guest, while the latter contented himself by returning a somewhat indifferent " Yes."

" Yes ! " echoed the Bishop of Halberstadt ! Why, I would not take any price for that animal, he is so tame and handsome. I have to thank my shepherd Conrad for this : he is the honestest fellow alive ; he is honour itself."

His reverend brother laughed aloud at this singular eulogy ; and when the other inquired what excited his mirth, he replied, " My dear friend, honour is a rare article in these days. In the course of my travels and my residence in the courts of princes I have acquired some knowledge of mankind, and do not so easily mistake one thing for another ; black for white ! no, they cannot impose upon me."

The Bishop of Halberstadt granted that he might be right in the main ; but for all that, he would swear that his shepherd Conrad did not impose upon him, that he was an honest man.

" Stop there," cried his guest ; " for I promise you he is not a hair better than others, only perhaps he is more cunning. Really honest servants are rarer than white ravens, and they are still less frequently to be met with, my friend, in the service of spiritual establishments. All of them deceive their masters ; some indeed are better than others, but all are rogues."

Bishop Henry opposed this heartless doctrine with all his might, for his extra glasses of wine had mounted into his head, and he lauded the honour and virtue of all his spiritual subjects; but more especially those of his shepherd, who had never told him an untruth, or been guilty of any wrong action during the whole time he had been in his service.

"What, never!" cried his guest in an ironical tone; "has he never lied, never circumvented, or cheated any one, much less you?"

"No," returned the bishop, with some warmth, "never. Conrad has never told me a lie, and never will."

"Never will," retorted his guest; "what, never! Now what will you bet me upon that? He'll lie, I warrant him!"

"Agreed; done!" cried the bishop, offering his hand. "It is a bet!"

They shook hands, and after some desultory conversation as to the value of the bet, it was agreed, for the wine was still in their heads, that the loser should forfeit a vat of wine to the winner, in which there should be one hundred and fifty fuders—German measure.

The space of three days was fixed upon, during which Conrad's honour was to be put to the test, and the Bishop of Halberstadt bound over his guest by note of hand, as well as by oath, not to give the least hint, either himself or by any third person, to the shepherd relating to the impending bet.

It was now late in the evening; and both these worthy prelates, having fared so well at dinner as well as after dinner, and feeling quite unable to renew the entertainment for that day, sighed for repose. So they took leave of each other for the night, each inwardly congratulating himself that by this lucky bet he had succeeded in securing a good stock of wine, out of which his reverend brother would in future be regaled without entrenching upon his own pocket; for both felt convinced that they must win.

Now in the train of the stranger bishop was a certain domestic of the name of Peter. He was a very complete rogue in his way, and had the art of making himself so agreeable to his master as to be esteemed a kind of humble companion and privy councillor in all little emergencies where the bishop was inclined to doubt his own spiritual judgment.

Just before his master retired to rest, it occurred to him that he would send for Peter. And so inveterate was his old habit of consultation now become, that, in spite of his bond, the moment Peter appeared he began to consult him, informing him of every circumstance that had passed, concluding with requesting his opinion as to how the wager might best be secured.

Peter, finding from his master's account the small estimation in which he held the servants of noble prelates, declaring that all were more or less rogues, had wit enough to see the dilemma in which he was placed. So he somewhat drily answered that he was sorry he was not capable of advising his master in an affair of such a particular kind as this.

The bishop, however, who had long known him better than he imagined, quickly perceived the ground of his reluctance to enter on the subject; and, feeling certain that the most greedy selfishness formed the chief ingredient in his servant's character, he plainly told him that if he would assist in securing the impending wager he should receive a handsome remuneration, in addition to a new scarlet cap.

This was intelligible language to Peter, and he opened his mouth, though, consistently with his character, it was only to observe upon the very trifling reward proposed, considering the immense amount of the wager in question; for, after all, what was a poor scarlet cap? In fact, the bishop was obliged to assure him that he did not intend to confine his gratitude to so slight a recompense before Peter would consent to put a hand to the job. But having made his terms, he was determined to spare nothing to bring the shepherd Conrad's honour into jeopardy. "Though he were a very phœnix of honesty," added he, "still he will have a fall."

On the following morning he rose with the determination to begin his machinations; and in a few hours he had learnt that Conrad had a sweetheart, the pretty Liese, to whom he was much attached. She would hear nothing of marriage, however, until he had a house of his own; and he was poor, and it would be the height of folly, in such circumstances, to load himself with the cares of a family.

All this Peter communicated to his master before dinner, and added that he had already obtained an interview with the fair Liese, and hence laid a plan to undermine the poor shepherd's integrity by means of the girl he loved. For this purpose he came to request a certain sum, which the bishop gave him.

He counted out the new shining pieces into his hand, reminding him at the same time to omit nothing that could tend to promote the success of their job. So Peter returned to finish his dialogue with the shepherd's sweetheart Liese, which was renewed as follows:

Peter. I am glad to hear, Liese, that Conrad has long been an admirer of yours : he is a brave, honest-hearted man.

Liese. It is easy to say yes ; but the ways and means are the main thing.

Peter. Oh, if he were really sincere, as no doubt he is, you need have no fear upon that head.

Liese. There you are mistaken, good man : we cannot live upon love, and money we have none.

Peter. Ah, does the shoe pinch there ?

Liese. Too true ! If Conrad had enough to buy a little house and a bit of land, it would alter the case. As it is, we must not think of marrying.

Peter. And why not ? I will undertake to give you as much as you want, provided you will assist me in return.

With these words Peter took out his purse and displayed a handful of money, which he threw upon a little table, so as almost to cover it. The money shone very temptingly in the maiden's eyes, and she longed to call it her own property. " Now," said the wily tempter, " the whole of this shall be yours when you agree to purchase for me the handsome ram belonging to Conrad's flock."

" Yes," said Liese, " but the ram does not belong to the shepherd."

"What signifies that ?" continued Peter. " He will find some means of obtaining it for you, at least if he loves you ; and you must take no denial."

" There you do him injustice," returned Liese. " I know he would lay down his life for me."

" Then put his affection to the proof only so far."

Liese, in addition to her wish to obtain the money, had now a curiosity to learn whether Conrad would make such a sacrifice to secure her affections. She promised the rogue that she would do everything in her power to engage Conrad to procure for him the handsome sheep, and Peter counted out the money, promising to bring more when he saw his purchase. Further to assure her, he said he would directly secure the little house and ground which she knew of before any other purchaser should appear.

In fact, he contrived to engage her so deeply in his web of villainy that she could not retract, and her only chance now lay in vanquishing Conrad's scruples about the removal of the sheep. In this his wily plan Peter had so far succeeded.

On the following day Liese decked herself out more elegantly than usual, and took her way towards the neighbourhood where Conrad was accustomed to pasture his sheep. As she approached the spot she pretended to be busily engaged in gathering herbs. Scarcely had Conrad got a sight of her than he ran to join her, and the tame sheep followed him. It was not long before he entered on the subject nearest his heart, inquiring earnestly when he might hope to call her his own.

But Liese answered him, far more coldly than usual, "I have heard enough of this, Conrad, a thousand times over; it is all nonsense, you know, until you can inform me that you have got a house and piece of ground where we may live together comfortably. Yes, you know my mind, and, until you can show me a house and field of our own, I shall never think of marrying."

Poor Conrad was turning sorrowfully away, quite cast down by this harsh treatment, such as he had never before received, when the artful maiden threw him an encouraging glance, adding, "A pretty specimen this of your love, Conrad, going off already in such a huff!"

"Good Lord," cried the shepherd, "how you torture one; first of all you find fault with me, and now you seem to doubt my love. I declare I would give my life for you, if that would be of any use. Only put me to the proof!"

"I do not want so much; but, as you desire it, I will just try whether your promises are worth anything."

The tame sheep at this moment thrust his head between the two lovers, and Liese gave him a piece of bread, which he began to eat.

"Then give me this pretty sheep here, Conrad. I am sure I can bring you a noble price for him."

The shepherd uttered an exclamation of surprise at the demand. At length he said, "Anything in the world, dear Liese, but not that. I never should be able to part with him, and if the bishop were to miss his tame ram as I drove home in the evening, and no longer stroked him with his own hand—no, I could never bear that. Take the best ten of my own from the flock; you are welcome to them, but leave the ram!"

"There, I said so," cried Liese, in an offended tone; "you men are all the same. Off with you, then, with all your sheep; for you will not show me the least favour, even when on the point of marriage; what might I expect afterwards? I see too well! So away! I will have nothing more to say to you."

With a frowning face she turned from him, though he entreated her with tears in his eyes not to exact so hard a proof of his affection. Sharp words—at least as harsh as lovers can use—now passed on both sides. The contest was long, but scarcely for a moment doubtful; for the maiden now acquainted Conrad that she had already agreed to dispose of the sheep, believing he would never refuse her; that further, she had accepted payment, and given earnest money, for the little property they had both so long wished for. In fact, she said, the sheep was sold and must be delivered up, cost what it would, for she had given her word and disposed of the purchase money.

This account she accompanied with a flood of tears, vowing that it was all owing to her affection for him, and now she was to be held up to the world as a liar and deceiver, and this she was resolved she would never outlive. The sole cause was her desire to secure the house and ground, where they might have spent many happy days; but now all her sweetest hopes were destroyed by his heartless obstinacy, which she would never bear.

"Were sheep never killed before?" she inquired of the wretched Conrad, as she concluded her lecture. "Are they never lost or stolen? Does the wolf never devour them now, as formerly? Speak!"

"I see it all," cried Conrad bitterly, quite vanquished by her reproaches and her tears, as he at the same time gave her his hand. "The sheep shall be delivered up to you before noon!" And in her turn Liese promised to become his wife at the month's end, and sealed this last contract with a kiss. The shepherd and his betrothed then took leave of each other, and Conrad gazed after her as long as she was in view.

Conrad, being now left alone, became more serious; his joy at the prospect of his marriage was sadly dashed by the thought of the scene that awaited him when the good bishop should first miss his tame sheep. How could he meet his eye, how muster courage to impose upon so excellent a master? He had been so long in his service, and thus to steal and lie at last—to steal his tame sheep, too, in which he took so much pleasure; it quite confounded all his ideas; he hardly knew whether he was dreaming or awake.

He stood cogitating on the spot where Liese had just before been gathering herbs. First, thought he, I shall have to speak to the bishop, and I must take care I am not taken by surprise and betray myself. He stuck his crook in the ground, then hung his coat over it, and placed his cap upon the top, declaring that he must try to act the part.

So he began to hold a dialogue with the bishop's effigy, in the following words, in which the tame sheep at his side often came in for a part: "God save you, Lord Bishop!" he cried out to the effigy. "Good-evening, Conrad," he went on; "where is the tame sheep?" "The ram, my Lord Bishop! the tame ram has overrun me. I have sought him everywhere. I have whistled for him as loud as I could, but he has never returned."

Conrad then whistled, and the ram began to bound and play with the counterfeit bishop before which the shepherd was bowing to the ground. "Alas," sighed Conrad, shaking his head, "this will never do! The poor fellow is too fond of bread to think of running away. The bishop will never believe it. No, no; I must hit upon something better. Well then—Ah, my Lord Bishop, such a misfortune, our handsome ram, poor Harne, is gone, stolen clean away!"

Just as he said these words, and bowed low before the bishop's image, poor Harne, as if in reply, gave him a pretty sharp push with his horns. "No, this is not the way either," exclaimed Conrad, as he turned angrily away from the hated spot; "it is not so easily done."

He next tried a variety of other means, all of which proved equally unsuccessful; and he shook his head, confessing that it was all of no use.

"Yet it must be done," he added; "it is to no purpose to think; at noon I am to deliver up poor Harne here, in order to save Liese's good name!"

Again he began to meditate, and after some time, in which he muttered deeply, searching for some loophole by which to make his escape, he suddenly cried with a more joyful and confident air:

"I have it, I have it now; it is the best, and honour wears longest in the end."

He threw his cloak over his shoulders, donned his cap, and drove his flock farther over the green. A little before noon, he went away, deeply sighing, with the favourite ram, in order to deliver him to Liese. Without troubling herself with any scruples, she in her turn gave him up to Peter, who had paid so high for him, and received the rest of the money, which she paid for the new house, while Peter hastened to his master. He acquainted him with his success, and the stranger bishop now chuckled in his sleeve at the idea of the approaching evening, when Conrad would appear as usual with his flock, and with a lie in his mouth, ready to impose upon his master. Peter seconded him in all his self-complacency and hopes of triumph over his host, omitting not, at the same time, to remind him respecting his promise of the new scarlet cap, and the other presents he was to receive in the morning. At the appointed hour the two bishops stationed themselves, as usual, in the courtyard of the castle. Conrad now appeared in view driving his flock from the field, and slowly approached the spot where the good prelates were waiting for him. The wily guest, with his servant Peter standing behind him, secretly congratulated himself upon the security of his wager, and both imagined they could trace in Conrad's features, as he approached, an expression of alarm, and the twinges of a conscience ill at rest.

Harne, the handsome ram, was nowhere to be seen, nor ran as usual to receive his allowance from the bishop, and feel the honour of his lordly hand. "Where is Harne?" inquired the bishop the moment that he missed him.

"I have sold him," returned Conrad, in an earnest and decided tone; "he is not here. Honour wears the longest, my good lord bishop. I always shaped my course by it, and I will not depart from it now."

Peter's countenance grew a wonderfully deal longer when he heard these words, and his master looked little better, both being woefully disappointed and cast down. But Bishop Henry of Halberstadt cried in a loud tone, while his face darkened with the most ominous frowns, "Idiot as thou art! how dared you to think of selling the tame ram without first obtaining my permission? but I will——"

"Most noble master," interrupted Conrad, "hear me patiently before you condemn me, let me beseech you! It was the maiden Liese who seduced me, exactly as Eve did Adam, and some arch villain hath likewise seduced Liese, exactly like the base fiend did Eve. If he will consent, however, to give me back the ram, I will not expose his name."

At the same time Conrad fixed his eyes upon Peter, who, full of rage and vexation, drew somewhat back; for he now saw full well that he should be accused of having thrown his master's money away for nothing, that he must go without his new scarlet cap, and all the other presents he had expected, while his tricks would be made manifest to the world.

"It was Liese," continued Conrad, "who engaged for the sale of Harne, or all this would never have happened" (at these words his master began to breathe, scenting which way the wind lay). " You know how long we have loved each other, only waiting to marry until we had got a little more beforehand. She has received so large a sum for the sheep as to enable her to buy house and land sufficient to maintain us both with industry and care. She engaged for all this, and when she had said, ' Yea, please your reverend honour, and I will marry you,' I could hardly get courage to say, ' No, you shall not,' for then I must have exposed her as an impostor to the world. With the priest's help and blessing she will soon be my wife ; and I am sure your reverence is too good not to permit the happiness of two human beings on account of the sale of one sheep ; and for a servant who has served you so long and faithfully. This is the whole truth of the matter, my lord bishop, and now deal with me as you will ; what is done is done, and Harne is gone. But do not punish me harder than your own conscience will warrant ; and do nothing to Liese, I beseech you. It was the base fiend blinded her, and all out of love for me, and I am in little better case myself."

These declarations appeared so hard of digestion to the bishop that he was just on the point of giving fresh rein to his anger, when his guest with a fierce look, turning towards Peter, said, " Thou jolterhead, then I have lost my bet after all, through thee ! " and he stamped indignantly with his foot.

" What say you there ? " inquired the bishop of his guest, as he heard this final confirmation of his suspicions. Upon this, the other could not avoid coming to an explanation of the whole affair, which afforded the Bishop of Halberstadt the greatest satisfaction. He the more easily forgave his shepherd, as by his excellent conduct he had secured him the wager, having had the honesty and the courage to tell the truth.

" Well, then, honour wears the longest ! " cried both the bishops in a breath ; and Conrad's master added, " As a due return for your honourable conduct I take upon myself the whole expense of your marriage with Liese, and divide the whole flock with you."

To this the stranger bishop added, " I shall not after this venture to be stingy. I freely give the shepherd back his ram ; the money I gave he may retain—it will serve as a wedding dower for his wife and the christening of the first child."

The Bishop of Halberstadt was shortly afterwards presented by his reverend friend with the large vat of wine, which he had fairly won.

JOHANNES H. D. ZSCHOKKE
1771–1848

THE BROKEN CUP

THAT Napoule is only a very little place on the bay of Cannes is true; yet it is pretty well known through all Provence. It lies in the shade of lofty evergreen palms and darker orange trees; but that alone would not make it renowned. Still they say that there are grown the most luscious grapes, the sweetest roses, and the handsomest girls. I don't know but it is so; in the meantime I believe it most readily. Pity that Napoule is so small, and cannot produce more luscious grapes, fragrant roses, and handsome maidens; especially, as we might then have some of them transplanted to our own country.

As, ever since the foundation of Napoule, all the Napoulese women have been beauties, so the little Marietta was a wonder of wonders, as the chronicles of the place declare. She was called the little Marietta; yet she was not smaller than a girl of seventeen or thereabout ought to be, seeing that her forehead just reached up to the lips of a grown man.

The chronicles aforesaid had very good ground for speaking of Marietta. I, had I stood in the shoes of the chronicler, would have done the same. For Marietta, who until lately had lived with her mother Manon at Avignon, when she came back to her birthplace, quite upset the whole village. Verily, not the houses, but the people and their heads; and not the heads of all the people, but of those particularly whose heads and hearts are always in danger when in the neighbourhood of two bright eyes. I know very well that such a position is no joke.

Mother Manon would have done much better if she had remained at Avignon. But she had been left a small inheritance, by which she received at Napoule an estate consisting of some vine-hills, and a house that lay in the shadow of a rock, between certain olive trees and African acacias. This is a kind of thing which no unprovided widow ever rejects; and, accordingly, in her own estimation, she was as rich and happy as though she were the Countess of Provence or something like it.

So much the worse was it for the good people of Napoule. They never suspected their misfortune, not having read in Homer how a single pretty woman had filled all Greece and Lesser Asia with discord and war.

. . . .

Marietta had scarcely been fourteen days in the house between the olive trees and the African acacias before every young man of Napoule knew that she lived there, and that there lived not in all Provence a more charming girl than the one in that house.

Went she through the village, sweeping lightly along like a dressed-up angel, her frock, with its pale-green bodice, and orange leaves and rosebuds upon the bosom of it, fluttering in the breeze, and flowers and ribbons waving about the straw bonnet, which shaded her beautiful features—yes, then the grave old men spake out, and the young ones were struck dumb. And everywhere, to the right and left, little windows and doors were opened with a " Good-morning," or a " Good-evening, Marietta," as it might be, while she nodded to the right and left with a pleasant smile.

If Marietta walked into church, all hearts (that is, of the young people) forgot Heaven ; all eyes turned from the saints, and the worshipping finger wandered idly among the pearls of the rosary. This must certainly have provoked much sorrow, at least among the more devout.

The maidens of Napoule particularly became very pious about this time, for they, most of all, took the matter to heart. And they were not to be blamed for it ; for since the advent of Marietta more than one prospective groom had become cold, and more than one worshipper of some beloved one quite inconstant. There were bickerings and reproaches on all sides, many tears, pertinent lectures, and even rejections. The talk was no longer of marriages, but of separations. They began to return their pledges of troth, rings, ribbons, etc. The old persons took part with their children ; criminations and strife spread from house to house ; it was most deplorable.

" Marietta is the cause of all," said the pious maidens first ; then the mothers said it ; next the fathers took it up ; and finally all—even the young men. But Marietta, shielded by her modesty and innocence, like the petals of the rosebud in its dark-green calix, did not suspect the mischief of which she was the occasion, and continued courteous to everybody. This touched the young men, who said, " Why condemn the pure and harmless child—she is not guilty!" Then the fathers said the same thing; then the mothers took it up, and finally all—even the pious maidens. For, let who would talk with Marietta, she was sure to gain their esteem. So before half a year had passed, everybody had spoken to her, and everybody loved her. But she did not suspect that she was the object of such general regard, as she had not before suspected that she was the object of dislike. Does the violet, hidden in the down-trodden grass, think how sweet it is?

Now every one wished to make amends for the injustice they had done Marietta. Sympathy deepened the tenderness of their attachment. Marietta found herself greeted everywhere in a more friendly way than ever; she was more cordially welcomed, more heartily invited to the rural sports and dances.

. . . .

All men, however, are not endowed with tender sympathy; some have hearts hardened like Pharaoh's. This arises, no doubt, from that natural depravity which has come upon men in consequence of the fall of Adam, or because, at their baptism, the devil is not brought sufficiently under subjection.

A remarkable example of this hardness of heart was given by one Colin, the richest farmer and proprietor in Napoule, whose vineyards and olive gardens, whose lemon and orange trees could hardly be counted in a day. One thing particularly demonstrates the perverseness of his disposition; he was twenty-seven years old, and had never yet asked for what purpose girls had been created!

True, all the people, especially damsels of a certain age, willingly forgave him this sin, and looked upon him as one of the best young men under the sun. His fine figure, his fresh, unembarrassed manner, his look, his laugh, enabled him to gain the favourable opinion of the aforesaid people, who would have forgiven him, had there been occasion, any one of the deadly sins. But the decision of such judges is not always to be trusted.

While both old and young at Napoule had become reconciled to the innocent Marietta, and proffered their sympathies to her, Colin was the only one who had no pity upon the poor child. If Marietta was talked of he became as dumb as a fish. If he met her in the street he would turn red and white with anger, and cast sidelong glances at her of the most malicious kind.

If at evening the young people met upon the seashore near the old castle ruins for sprightly pastimes, or rural dances, or to sing catches, Colin was the merriest among them. But as soon as Marietta arrived the rascally fellow was silent, and all the gold in the world couldn't have made him sing. What a pity, when he had such a fine voice! Everybody listened to it so willingly, and its store of songs was endless.

All the maidens looked kindly upon Colin, and he was friendly with all of them. He had, as we have said, a roguish glance, which the lasses feared and loved; and it was so sweet they would like to have had it painted. But, as might naturally be expected, the offended Marietta did not look graciously upon him. And in that she was perfectly right. Whether he smiled or not, it was all the same to her. As to his roguish glance, why, she would never hear it mentioned; and therein too she was perfectly right. When he told a tale (and he knew thousands) and everybody listened, she nudged her neighbour, or perhaps threw tufts of grass at Peter or Paul, and laughed and chattered, and did not listen to Colin at all. This behaviour quite provoked the proud fellow, so that he would break off in the middle of his story and stalk sullenly away.

Revenge is sweet. The daughter of Mother Manon well knew how to triumph. Yet Marietta was a right good child and quite too tender-hearted. If Colin was silent, it gave her pain. If he was downcast, she laughed no more. If he went away, she did not stay long behind, but hurried to her home, and wept tears of repentance, more beautiful than those of the Magdalen, although she had not sinned like the Magdalen.

. . . .

Father Jerome, the pastor of Napoule, was an old man of seventy, who possessed all the virtues of a saint, and only one failing, which was, that by reason of his advanced years he was hard of hearing. But, on that very account, his homilies were more acceptable to the children of his baptism and blessing. True, he preached only of two subjects, as if they comprehended the whole of religion. It was either "Little children, love one another," or it was "Mysterious are the ways of Providence." And truly there is so much Faith, Love and Hope in these that one might at a pinch be saved by them. The little children loved one another most obediently, and trusted in the ways of Providence. Only Colin, with his flinty heart, would know nothing of either: for even when he professed to be friendly, he entertained the deepest malice.

The Napoulese went to the annual market or fair of the city of Vence. It was truly a joyful time, and though they had but little gold to buy with, there were many goods to look at. Now Marietta and Mother Manon went to the fair with the rest, and Colin was also there. He bought a great many curiosities and trifles for his friends—but he would not spend a farthing for Marietta. And yet he was always at her elbow, though he did not speak to her, nor she to him. It was easy to see that he was brooding over some scheme of wickedness.

Mother Manon stood gazing before a shop, when she suddenly exclaimed:

"Oh! Marietta, see that beautiful cup! A queen would not be ashamed to raise it to her lips. Only see: the edge is of dazzling gold, and the flowers upon it could not bloom more beautifully in the garden, although they are only painted. And in the midst of this Paradise! pray see, Marietta, how the apples are smiling on the trees. They are verily tempting. And Adam cannot withstand it, as the enchanting Eve offers him one for food! And do see how prettily the little frisking lamb skips around the old tiger, and the snow-white dove with her golden throat stands there before the vulture, as if she would caress him!"

Marietta could not satisfy herself with looking. "Had I such a cup, mother!" she said, "it is far too beautiful to drink out of: I would place my flowers in it and constantly peep into Paradise. We are at the fair in Vence, but when I look on the picture I feel as if I were in Paradise."

So spoke Marietta, and called her companions to the spot to share her admiration of the cup: but the young men soon joined the maidens, until at length almost half the inhabitants of Napoule were assembled before the wonderfully beautiful cup. But miraculously beautiful was it mainly from its inestimable, translucent porcelain, with gilded handles and glowing colours. They asked the merchant timidly, "Sir, what is the price of it?" And he answered, "Among friends, it is worth a hundred livres." Then they all became silent, and went away in despair. When the Napoulese were all gone from the front of the shop, Colin came there by stealth, threw the merchant a hundred livres upon the counter, had the cup put in a box well packed with cotton, and then carried it off. What evil plans he had in view no one would have surmised.

Near Napoule, on his way home, it being already dusk, he met old

Jacques, the Justice's servant, returning from the fields. Jacques was a very good man, but excessively stupid.

" I will give thee money enough to get something to drink, Jacques," said Colin, " if thou wilt bear this box to Manon's house, and leave it there ; and if any one should see thee, and inquire from whom the box came, say, ' A stranger gave it to me.' But never disclose my name, or I will always detest thee."

Jacques promised this, took the drink-money and the box, and went with it toward the little dwelling between the olive trees and the African acacias.

. . . .

Before he arrived there he encountered his master, Justice Hautmartin, who asked, " Jacques, what art thou carrying ? "

" A box for Mother Manon. But, sir, I cannot say from whom it comes."

" Why not ? "

" Because Colin would always detest me."

" It is well that thou canst keep a secret. But it is already late ; give me the box, for I am going to-morrow to see Mother Manon ; I will deliver it to her and not betray that it came from Colin. It will save thee a walk, and furnish me a good excuse for calling on the old lady."

Jacques gave the box to his master, whom he was accustomed to obey implicitly in all things. The justice bore it into his chamber, and examined it by the light with some curiosity. On the lid was neatly written with red chalk : " For the lovely and dear Marietta." But Monsieur Hautmartin well knew that this was some of Colin's mischief, and that some knavish trick lurked under the whole. He therefore opened the box carefully for fear that a mouse or rat should be concealed within. When he beheld the wondrous cup, which he had seen at Vence, he was dreadfully shocked, for Monsieur Hautmartin was a skilful casuist, and knew that the inventions and devices of the human heart are evil from our youth upward. He saw at once that Colin designed this cup as a means of bringing misfortune upon Marietta : perhaps to give out, when it should be in her possession, that it was the present of some successful lover in the town, or the like, so that all decent people would thereafter keep aloof from Marietta. Therefore Monsieur Hautmartin resolved, in order to prevent any evil reports, to profess himself the giver. Moreover, he loved Marietta, and would gladly have seen her observe more strictly toward himself the sayings of the grey-headed priest Jerome, " Little children, love one another." In truth, Monsieur Hautmartin was a little child of fifty years old, and Marietta did not think the saying applied particularly to him. Mother Manon, on the contrary, thought that the Justice was a clever little child, he had gold and a high reputation from one end of Napoule to the other. And when the Justice spoke of marriage, and Marietta ran away in affright, Mother Manon remained sitting, and had no fear for the tall, staid gentleman. It must also be confessed there were no faults in his person. And although Colin might be the handsomest man in the village, yet the Justice far surpassed him in two things, namely, in the number of years, and in a very, very big nose. Yes, this nose, which always went before the Justice like a herald to proclaim his approach, was a real elephant among human noses.

With this proboscis, his good purpose, and the cup, the Justice went the following morning to the house between the olive trees and the African acacias.

" For the beautiful Marietta," said he, " I hold nothing too costly. Yesterday you admired the cup at Vence ; to-day allow me, lovely Marietta, to lay it and my devoted heart at your feet."

Manon and Marietta were transported beyond measure when they beheld the cup. Manon's eyes glistened with delight, but Marietta turned and said, " I can take neither your heart nor your cup."

Then Mother Manon was angry, and cried out, " But I accept both heart and cup. Oh, thou little fool, how long wilt thou despise thy good fortune ! For whom dost thou tarry? Will a count of Provence make thee his bride, that thou scornest the Justice of Napoule ? I know better how to look after my interests. Monsieur Hautmartin, I deem it an honour to call thee my son-in-law."

Then Marietta went out and wept bitterly, and hated the beautiful cup with all her heart.

But the Justice, drawing the palm of his flabby hand over his nose, spoke thus judiciously :

" Mother Manon, hurry nothing. The dove will at length, when it learns to know me better, give way. I am not impetuous. I have some skill among women, and before a quarter of a year passes by I will insinuate myself into Marietta's good graces."

" Thy nose is too large for that," whispered Marietta, who listened outside the door and laughed to herself. In fact, the quarter of a year passed by and Monsieur Hautmartin had not yet pierced the heart even with the tip of his nose.

During this quarter of a year Marietta had other affairs to attend to. The cup gave her much vexation and trouble, and something else besides.

For a fortnight nothing else was talked of in Napoule, and every one said it is a present from the Justice, and the marriage is already agreed upon. Marietta solemnly declared to all her companions that she would rather plunge to the bottom of the sea than marry the Justice, but the maidens continued to banter her all the more, saying, "Oh, how blissful it must be to repose in the shadow of his nose!" This was her first vexation.

Then Mother Manon had the cruelty to force Marietta to rinse out the cup every morning at the spring under the rock and to fill it with fresh flowers. She hoped by this to accustom Marietta to the cup and heart of the giver. But Marietta continued to hate both the gift and giver, and her work at the spring became an actual punishment. Second vexation.

Then when, in the morning, she came to the spring, twice every week she found on the rock, immediately over it, some most beautiful flowers, handsomely arranged, all ready for the decoration of the cup. And on the flower-stalks a strip of paper was always tied, on which was written, "Dear Marietta." Now no one need expect to impose upon little Marietta as if magicians and fairies were still in the world. Consequently she knew that both the flowers and papers must have come from Monsieur Hautmartin. Marietta, indeed, would not smell them because the living breath from out of the Justice's nose had perfumed them. Nevertheless she took the flowers, because they were finer than wild flowers, and tore the slip of paper into a thousand pieces, which she strewed upon the spot where the flowers usually lay. But this did not vex Justice Hautmartin, whose love was unparalleled in its kind as his nose was in its kind. Third vexation.

At length it came out in conversation with Monsieur Hautmartin that he was not the giver of the beautiful flowers. Then who could it be? Marietta was utterly astounded at the unexpected discovery. Thenceforth she took the flowers from the rock more kindly; but, further, Marietta was—what maidens are not wont to be—very inquisitive. She conjectured first this and then that young man in Napoule. Yet her conjectures were in vain. She looked and listened far into the night ; she rose earlier than usual. But she looked and listened in vain. And still twice a week in the morning the miraculous flowers lay upon the rock, and upon the strip of paper wound round them she always read the silent sigh, " Dear Marietta ! " Such an incident would have made even the most indifferent inquisitive. But curiosity at length became a burning pain. Fourth vexation.

. . . .

Now Father Jerome, on Sunday, had again preached from the text : " Mysterious are the dispensations of Providence." And little Marietta thought, " If Providence would only dispense that I might at length find out who is the flower dispenser. Father Jerome was never wrong."

On a summer night, when it was far too warm to rest, Marietta awoke very early, and could not resume her sleep. Therefore she sprang joyously from her couch as the first streaks of dawn flashed against the window of her little chamber, over the waves of the sea and the Lerinian Isles, dressed herself, and went out to wash her forehead, breast, and arms in the cool spring. She took her hat with her, intending to take a walk by the seashore, as she knew of a retired place for bathing.

In order to reach this retired spot it was necessary to pass over the rocks behind the house, and thence down through the orange and palm trees. On this occasion Marietta could not pass through them ; for under the youngest and most slender of the palms lay a tall young man in profound sleep—near him a nosegay of most splendid flowers. A white paper lay thereon, from which probably a sigh was again breathing. How could Marietta get by there ?

She stood still, trembling with fright. She would go home again. Hardly had she retreated a couple of steps, ere she looked again at the sleeper, and remained motionless. Yet the distance prevented her from recognising his face. Now the mystery was to be solved, or never. She tripped lightly nearer to the palms ; but he seemed to stir—then she ran again toward the cottage. His movements were but the fearful imaginings of Marietta. Now she returned again on her way toward the palms ; but his sleep might perhaps be only dissembled—swiftly she ran toward the cottage—but who would flee for a mere probability ? She trod more boldly the path toward the palms.

With these fluctuations of her timid and joyous spirit, between fright and curiosity, with these to-and-fro trippings between the house and the palm trees, she at length nearly approached the sleeper; at the same time curiosity became more powerful than fear.

"What is he to me? My way leads me directly past him. Whether he sleeps or wakes, I will go straight on." So thought Manon's daughter. But she passed not by, but stood looking directly in the face of the flower-giver, in order to be certain who it was. Besides, he slept as if it were the first time in a month. And who was it? Now, who else should it be but the arch, wicked Colin.

So it was *he* who had annoyed the gentle maiden, and given her so much trouble with Monsieur Hautmartin, because he bore a grudge against her; he had been the one who had teased her with flowers, in order to torture her curiosity. Wherefore? He hated Marietta. He behaved himself always most shamefully toward the poor child. He avoided her when he could; and when he could not, he grieved the good-natured little one. With all the other maidens of Napoule he was more chatty, friendly, courteous, than toward Marietta. Consider—he had never once asked her to dance, and yet she danced bewitchingly.

Now there he lay, surprised, taken in the act. Revenge swelled in Marietta's bosom. What disgrace could she subject him to? She took the nosegay, unloosened it, strewed his present over the sleeper in scorn. But the paper, on which appeared again the sigh, "Dear Marietta!" she retained, and thrust quickly into her bosom. She wished to preserve this proof of his handwriting. Marietta was sly. Now she would go away. But her revenge was not yet satisfied. She could not leave the place without returning Colin's ill-will. She took the violet-coloured silken ribbon from her hat, and threw it lightly around the sleeper's arm and around the tree, and with three knots tied Colin fast. Now when he awoke, how astonished he would be! How his curiosity would torment him to ascertain who had played him this trick! He could not possibly know. So much the better; it served him right. She seemed to regret her work when she had finished it. Her bosom throbbed impetuously. Indeed, I believe that a little tear filled her eye, as she compassionately gazed upon the guilty one. Slowly she retreated to the orange grove by the rocks—she looked around often—slowly ascended the rocks, looking down among the palm trees as she ascended. Then she hastened to Mother Manon, who was calling her.

. . . .

That very day Colin practised new mischief. What did he? He wished to shame the poor Marietta publicly. Ah! she never thought that every one in Napoule knew her violet-coloured ribbon! Colin remembered it but too well. Proudly he bound it around his hat, and exhibited it to the gaze of all the world as a conquest. And male and female cried out, " He has received it from Marietta." And all the maidens said angrily, " The reprobate!" And all the young men who liked to see Marietta cried out, " The reprobate!"

" How! Mother Manon?" shrieked the Justice Hautmartin when he came to her house, and he shrieked so loudly that it re-echoed wonderfully through his nose. " How! Do you suffer this? my betrothed presents the young proprietor Colin with her hat-band! It is high time that we celebrate our nuptials. When that is over, then I shall have a right to speak."

" You have a right!" answered Mother Manon. " If things are so, the marriage must take place forthwith. When that is done, all will go right."

" But, Mother Manon, Marietta always refuses to give me her consent."

" Prepare the marriage feast."

" But she will not even look kindly at me; and when I seat myself at her side, the little savage jumps up and runs away."

" Justice, only prepare the marriage feast."

" But if Marietta resists——"

" We will take her by surprise. We will go to Father Jerome on Monday morning early, and he shall quietly celebrate the marriage. This we can easily accomplish with him. I am her mother, you the first judicial person in Napoule. He must obey. Marietta need know nothing about it. Early on Monday morning I will send her to Father Jerome all alone, with a message so that she will suspect nothing. Then the priest shall speak earnestly to her. Half an hour afterward we two will come. Then swiftly to the altar. And even if Marietta should then say No, what does it matter? The old priest can hear nothing. But till then, mum to Marietta and all Napoule."

So the secret remained with the two. Marietta dreamed not of the good luck which was in store for her. She thought only of Colin's wickedness, which had made her the common talk of the whole place. Oh! how she repented her heedlessness about the ribbon; and yet in her heart she forgave the reprobate his crime. Marietta was far too good. She told her mother, she told all her playmates: "Colin has found my lost band. I never gave it to him. He only wishes to vex me with it. You all know that Colin was always ill-disposed toward me, and always sought to mortify me!"

Ah! the poor child! she knew not what new abomination the malicious fellow was again contriving.

. . . .

Early in the morning Marietta went to the spring with the cup. There were no flowers yet on the rock. It was still much too early; for the sun had scarcely risen from the sea.

Footsteps were heard. Colin came in sight, the flowers in his hand. Marietta became very red. Colin stammered out: "Good-morning, Marietta," but the greeting came not from his heart.

"Why dost thou wear my ribbon so publicly, Colin?" said Marietta, and placed the cup upon the rock. "I did not give it thee."

"Thou didst not give it to me, dear Marietta?" asked he, and inward rage made him deadly pale.

Marietta was ashamed of the falsehood, drooped her eyelids, and said after a while: "Well, I did give it thee, yet thou shouldst not have worn it. Give it back."

Slowly he untied it; his anger was so great that he could not prevent the tears from filling his eyes, nor the sighs from escaping his breast. "Dear Marietta, leave thy ribbon with me," said he softly.

"No," answered she.

Then his suppressed passion changed into desperation. Sighing, he looked toward heaven, then sadly on Marietta, who, silent and abashed, stood by the spring with downcast eyes.

He wound the violet-coloured ribbon around the stalks of the flowers, and said; "There, take them all," and threw the flowers so spitefully against the magnificent cup upon the rock that it was thrown down and dashed to pieces. Maliciously he fled away.

Mother Manon, lurking behind the window, had seen and heard all. When the cup broke, hearing and sight left her. She was scarcely able to speak for very horror. And as she pushed with all her strength against the narrow window, to shout after the guilty one, it gave way, and with one crash fell to earth and was shattered in pieces.

So much ill-luck would have discomposed any other woman. But Manon soon recovered herself. "How lucky that I was a witness to this roguery!" exclaimed she; "he must to the Justice—he shall replace both cup and window-sash with his gold. It will give a rich dowry to Marietta." But when Marietta brought in the fragments of the shattered cup, when Manon saw the Paradise lost, the good man Adam without a head, and of Eve not a solitary limb remaining, the serpent unhurt, triumphing, the tiger safe, but the little lamb gone even to the very tail, as if the tiger had swallowed it, then Mother Manon screamed forth curses against Colin, and said : " One can easily see that this *fall* came from the hand of the devil."

. . . .

She took the cup in one hand, Marietta in the other, and went, about nine o'clock, to where Monsieur Hautmartin was wont to sit in judgment. She there made a great outcry, and showed the broken cup and the Paradise lost. Marietta wept bitterly.

The Justice, when he saw the broken cup and his beautiful bride in tears, flew into so violent a rage toward Colin that his nose was as violet-coloured as Marietta's well-known hat-band. He immediately despatched his bailiffs to bring the criminal before him.

Colin came, overwhelmed with grief. Mother Manon now repeated her complaint with great eloquence before Justice, bailiffs and scribes. But Colin listened not. He stepped to Marietta and whispered to her : " Forgive me, dear Marietta, as I forgive thee. I broke thy cup unintentionally ; but thou, thou hast broken my heart ! "

" What whispering is that ? " cried Justice Hautmartin, with magisterial authority. " Hearken to this accusation, and defend yourself."

" I have naught to defend. I broke the cup against my will," said Colin.

" That I verily believe," said Marietta, sobbing. " I am as guilty as he ; for I offended him—then he threw the ribbon and flowers to me. He could not help it."

" Well ! " cried Mother Manon. " Do you intend to defend him ? Mr. Justice, pronounce his sentence. He has broken the cup, and he does not deny it."

" Since you cannot deny it, Mr. Colin," said the Justice, " you must pay three hundred livres for the cup, for it is worth that ; and then for——"

" No," interrupted Colin, " it is not worth that. I bought it at Vence for Marietta for a hundred livres."

" You bought it, sir brazen face ? " shrieked the Justice, and his whole face became like Marietta's hat-band. He could not and would not say more, for he dreaded a disagreeable investigation of the matter.

But Colin was vexed at the imputation, and said: "I sent this cup on the evening of the fair, by your own servant, to Marietta. There stands Jacques in the door. Speak, Jacques, did I not give thee the box to carry to Mother Manon?"

Monsieur Hautmartin wished to interrupt this conversation by speaking loudly. But the simple Jacques said: "Only recollect, Justice, you took away Colin's box from me, and carried what was in it to Mother Manon. The box lies there under the papers."

Then the bailiffs were ordered to remove the simpleton; and Colin was also directed to retire, until he should be sent for again.

"Very well, Mr. Justice," interposed Colin, "but this business shall be your last in Napoule. I know this, that you would ingratiate yourself with Mother Manon and Marietta by means of my property. When you want me, you will have to ride to Grasse to the Governor's." With that, Colin departed.

Monsieur Hautmartin was quite puzzled with this affair, and in his confusion knew not what he was about. Manon shook her head. The affair was dark and mysterious to her. "Who will now pay me for the broken cup?" she asked.

"To me," said Marietta, with glowing, brightened countenance, "to *me* it is already paid for."

. . . .

Colin rode that same day to the Governor at Grasse, and came back early the next morning. But Justice Hautmartin only laughed at him, and removed all of Mother Manon's suspicions by swearing he would let his nose be cut off if Colin did not pay three hundred livres for the broken cup. He also went with Mother Manon to talk with Father Jerome about the marriage, and impressed upon him the necessity of earnestly setting before Marietta her duty as an obedient daughter in not opposing the will of her mother. This the pious old man promised, although he understood not the half of what they shouted in his ear.

When Monday morning came Mother Manon said to her daughter: "Dress yourself handsomely, and carry this myrtle wreath to Father Jerome; he wants it for a bride." Marietta dressed herself in her Sunday clothes, took the myrtle wreath unsuspiciously, and carried it to Father Jerome.

On the way Colin met her, and greeted her joyfully, though timidly; and when she told him where she was taking the wreath, Colin said: "I am going the same way, for I am carrying the money for the church's tenths to the priest." And as they went on he took her hand silently, and both trembled as if they designed some crime against each other.

"Hast thou forgiven me?" whispered Colin, anxiously. "Ah! Marietta, what have I done to thee, that thou art so cruel toward me?"

She could only say: "Be quiet, Colin, you shall have the ribbon again; and I will preserve the cup since it came from you! Did it really come from you?"

"Ah! Marietta, canst thou doubt it? All I have I would gladly give thee. Wilt thou, hereafter, be as kind to me as thou art to others?"

She replied not. But as she entered the parsonage she looked aside at him, and when she saw his fine eyes filled with tears, she whispered softly: "Dear Colin!" Then he bent down and kissed her hand. With this the door of a chamber opened and Father Jerome, with venerable aspect, stood before them. The young couple held fast to each other. I know not whether this was the effect of the hand-kissing, or the awe they felt for the sage.

Marietta handed him the myrtle wreath. He laid it upon her head and said: "Little children, love one another"; and then urged the good maiden, in the most touching and pathetic manner, to love Colin. For the old gentleman, from his hardness of hearing, had either mistaken the name of the bridegroom, or forgotten it, and thought Colin must be the bridegroom.

Then Marietta's heart softened under the exhortation, and with tears and sobs she exclaimed: "Ah! I have loved him for a long time, but he hates me."

"I hate thee, Marietta?" cried Colin. "My soul has lived only in thee since thou camest to Napoule. Oh! Marietta, how could I hope and believe that thou didst love me? Does not all Napoule worship thee?"

"Why, then, dost thou avoid me, Colin, and prefer all my companions before me?"

"Oh! Marietta, I feared and trembled with love and anxiety when I beheld thee; I had not the courage to approach thee; and when I was away from thee I was most miserable."

As they talked thus with each other the good father thought they were quarrelling; and he threw his arms around them, brought them together, and said imploringly: "Little children, love one another."

Then Marietta sank on Colin's breast, and Colin threw his arms around her, and both faces beamed with rapture. They forgot the priest, the whole world. Each was sunk into the other. Both had so completely lost their recollection that, unwittingly, they followed the delightful Father Jerome into the church and before the altar.

"Marietta!" sighed he.

"Colin!" sighed she.

In the church there were many devout worshippers; but they witnessed Colin's and Marietta's marriage with amazement. Many ran out before the close of the ceremony, to spread the news throughout Napoule: "Colin and Marietta are married."

When the solemnisation was over, Father Jerome rejoiced that he had succeeded so well, and that such little opposition had been made by the parties. He led them into the parsonage.

. . . .

Then Mother Manon arrived, breathless; she had waited at home a long time for the bridegroom. He had not arrived. At the last stroke of the clock she grew anxious and went to Monsieur Hautmartin's. There a new surprise awaited her. She learned that the Governor, together with the officers of the Viguerie, had appeared and taken possession of the accounts, chests and papers of the Justice and at the same time arrested Monsieur Hautmartin.

"This, surely, is the work of that wicked Colin," thought she, and hurried to the parsonage in order to apologise to Father Jerome for delaying the marriage. The good grey-headed old man advanced toward her, proud of his work, and leading by the hand the newly-married pair.

Now Mother Manon lost her wits and her speech in good earnest when she learned what had happened. But Colin had more thoughts and power of speech than in his whole previous life. He told of his love and the broken cup, the falsehood of the Justice, and how he had unmasked this unjust magistrate in the Viguerie at Grasse. Then he besought Mother Manon's blessing, since all this had happened without any fault on the part of Marietta or himself.

Father Jerome, who for a long while could not make out what had happened, when he received a full explanation of the marriage through mistake, piously folded his hands and exclaimed, with uplifted eyes: "Wonderful are the dispensations of Providence!" Colin and Marietta kissed his hands; Mother Manon, through sheer veneration of heaven, gave the young couple her blessing, but remarked incidentally that her head seemed turned round.

Mother Manon herself was pleased with her son-in-law when she came to know the full extent of his property, and especially when she found that Monsieur Hautmartin and his nose had been arrested.

"But am I then really a wife?" asked Marietta; "and really Colin's wife?"

Mother Manon nodded her head, and Marietta hung upon Colin's arm. Thus they went to Colin's farm, to his dwelling-house, through the garden.

"Look at the flowers, Marietta," said Colin; "how carefully I cultivated them for your cup!"

Colin, who had not expected so pleasant an event, now prepared a wedding feast on the spur of the occasion. Two days was it continued. All Napoule was feasted. Who shall describe Colin's extravagance?

The broken cup is preserved in the family to the present day as a memorial and sacred relic.

HOW THE VICAR CAME ROUND

JOHANNES H. D. ZSCHOKKE

THE Frau Obersteuerrätin was "auntie" to the whole world; and indeed she deserved the name, for she was a motherly friend, counsellor and helper to all who came within her domain; she was the best and most charitable of women, judging mildly of the weaknesses of others so long as her own little weaknesses were respected. She overlooked the eccentricities of her clerical brother, which he committed in a state of absent-mindedness, and she did not raise any objections to Susie's marvellous *naïveté*, though often enough it caused her bitter dilemmas.

It was a warm May day on which the Vicar entered the room with his usual greeting: "Good-morning, Auntie—good-morning, Susie."

Auntie nodded pleasantly. Susie, who was sitting by her on the sofa, knitting a white stocking, arose, dropped a little familiar curtsey, and said: "*Votre servante*, Uncle."

"But, Heaven preserve us, what is the matter with you to-day, Vicar?" said Aunt Rosmarin.

"How so?" queried the Vicar, putting his hands in all of his pockets in a vain search for a handkerchief with which to wipe the perspiration from his brow.

"It's very likely you have your wig in your pocket," said Auntie, "for your handkerchief is on your head."

"On my head," exclaimed the Vicar in surprise, and putting his hand there he found it. "I shouldn't be greatly surprised if you were right, Auntie; it's a hot, hot day; the sun was burning, my back was burning; I came from town, so I took off my wig to cool my head, spread my handkerchief over the latter, and lay down in a corn-field."

Again he began to search his pockets, while Susie made room for him on the sofa, and went out to get him a refreshing drink of water and raspberry syrup.

"What are you looking for, Vicar?" asked Auntie.

"If I mistake not, I brought a letter for you from town; but what has become of it is more than I can tell. I think it is from the Burgomaster. Seek and ye shall find."

"But, Vicar, first of all, put on your wig—this is very indecent. It is an insult to your congregation to walk about bald-headed."

"I should hope not. But in that case I trust that there would be bears to obey me, like the prophet Elisha, and devour all bad boys who would make bold to have a laugh at me. But, *ad vocem*, my wig, Auntie; what did you do with it?"

"What did I do with it? You did not entrust it to my keeping. Perhaps you lost it on the way!"

"Heaven preserve us! It was my best wig. You are right, Auntie; it is lying in the grass, together with the Burgomaster's letter, precisely on the spot where I myself lay a quarter of an hour ago, in the shadow of the corn."

Auntie seized her bell. The maid appeared; the Inspector was called, and ordered to send for the wig and the letter—as quickly as possible. Auntie was quite as impatient to hide the Vicar's baldness as to read the Burgomaster's letter. The shape of the wig, as well as colour and address of the letter, were explicitly described to the Inspector, and he forthwith sent two grooms, four threshers, and one dairy-boy out upon all roads, footpaths, and byways that run between Nieder-Fahren and Waiblingen. He stationed himself upon the hill by the wind-mill and reconnoitred the field of action through a telescope. Such excellent arrangements could not fail to bring about the desired result. In half an hour the seven messengers returned to the house led by the wig, the letter, and the Inspector.

Sure enough the letter was from the Burgomaster. It contained nothing less than a formal invitation to the Frau Obersteuerrätin, together with her brother and Fräulein Susie and the Inspector Säblein, to the wedding of the Burgomaster's eldest daughter.

Although Auntie felt very much flattered by this attention of the Burgomaster, with whom she was but slightly acquainted, there were some difficulties in the way which must needs be talked over in a family council.

Auntie was very much averse to bringing Susie into contact in any way with the young gentlemen of Waiblingen. First of all, Susie was seventeen years old—a fact which did not seem at all portentous to the child, but all the more so to her cautious aunt. Second, Susie was beautiful as any Susanna, not excepting the one in the Old Testament. Thirdly, she had the prospect of inheriting a considerable fortune, and Auntie had no notion of giving up her darling to the first-comer. Fourthly, Susie was exceedingly inexperienced, though she was not wanting in the usual measure of laudable curiosity.

The young men of Waiblingen were in no way suited to be the companions of such a girl. First, because a great many of them were handsome, which is a very bad thing; and secondly, they were all great lovers of comedies and novels; they kept up an amateur stage; and at Waiblingen two booksellers made their living with circulating libraries—a bad sign of our times! Thirdly, even though one might have forgiven them their sleek faces and romantic tendencies, few of them had a fortune that would weigh in the scales against Aunt Rosmarin's possessions, nor were they of a rank to be compared with the title of Obersteuerrat.

Auntie had pondered this question long since in the silence of her own heart, and she had come to the conclusion that it was best to take defensive measures against the elegant world of Waiblingen. Susie seldom went there, and still seldomer were there any young guests invited to Nieder-Fahren.

After ripe consideration it was decided in the family council, in which the Inspector also took part, to go to the wedding at the Burgomaster's, but not without the utmost caution.

Auntie undertook to call Susie's attention to the dangers arising out of the affections. The Vicar was to add spiritual admonition, and the Inspector—who had the reputation of having been a good waltzer in his younger years, while now he was unfortunately a bachelor of fifty-six—promised to renew Susie's dancing-lessons. At the wedding all three pledged each other to do their best, and not lose the damsel out of sight.

Hereupon tailors, shoemakers and milliners were put in a fair way of getting a living. Auntie was desirous of doing whatever was due to her rank, and she also had the pardonable pride of showing off Susie's beauty to the best advantage.

Susie was delighted with the elaborate preparations—all this was a new experience. She put her dancing-master quite out of breath, and her only regret was that his feet being fifty-six years old were not as flexible as hers being seventeen. Joy and nature taught her to dance; but Säblein took it all upon his account. He was nothing loath to practise his noble half-forgotten art, the less so as the family council had decreed that he alone should be Susie's partner at the wedding.

Unfortunately this plan miscarried, and the reason was this. The day before the wedding all the dances were to be reviewed once more under the supervision of the Vicar and Auntie. Before the spectators came, Säblein exerted himself more than was good for him to dance at least no worse than his clever pupil. She floated about like a butterfly, and in her rapture took many a step which was no less graceful for not coming under any rule. Säblein, in an ecstasy of delight, rashly undertook to show her the acme of his art. Years ago he could dance *entrechats*—ambition pricked him to make a trial once more. His first attempt was half a failure, his second was a whole one. His lank, thin-whittled legs, which had never been a cause of reproach to him, got so hopelessly and abnormally entangled that, the rest of his body keeping in motion, a disaster was inevitable. The unfortunate dancing-master fell in a most *un*masterly manner upon the floor, and as a falling pine uproots all blooming bushes that surround it, so he pulled down the little sylph that was frolicking about him.

The Vicar, just about to open the door from without, heard the fall, which shook the very foundations of the house, and entered hastily. It was partly this haste and partly the Vicar's near-sightedness, which he was wont to forget in his absent-mindedness, which became the cause of a second accident. He stepped upon the dancing-master's leg, which the latter drew back with pardonable abruptness, thereby robbing the Vicar of his equilibrium. Before he had time to beg pardon he lay upon the floor along with the others. While his powdered wig was propelled by the rapid motion far under the sofa, his short legs performed some wonderful antics, and at last turned up their soles toward Heaven, as if imploring its aid.

The whole occurrence was a very short one. The Vicar was the first to gather himself up, and, mistaking Susie's snowy, befrilled cap for his escaped wig, he seized it without more ado, and covered his head therewith because he heard the Obersteuerrätin at the door. Susie was on her feet too before Auntie entered. But Säblein sat upon the floor making horrible faces, for he had hurt his hip.

"Great heavens!" cried Aunt Rosmarin, clapping her hands together, and looking now at the Inspector's painful grimaces, now at her brother's head in a woman's cap. "Are you playing a farce?

Are you forgetful of all decency? Do you call this good breeding? and especially you, Vicar?" . . .

"And pray, why is it especially I?" he asked with a touch of sensitiveness, for he did not greatly like his sister's sermons.

Here Susie gained a hearing, and quickly restored peace by giving her perplexed aunt the explanation to this riddle, and laughingly exchanging her cap for the wig.

This apparently unimportant occurrence was the first cause to all following misfortunes; for Säblein went limping about for many days, and consequently could not dance at the wedding.

. . . .

Aunt Rosmarin had her suspicions when she saw Susie, now swimming in bliss, now abject and mournful, or when she heard how Susie went walking in the park evening after evening, and when she herself, putting aside her dread of rheumatism, secretly followed her there, but always found Susie alone.

Auntie shook her head, and said to her brother: "I believe, Vicar, our little Baroness is in love." She had hit it, but wise Auntie never thought of the Baron. "We must keep our eyes on this marvellously mysterious child, for she will confess nothing to me. It is a delicate task, I know, and I myself am too old to run after her in the park every day the Lord makes. And, of course, Vicar, it is not a matter to be entrusted to the domestics; that were contrary to all dignity and order. But at the same time she must be watched, for these constant visits to the park for the last fortnight must have some good reason."

"Trust me, Auntie," said the Vicar, "trust me; I will guard the park like a spy. Murder shall out. This is just the sort of thing that suits me."

The plans were laid with great subtlety. The Vicar looked unconcerned in Susie's presence, and the following day at sunset he started upon his errand.

He was indeed very lucky, for the Baron was really in the park. He was twice lucky, for it so happened that he entered the park from the side where it touched the woods, and where the Baron was wont to enter it. He was in the habit of leaving his horse there, and giving it to the servant to hold.

The servant, finding his task decidedly dull, had to-day tied the Baron's horse to a young birch tree and gone about his own affairs. The Vicar looked at the elegantly-equipped noble steed from all sides, and nodding his head thoughtfully, unfastened it, saying to himself, " I'll take it home to our stable ; the owner will no doubt apply for it, and all the rest will follow. In truth, it's a shrewd plan ! "

But there was an unfavourable circumstance. There seemed to be a secret understanding between the horse and his master. He most decidedly objected to being pulled along by the bridle ; no amount of patting and caressing had any effect ; he planted his fore-legs firmly on the ground and pulled his head back.

" Friend," said the Vicar, " at best you are but a beast, and you have no eyes behind your ears. I'll wager you will go willingly." With that he climbed upon the noble animal's back, which stood as patient as a lamb. To be sure it was thirty years or more since the good Vicar had been on horseback, and, moreover, his legs were about two inches too short for the stirrups ; but then it was to be but a few moments' ride, and it was well to show Aunt Rosmarin that he had not forgotten the chivalrous arts over his theology. Over and above all this there was danger in delay.

So he belaboured the horse's shanks with his boots, and the steed, taken aback by such ill-treatment, at once began to canter along the woody path, across the field into the open road, having for weeks past traversed no other way than this with the Baron. The Vicar, in danger of losing his balance, with laudable precaution clasped his fingers in the mane of his Pegasus. Finding himself upon the road, however, instead of parading under Auntie's window, he tried to grasp the bridle. Over this attempt he came very near losing both stirrups. Making sure of these once more, he let the bridle alone. For a while these two purposes warred with each other, and between times he admonished the fiery horse with many caresses to stand still. But it was all in vain ; and when in his despair he pulled the rein too tight, at the same time clasping the horse's sides firmly with his legs, it forthwith rose upon its hind feet, and, to his inexpressible horror, began to walk about like a human being, and perform tricks which were positively not to the Vicar's taste just at that moment.

He now succumbed to fate and to his horse, clinging to the latter with hands and feet while it sped along at a full gallop till the poor Vicar was deaf and blind with dizziness.

" Out of the depths have I cried unto Thee," he sighed. " If this isn't the very devil himself ! Had I but left the beast standing where it was how happy should I be ! "

It so happened that right here the road had been barred by peasants in honour of the grazing cattle.

" Te Deum laudamus ! " cried the Vicar. " Here surely this rascal of a horse will come to a stand." But the steed leaped over as if he had wings, so that the horseman's hair stood on end, and his hat and wig took flight in horror. " I have learned to ride better than you, for I still hold my seat," said the good Vicar in Christian tranquillity to the truants, not venturing to turn and look after them.

" Whither, in the Lord's name ? Twice four-and-twenty hours at this rate and we shall have spanned this terrestrial globe and come out on the other side at Nieder-Fahren." As he was saying this they approached a bridge. The Vicar, in terror lest the horse in its blind rage might miss the bridge and leap into the stream, tugged frantically at the rein on the side nearest to the bridge. But he tugged too long ; the provoking animal thereupon left the bridge lying at the right, and jumped into the water. The Vicar came very near fainting away when he became aware of floating between heaven and water, and felt the waves penetrate his black silk stockings, and soon after his velvet breeches, until they played about his hips.

The horse, which was a capital swimmer, reached the opposite shore in safety, regained the road, and jauntily continued its journey until it reached Schloss Malzen, where it darted joyfully with the Vicar into the open door of the stable, standing still at last in its own familiar stall. The servants in the courtyard ran in after him, helped the rider out of the saddle, and anxiously inquired how he had come into possession of the Baron's horse.

An unspeakable sense of blissful security seized the much-tried clergyman as once more he felt *terra firma* beneath his feet. Deprived of his hat and his wig, to be sure, and the lower half of his body dripping with water, far from home, the approaching night before him, and upon the domain of the arch-enemy of Nieder-Fahren—all these circumstances served to make the situation not altogether agreeable. But what cared he so long as his life was saved ?

While the servants were storming the breathless gentleman with questions the Baron's steward appeared upon the scene, and hospitably urged him to come into the house. As upon his request a carriage was promised him to take him back to Nieder-Fahren, he consented to enter and rest before his departure. Meanwhile nearly two hours passed ; no carriage appeared, and the Vicar began to wax suspicious lest he was being treated as a prisoner for having run away with the horse, although he had repeatedly affirmed that it was he who had been run away with. He finally decided to take flight. He arose, and was about to open the door, when Baron Pompeius von Malzen entered, having arrived upon his lackey's horse while the despairing lackey was on a search for the Baron's steed through the whole of Ober and Nieder-Fahren. The Baron, recognising the worthy uncle of his wife—the tale concerning the arrival of the horse with a wigless and decidedly damp clergyman had been related to him in the courtyard—at once escorted him to a better room, ordered dry clothing, and gave the Vicar time to change his garments. His departure was quite out of the question for that night; the Baron would not let the opportunity escape him to heap coals of fire upon the head of one of his adversaries, to entertain him sumptuously, and overwhelm him with courtesies.

Susie's uncle, surprised at the Baron's cordial manner, soon felt very comfortable behind smoking viands and bottles of Burgundy. Still, however soft and firm he sat upon the luxurious cushions of his chair, he could not for the whole evening rid himself of the notion, as he said, of having " the devilish beast " between his legs.

" At the same time I am more grateful to my good horse than I can tell you," said the Baron, " for bringing me the uncle of my beloved wife. I have long wished for the honour of your acquaintance, so that I might beg for your kind intercession. I adore my wife, and a separation is about to be forced upon us. My wife has forgiven me—nay, more, she loves me; she does not desire a separation, and yet——"

" Loves you? Does not desire a separation? " cried the Vicar, shaking his head, which was adorned with the Baron's best cotton nightcap.

" Will you have proofs? " said the Baron. " Ah, I will be frank with our dear uncle. You shall know all. This hour may decide our life's happiness." He thereupon went and fetched Susie's letters.

And indeed from his niece's letters the Vicar saw that between her and the Baron there was eternal peace, and a great deal more that is eternal. He seemed greatly touched as he laid the letters down; he stretched out his hand across the table and said:

" Baron, I for my part will make peace with you. Susie shall be yours, and the law-suit may go to the dogs. But we must handle Aunt Rosmarin carefully. She is a dear, good woman, but she has peculiar ideas about some things. Up to this day I was a raging Saul, henceforth I shall be a gentle Paul, and shall begin at once upon my work of conversion. The Baron jumped up, embracing and kissing brave Saul in a rapture of delight.

. . . .

Meanwhile Aunt Rosmarin had heard her brother relate the story of his adventure. When he told her how he found the horse, her eyes sparkled with pleasure at the discovery. The fact of his getting into the saddle she accompanied with the remark: "You don't know how to ride. Every cobbler to his last!" When he came to his aerial flight across the bar, and his swim through the stream, she jumped up, nervously seized her brother's two hands and cried, "For heaven's sake, what dangers were you subject to?" And she did not regain her composure until he halted before the horse's crib. Then, as the Baron came in, her face lengthened; the warmer the Vicar grew in chanting his praises the cooler was Aunt Rosmarin. And when he had the audacity to add, "Susie does not seem to dislike the Baron; seems to me we had better let the law-suit go, and let things take their course," Auntie shook her head, while she gazed at her brother from top to toe with wide-open eyes.

"Well, I never!" said she. "I fear me the ride and the fright have done you some injury. If the Baron did not turn you out into the pitch-dark night, giving you lodging and food instead, he did no more than heathens and barbarians would have done. You need not think I'll give him Susie for his roasts and his Burgundy. A weak sort of man you must be to be willing to sacrifice your principles and all the disgrace and sorrow our family has suffered through the Baron for one poor supper."

Then did the Vicar arise in indignation and say, "Why, Aunt Rosmarin, has all Christian charity gone out of you? I wish then that *you* had ridden the Baron's horse in my stead; I wish *you* had been called upon to fly through the air, and to swim through the surging billows, to make the acquaintance of an honourable man. Then you would think different."

Aunt Rosmarin thought her brother's remarkable wish very improper, as well as insulting. She thereupon gave him a lecture lasting three hours, and having for its perpetual refrain, "I will not hear another word about the Baron. In future I shall act alone, in strict accordance with my principles."

CASPAR FRIEDRICH GOTTSCHALCK
c. 1772

THE UNLUCKY MISER

DURING the Thirty Years' War the neighbouring dwellers of the mountain hastily removed their money and other property into the castle of Questenberg, the better to secure it from military violence and depredations. The whole of these treasures are still said to lie concealed in a large brewing copper buried in one of the subterranean vaults, and cautiously guarded by a spectre of the castle.

Now it so happened that one Sunday an inhabitant of the place directed his steps towards the old castle, contemplated, as a rustic does, the overhanging ruins, explored all the places round, until at length he came to one which seemed gradually to descend into the earth. He made his way through the rank-growing grass and shrubs around, ventured still farther and farther, and at last approached the entrance to a dark passage. His curiosity led him to proceed ; he was now fairly underground, and beheld, where scarcely a ray of light was visible, a round opening in the earth. As he was standing close to the side, a spectre appeared wrapped in a large mantle. The place became suddenly bright ; and the affrighted rustic saw before him the famed old brewing copper, filled with shining gold pieces, of which he had heard so much from the lips of his great-grandmother.

He was sadly perplexed to know what to do, whether he should go, or venture to take a piece. Just then the spirit spoke : " You may take one, and come again every day for the same, but take only one at a time—no more ! "

Upon this he disappeared, and the man laid hands upon the gold piece. With a beating heart, half pleasure, and half dread, he hastened back again, set a mark upon the place, and so went, gazing a thousand times upon the spectre's present by the way, to his own house. The day following, he repeated the pleasant experiment ; the spirit indeed was not there, but there was the brewing vessel full of gold. He took another piece and went his way, and thus it continued the second, the third and fourth day; each bringing its tribute of a gold piece for more than the space of a year.

His humble abode became gradually metamorphosed into a stately building; many acres of ground were added, herds were seen pasturing in his fields, and no rustic in the village could do the things which he did. But the more his property increased, the more nettlesome did our rustic become. "Wherefore," said he, "should I labour? I who may sit down and take my ease?"

With this view he hired both men and maid-servants to cultivate his grounds, while he was seated in a new arm-chair, or rode out on a pretty hackney to view his crops of corn which he himself used formerly to sow. In fact his daily visit to the great brewing copper constituted his sole exertion. Mammon was hourly taking stronger possession of his soul; his pride began to equal his avarice; and though a gold piece was worth nearly twenty dollars, the thought came into his mind that it was growing rather a heavy job to walk, or more properly, to climb uphill daily for the sake of a single gold piece, so steep too as it was, and he inwardly resolved to bring back two pieces the very next time.

This he did, and continued the practice for above a month. Yet still not content with this double pay, he said to himself:

"Oh, lord, what a bore it is to carry on this eternal daily labour, all for the sake of a couple of gold pieces. It is quite clear that the whole of the treasure is meant for me, and whether I receive it all at once, or by dribbling it out thus without end, it comes to the same thing. So I will go, heaven willing, and empty this fine brewing copper at a single swoop, and henceforward I shall need to give myself no further trouble!"

Accordingly he took a number of bags, and went panting with them up the mountain: for he had grown fat and pursy with too much leisure and good living, so that he was quite exhausted by the time he reached the well-known entrance. He sat himself down to recover breath, and was glad to think that these plaguy journeys would now be at an end, beginning even to speculate what he should next undertake, when he beheld the whole of the bags well stuffed standing in his own house; whether a noble manor, becoming a knight, should be his; whether he would first set up his coach and four; what a grand table he would keep; what noble guests around him; and how he would carouse with them in spite of the knight of the neighbouring castle of Kyffhausen and all his kin.

With this he stood bolt upright, took his sacks, and disappeared along the dark passage. Now he stood close to the brewing copper, which, in spite of all he had gradually deducted out of it, appeared to be newly filled up to the very brim with gold. He knelt down with his first bag at the side, put both his hands into the gold, and was on the point of making the first draught for his sack, when behold, suddenly the whole vessel fell out of his grasp with hideous din, deep and deeper into the vault; fire-brands and brimstone blazed around him, and the disappointed wretch fell back almost in a swoon.

Away went all the treasure; and along with it all his glorious dreams and all his castles in the air. No brewing copper appeared more, though his cupidity was great as before, which he might easily have satisfied with a gold piece daily, had he known how to rest content when he was well.

It is thus that avarice revenges itself upon its worshippers.

LUDWIG TIECK
1773–1853

THE ELVES

"WHERE is our little Mary?" said the father.

"She is playing out upon the green there, with our neighbour's boy," replied the mother.

"I wish they may not run away and lose themselves," said he; "they are so thoughtless."

The mother looked for the little ones, and brought them their evening luncheon. "It is warm," said the boy; "and Mary had a longing for the red cherries."

"Have a care, children," said the mother, "and do not run too far from home, and not into the wood; father and I are going to the fields."

Little Andres answered: "Never fear, the wood frightens us; we shall sit here by the house, where there are people near us."

The mother went in, and soon came out again with her husband. They locked the door, and turned towards the fields to look after their labourers, and see their hay-harvest in the meadow. Their house lay upon a little green height, encircled by a pretty ring of paling, which likewise enclosed their fruit and flower garden. The hamlet stretched somewhat deeper down, and on the other side lay the castle of the Count. Martin rented the large farm from this nobleman; and was living in contentment with his wife and only child; for he yearly saved some money, and had the prospect of becoming a man of substance by his industry, for the ground was productive, and the Count not illiberal.

As he walked with his wife to the fields, he gazed cheerfully round, and said, "What a different look this quarter has, Brigitta, from the place we lived in formerly! Here it is all so green; the whole village is bedecked with thick-spreading fruit trees; the ground is full of beautiful herbs and flowers; all the houses are cheerful and cleanly, the inhabitants are at their ease: nay, I could almost fancy that the woods are greener here than elsewhere, and the sky bluer; and, so far as the eye can reach, you have pleasure and delight in beholding the bountiful earth."

"And whenever you cross the stream," said Brigitta, "you are, as it were, in another world, all is so dreary and withered; but every traveller declares that our village is the fairest in the country far and near."

"All but that fir-ground," said her husband; "do but look back to it, how dark and dismal that solitary spot is lying in the gay scene; the dingy fir trees with the smoky huts behind them, the ruined stalls, the brook flowing past with a sluggish melancholy."

"It is true," replied Brigitta; "if you but approach that spot, you grow disconsolate and sad, you know not why. What sort of people can they be that live there, and keep themselves so separate from the rest of us, as if they had an evil conscience?"

"A miserable crew," replied the young farmer: "gipsies, seemingly, that steal and cheat in other quarters, and have their hoard and hiding-place here. I wonder only that his lordship suffers them."

"Who knows," said the wife, with an accent of pity, "but perhaps they may be poor people, wishing, out of shame, to conceal their poverty; for, after all, no one can say aught ill of them; the only thing is, that they do not go to church, and none knows how they live; for the little garden, which indeed seems altogether waste, cannot possibly support them; and fields they have none."

"God knows," said Martin, as they went along, "what trade they follow; no mortal comes to them; for the place they live in is as if bewitched and excommunicated, so that even our wildest fellows will not venture into it."

Such conversation they pursued while walking to the fields. That gloomy spot they spoke of lay aside from the hamlet. In a dell, begirt with firs, you might behold a hut, and various ruined office-houses; rarely was smoke seen to mount from it, still more rarely did men appear there; though at times curious people, venturing somewhat nearer, had perceived upon the bench before the hut some hideous women, in ragged clothes, dandling in their arms some children equally dirty and ill-favoured; black dogs were running up and down upon the boundary; and, of an evening, a man of monstrous size was seen to cross the foot-bridge of the brook and disappear in the hut; and in the darkness various shapes were observed, moving like shadows round a fire in the open air. This piece of ground, the firs, and the ruined huts formed in truth a strange contrast with the bright green landscape, the white houses of the hamlet, and the stately new-built castle.

The two little ones had now eaten their fruit; it came into their heads to run races; and the little nimble Mary always got the start of the less active Andres. "It is not fair," cried Andres at last: "let us try it for some length, then we shall see who wins."

"As thou wilt," said Mary; "only to the brook we must not run."

"No," said Andres; "but there, on the hill, stands the large pear tree, a quarter of a mile from this. I shall run by the left, round past the fir-ground; thou canst try it by the right over the fields; so we do not meet till we get up, and then we shall see which of us is swifter."

"Done," cried Mary, and began to run; "for we shall not mar one another by the way, and my father says it is as far to the hill by that side of the gipsies' house as by this."

Andres had already started, and Mary, turning to the right, could no longer see him. "It is very silly," said she to herself. "I have only to take heart, and run along the bridge, past the hut, and through the yard, and I shall certainly be first." She was already standing by the brook and the clump of firs. "Shall I? No: it is too frightful," said she. A little white dog was standing on the farther side, and barking with might and main. In her terror, Mary thought the dog some monster, and sprang back. "Fy! fy!" said she: "the dolt is gone half-way by this time, while I stand here considering." The little dog kept barking, and, as she looked at it more narrowly, it seemed no longer frightful, but, on the contrary, quite pretty: it had a red collar round its neck, with a glittering bell; and as it raised its head, and shook itself in barking, the little bell sounded with the finest tinkle. "Well, I must risk it!" cried she: "I will run for life; quick, quick, I am through; certainly to Heaven, they cannot eat me up alive in half a minute!" And with this, the gay, courageous little Mary sprang along the foot-bridge; passed the dog, which ceased its barking and began to fawn on her; and in a moment she was standing on the other bank, and the black firs all round concealed from view her father's house and the rest of the landscape.

But what was her astonishment when here! The loveliest, most variegated flower-garden lay round her; tulips, roses and lilies were glittering in the fairest colours; blue and gold-red butterflies were wavering in the blossoms; cages of shining wire were hung on the espaliers, with many-coloured birds in them, singing beautiful songs; and children, in short white frocks, with flowing yellow hair and brilliant eyes, were frolicking about; some playing with lambkins, some feeding the birds, or gathering flowers, and giving them to one another; some, again, were eating cherries, grapes and ruddy apricots. No hut was to be seen; but instead of it, a large fair house, with a brazen door and lofty statues, stood glancing in the middle of the space. Mary was confounded with surprise, and knew not what to think; but, not being bashful, she went right up to the first of the children, held out her hand, and wished the little creature good even.

"Art thou come to visit us, then?" said the glittering child; "I saw thee running, playing on the other side, but thou wert frightened for our little dog."

"So you are not gipsies and rogues," said Mary, "as Andres always told me! He is a stupid thing, and talks of much he does not understand."

"Stay with us," said the strange little girl; "thou wilt like it well."

"But we are running a race."

"Thou wilt find thy comrade soon enough. There, take and eat."

Mary ate, and found the fruit more sweet than any she had ever tasted in her life before; and Andres, and the race, and the prohibition of her parents, were entirely forgotten.

A stately woman, in a shining robe, came towards them, and asked about the stranger child. "Fairest lady," said Mary, "I came running hither by chance, and now they wish to keep me."

"Thou art aware, Zerina," said the lady, "that she can be here but for a little while; besides, thou shouldst have asked my leave."

"I thought," said Zerina, "when I saw her admitted across the bridge, that I might do it; we have often seen her running in the fields, and thou thyself hast taken pleasure in her lively temper. She will have to leave us soon enough."

"No, I will stay here," said the little stranger; "for here it is so beautiful, and here I shall find the prettiest playthings, and store of berries and cherries to boot. On the other side it is not half so grand."

The gold-robed lady went away with a smile; and many of the children now came bounding round the happy Mary in their mirth, and twitched her, and incited her to dance; others brought her lambs, or curious playthings; others made music on instruments, and sang to it.

She kept, however, by the playmate who had first met her; for Zerina was the kindest and loveliest of them all. Little Mary cried and cried again: "I will stay with you for ever; I will stay with you, and you shall be my sisters"; at which the children all laughed, and embraced her. "Now, we shall have a royal sport," said Zerina. She ran into the palace, and returned with a little golden box, in which lay a quantity of seeds, like glittering dust. She lifted of it with her little hand, and scattered some grains on the green earth. Instantly the grass began to move, as in waves; and, after a few moments, bright rose-bushes started from the ground, shot rapidly up, and budded all at once, while the sweetest perfume filled the place. Mary also took a little of the dust, and, having scattered it, she saw white lilies, and the most variegated pinks, pushing up. At a signal from Zerina, the flowers disappeared, and others rose in their room. "Now," said Zerina, "look for something greater." She laid two pine-seeds in the ground, and stamped them in sharply with her foot. Two green bushes stood before them. "Grasp me fast," said she; and Mary threw her arms about the slender form. She felt herself borne upwards; for the trees were springing under them with the greatest speed; the tall pines waved to and fro, and the two children held each other fast embraced, swinging this way and that in the red clouds of the twilight, and kissed each other; while the rest were climbing up and down the trunks with quick dexterity, pushing and teasing one another with loud laughter when they met; if any one fell down in the press, it flew through the air, and sank slowly and surely to the ground. At length Mary was beginning to be frightened; and the other little child sang a few loud tones, and the trees again sank down, and set them on the ground as gradually as they had lifted them before to the clouds.

They next went through the brazen door of the palace. Here many fair women, elderly and young, were sitting in the round hall, partaking of the fairest fruits, and listening to glorious invisible music. In the vaulting of the ceiling, palms, flowers and groves stood painted, among which little figures of children were sporting and winding in every graceful posture; and with the tones of the music, the images altered and glowed with the most burning colours; now the blue and green were sparkling like radiant light, now these tints faded back in paleness, the purple flamed up, and the gold took fire ; and then the naked children seemed to be alive among the flower-garlands, and to draw breath, and emit it through their ruby-coloured lips ; so that by fits you could see the glance of their little white teeth, and the lighting up of their azure eyes.

From the hall, a stair of brass led down to a subterranean chamber. Here lay much gold and silver, and precious stones of every hue shone out between them. Strange vessels stood along the walls, and all seemed filled with costly things. The gold was worked into many forms, and glittered with the friendliest red. Many little dwarfs were busied sorting the pieces from the heap, and putting them in the vessels ; others, hunchbacked, and bandy-legged, with long red noses, were tottering slowly along, half-bent to the ground, under full sacks, which they bore as millers do their grain, and, with much panting, shaking out the gold-dust on the ground. Then they darted awkwardly to the right and left, and caught the rolling balls that were like to run away ; and it happened now and then that one in his eagerness overset the other, so that both fell heavily and clumsily to the ground. They made angry faces, and looked askance as Mary laughed at their gestures and their ugliness. Behind them sat an old crumpled little man, whom Zerina reverently greeted ; he thanked her with a grave inclination of his head. He held a sceptre in his hand, and wore a crown upon his brow, and all the other dwarfs appeared to regard him as their master, and obey his nod.

" What, more wanted ? " asked he, with a surly voice, as the children came a little nearer. Mary was afraid, and did not speak ; but her companion answered, they were only come to look about them in the chambers. " Still your old child's tricks ! " replied the dwarf. " Will there never be an end to idleness ? " With this, he turned again to his employment, kept his people weighing and sorting the ingots ; some he sent away on errands, some he chid with angry tones.

" Who is the gentleman ? " said Mary.

" Our Metal-Prince," replied Zerina, as they walked along.

They seemed once more to reach the open air, for they were standing by a lake, yet no sun appeared, and they saw no sky above their heads. A little boat received them, and Zerina steered it diligently forwards. It shot rapidly along. On gaining the middle of the lake, the stranger saw that multitudes of pipes, channels and brooks were spreading from the little sea in every direction. " These waters to the right," said Zerina, " flow beneath your garden, and this is why it blooms so freshly ; by the other side we get down into the great stream." On a sudden, out of all the channels, and from every quarter of the lake, came a crowd of little children swimming up ; some wore garlands of sedge and water-lily ; some had red stems of coral, others were blowing on crooked shells ; a tumultuous noise echoed merrily from the dark shores ; among the children might be seen the fairest women sporting in the waters, and often several of the children sprang about some one of them, and with kisses hung upon her neck and shoulders. All saluted the strangers ; and these steered onwards through the revelry out of the lake, into a little river, which grew narrower and narrower. At last the boat came aground. The strangers took their leave, and Zerina knocked against the cliff. This opened like a door, and a female form, all red, assisted them to mount. " Are you all brisk here ? " inquired Zerina.

" They are just at work," replied the other, " and happy as they could wish ; indeed, the heat is very pleasant."

They went up a winding stair, and on a sudden Mary found herself in a most resplendent hall, so that, as she entered, her eyes were dazzled by the radiance. Flame-coloured tapestry covered the walls with a purple glow ; and when her eye had grown a little used to it, the stranger saw, to her astonishment, that, in the tapestry, there were figures moving up and down in dancing joyfulness ; in form so beautiful, and of so fair proportions, that nothing could be seen more graceful ; their bodies were as of red crystal, so that it appeared as if the blood were visible within them, flowing and playing in its courses. They smiled on the stranger, and saluted her with various bows ; but as Mary was about approaching nearer them, Zerina plucked her sharply back, crying : " Thou wilt burn thyself, my little Mary, for the whole of it is fire."

Mary felt the heat. " Why do the pretty creatures not come out," said she, " and play with us ? "

" As thou livest in the Air," replied the other, " so are they obliged to stay continually in Fire, and would faint and languish if they left it. Look now, how glad they are, how they laugh and shout ; those down below spread out the fire-floods everywhere beneath the earth, and thereby the flowers, and fruits and wine are made to flourish ; these red streams, again, are to run beside the brooks of water ; and thus the fiery creatures are kept ever busy and glad. But for thee it is too hot here; let us return to the garden."

In the garden, the scene had changed since they left it. The moonshine was lying on every flower; the birds were silent, and the children were asleep in complicated groups, among the green groves. Mary and her friend, however, did not feel fatigue, but walked about in the warm summer night, in abundant talk, till morning.

When the day dawned, they refreshed themselves on fruit and milk, and Mary said: "Suppose we go, by way of change, to the firs, and see how things look there?"

"With all my heart," replied Zerina; "thou wilt see our watchmen, too, and they will surely please thee; they are standing up among the trees on the mound." The two proceeded through the flower garden by pleasant groves, full of nightingales; then they ascended a vine hill; and at last, after long following the windings of a clear brook, arrived at the firs, and the height which bounded the domain. "How does it come," said Mary, "that we have to walk so far here, when, without, the circuit is so narrow?"

"I know not," said her friend; "but so it is."

They mounted to the dark firs, and a chill wind blew from without in their faces; a haze seemed lying far and wide over the landscape. On the top were many strange forms standing; with mealy, dusty faces; their misshapen heads not unlike those of white owls; they were clad in folded cloaks of shaggy wool; they held umbrellas of curious skins stretched out above them; and they waved and fanned themselves incessantly with large bat's wings, which flared out curiously beside the woollen roquelaures. "I could laugh, yet I am frightened," cried Mary.

"These are our good trusty watchmen," said her playmate; "they stand here and wave their fans, that cold anxiety and inexplicable fear may fall on every one that attempts to approach us. They are covered so, because without it is now cold and rainy, which they cannot bear. But snow, or wind, or cold air never reaches down to us; here is an everlasting spring and summer: yet if these poor people on the top were not frequently relieved, they would certainly perish."

"But who are you, then?" said Mary, while again descending to the flowery fragrance; "or have you no name at all?"

"We are called the Elves," replied the friendly child; "people talk about us in the Earth, as I have heard."

They now perceived a mighty bustle on the green. "The fair Bird is come!" cried the children to them: all hastened to the hall. Here, as they approached, young and old were crowding over the threshold, all shouting for joy; and from within resounded a triumphant peal of music. Having entered, they perceived the vast circuit filled with the most varied forms, and all were looking upwards to a large Bird with glancing plumage, that was sweeping slowly round in the dome, and in its stately flight describing many a circle. The music sounded more gaily than before; the colours and lights alternated more rapidly. At last the music ceased; and the Bird, with a rustling noise, floated down upon a glittering crown that hung hovering in air under the high window, by which the hall was lighted from above. His plumage was purple and green, and shining golden streaks played through it; on his head there waved a diadem of feathers, so resplendent that they glanced like jewels. His bill was red, and his legs of a glancing blue. As he moved, the tints gleamed through each other, and the eye was charmed with their radiance. His size was as that of an eagle. But now he opened his glittering beak; and sweetest melodies came pouring from his moved breast, in finer tones than the love-sick nightingale gives forth; still stronger rose the song, and streamed like floods of Light, so that all, the very children themselves, were moved by it to tears of joy and rapture. When he ceased, all bowed before him; he again flew round the dome in circles, then darted through the door, and soared into the light heaven, where he shone far up like a red point, and then soon vanished from their eyes.

"Why are ye all so glad?" inquired Mary, bending to her fair playmate, who seemed smaller than yesterday.

"The King is coming!" said the little one; "many of us have never seen him, and whithersoever he turns his face, there is happiness and mirth; we have long looked for him, more anxiously than you look for spring when winter lingers with you; and now he has announced, by his fair herald, that he is at hand. This wise and glorious Bird, that has been sent to us by the King, is called Phœnix; he dwells far off in Arabia, on a tree, which there is no other that resembles on Earth, as in like manner there is no second Phœnix. When he feels himself grown old, he builds a pile of balm and incense, kindles it, and dies singing; and then, from the fragrant ashes, soars up the renewed Phœnix with unlessened beauty. It is seldom he so wings his course that men behold him; and when once in centuries this does occur, they note it in their annals, and expect remarkable events. But now, my friend, thou and I must part ; for the sight of the King is not permitted thee."

Then the lady with the golden robe came through the throng, and beckoning Mary to her, led her into a sequestered walk. "Thou must leave us, my dear child," said she ; "the King is to hold his court here for twenty years, perhaps longer ; and fruitfulness and blessings will spread far over the land, but chiefly here beside us ; all the brooks and rivulets will become more bountiful, all the fields and gardens richer, the wine more generous, the meadows more fertile, and the woods more fresh and green ; a milder air will blow, no hail shall hurt, no flood shall threaten. Take this ring, and think of us : but beware of telling any one of our existence ; or we must fly this land, and thou and all around will lose the happiness and blessing of our neighbourhood. Once more, kiss thy playmate, and farewell." They issued from the walk ; Zerina wept, Mary stooped to embrace her, and they parted. Already she was on the narrow bridge ; the cold air was blowing on her back from the firs ; the little dog barked with all its might, and rang its little bell ; she looked round, then hastened over, for the darkness of the firs, the bleakness of the ruined huts, the shadows of the twilight, were filling her with terror.

"What a night my parents must have had on my account ! " said she within herself, as she stept on the green ; "and I dare not tell them where I have been, or what wonders I have witnessed, nor indeed would they believe me." Two men passing by saluted her, and as they went along, she heard them say : "What a pretty girl ! Where can she come from ? " With quickened steps she approached the house : but the trees which were hanging last night loaded with fruit were now standing dry and leafless ; the house was differently painted, and a new barn had been built beside it. Mary was amazed, and thought she must be dreaming. In this perplexity she opened the door ; and behind the table sat her father, between an unknown woman and a stranger youth. "Good God ! Father," cried she, "where is my mother ? "

"Thy mother ! " said the woman, with a forecasting tone, and sprang towards her : "Ha, thou surely canst not—Yes, indeed, indeed thou art my lost, long-lost dear, only Mary ! " She had recognised her by a little brown mole beneath the chin, as well as by her eyes and shape. All embraced her, all were moved with joy, and the parents wept. Mary was astonished that she almost reached to her father's stature; and she could not understand how her mother had become so changed and faded; she asked the name of the stranger youth. "It is our neighbour's Andres," said Martin. "How comest thou to us again, so unexpectedly, after seven long years? Where hast thou been? Why didst thou never send us tidings of thee?"

"Seven years!" said Mary, and could not order her ideas and recollections. "Seven whole years?"

"Yes, yes," said Andres, laughing, and shaking her trustfully by the hand; "I have won the race, good Mary; I was at the pear tree and back again seven years ago, and thou, sluggish creature, art but just returned!"

They again asked, they pressed her; but remembering her instruction, she could answer nothing. It was they themselves chiefly that, by degrees, shaped a story for her: How, having lost her way, she had been taken up by a coach, and carried to a strange remote part, where she could not give the people any notion of her parents' residence; how she was conducted to a distant town, where certain worthy persons brought her up, and loved her; how they had lately died, and at length she had recollected her birthplace, and so returned. "No matter how it is!" exclaimed her mother; "enough that we have thee again, my little daughter, my own, my all!"

Andres waited supper, and Mary could not be at home in anything she saw. The house seemed small and dark; she felt astonished at her dress, which was clean and simple, but appeared quite foreign; she looked at the ring on her finger, and the gold of it glittered strangely, enclosing a stone of burning red. To her father's question, she replied that the ring also was a present from her benefactors.

She was glad when the hour of sleep arrived, and she hastened to her bed. Next morning she felt much more collected; she had now arranged her thoughts a little, and could better stand the questions of the people in the village, all of whom came in to bid her welcome. Andres was there too with the earliest, active, glad, and serviceable beyond all others. The blooming maiden of fifteen had made a deep impression on him; he had passed a sleepless night. The people of the castle likewise sent for Mary, and she had once more to tell her story to them, which was now grown quite familiar to her. The old Count and his Lady were surprised at her good breeding; she was modest, but not embarrassed; she made answer courteously in good phrases to all their questions; all fear of noble persons and their equipage had passed away from her; for when she measured these halls and forms by the wonders and the high beauty she had seen with the Elves in their hidden abode, this earthly splendour seemed but dim to her, the presence of men was almost mean. The young lords were charmed with her beauty.

It was now February. The trees were budding earlier than usual; the nightingale had never come so soon; the spring rose fairer in the land than the oldest men could recollect it. In every quarter, little brooks gushed out to irrigate the pastures and meadows; the hills seemed heaving, the vines rose higher and higher, the fruit trees blossomed as they had never done; and a swelling fragrant blessedness hung suspended heavily in rosy clouds over the scene. All prospered beyond expectation; no rude day, no tempest injured the fruits; the wine flowed blushing in immense grapes; and the inhabitants of the place felt astonished, and were captivated as in a sweet dream. The next year was like its forerunner; but men had now become accustomed to the marvellous. In autumn, Mary yielded to the pressing entreaties of Andres and her parents; she was betrothed to him, and in winter they were married.

She often thought with inward longing of her residence behind the fir trees; she continued serious and still. Beautiful as all that lay around her was, she knew of something yet more beautiful; and from the remembrance of this, a faint regret attuned her nature to soft melancholy. It smote her painfully when her father and mother talked about the gipsies and vagabonds that dwelt in the dark spot of ground. Often she was on the point of speaking out in defence of those good beings, whom she knew to be the benefactors of the land; especially to Andres, who appeared to take delight in zealously abusing them: yet still she repressed the word that was struggling to escape her bosom. So passed this year; in the next she was solaced by a little daughter, whom she named Elfrida, thinking of the designation of her friendly Elves.

The young people lived with Martin and Brigitta, the house being large enough for all; and helped their parents in conducting their now extended husbandry. The little Elfrida soon displayed peculiar faculties and gifts; for she could walk at a very early age, and could speak perfectly before she was a twelvemonth old; and after some few years she had become so wise and clever, and of such wondrous beauty, that all people regarded her with astonishment; and her mother could not keep away the thought that her child resembled one of those shining little ones in the space behind the firs. Elfrida cared not to be with other children; but seemed to avoid, with a sort of horror, their tumultuous amusements, and liked best to be alone. She would then retire into a corner of the garden, and read, or work diligently with her needle; often also you might see her sitting, as if deep sunk in thought; or violently walking up and down the alleys, speaking to herself. Her parents readily allowed her to have her will in these things, for she was healthy, and waxed apace; only her strange sagacious answers and observations often made them anxious. "Such wise children do not grow to age," her grandmother, Brigitta, many times observed; "they are too good for this world; the child, besides, is beautiful beyond nature, and will never find its proper place on Earth."

The little girl had this peculiarity, that she was very loath to let herself be served by any one, but endeavoured to do everything herself. She was almost the earliest riser in the house; she washed herself carefully, and dressed without assistance: at night she was equally careful; she took special heed to pack up her clothes and washes with her own hands, allowing no one, not even her mother, to meddle with her articles. The mother humoured her in this caprice, not thinking it of any consequence. But what was her astonishment when, happening one holiday to insist, regardless of Elfrida's tears and screams, on dressing her out for a visit to the castle, she found upon her breast, suspended by a string, a piece of gold of a strange form, which she directly recognised as one of that sort she had seen in such abundance in the subterranean vault! The little thing was greatly frightened, and at last confessed that she had found it in the garden, and as she liked it much, had kept it carefully: she at the same time prayed so earnestly and pressingly to have it back, that Mary fastened it again on its former place, and, full of thoughts, went out with her in silence to the castle.

Sidewards from the farm-house lay some offices for the storing of produce and implements; and behind these there was a little green, with an old grove, now visited by no one, as, from the new arrangement of the buildings, it lay too far from the garden. In this solitude Elfrida delighted most; and it occurred to nobody to interrupt her here, so that frequently her parents did not see her for half a day. One afternoon her mother chanced to be in these buildings, seeking for some lost article among the lumber, and she noticed that a beam of light was coming in, through a chink in the wall. She took a thought of looking through this aperture, and seeing what her child was busied with; and it happened that a stone was lying loose, and could be pushed aside, so that she obtained a view right into the grove. Elfrida was sitting there on a little bench, and beside her the well-known Zerina; and the children were playing and amusing one another in the kindliest unity. The Elf embraced her beautiful companion, and said mournfully: "Ah! dear little creature, as I sport with thee, so have I sported with thy mother, when she was a child; but you mortals so soon grow tall and thoughtful! It is very hard: wert thou but to be a child as long as I!"

"Willingly would I do it," said Elfrida; "but they all say I shall come to sense, and give over playing altogether; for I have great gifts, as they think, for growing wise. Ah! and then I shall see thee no more, thou dear Zerina! Yet it is with us, as with the fruit-tree flowers: how glorious the blossoming apple tree, with its red bursting buds! It looks so stately and broad, and every one that passes under it thinks, surely something great will come of it; then the sun grows hot, and the buds come joyfully forth; but the wicked kernel is already there, which pushes off and casts away the fair flower's dress; and now, in pain and waxing, it can do nothing more, but must grow to fruit in harvest. An apple, to be sure, is pretty and refreshing; yet nothing to the blossom of spring. So is it also with us mortals: I am not glad in the least at growing to be a tall girl. Ah! could I but once visit you!"

"Since the King is with us," said Zerina, "it is quite impossible; but I will come to thee, my darling, often, often, and none shall see me either here or there. I will pass invisible through the air, or fly over to thee like a bird: Oh! we will be much, much together, while thou art still little. What can I do to please thee?"

"Thou must like me very dearly," said Elfrida, "as I like thee in my heart: but come, let us make another rose."

Zerina took the well-known box from her bosom, threw two grains from it on the ground, and instantly a green bush stood before them, with two deep-red roses, bending their heads, as if to kiss each other. The children plucked them smiling, and the bush disappeared. "Oh that it would not die so soon!" said Elfrida; "this red child, this wonder of the Earth!"

"Give it me here," said the little Elf; then breathed thrice upon the budding rose, and kissed it thrice. "Now," said she, giving back the rose, "it will continue fresh and blooming till winter."

"I will keep it," said Elfrida, "as an image of thee; I will guard it in my little room, and kiss it night and morning, as if it were thyself."

"The sun is setting," said the other, "I must home." They embraced again, and Zerina vanished.

In the evening, Mary clasped her child to her breast with a feeling of alarm and veneration. She henceforth allowed the good little girl more liberty than formerly; and often calmed her husband, when he came to search for the child, which for some time he was wont to do, as her retiredness did not please him, and he feared that, in the end, it might make her silly, or even pervert her understanding. The mother often glided to the chink; and almost always found the bright Elf beside her child, employed in sport, or in earnest conversation.

"Wouldst thou like to fly?" inquired Zerina, once.

"Oh, well! How well!" replied Elfrida; and the fairy clasped her mortal playmate in her arms, and mounted with her from the ground, till they hovered above the grove. The mother, in alarm, forgot herself, and pushed out her head in terror to look after them; when Zerina, from the air, held up her finger, and threatened, yet smiled; then descended with the child, embraced her, and disappeared. After this, it happened more than once that Mary was observed by her; and every time, the shining little creature shook her head, or threatened, yet with friendly looks.

Often, in disputing with her husband, Mary had said in her zeal: "Thou dost injustice to the poor people in the hut!" But when Andres pressed her to explain why she differed in opinion from the whole village, nay, from his Lordship himself, and how she could understand it better than the whole of them, she still broke off embarrassed, and became silent. One day, after dinner, Andres grew more violent than ever; and maintained that, by one means or another, the crew must be packed away, as a nuisance to the country; when his wife in anger said to him: "Hush! for they are benefactors to thee and to every one of us."

"Benefactors!" cried the other in astonishment. "These rogues and vagabonds!"

In her indignation, she was now at last tempted to relate to him, under promise of the strictest secrecy, the history of her youth: and as Andres at every word grew more incredulous, and shook his head in mockery, she took him by the hand and led him to the chink, where, to his amazement, he beheld the glittering Elf sporting with his child, and caressing her in the grove. He knew not what to say; an exclamation of astonishment escaped him, and Zerina raised her eyes. On the instant she grew pale, and trembled violently; not with friendly, but with indignant looks, she made the sign of threatening, and then said to Elfrida: "Thou canst not help it, dearest heart; but they will never learn sense, wise as they believe themselves." She embraced the little one with stormy haste; and then, in the shape of a raven, flew with hoarse cries over the garden, towards the firs.

In the evening, the little one was very still, she kissed her rose with tears; Mary felt depressed and frightened, Andres scarcely spoke. It grew dark. Suddenly there went a rustling through the trees; birds flew to and fro with wild screaming, thunder was heard to roll, the Earth shook, and tones of lamentation moaned in the air. Andres and his wife had not courage to rise; they shrouded themselves within the curtains, and with fear and trembling awaited the day. Towards morning it grew calmer; and all was silent when the sun, with his cheerful light, rose over the wood.

Andres dressed himself, and Mary now observed that the stone of the ring upon her finger had become quite pale. On opening the door, the sun shone clear on their faces, but the scene around them they could scarcely recognise. The freshness of the wood was gone; the hills were shrunk, the brooks were flowing languidly with scanty streams, the sky seemed grey; and when you turned to the firs, they were standing there, no darker or more dreary than the other trees. The huts behind them were no longer frightful; and several inhabitants of the village came and told about the fearful night, and how they had been across the spot where the gipsies had lived; how these people must have left the place at last, for their huts were standing empty, and within had quite a common look, just like the dwellings of other poor people: some of their household gear was left behind.

Elfrida in secret said to her mother: "I could not sleep last night; and in my fright at the noise, I was praying from the bottom of my heart, when the door suddenly opened, and my playmate entered to take leave of me. She had a travelling-pouch slung round her, a hat on her head, and a large staff in her hand. She was very angry at thee; since on thy account she had now to suffer the severest and most painful punishments, as she had always been so fond of thee; for all of them, she said, were very loath to leave this quarter."

Mary forbade her to speak of this; and now the ferryman came across the river, and told them new wonders. As it was growing dark, a stranger man of large size had come to him, and hired his boat till sunrise; and with this condition, that the boatman should remain quiet in his house, at least should not cross the threshold of his door. "I was frightened," continued the old man, "and the strange bargain would not let me sleep. I slipped softly to the window, and looked towards the river. Great clouds were driving restlessly through the sky, and the distant woods were rustling fearfully; it was as if my cottage shook, and moans and lamentations glided round it. On a sudden I perceived a white streaming light, that grew broader and broader, like many thousands of falling stars; sparkling and waving, it proceeded forward from the dark fir ground, moved over the fields, and spread itself along towards the river. Then I heard a trampling, a jingling, a bustling, and rushing, nearer and nearer; it went forwards to my boat, and all stept into it, men and women, as it seemed, and children; and the tall stranger ferried them over. In the river were by the boat swimming many thousands of glittering forms; in the air, white clouds and lights were wavering; and all lamented and bewailed that they must travel forth so far, far away, and leave their beloved dwelling. The noise of the rudder and the water creaked and gurgled between whiles, and then suddenly there would be silence. Many a time the boat landed, and went back, and was again laden; many heavy casks, too, they took along with them, which multitudes of horrid-looking little fellows carried and rolled; whether they were devils or goblins, Heaven only knows. Then came, in waving brightness, a stately freight; it seemed an old man mounted on a small white horse, and all were crowding round him. I saw nothing of the horse but its head; for the rest of it was covered with costly glittering cloths and trappings: on his brow the old man had a crown, so bright, that as he came across I thought the sun was rising there, and the redness of the dawn glimmering in my eyes. Thus it went on all night; I at last fell asleep in the tumult, half in joy, half in terror. In the morning all was still; but the river is, as it were, run off, and I know not how I am to steer my boat in it now."

The same year there came a blight; the woods died away, the springs ran dry; and the scene, which had once been the joy of every traveller, was in autumn standing waste, naked, and bald; scarcely showing here and there, in the sea of sand, a spot or two where grass, with a dingy greenness, still grew up. The fruit trees all withered, the vines faded away, and the aspect of the place became so melancholy that the Count, with his people, next year left the castle, which in time decayed and fell to ruins.

Elfrida gazed on her rose day and night with deep longing, and thought of her kind playmate; and as it drooped and withered, so did she also hang her head; and before the spring, the little maiden had herself faded away. Mary often stood upon the spot before the hut, and wept for the happiness that had departed. She wasted herself away like her child, and in a few years she too was gone. Old Martin, with his son-in-law, returned to the quarter where he had lived before.

E. T. W. HOFFMANN
1776–1822

THE CREMONA VIOLIN

COUNCILLOR KRESPEL was one of the strangest, oddest men I ever met with in my life. When I went to live in H—— for a time the whole town was full of talk about him, as he happened to be just then in the midst of one of the very craziest of his schemes. Krespel had the reputation of being both a clever, learned lawyer and a skilful diplomatist. One of the reigning princes of Germany—not, however, one of the most powerful—had appealed to him for assistance in drawing up a memorial, which he was desirous of presenting at the Imperial Court with the view of furthering his legitimate claims upon a certain strip of territory. The project was crowned with the happiest success; and as Krespel had once complained that he could never find a dwelling sufficiently comfortable to suit him, the prince, to reward him for the memorial, undertook to defray the cost of building a house which Krespel might erect just as he pleased. Moreover, the prince was willing to purchase any site that he should fancy. This offer, however, the Councillor would not accept; he insisted that the house should be built in his garden, situated in a very beautiful neighbourhood outside the town walls. So he bought all kinds of materials and had them carted out. Then he might have been seen day after day, attired in his curious garments (which he had made himself according to certain fixed rules of his own), slaking the lime, riddling the sand, packing up the bricks and stones in regular heaps, and so on. All this he did without once consulting an architect or thinking about a plan. One fine day, however, he went to an experienced builder of the town and requested him to be in his garden at daybreak the next morning, with all his journeymen and apprentices, and a large body of labourers, etc., to build him his house. Naturally the builder asked for the architect's plan, and was not a little astonished when Krespel replied that none was needed, and that things would turn out all right in the end, just as he wanted them. Next morning, when the builder and his men came to the place, they found a trench drawn out in the shape of an exact square; and Krespel said, " Here's where you must lay the foundations ; then carry up the walls until I say they are high enough." " Without windows and doors, and without partition walls ? " broke in the builder, as if alarmed at Krespel's mad folly. " Do what I tell you, my dear sir," replied the Councillor quite calmly ; " leave the rest to me ; it will be all right." It was only the promise of high pay that could induce the builder to proceed with the ridiculous building , but none has ever been erected under merrier circumstances. As there was an abundant supply of food and drink, the workmen never left their work ; and amidst their continuous laughter the four walls were run up with incredible quickness, until one day Krespel cried, " Stop ! " Then the workmen, laying down trowel and hammer, came down from the scaffoldings and gathered round Krespel in a circle, whilst every laughing face was asking, " Well, and what now ? " " Make way ! " cried Krespel ; and then running to one end of the garden, he strode slowly towards the square of brickwork. When he came close to the wall he shook his head in a dissatisfied manner, ran to the other end of the garden, again strode slowly towards the brickwork square, and proceeded to act as before. These tactics he pursued several times, until at length, running his sharp nose hard against the wall, he cried, " Come here, come here, men ! break me a door in here ! Here's where I want a door made ! " He gave the exact dimensions in feet and inches, and they did as he bid them. Then he stepped inside the structure, and smiled with satisfaction as the builder remarked that the walls were just the height of a good two-storeyed house. Krespel walked thoughtfully backwards and forwards across the space within, the bricklayers behind him with hammers and picks, and wherever he cried, " Make a window here, six feet high by four feet broad ! " " There a little window, three feet by two ! " a hole was made in a trice.

It was at this stage of the proceedings that I came to H—— ; and it was highly amusing to see how hundreds of people stood round about the garden and raised a loud shout whenever the stones flew out and a new window appeared where nobody had for a moment expected it. And in the same manner Krespel proceeded with the buildings and fittings of the rest of the house, and with all the work necessary to that end ; everything had to be done on the spot in accordance with the instructions which the Councillor gave from time to time. However, the absurdity of the whole business, the growing conviction that things would in the end turn out better than might have been expected, but above all, Krespel's generosity—which, indeed, cost him nothing—kept them all in good-humour. Thus were the difficulties overcome which necessarily arose out of this eccentric way of building, and in a short time there was a completely finished house, its outside, indeed, presenting a most extraordinary appearance, no two windows, etc., being alike, but on the other hand the interior arrangements suggested a peculiar feeling of comfort. All who entered the house bore witness to the truth of this; and I, too, experienced it myself when I was taken in by Krespel after I had become more intimate with him. For hitherto I had not exchanged a word with this eccentric man; his building had occupied him so much that he had not even once been to Professor M——'s to dinner, as he was in the habit of doing on Tuesdays. Indeed, in reply to a special invitation, he sent word that he should not set foot over the threshold before the house-warming of his new building took place. All his friends and acquaintances, therefore, confidently looked forward to a great banquet; but Krespel invited nobody except the masters, journeymen, apprentices, and labourers who had built the house. He entertained them with the choicest viands; bricklayers' apprentices devoured partridge pies regardless of consequences; young joiners polished off roast pheasants with the greatest success; whilst hungry labourers helped themselves for once to the choicest morsels of *truffes fricassées*. In the evening their wives and daughters came, and there was a great ball. After waltzing a short while with the wives of the masters, Krespel sat down amongst the town musicians, took a violin in his hand, and directed the orchestra until daylight.

On the Tuesday after this festival, which exhibited Councillor Krespel in the character of a friend of the people, I at length saw him appear, to my no little joy, at Professor M——'s. Anything more strange and fantastic than Krespel's behaviour it would be impossible to find. He was so stiff and awkward in his movements, that he looked every moment as if he would run up against something or do some damage. But he did not; and the lady of the house seemed to be well aware that he would not, for she did not grow a shade paler when he rushed with heavy steps round a table crowded with beautiful cups, or when he manœuvred near a large mirror that reached down to the floor, or even when he seized a flower-pot of beautifully painted porcelain and swung it round in the air as if desirous of making its colours play. Moreover, before dinner he subjected everything in the

Professor's room to a most minute examination ; he also took down a picture from the wall and hung it up again, standing on one of the cushioned chairs to do so. At the same time he talked a good deal and vehemently ; at one time his thoughts kept leaping, as it were, from one subject to another (this was most conspicuous during dinner) ; at another, he was unable to have done with an idea ; seizing upon it again and again, he gave it all sorts of wonderful twists and turns, and couldn't get back into the ordinary track until something else took hold of his fancy. Sometimes his voice was rough and harsh and screeching, and sometimes it was low and drawling and singing ; but at no time did it harmonise with what he was talking about. Music was the subject of conversation ; the praises of a new composer were being sung, when Krespel, smiling, said in his low, singing tones, " I wish the devil with his pitchfork would hurl that atrocious garbler of music millions of fathoms down to the bottomless pit of hell ! " Then he burst out passionately and wildly, " She is an angel of heaven, nothing but pure God-given music !—the paragon and queen of song ! " —and tears stood in his eyes. To understand this, we had to go back to a celebrated *artiste*, who had been the subject of conversation an hour before.

Just at this time a roast hare was on the table ; I noticed that Krespel carefully removed every particle of meat from the bones on his plate, and was most particular in his inquiries after the hare's feet ; these the Professor's little five-year-old daughter now brought to him with a very pretty smile. Besides, the children had cast many friendly glances towards Krespel during dinner ; now they rose and drew nearer to him, yet not without signs of timorous awe. What's the meaning of that ? thought I to myself. Dessert was brought in ; then the Councillor took a little box from his pocket, in which he had a miniature lathe of steel. This he immediately screwed fast to the table, and turning the bones with incredible skill and rapidity, he made all sorts of little fancy boxes and balls, which the children received with cries of delight. Just as we were rising from table, the Professor's niece asked, " And what is our Antonia doing ? " Krespel's face was like that of one who has bitten of a sour orange and wants to look as if it were a sweet one ; but this expression soon changed into the likeness of a hideous mask, whilst he laughed behind it with downright, bitter, fierce, and, as it seemed to me, satanic scorn. " Our Antonia ? our dear Antonia ? " he asked in his drawling, disagreeable, singing way.

The Professor hastened to intervene ; in the reproving glance which he gave his niece I read that she had touched a point likely to stir up unpleasant memories in Krespel's heart. " How are you getting on with your violins ? " interposed the Professor in a jovial manner, taking the Councillor by both hands. Then Krespel's countenance cleared up, and with a firm voice he replied, " Capitally, Professor ; you recollect my telling you of the lucky chance which threw that splendid Amati[1] into my hands. Well, I've only cut it open to-day—not before to-day. I hope Antonia has carefully taken the rest of it to pieces." " Antonia is a good child," remarked the Professor. " Yes, indeed, that she is," cried the Councillor, whisking himself round ; then, seizing his hat and stick, he hastily rushed out of the room. I saw in the mirror how that tears were standing in his eyes.

As soon as the Councillor was gone, I at once urged the Professor to explain to me what Krespel had to do with violins, and particularly with Antonia. " Well," replied the Professor, " not only is the Councillor a remarkably eccentric fellow altogether, but he practises violin-making in his own crack-brained way." " Violin-making ! " I exclaimed, perfectly astonished. " Yes," continued the Professor, " according to the judgment of men who understand the thing, Krespel makes the very best violins that can be found nowadays ; formerly he would frequently let other people play on those in which he had been especially successful, but that's been all over and done with now for a long time. As soon as he has finished a violin he plays on it himself for one or two hours, with very remarkable power and with the most exquisite expression, then he hangs it up beside the rest, and never touches it again or suffers anybody else to touch it. If a violin by any of the eminent old masters is hunted up anywhere, the Councillor buys it immediately, no matter what the price put upon it. But he plays it as he does his own violins, only once ; then he takes it to pieces in order to examine closely its inner structure, and should he fancy he hasn't found exactly what he sought for, he in a pet throws the pieces into a big chest, which is already full of the remains of broken violins." " But who and what is Antonia ? " I inquired hastily and impetuously. " Well, now, that," continued the Professor, " that is a thing which

[1] The Amati were a celebrated family of violin-makers of the sixteenth and seventeenth centuries, belonging to Cremona in Italy. They form the connecting link between the Brescian school of makers and the greatest of all makers, Straduarius and Guarnerius.

might very well make me conceive an unconquerable aversion to the Councillor, were I not convinced that there is some peculiar secret behind it, for he is such a good-natured fellow at bottom as to be sometimes guilty of weakness. When we came to H——, several years ago, he led the life of an anchorite, along with an old housekeeper, in —— Street. Soon, by his oddities, he excited the curiosity of his neighbours ; and immediately he became aware of this, he sought and made acquaintances. Not only in my house but everywhere we became so accustomed to him that he grew to be indispensable. In spite of his rude exterior, even the children liked him, without ever proving a nuisance to him ; for, notwithstanding all their friendly passages together, they always retained a certain timorous awe of him, which secured him against all over-familiarity. You have to-day had an example of the way in which he wins their hearts by his ready skill in various things. We all took him at first for a crusty old bachelor, and he never contradicted us. After he had been living here some time, he went away, nobody knew where, and returned at the end of some months. The evening following his return his windows were lit up to an unusual extent ! This alone was sufficient to arouse his neighbours' attention, and they soon heard the surpassingly beautiful voice of a female singing to the accompaniment of a piano. Then the music of a violin was heard chiming in and entering upon a keen ardent contest with the voice. They knew at once that the player was the Councillor. I myself mixed in the large crowd which had gathered in front of his house to listen to this extraordinary concert ; and I must confess that, besides this voice and the peculiar, deep, soul-stirring impression which the execution made upon me, the singing of the most celebrated *artistes* whom I had ever heard seemed to me feeble and void of expression. Until then I had had no conception of such long-sustained notes, of such nightingale trills, of such undulations of musical sound, of such swelling up to the strength of organ-notes, of such dying away to the faintest whisper. There was not one whom the sweet witchery did not enthral ; and when the singer ceased, nothing but soft sighs broke the impressive silence. Somewhere about midnight the Councillor was heard talking violently, and another male voice seemed, to judge from the tones, to be reproaching him, whilst at intervals the broken words of a sobbing girl could be detected. The Councillor continued to shout with increasing violence, until he fell into that drawling, singing way that you know. He was interrupted by a loud scream from the girl, and then all was as still as death. Suddenly a loud racket was heard on the stairs ; a young man rushed out sobbing, threw himself into a post-chaise which stood below, and drove rapidly away. The next day the Councillor was very cheerful, and nobody had the courage to question him about the events of the previous night. But on inquiring of the housekeeper, we gathered that the Councillor had brought home with him an extraordinarily pretty young lady whom he called Antonia, and she it was who had sung so beautifully. A young man also had come along with them ; he had treated Antonia very tenderly, and must evidently have been her betrothed. But he, since the Councillor peremptorily insisted on it, had had to go away again in a hurry. What the relations between Antonia and the Councillor are has remained until now a secret, but this much is certain, that he tyrannises over the poor girl in the most hateful fashion. He watches her as Doctor Bartholo watches his ward in the *Barber of Seville* ; she hardly dare show herself at the window ; and if, yielding now and again to her earnest entreaties, he takes her into society, he follows her with Argus eyes, and will on no account suffer a musical note to be sounded, far less let Antonia sing—indeed, she is not permitted to sing in his own house. Antonia's singing on that memorable night has therefore come to be regarded by the townspeople in the light of a tradition of some marvellous wonder that suffices to stir the heart and the fancy ; and even those who did not hear it often exclaim, whenever any other singer attempts to display her powers in the place, 'What sort of a wretched squeaking do you call that ? Nobody but Antonia knows how to sing.' "

Having a singular weakness for such-like fantastic histories, I found it necessary, as may easily be imagined, to make Antonia's acquaintance. I had myself often enough heard the popular sayings about her singing, but had never imagined that that exquisite *artiste* was living in the place, held a captive in the bonds of this eccentric Krespel like the victim of a tyrannous sorcerer. Naturally enough I heard in my dreams on the following night Antonia's marvellous voice, and as she besought me in the most touching manner in a glorious *adagio* movement (very ridiculously it seemed to me, as if I had composed it myself) to save her—I soon resolved, like a second Astolpho,[1]

[1] A reference to Ariosto's *Orlando Furioso.* Astolpho, an English cousin of Orlando, was a great boaster, but generous, courteous, gay, and remarkably handsome ; he was carried to Alcina's island on the back of a whale.

to penetrate into Krespel's house, as if into another Alcina's magic castle, and deliver the queen of song from her ignominious fetters.

It all came about in a different way from what I had expected ; I had seen the Councillor scarcely more than two or three times, and eagerly discussed with him the best method of constructing violins, when he invited me to call and see him. I did so ; and he showed me his treasures of violins. There were fully thirty of them hanging up in a closet ; one amongst them bore conspicuously all the marks of great antiquity (a carved lion's head, etc.), and, hung up higher than the rest, and surmounted by a crown of flowers, it seemed to exercise a queenly supremacy over them. " This violin," said Krespel, on my making some inquiry relative to it, " this violin is a very remarkable and curious specimen of the work of some unknown master, probably of Tartini's [1] age. I am perfectly convinced that there is something especially exceptional in its inner construction, and that, if I took it to pieces, a secret would be revealed to me which I have long been seeking to discover, but—laugh at me if you like—this senseless thing which only gives signs of life and sound as I make it, often speaks to me in a strange way of itself. The first time I played upon it I somehow fancied that I was only the magnetiser who has the power of moving his subject to reveal of his own accord in words the visions of his inner nature. Don't go away with the belief that I am such a fool as to attach even the slightest importance to such fantastic notions, and yet it's certainly strange that I could never prevail upon myself to cut open that dumb lifeless thing there. I am very pleased now that I have not cut it open, for since Antonia has been with me I sometimes play to her upon this violin. For Antonia is fond of it—very fond of it." As the Councillor uttered these words with visible signs of emotion, I felt encouraged to hazard the question, " Will you not play it to me, Councillor ? " Krespel made a wry face, and falling into his drawling, singing way, said, " No, my good sir ! " and that was an end of the matter. Then I had to look at all sorts of rare curiosities, the greater part of them childish trifles ; at last, thrusting his arm into a chest, he brought out a folded piece of paper, which he pressed into

[1] Giuseppe Tartini, born in 1692, died in 1770, was one of the most celebrated violinists of the eighteenth century, and the discoverer (in 1714) of " resultant tones," or " Tartini's tones," as they are frequently called. Most of his life was spent at Padua. He did much to advance the art of the violinist, both by his compositions for that instrument and by his treatise on its capabilities.

my hand, adding solemnly, " You are a lover of art ; take this present as a priceless memento, which you must value at all times above everything else." Therewith he took me by the shoulders and gently pushed me towards the door, embracing me on the threshold. That is to say, I was in a symbolical manner virtually kicked out of doors. Unfolding the paper, I found a piece of a first string of a violin about an eighth of an inch in length, with the words, " A piece of the treble string with which the deceased Stamitz [1] strung his violin for the last concert at which he ever played."

This summary dismissal at mention of Antonia's name led me to infer that I should never see her ; but I was mistaken, for on my second visit to the Councillor's I found her in his room, assisting him to put a violin together. At first sight Antonia did not make a strong impression ; but soon I found it impossible to tear myself away from her blue eyes, her sweet rosy lips, her uncommonly graceful, lovely form. She was very pale ; but a shrewd remark or a merry sally would call up a winning smile on her face and suffuse her cheeks with a deep burning flush, which, however, soon faded away to a faint rosy glow. My conversation with her was quite unconstrained, and yet I saw nothing whatever of the Argus-like watchings on Krespel's part which the Professor had imputed to him ; on the contrary, his behaviour moved along the customary lines, nay, he even seemed to approve of my conversation with Antonia. So I often stepped in to see the Councillor ; and as we became accustomed to each other's society, a singular feeling of homeliness, taking possession of our little circle of three, filled our hearts with inward happiness. I still continued to derive exquisite enjoyment from the Councillor's strange crotchets and oddities ; but it was of course Antonia's irresistible charms alone which attracted me, and led me to put up with a good deal which I should otherwise, in the frame of mind in which I then was, have impatiently shunned. For it only too often happened that in the Councillor's characteristic extravagance there was mingled much that was dull and tiresome ; and it was in a special degree irritating to me that, as often as I turned the conversation upon music, and particularly upon singing, he was sure to interrupt me, with that

[1] This was the name of a well-known musical family from Bohemia. Karl Stamitz is the one here possibly meant, since he died about eighteen or twenty years previous to the publication of this tale.

sardonic smile upon his face and those repulsive singing tones of his, by some remark of a quite opposite tendency, very often of a commonplace character. From the great distress which at such times Antonia's glances betrayed, I perceived that he only did it to deprive me of a pretext for calling upon her for a song. But I didn't relinquish my design. The hindrances which the Councillor threw in my way only strengthened my resolution to overcome them ; I *must* hear Antonia sing if I was not to pine away in reveries and dim aspirations for want of hearing her.

One evening Krespel was in an uncommonly good-humour ; he had been taking an old Cremona violin to pieces, and had discovered that the sound-post was fixed half a line more obliquely than usual—an important discovery !—one of incalculable advantage in the practical work of making violins ! I succeeded in setting him off at full speed on his hobby of the true art of violin-playing. Mention of the way in which the old masters picked up their dexterity in execution from really great singers (which was what Krespel happened just then to be expatiating upon) naturally paved the way for the remark that now the practice was the exact opposite of this, the vocal score erroneously following the affected and abrupt transitions and rapid scaling of the instrumentalists. " What is more nonsensical," I cried, leaping from my chair, running to the piano, and opening it quickly—" what is more nonsensical than such an execrable style as this, which, far from being music, is much more like the noise of peas rolling across the floor ? " At the same time I sang several of the modern *fermatas*, which rush up and down and hum like a well-spun peg-top, striking a few villainous chords by way of accompaniment. Krespel laughed outrageously and screamed : " Ha ! ha ! methinks I hear our German-Italians or our Italian-Germans struggling with an aria from Pucitta,[1] or Portogallo,[2] or some other *Maestro di capella*, or rather *schiavo d'un primo uomo*." [3] Now, thought I, now's the time ; so turning to Antonia, I remarked, " Antonia knows nothing of such singing as that, I believe ? " At the

[1] Vincenzo Pucitta (1778–1861) was an Italian opera composer, whose music " shows great facility, but no invention." He also wrote several songs.

[2] Il Portogallo was the Italian sobriquet of a Portuguese musician named Mark Anthony Simâo (1763–1829). He lived alternately in Italy and Portugal, and wrote several operas.

[3] Literally, " The slave of a *primo uomo*," *primo uomo* being the masculine form corresponding to *prima donna*, that is, a singer of hero's parts in operatic music. At one time also female parts were sung and acted by men or boys.

same time I struck up one of old Leonardo Leo's [1] beautiful soul-stirring songs. Then Antonia's cheeks glowed; heavenly radiance sparkled in her eyes, which grew full of reawakened inspiration; she hastened to the piano; she opened her lips; but at that very moment Krespel pushed her away, grasped me by the shoulders, and with a shriek that rose up to a tenor pitch, cried, "My son—my son—my son!" And then he immediately went on, singing very softly, and grasping my hand with a bow that was the pink of politeness, "In very truth, my esteemed and honourable student-friend, in very truth, it would be a violation of the codes of social intercourse, as well as of all good manners, were I to express aloud and in a stirring way my wish that here, on this very spot, the devil from hell would softly break your neck with his burning claws, and so in a sense make short work of you; but, setting that aside, you must acknowledge, my dearest friend, that it is rapidly growing dark, and there are no lamps burning to-night, so that, even though I did not kick you downstairs at once, your darling limbs might still run a risk of suffering damage. Go home by all means; and cherish a kind remembrance of your faithful friend, if it should happen that you never—pray understand me—if you should never see him in his own house again." Therewith he embraced me, and, still keeping fast hold of me, turned with me slowly towards the door, so that I could not get another single look at Antonia. Of course it is plain enough that in my position I couldn't thrash the Councillor, though that is what he really deserved. The Professor enjoyed a good laugh at my expense, and assured me that I had ruined for ever all hopes of retaining the Councillor's friendship. Antonia was too dear to me, I might say too holy, for me to go and play the part of the languishing lover and stand gazing up at her window, or to fill the rôle of the love-sick adventurer. Completely upset, I went away from H——; but, as is usual in such cases, the brilliant colours of the picture of my fancy faded, and the recollection of Antonia, as well as of Antonia's singing (which I had never heard), often fell upon my heart like a soft faint trembling blight, comforting me.

Two years afterwards I received an appointment in B——, and set out on a journey to the south of Germany. The towers of H—— rose before me in the red vaporous glow of the evening; the nearer I came

[1] Leonardo Leo, the chief Neapolitan representative of Italian music in the first part of the eighteenth century, and author of more than forty operas and nearly one hundred compositions for the Church.

the more was I oppressed by an indescribable feeling of the most agonizing distress ; it lay upon me like a heavy burden ; I could not breathe ; I was obliged to get out of my carriage into the open air. But my anguish continued to increase until it became actual physical pain. Soon I seemed to hear the strains of a solemn chorale floating in the air ; the sounds continued to grow more distinct ; I realised the fact that they were men's voices chanting a church chorale. " What's that ? what's that ? " I cried, a burning stab darting as it were through my breast. "Don't you see ?" replied the coachman, who was driving along beside me, " why, don't you see ? They're burying somebody up yonder in yon churchyard." And indeed we were near the churchyard ; I saw a circle of men clothed in black standing round a grave, which was on the point of being closed. Tears started to my eyes ; I somehow fancied they were burying there all the joy and all the happiness of life. Moving on rapidly down the hill, I was no longer able to see into the churchyard ; the chorale came to an end, and I perceived not far distant from the gate some of the mourners returning from the funeral. The Professor, with his niece on his arm, both in deep mourning, went close past me without noticing me. The young lady had her handkerchief pressed close to her eyes, and was weeping bitterly. In the frame of mind in which I then was I could not possibly go into the town, so I sent on my servant with the carriage to the hotel where I usually put up, whilst I took a turn in the familiar neighbourhood to get rid of a mood that was possibly only due to physical causes, such as heating on the journey, etc. On arriving at a well-known avenue, which leads to a pleasure resort, I came upon a most extraordinary spectacle. Councillor Krespel was being conducted by two mourners, from whom he appeared to be endeavouring to make his escape by all sorts of strange twists and turns. As usual, he was dressed in his own curious home-made grey coat ; but from his little cocked-hat, which he wore perched over one ear in military fashion, a long narrow ribbon of black crape fluttered backwards and forwards in the wind. Around his waist he had buckled a black sword-belt ; but instead of a sword he had stuck a long fiddle-bow into it. A creepy shudder ran through my limbs : " He's insane," thought I, as I slowly followed them. The Councillor's companions led him as far as his house, where he embraced them, laughing loudly. They left him ; and then his glance fell upon me, for I now stood near him. He stared at me fixedly for some time ; then he cried in a hollow voice,

" Welcome, my student friend! you also understand it!" Therewith he took me by the arm and pulled me into the house, up the steps, into the room where the violins hung. They were all draped in black crape; the violin of the old master was missing; in its place was a cypress wreath. I knew what had happened. "Antonia! Antonia!" I cried, in inconsolable grief. The Councillor, with his arms crossed on his breast, stood beside me, as if turned into stone. I pointed to the cypress wreath. "When she died," said he, in a very hoarse solemn voice, "when she died, the sound-post of that violin broke into pieces with a ringing crack, and the sound-board was split from end to end. The faithful instrument could only live with her and in her; it lies beside her in the coffin, it has been buried with her." Deeply agitated, I sank down upon a chair, whilst the Councillor began to sing a gay song in a husky voice; it was truly horrible to see him hopping about on one foot, and the crape string (he still had his hat on) flying about the room and up to the violins hanging on the walls. Indeed, I could not repress a loud cry that rose to my lips when, on the Councillor making an abrupt turn, the crape came all over me; I fancied he wanted to envelop me in it and drag me down into the horrible dark depths of insanity. Suddenly he stood still and addressed me in his singing way, "My son! my son! why do you call out? Have you espied the angel of death? That always precedes the ceremony." Stepping into the middle of the room, he took the violin-bow out of his sword-belt, and, holding it over his head with both hands, broke it into a thousand pieces. Then, with a loud laugh, he cried, "Now you imagine my sentence is pronounced, don't you, my son? but it's nothing of the kind—not at all! not at all! Now I'm free—free—free—hurrah! I'm free! Now I shall make no more violins—no more violins—hurrah! no more violins!" This he sang to a horrible mirthful tune, again spinning round on one foot. Perfectly aghast, I was making the best of my way to the door, when he held me fast, saying quite calmly, "Stay, my student friend, pray don't think from this outbreak of grief, which is torturing me as if with the agonies of death, that I am insane; I only do it because a short time ago I made myself a dressing-gown in which I wanted to look like Fate or like God!" The Councillor then went on with a medley of silly and awful rubbish, until he fell down utterly exhausted; I called up the old housekeeper, and was very pleased to find myself in the open air again.

I never doubted for a moment that Krespel had become insane;

the Professor, however, asserted the contrary. "There are men," he remarked, "from whom nature or a special destiny has taken away the cover behind which the mad folly of the rest of us runs its course unobserved. They are like thin-skinned insects, which, as we watch the restless play of their muscles, seem to be misshapen, while nevertheless everything soon comes back into its proper form again. All that with us remains thought passes over with Krespel into action. That bitter scorn which the spirit that is wrapped up in the doings and dealings of the earth often has at hand, Krespel gives vent to in outrageous gestures and agile caprioles. But these are his lightning conductor. What comes up out of the earth he gives again to the earth, but what is divine, that he keeps; and so I believe that his inner consciousness, in spite of the apparent madness which springs from it to the surface, is as right as a trivet. To be sure, Antonia's sudden death grieves him sore, but I warrant that to-morrow will see him going along in his old jog-trot way as usual." And the Professor's prediction was almost literally fulfilled. Next day the Councillor appeared to be just as he formerly was, only he averred that he would never make another violin, nor yet ever play on another. And, as I learned later, he kept his word.

Hints which the Professor let fall confirmed my own private conviction that the so carefully guarded secret of the Councillor's relations to Antonia, nay, that even her death, was a crime which must weigh heavily upon him, a crime that could not be atoned for. I determined that I would not leave H—— without taxing him with the offence which I conceived him to be guilty of; I determined to shake his heart down to its very roots, and so compel him to make open confession of the terrible deed. The more I reflected upon the matter, the clearer it grew in my own mind that Krespel must be a villain, and in the same proportion did my intended reproach, which assumed of itself the form of a real rhetorical masterpiece, wax more fiery and more impressive. Thus equipped and mightily incensed I hurried to his house. I found him with a calm smiling countenance making playthings. "How can peace," I burst out—"how can peace find lodgment even for a single moment in your breast, so long as the memory of your horrible deed preys like a serpent upon you?" He gazed at me in amazement, and laid his chisel aside. "What do you mean, my dear sir?" he asked; "pray take a seat." But my indignation chafing me more and more, I went on to accuse him directly of having murdered Antonia, and to threaten him with the vengeance of the Eternal.

Further, as a newly full-fledged lawyer, full of my profession, I went so far as to give him to understand that I would leave no stone unturned to get a clue to the business, and so deliver him here in this world into the hands of an earthly judge. I must confess that I was considerably disconcerted when, at the conclusion of my violent and pompous harangue, the Councillor, without answering so much as a single word, calmly fixed his eyes upon me as though expecting me to go on again. And this I did indeed attempt to do, but it sounded so ill-founded and so stupid as well that I soon grew silent again. Krespel gloated over my embarrassment, whilst a malicious ironical smile flitted across his face. Then he grew very grave, and addressed me in solemn tones. " Young man, no doubt you think I am foolish, insane ; that I can pardon you, since we are both confined in the same mad-house ; and you only blame me for deluding myself with the idea that I am God the Father because you imagine yourself to be God the Son. But how do you dare desire to insinuate yourself into the secrets and lay bare the hidden motives of a life that is strange to you and that must continue so ? She has gone and the mystery is solved." He ceased speaking, rose, and traversed the room backwards and forwards several times. I ventured to ask for an explanation ; he fixed his eyes upon me, grasped me by the hand, and led me to the window, which he threw wide open. Propping himself upon his arms, he leaned out, and, looking down into the garden, told me the history of his life. When he finished I left him, touched and ashamed.

In a few words, his relations with Antonia rose in the following way. Twenty years before, the Councillor had been led into Italy by his favourite engrossing passion of hunting up and buying the best violins of the old masters. At that time he had not yet begun to make them himself, and so of course he had not begun to take to pieces those which he bought. In Venice he heard the celebrated singer, Angela ——i, who at that time was playing with splendid success as *prima donna* at St. Benedict's Theatre. His enthusiasm was awakened, not only in her art—which Signora Angela had indeed brought to a high pitch of perfection—but in her angelic beauty as well. He sought her acquaintance ; and in spite of all his rugged manners he succeeded in winning her heart, principally through his bold and yet at the same time masterly violin-playing. Close intimacy led in a few weeks to marriage, which, however, was kept a secret, because Angela was unwilling to sever her connection with the theatre, neither did she wish to part with her professional name, that by which she was celebrated, nor to add to it the cacophonous " Krespel." With the most extravagant irony he described to me what a strange life of worry and torture Angela led him as soon as she became his wife. Krespel was of opinion that more capriciousness and waywardness were concentrated in Angela's little person than in all the rest of the *prima donnas* in the world put together. If he now and again presumed to stand up in his own defence, she let loose a whole army of abbots, musical composers, and students upon him, who, ignorant of his true connection with Angela, soundly rated him as a most intolerable, ungallant lover for not submitting to all the Signora's caprices. It was just after one of these stormy scenes that Krespel fled to Angela's country-seat to try and forget in playing fantasias on his Cremona violin the annoyances of the day. But he had not been there long before the Signora, who had followed hard after him, stepped into the room. She was in an affectionate humour; she embraced her husband, overwhelmed him with sweet and languishing glances, and rested her pretty head on his shoulder. But Krespel, carried away into the world of music, continued to play on until the walls echoed again; thus he chanced to touch the Signora somewhat ungently with his arm and the fiddle-bow. She leapt back full of fury, shrieking that he was a " German brute," snatched the violin from his hands, and dashed it on the marble table into a thousand pieces. Krespel stood like a statue of stone before her; but then, as if awakening out of a dream, he seized her with the strength of a giant and threw her out of the window of her own house, and, without troubling himself about anything more, fled back to Venice—to Germany. It was not, however, until some time had elapsed that he had a clear recollection of what he had done; although he knew that the window was scarcely five feet from the ground, and although he was fully cognisant of the necessity, under the above-mentioned circumstances, of throwing the Signora out of the window, he yet felt troubled by a sense of painful uneasiness, and the more so since she had imparted to him in no ambiguous terms an interesting secret as to her condition. He hardly dared to make inquiries; and he was not a little surprised about eight months afterwards at receiving a tender letter from his beloved wife, in which she made not the slightest allusion to what had taken place in her country-house, only adding to the intelligence that she had been safely delivered of a sweet little daughter the heartfelt prayer that her dear husband and now a happy father would come at once to Venice. That, however, Krespel did not do ; rather he appealed to a confidential friend for a more circumstantial account of the details, and learned that the Signora had alighted upon the soft grass as lightly as a bird, and that the sole consequences of the fall or shock had been psychic. That is to say, after Krespel's heroic deed she had become completely altered ; she never showed a trace of caprice, of her former freaks, or of her teasing habits ; and the composer who wrote for the next carnival was the happiest fellow under the sun, since the Signora was willing to sing his music without the scores and hundreds of changes which she at other times had insisted upon. " To be sure," added his friend, " there was every reason for preserving the secret of Angela's cure, else every day would see lady singers flying through windows." The Councillor was not a little excited at this news ; he engaged horses ; he took his seat in the carriage. " Stop ! " he cried suddenly. " Why, there's not a shadow of doubt," he murmured to himself, " that as soon as Angela sets eyes upon me again, the evil spirit will recover his power and once more take possession of her. And since I have already thrown her out of the window, what could I do if a similar case were to occur again ? What would there be left for me to do ? " He got out of the carriage, and wrote an affectionate letter to his wife, making graceful allusion to her tenderness in especially dwelling upon the fact that his tiny daughter had, like him, a little mole behind the ear, and—remained in Germany. Now ensued an active correspondence between them. Assurances of unchanged affection—invitations—laments over the absence of the beloved one—thwarted wishes—hopes, etc.—flew backwards and forwards from Venice to H——, from H—— to Venice. At length Angela came to Germany, and, as is well known, sang with brilliant success as *prima donna* at the great theatre in F——. Despite the fact that she was no longer young, she won all hearts by the irresistible charm of her wonderfully splendid singing. At that time she had not lost her voice in the least degree. Meanwhile, Antonia had been growing up ; and her mother never tired of writing to tell her father how that a singer of the first rank was developing in her. Krespel's friends in F—— also confirmed this intelligence, and urged him to come for once to F—— to see and admire this uncommon sight of two such glorious singers. They had not the slightest suspicion of the close relations in which Krespel stood to the pair. Willingly would he have seen with his own eyes the daughter who occupied so large a place in his heart, and who moreover often appeared to him in his dreams; but as often as he thought upon his wife he felt very uncomfortable, and so he remained at home amongst his broken violins.

There was a certain promising young composer, B—— of F——, who was found to have suddenly disappeared, nobody knew where. This young man fell so deeply in love with Antonia that, as she returned his love, he earnestly besought her mother to consent to an immediate union, sanctified as it would further be by art. Angela had nothing to urge against his suit; and the Councillor the more readily gave his consent that the young composer's productions had found favour before his rigorous critical judgment. Krespel was expecting to hear of the consummation of the marriage, when he received instead a black-sealed envelope addressed in a strange hand. Doctor R—— conveyed to the Councillor the sad intelligence that Angela had fallen seriously ill in consequence of a cold caught at the theatre, and that during the night immediately preceding what was to have been Antonia's wedding-day, she had died. To him, the Doctor, Angela had disclosed the fact that she was Krespel's wife, and that Antonia was his daughter; he, Krespel, had better hasten therefore to take charge of the orphan. Notwithstanding that the Councillor was a good deal upset by this news of Angela's death, he soon began to feel that an antipathetic, disturbing influence had departed out of his life, and that now for the first time he could begin to breathe freely. The very same day he set out for F——. You could not credit how heartrending was the Councillor's description of the moment when he first saw Antonia. Even in the fantastic oddities of his expression there was such a marvellous power of description that I am unable to give even so much as a faint indication of it. Antonia inherited all her mother's amiability and all her mother's charms, but not the repellent reverse of the medal. There was no chronic moral ulcer, which might break out from time to time. Antonia's betrothed put in an appearance, whilst Antonia herself, fathoming with happy instinct the deeper-lying character of her wonderful father, sang one of old Padre Martini's [1] motets, which, she knew, Krespel in the heyday of his courtship had never grown tired

[1] Giambattista Martini, more commonly called Padre Martini, of Bologna, formed an influential school of music there in the latter half of the eighteenth century. He wrote vocal and instrumental pieces for both the church and the theatre. He was also a learned historian of music. He has the merit of having discerned and encouraged the genius of Mozart when, a boy of fourteen, he visited Bologna in 1770.

of hearing her mother sing. The tears ran in streams down Krespel's cheeks; even Angela he had never heard sing like that. Antonia's voice was of a very remarkable and altogether peculiar timbre: at one time it was like the sighing of an Æolian harp, at another like the warbled gush of the nightingale. It seemed as if there was not room for such notes in the human breast. Antonia, blushing with joy and happiness, sang on and on—all her most beautiful songs, B—— playing between whiles as only enthusiasm that is intoxicated with delight can play. Krespel was at first transported with rapture, then he grew thoughtful—still—absorbed in reflection. At length he leapt to his feet, pressed Antonia to his heart, and begged her in a low husky voice, "Sing no more if you love me—my heart is bursting—I fear—I fear—don't sing again."

"No!" remarked the Councillor next day to Doctor R——, "when, as she sang, her blushes gathered into two dark red spots on her pale cheeks, I knew it had nothing to do with your nonsensical family likenesses, I knew it was what I dreaded." The Doctor, whose countenance had shown signs of deep distress from the very beginning of the conversation, replied, "Whether it arises from a too early taxing of her powers of song, or whether the fault is Nature's—enough, Antonia labours under an organic failure in the chest, while it is from it, too, that her voice derives its wonderful power and its singular timbre, which I might almost say transcend the limits of human capabilities of song. But it bears the announcement of her early death; for, if she continues to sing, I wouldn't give her at the most more than six months longer to live." Krespel's heart was lacerated as if by the stabs of hundreds of stinging knives. It was as though his life had been for the first time overshadowed by a beautiful tree full of the most magnificent blossoms, and now it was to be sawn to pieces at the roots, so that it could not grow green and blossom any more. His resolution was taken. He told Antonia all; he put the alternatives before her—whether she would follow her betrothed and yield to his and the world's seductions, but with the certainty of dying early, or whether she would spread round her father in his old days that joy and peace which had hitherto been unknown to him, and so secure a long life. She threw herself sobbing into his arms, and he, knowing the heartrending trial that was before her, did not press for a more explicit declaration. He talked the matter over with her betrothed; but, notwithstanding that the latter averred that no note should ever cross Antonia's lips, the

Councillor was only too well aware that even B—— could not resist the temptation of hearing her sing, at any rate arias of his own composition. And the world, the musical public, even though acquainted with the nature of the singer's affliction, would certainly not relinquish its claims to hear her, for in cases where pleasure is concerned people of this class are very selfish and cruel. The Councillor disappeared from F—— along with Antonia, and came to H——. B—— was in despair when he learned that they had gone. He set out on their track, overtook them, and arrived at H—— at the same time that they did. "Let me see him only once, and then die!" entreated Antonia. "Die! die!" cried Krespel, wild with anger, an icy shudder running through him. His daughter, the only creature in the wide world who had awakened in him the springs of unknown joy, who alone had reconciled him to life, tore herself away from his heart, and he—he suffered the terrible trial to take place. B—— sat down to the piano; Antonia sang; Krespel fiddled away merrily, until the two red spots showed themselves on Antonia's cheeks. Then he bade her stop; and as B—— was taking leave of his betrothed, she suddenly fell to the floor with a loud scream. "I thought," continued Krespel in his narration, "I thought that she was, as I had anticipated, really dead; but as I had prepared myself for the worst, my calmness did not leave me, nor my self-command desert me. I grasped B——, who stood like a silly sheep in his dismay, by the shoulders, and said (here the Councillor fell into his singing tone), 'Now that you, my estimable pianoforte-player, have, as you wished and desired, really murdered your betrothed, you may quietly take your departure; at least have the goodness to make yourself scarce before I run my bright hanger through your heart. My daughter, who, as you see, is rather pale, could very well do with some colour from your precious blood. Make haste and run, for I might also hurl a nimble knife or two after you.' I must, I suppose, have looked rather formidable as I uttered these words, for, with a cry of the greatest terror, B—— tore himself loose from my grasp, rushed out of the room, and down the steps." Directly after B—— was gone, when the Councillor tried to lift up his daughter, who lay unconscious on the floor, she opened her eyes with a deep sigh, but soon closed them again as if about to die. Then Krespel's grief found vent aloud, and would not be comforted. The doctor, whom the old housekeeper had called in, pronounced Antonia's case a somewhat serious but by no means dangerous attack;

and she did indeed recover more quickly than her father had dared to hope. She now clung to him with the most confiding childlike affection; she entered into his favourite hobbies—into his mad schemes and whims. She helped him take old violins to pieces and glue new ones together. "I won't sing again any more, but live for you," she often said, sweetly smiling upon him, after she had been asked to sing and had refused. Such appeals, however, the Councillor was anxious to spare her as much as possible; therefore it was that he was unwilling to take her into society, and solicitously shunned all music. He well understood how painful it must be for her to forgo altogether the exercise of that art which she had brought to such a pitch of perfection. When the Councillor bought the wonderful violin that he had buried with Antonia, and was about to take it to pieces, she met him with such sadness in her face and softly breathed the petition, "What! this as well?" By some power, which he could not explain, he felt impelled to leave this particular instrument unbroken, and to play upon it. Scarcely had he drawn the first few notes from it than Antonia cried aloud with joy, "Why, that's me!—now I shall sing again." And, in truth, there was something remarkably striking about the clear, silvery, bell-like tones of the violin; they seemed to have been engendered in the human soul. Krespel's heart was deeply moved; he played, too, better than ever. As he ran up and down the scale, playing bold passages with consummate power and expression, she clapped her hands together and cried with delight, "I did that well! I did that well!"

From this time onwards her life was filled with peace and cheerfulness. She often said to the Councillor, "I should like to sing something, father." Then Krespel would take his violin down from the wall and play her most beautiful songs, and her heart was right glad and happy. Shortly before my arrival in H—— the Councillor fancied one night that he heard somebody playing the piano in the adjoining room, and he soon made out distinctly that B—— was flourishing on the instrument in his usual style. He wished to get up, but felt himself held down as if by a dead weight, and lying as if fettered in iron bonds; he was utterly unable to move an inch. Then Antonia's voice was heard singing low and soft; soon, however, it began to rise and rise in volume until it became an ear-splitting *fortissimo*; and at length she passed over into a powerfully impressive song which B—— had once composed for her in the devotional style of the old masters.

Krespel described his condition as being incomprehensible, for terrible anguish was mingled with a delight he had never experienced before. All at once he was surrounded by a dazzling brightness, in which he beheld B—— and Antonia locked in a close embrace, and gazing at each other in a rapture of ecstasy. The music of the song and of the pianoforte accompanying it went on without any visible signs that Antonia sang or that B—— touched the instrument. Then the Councillor fell into a sort of dead faint, whilst the images vanished away. On awakening he still felt the terrible anguish of his dream. He rushed into Antonia's room. She lay on the sofa, her eyes closed, a sweet angelic smile on her face, her hands devoutly folded, and looking as if asleep and dreaming of the joys and raptures of heaven. But she was—dead.

DE LA MOTTE FOUQUÉ
1777–1843

THE FIELD OF TERROR

IT happened that some little time before the Peace of Westphalia there assembled at the foot of the Riesenberg, in a beautiful part of the country of Silesia, a number of persons who were the relations, and had lately succeeded to the property, of an opulent, deceased farmer. This man had died without children, and had left several farms and fields scattered about that fertile country, and his heirs were now met together to divide the inheritance.

For this purpose they had assembled in a barn in one of the principal villages, and they found no difficulty among themselves as to the allotment of every part of the estate, except with regard to a particular field which was known by the name of the Haunted Field, in consequence of the wonderful stories that were told respecting it.

This field was now entirely overgrown with wild flowers and weeds, which nevertheless from their strong growth betokened at the same time the excellent nature of the land, and its desolate and neglected condition. For many years had now passed since it had been disturbed by the ploughshare, or received the seed from the hands of the industrious husbandman ; as it was related that no sooner had the ploughman at any time entered within its bounds than the oxen became frantic under the yoke, and ran off in affright, and that the ploughman and the seedsman, struck with the like panic, would fly in dismay, affirming that some supernatural beings, under pretence of assisting them in their labours, approached them with such hideous aspects that no one could look on them and keep their senses.

The question now arose to whom this Haunted Field should be allotted. Every one felt an insurmountable objection to it himself, but thought his neighbour might perhaps manage it, and, as is the way of the world, was desirous of shifting the burden off his own shoulders. They could, however, come to no agreement, and it was now late in the evening and time to depart when one of them proposed an expedient which he hoped would satisfy all parties.

" We are bound," he said, " agreeably to the testator's will, to bestow a legacy on his poor cousin who dwells in this village. The maiden is, to be sure, only very distantly related to the departed, yet she is virtuous and frugal, and well deserving of a good husband, and goes by the name of 'the pretty Sabine.' Now I propose that we present this maiden with the Haunted Field, and we shall in that way discharge the wishes of our lamented relation, and it may perhaps prove a rich dowry to her if she can find a husband that will venture to cultivate it."

They were all delighted at this proposal, and immediately dispatched one of their number to communicate to the cousin the intelligence of their bounty.

It was about the same time in the evening that Sabine heard, in the twilight, a gentle tap at her cottage window, and on asking who knocked, was answered by a voice, at the first sound of which the rustic bolt was drawn back and the little window thrown open. It was the brave young Frederick whom she had been long expecting, and who, being born as poor as herself, had for the last ten years devoted himself to the wars in order to win some little subsistence to compass his marriage with the pretty Sabine, whose kind heart was all his own.

It was a delightful picture to see Sabine leaning out of her wired lattice with tears of joy starting in her beautiful eyes, and the brave young Frederick looking up to her and proffering her his faith.

"Ah! Frederick," she said, "God be praised, thou art returned safe; this has been my constant prayer morn and evening; and tell me, Frederick, have you made your fortune in the campaign?"

"Fortunes are not so soon won," said Frederick, shaking his head and smiling, "and prizes do not fall to every one. However, I am better off than when I departed, and if you have a bold heart I think you may venture to marry."

"Ah!" sighed Sabine, "thou kind-hearted Frederick, to take a poor naked orphan for better or worse."

"Nay," said Frederick, "give me but one friendly yes, and promise to be mine, and I will warrant we shall thrive and live like princes."

"And hast thou got thy discharge and art no longer a soldier?"

Frederick, looking into the knapsack that held his treasures, brought out a silver medal, which he reached to Sabine, and as she received it, the light of the little lamp in her chamber fell on the piece. There was a burst drum figured in an old-fashioned manner, and over it was written the words—"God be praised, the war is ended."

"Perhaps," added Frederick, helping her to decipher the medal;

"in truth it is not yet peace, but we shall have no more fighting at present, and our colonel has discharged his men."

At this intelligence Sabine held out her hand as a pledge of her affection to her lover, and invited her betrothed to come into her little chamber, where he seated himself down by her side and related how he had won his gold and silver in honourable battle, and in the open field, from a foreign officer of rank whom he had made prisoner, and obtained the money as his ransom. After an approving smile conferred on her brave soldier, the industrious maiden took up her spindle, rejoicing that there was no ill-gotten gain belonging to either of them.

Just at this moment the cousin arrived to communicate the message entrusted to him. Sabine, with maidenly blushes, presented to him the stranger as her intended husband, and the cousin added:

"This is well! I am arrived just in time, for if your betrothed has not brought back a fortune from the wars, this will be a welcome gift, which I am directed to present to you in the name of your relations, as it was the will of the testator that you should be remembered in some way or other."

Frederick was too much offended at the boasting manner in which this communication was made to testify any joy on the occasion. But Sabine, in a humble manner, thanked God for His gracious dispensation, and ignorant of the evil motives of mankind, she, with a joyful heart, bowed her head in token of her great satisfaction.

But when she heard that the Haunted Field was assigned to her as her portion, and in satisfaction of her just claims, the sordid behaviour of her relations struck her to the soul, and she could not restrain her tears at the grievous disappointment.

The cousin, with a malicious smile, said he was grieved to find she thought herself wronged, as it was in fact a much larger share of the inheritance than really of right belonged to her. And, thus speaking, he was taking his departure, but Frederick interrupted him, and addressing him in a cool and deliberate manner:

"Sir," said he, "I see you are disposed to make a jest of this matter, and that you have all conspired together not to give my young bride a single farthing. But we will accept your present in God's name, in the hope that, in the hands of a brave and active soldier, the Haunted Field may be a better bargain than a parcel of covetous, envious old relations wish it to be."

The cousin, abashed at the presence of the bold young man, returned no answer, and made the best of his way back. The bridegroom then kissed the tears from the eyes of his young bride,[1] and hastened away to the priest to arrange matters for the marriage.

After the lapse of a few weeks Frederick and Sabine became man and wife, and commenced their slender housekeeping. The young man had expended the greater part of his gold and silver pieces in the purchase of a yoke of fine oxen, and in the buying of seed and implements requisite for his husbandry, reserving no more than sufficient to support himself and his wife in the most frugal manner until they should be enriched by the next year's harvest.

As Frederick with his oxen and plough now took his departure for the field, he looked back and smiled at his good Sabine, saying that he was now about to lay out his gold, and that next year he should have it all back, and to spare. Sabine looked anxiously after him, wishing in her own heart that he might return home in safety.

And home truly he came, and that, too, before the ringing of the curfew, but by no means so full of cheer as when he set out joyfully singing in the morning. He was himself dragging along the plough, which was battered and broken, and was at the same time leading one of his oxen lame and wounded along with him, and himself bleeding on the shoulders and head. Still, his soldier-like courage did not fail him, and calling on his wife with a cheerful countenance :

" Prepare for salting," he said, " for this goblin in the Haunted Field has provided us with an abundance of beef. This ox that I have brought back with me has run mad, and injured himself so much that he will not be fit for any further work. The other ran off to the mountain, and there I saw him plunge from a steep rock into the river below, where I fancy he now lies at the bottom."

" Oh ! these cousins, these wicked cousins ! " cried Sabine, weeping, " already has their accursed present robbed thee of thy hard-earned gold, and, what is more, thou art thyself hurt and bleeding, my brave young soldier ! "

" My hurt is of no consequence," said Frederick, " it was but the oxen that crushed me between them when they ran mad, and I endeavoured to stop them : but it matters not grieving, and in the morning I will start afresh."

[1] In Germany the appellations of Bride and Bridegroom are attached to the respective parties on their betrothal.

Sabine was now so terrified at what had happened that she endeavoured to dissuade her husband from any further attempt at cultivating the unlucky field. But he declared in reply that the field should have no rest as long as he lived, and "land that one cannot plough one must delve," said he, "and I think this goblin will not frighten a good steady soldier in the way he does a poor brute animal."

He then slaughtered the wounded beast and cut him up, and the next morning, as soon as Sabine was ready to begin salting the meat, Frederick was again on his way to the Haunted Field, and departed with his pickaxe and his spade, with as good a heart as on the morning before he had set out with his good yoke of oxen and his new shining plough.

He returned from his work in the evening as on the previous day. He looked pale and wearied, but was in good spirits.

"This is rather hard work," said he, laughing, "for there comes a lubberly goblin, first on this side, then on that, bantering me with his foolish talk and tricks ; but he seemed to wonder at last that I took no heed of him, and from that I begin to get fresh courage. Besides, what has an industrious man to fear that goes straight forward and minds his work ? "

Many days now passed away in the same manner. The brave Frederick continued unwearied, delving and sowing and destroying the weeds. And he had now cultivated a good portion of the Haunted Field by the aid of his spade alone, for he never relaxed in his exertions, and his land began to promise a crop, if not very rich, still a handsome return for his trouble ; and he now cut his corn and carried it all home himself, for his land was yet too poor to afford him reapers to help him, and he would not let Sabine venture into the field, more particularly as he was expecting her soon to present him with an infant. The child was born, and in three years two more came, and so his life went on without any remarkable occurrence.

By hard striving and industry he compelled the Haunted Field to yield him one crop after another, and thus, like an honest man, redeemed his word to Sabine, that he would find sufficient to support her.

It happened one evening at harvest time that Frederick had remained at work until near dark, when all at once he perceived at his side a strongly-built, swarthy-looking man like a collier, with a huge furnace-iron in his hand, who said to Frederick :

"What ! are there no oxen left in the land that thou workest with thine own hands? Thou shouldst be a rich farmer if one may judge from the extent of thy land."

Frederick well knew who it was that thus addressed him, and did as people are accustomed to do on these occasions, that is, held his tongue and worked even the harder, and tried to turn his thoughts another way.

But the goblin did not on this occasion disappear as these beings commonly do when they are thus treated, in order to appear afterwards in a more hideous form, but again addressed Frederick, and said in a friendly tone:

"Friend, thou wrongest both me and thyself. Answer me truly and sincerely; perhaps I may find a cure for thy misfortunes."

"Well, then, in God's name speak," said Frederick, "and if there be mischief in thy words the blame be with thee."

Frederick then rose from his work and related in a true manner to the collier all that had happened since he took possession of the field, nor did he conceal his hatred to the goblin, and how difficult it was, owing to his persecution, to work out a subsistence with his bare pick-axe and spade, and support his family.

The collier heard all with a serious countenance. He then stood still for some time in a musing attitude, and at last spoke as follows:

"It seems, friend, that thou knowest who I am, and that is commendable in thee, that thou hast not sacrificed the truth but spoken boldly out, notwithstanding thou hast so much cause to be angry with me; and to confess the truth thou hast indeed had too much reason. But now, since I find thee a right honest churl, I will make thee an offer that will recompense thee for all that is past. Thou must know, then, that when I have had my fill of sport in woods and mountains, I have a fancy to dwell in a comfortable house, and live a sober and orderly life for some half-year or so. How, now, if thou wert to engage me as thy servant for the next six months?"

"Now that is ill done," said Frederick, "to banter an honest man in this way."

"No! no!" said the other, "it is no bantering—I am really serious; thou shalt find me a truly hard-working drudge, and as long as I serve thee, no hobgoblin will venture to be seen in the Haunted Field, so that thou mayest work thy oxen there without interruption."

"That I should like well," said Frederick, after some thought, "if

I only knew whether thou wouldst keep thy word, and moreover if it is right to deal with thee."

" That you must settle yourself," said the stranger, " but my word will never be broken as long as the Riesenberg stands ; and, moreover, I am not a malicious-minded spirit—somewhat sportive, and tricksy, and wild, but that is all."

" Why, then," said Frederick, " thou must needs be the famous Rubezahl ! "

" When thou thinkest so," said the collier, interrupting him, " learn that that powerful spirit will not allow of a name so ignominious, but calls himself the Monarch of the Hills."

" That would be a droll affair," said Frederick, laughing, " to have the King of the Hills for my serving-man."

" Thou mayest call me Waldmann, then," answered the other.

Frederick now stood considering for a considerable time, and at last said, " Well ! so be it—I don't think I do wrong in engaging thee ; I have often observed that people employ irrational animals to turn the spit and do other household offices ; why not a goblin ? "

The collier uttered a hearty laugh, and said, " Now such an offer was never made by any of my kind before. But that I heed not—'tis my humour, and so 'tis a bargain, my honoured master ! "

Frederick, however, made it a condition that his new servant should on no account whatever discover to Sabine or the children that he had lived in the Haunted Field, or in the old caverns of the Riesenberg ; nor at any time play any goblin tricks about the house or farm. Waldmann pledged his word to all this, so the matter was concluded, and home they both went together in a friendly mood.

Sabine was not a little surprised at this addition to their household, and could scarcely look upon the swarthy gigantic servant without fear. The children were at first so much alarmed that they would not venture out of doors when he was at work in the garden or in the croft ; but his quiet and good-natured and friendly behaviour soon reconciled all the household ; and if he now and then had a frolicsome fit, and chased the dog and the fowls, they thought it only sportiveness and good-humour, and a single word from the master was sufficient to bring him back into his usual bounds.

Frederick, now relying on the promise of the spirit of the mountain, inconsiderately expended his long-treasured gold in the purchase of two fine new oxen, and again went joyfully forth to his field with his plough newly repaired. Sabine looked after him anxiously, and anxiously awaited his return at night, fearing that he might again have all his prospects blighted, and be worse hurt himself than on the former occasion. But with the curfew, home came Frederick, singing through the village, driving before him his yoke of fine oxen, and kissed in great glee his wife and children, and shook his servant kindly by the hand.

Waldmann also often took out the oxen to plough, while Frederick laboured in the garden or in the barn. The greater part of the Haunted Field was now cultivated, and everything went on prosperously, to the surprise of all the inhabitants of the village, and to the chagrin of the envious relations.

The harvest was now finished, and winter approaching, when Frederick went one day with his team to gather wood for the hearth and the oven. It so happened, too, that Sabine was at the same time called away to see a poor widow in the neighbourhood who lay ill of a fever, and whom she was accustomed to befriend to the best of her means. She knew not well what to do with her children, but Waldmann desired her to leave them in his care, and as she knew that they were always amused with his tales she did so, and departed on her pious errand.

In about an hour's time from this, Frederick returned home from the forest. He placed his waggon in the shed, and put up his oxen in their stalls, and was cheerfully turning his steps to the house to warm his benumbed limbs at the fire, when the piercing cries of his children suddenly alarmed his ears. He rushed into the house, burst open the kitchen door, and there found all the children shrieking, and pushed together behind the oven, and Waldmann madly laughing and leaping about, making hideous faces, and his hair all in fire and flames.

" What's to be done here ? " said the master in an angry tone. The fire was instantly extinguished on Waldmann's head, and he stood in a humble posture before his master, excusing himself by saying that he was only amusing the children. But the children ran crying to their father, and told him that he had terrified them with frightful faces, and ran to them now with a ram's head and now a dog's. " 'Tis enough," said Frederick to him, " depart, friend—we dwell no longer under the same roof."

And he therewith took him by the arm, and pushed him out of the house and beyond the garden, telling the children to remain quiet in the chamber and not terrify themselves any more, as their father was now come and they were as safe as in Abraham's bosom.

The strange servant made no resistance, but as he now stood beside Frederick on the wintry ground he said laughing, "Hear! master! suppose we strike a fresh bargain. I have, I confess, made a great disturbance, but it shall not happen again; I fell unfortunately into a fit of my old humour."

"For your own pleasure," said Frederick, "but you might have terrified my children out of their senses. There is an end of our contract."

"My half-year is not yet expired," said Waldmann, arguing, "and I insist on going back to the house."

"Thou shalt not again touch my threshold," said Frederick; "thou hast broken the contract by playing thy accursed pranks; but I will pay thee thy full wages—there they are—take them and depart."

"My full wages," said the goblin with a contemptuous laugh "hast thou then forgotten my treasures in the mountains?"

"'Tis more on my own account than thine," said Frederick; "I don't wish to remain in any one's debt." And with that he forced the money into Waldmann's pocket.

"And what will become of the Haunted Field?" said Waldmann, with an angry look.

"What God wills," said Frederick. "I would rather lose fifty fields than that you should injure one hair of my children's heads. Away with thee, or I shall serve thee in a manner thou wilt not like."

"Softly," said the goblin; "when spirits such as I assume a man's form it is generally a strong one, and thou mightest perhaps come the worst off in such a contest, and then God be merciful to thee!"

"That He has ever been, and has given me a good strength of arm as thou shalt find. Back to thy mountains, thou odious brute—I warn thee for the last time."

On this the goblin attacked Frederick in a furious manner, and an obstinate contest ensued. They wrestled and threw each other without the victory being decided for the one or the other, until at last Frederick by a masterly stroke brought his opponent to the ground, and kneeling on his breast he began to beat him with his fists, exclaiming, "I'll teach thee how to attack thy master, thou accursed mountain spirit!"

Rubezahl, however, laughed so heartily at this, that Frederick, thinking that he was mocking him, repeated his blows with renewed vigour, until the goblin at last cried out, " Enough, enough ! I was not laughing at thee, but at myself, and cry mercy ! "

" That's another matter," said Frederick ; " rise then." And he helped him up on his legs.

" I have had a sufficient trial of human life," said the spirit, laughing ; " none of my kind, I think, ever carried the sport so far. But hark ! friend, thou must nevertheless allow I made a brave resistance ; for thou knowest I could easily have called a host of mountain spirits to my aid had I so pleased. Truly I am almost killed with laughing."

Frederick stood regarding the merry Rubezahl, and said, " You will, I fancy, bear me a grudge, and send me ill-luck not only in the Haunted Field, but in other matters ; but still I cannot repent of what I have done. I have only exercised my just authority and protected my children. Were it to happen again I should treat thee in the same way."

" No, no," said Rubezahl, " do not give yourself that trouble—I have had enough for this time. But listen to my words—go on working thy Haunted Field, and I promise thee not the shadow of a goblin shall henceforth be seen in it as long as the Riesenberg stands, and so farewell and prosper, my honest strong-fisted master."

And on this, with a familiar nod, he disappeared, and Frederick, during the remainder of his life, never saw him again. But Rubezahl kept his word to the full and more.

An unheard-of prosperity began to manifest itself in all the affairs of Frederick, and he became in a short time the richest farmer in the village. And when the children played in the Haunted Field, which both they and Sabine now walked in without fear, they would often relate how the good Waldmann had appeared to them and told them humorous tales, and how they found choice confectionaries, or beautiful carved toys, or golden ducats in their pockets on their return home.

BROTHERS GRIMM

JAKOB 1785–1863. WILHELM 1786–1859

TOM THUMB

THERE was once a poor woodman sitting by the fire in his cottage, and his wife sat by his side spinning.

" How lonely it is," said he, " for you and me to sit here by ourselves without any children to play about and amuse us, while other people seem so happy and merry with their children ! "

" What you say is very true," said his wife, sighing and turning round her wheel ; " how happy should I be if I had but one child ! and if it were ever so small, nay, if it were no bigger than my thumb, I should be very happy, and love it dearly."

Now it came to pass that this good woman's wish was fulfilled just as she desired ; for, some time afterwards, she had a little boy who was quite healthy and strong, but not much bigger than my thumb.

So they said, " Well, we cannot say we have not got what we wished for, and, little as he is, we will love him dearly " ; and they called him Tom Thumb.

They gave him plenty of food, yet he never grew bigger, but remained just the same size as when he was born ; still his eyes were sharp and sparkling, and he soon showed himself to be a clever little fellow, who always knew well what he was about.

One day, as the woodman was getting ready to go into the wood to cut fuel, he said, " I wish I had some one to bring the cart after me, for I want to make haste."

" O father ! " cried Tom, " I will take care of that ; the cart shall be in the wood by the time you want it."

Then the woodman laughed and said, " How can that be ? You cannot reach up to the horse's bridle."

" Never mind that, father," said Tom ; " if my mother will only harness the horse, I will get into his ear, and tell him which way to go."

" Well," said the father, " we will try for once."

When the time came, the mother harnessed the horse to the cart and put Tom into his ear ; and as he sat there, the little man told the beast how to go, crying out, " Go on ! " and " Stop ! " as he wanted ;

so the horse went on just as if the woodman had driven it himself into the wood. It happened that, as the horse was going a little too fast, and Tom was calling out, " Gently! gently!" two strangers came up.

" What an odd thing that is!" said one; " there is a cart going along, and I hear a carter talking to the horse, but can see no one."

" That is strange," said the other; " let us follow the cart and see where it goes."

So they went on into the wood, till at last they came to the place where the woodman was.

Then Tom Thumb, seeing his father, cried out, " See, father, here I am with the cart, all right and safe; now take me down."

So his father took hold of the horse with one hand, and with the other took his son out of the ear; then he put him down upon a straw, where he sat as merry as you please.

The two strangers were all this time looking on, and did not know what to say for wonder. At last one took the other aside and said, " That little urchin will make our fortune if we can get him, and carry him about from town to town as a show: we must buy him."

So they went to the woodman and asked him what he would take for the little man: " He will be better off," said they, " with us than with you."

" I won't sell him at all," said the father; " my own flesh and blood is dearer to me than all the silver and gold in the world."

But Tom, hearing of the bargain they wished to make, crept up his father's coat to his shoulder, and whispered in his ear, " Take the money, father, and let them have me; I'll soon come back to you."

So the woodman at last agreed to sell Tom to the strangers for a large piece of gold.

" Where do you like to sit?" said one of them.

" Oh, put me on the rim of your hat, that will be a nice gallery for me; I can walk about there, and see the country as we go along."

So they did as he wished; and when Tom had taken leave of his father, they took him away with them. They journeyed on till it began to be dusky, and then the little man said, " Let me get down, I'm tired."

So the man took off his hat and set him down on a clod of earth in a ploughed field by the side of the road. But Tom ran about amongst the furrows, and at last slipped into an old mouse-hole.

" Good-night, masters," said he, " I'm off! Mind and look sharp after me the next time."

They ran directly to the place, and poked the ends of their sticks into the mouse-hole, but all in vain. Tom only crawled farther and farther in, and at last it became quite dark, so that they were obliged to go their way without their prize, as sulky as you please.

When Tom found they were gone, he came out of his hiding-place. "What dangerous walking it is," said he, "in this ploughed field! If I were to fall from one of these great clods, I should certainly break my neck."

At last, by good luck, he found a large empty snail-shell. "This is lucky," said he, "I can sleep here very well," and in he crept.

Just as he was falling asleep he heard two men passing, and one said to the other, "How shall we manage to steal that rich parson's silver and gold?"

"I'll tell you," cried Tom.

"What noise was that?" said the thief, frightened. "I am sure I heard some one speak."

They stood still listening, and Tom said, "Take me with you, and I'll soon show you how to get the parson's money."

"But where are you?" said they.

"Look about on the ground," answered he, "and listen where the sound comes from."

At last the thieves found him out, and lifted him in their hands. "You little urchin!" said they, "what can you do for us?"

"Why, I can get between the iron window-bars of the parson's house and throw out whatever you want."

"That's a good thought," said the thieves; "come along, we shall see what you can do."

When they came to the parson's house, Tom slipped through the window-bars into the room, and then called out as loud as he could bawl, "Will you have all that is here?"

At this the thieves were frightened, and said, "Softly, softly! Speak low, that you may not awaken anybody."

But Tom pretended not to understand them, and bawled out again, "How much will you have? Shall I throw it all out?"

Now the cook lay in the next room, and hearing a noise she raised herself in her bed and listened. Meantime the thieves were frightened, and ran off to a little distance; but at last they plucked up courage and said, "The little urchin is only trying to make a fool of us."

So they came back and whispered softly to him, saying, "Now let us have no more of your jokes, but throw out some of the money."

Then Tom called out as loud as he could, "Very well: hold your hands, here it comes."

The cook heard this quite plain, so she sprang out of bed and ran to open the door. The thieves ran off as if a wolf was at their tails; and the maid, having groped about and found nothing, went away for a light.

By the time she returned, Tom had slipped into the barn; and when the cook had looked about and searched every hole and corner, and found nobody, she went to bed, thinking she must have been dreaming with her eyes open. The little man crawled about in the hay-loft, and at last found a glorious place to finish his night's rest in; so he laid himself down, meaning to sleep till daylight, and then find his way home to his father and mother.

But alas! how cruelly was he disappointed! what crosses and sorrows happen in this world! The cook got up early before day-break to feed the cows: she went straight to the hay-loft, and carried away a large bundle of hay with the little man in the middle of it fast asleep. He still, however, slept on, and did not awake till he found himself in the mouth of the cow, who had taken him up with a mouthful of hay. "Good lack-a-day!" said he. "How did I manage to tumble into the mill?"

But he soon found out where he really was, and was obliged to have all his wits about him in order that he might not get between the cow's teeth and so be crushed to death. At last down he went into her stomach. "It is rather dark here," said he; "they forgot to build windows in this room to let the sun in; a candle would be no bad thing."

Though he made the best of his bad luck, he did not like his quarters at all; and the worst of it was, that more and more hay was always coming down, and the space in which he was became smaller and smaller. At last he cried out as loud as he could, "Don't bring me any more hay! Don't bring me any more hay!"

The maid happened to be just then milking the cow, and hearing some one speak and seeing nobody, and yet being quite sure it was the same voice that she had heard in the night, she was so frightened that she fell off her stool and overset the milk-pail. She ran off as fast as she could to her master the parson, and said, " Sir, sir, the cow is talking ! "

But the parson said, " Woman, thou art surely mad ! " However, he went with her into the cow-house to see what was the matter. Scarcely had they set their foot on the threshold when Tom called out, " Don't bring me any more hay ! "

Then the parson himself was frightened ; and thinking the cow was surely bewitched, ordered that she should be killed directly. So the cow was killed, and the stomach, in which Tom lay, was thrown out upon a dunghill.

Tom soon set to work to get out, which was not a very easy task ; but at last, just as he made room to get his head out, a new misfortune befell him : a hungry wolf sprang out, and swallowed the whole stomach, with Tom in it, at a single gulp, and ran away.

Tom, however, was not disheartened ; and thinking the wolf would not dislike having a chat with him as he was going along, he called out, " My good friend, I can show you a famous treat."

" Where's that ? " said the wolf.

" In such and such a house," said Tom, describing his father's house, " you can crawl through the drain into the kitchen, and there you will find cakes, ham, beef, and everything your heart can desire."

The wolf did not want to be asked twice ; so that very night he went to the house and crawled through the drain into the kitchen, and ate and drank there to his heart's content. As soon as he was satisfied, he wanted to get away ; but he had eaten so much that he could not get out the same way that he came in. This was just what Tom had reckoned upon ; and he now began to set up a great shout, making all the noise he could.

" Will you be quiet ? " said the wolf : " you'll awaken everybody in the house."

" What's that to me ? " said the little man : " you have had your frolic, now I've a mind to be merry myself " ; and he began again singing and shouting as loud as he could.

The woodman and his wife, being awakened by the noise, peeped through a crack in the door ; but when they saw that the wolf was there, you may well suppose that they were terribly frightened ; and the woodman ran for his axe, and gave his wife a scythe. " Now do you stay behind," said the woodman, " and when I have knocked him on the head, do you rip up his belly for him with the scythe."

Tom heard all this, and said, " Father, father! I am here, the wolf has swallowed me"; and his father said, " Heaven be praised! we have found our dear child again," and he told his wife not to use the scythe, for fear she should hurt him.

Then he aimed a great blow, and struck the wolf on the head, and killed him on the spot; and when he was dead they cut open his body and set Tommy free.

" Ah!" said the father, " what fears we have had for you!"

" Yes, father," answered he. " I have travelled all over the world since we parted, in one way or other; and now I am very glad to get fresh air again."

" Why, where have you been?" said his father.

" I have been in a mouse-hole, in a snail-shell, down a cow's throat, and in the wolf's belly; and yet here I am again, safe and sound."

" Well," said they, " we will not sell you again for all the riches in the world."

So they hugged and kissed their dear little son, and gave him plenty to eat and drink, and fetched new clothes for him, for his old ones were quite spoiled on his journey.

THE TWELVE DANCING PRINCESSES

Brothers Grimm

THERE was once a king who had twelve lovely daughters. They slept in twelve beds all in one room, and when they went to bed the doors were shut and locked up ; but every morning their shoes were found to be quite worn through, as if they had been danced in all night, and yet nobody could find how it happened, or where they had been.

Then the king made it known to all the land, that if any person could discover the secret, and find out where it was that the princesses danced at night, he should have the one he liked best for his wife, and should be king after his death ; but whoever tried and did not succeed after three days and nights should be put to death.

A king's son soon came. He was well entertained, and in the evening was taken to the chamber next to the one where the princesses lay in their twelve beds. There he was to sit and watch where they went to dance ; and in order that nothing might pass without his hearing it, the door of his chamber was left open. But the king's son soon fell asleep, and when he awoke in the morning he found that the princesses had all been dancing, for the soles of their shoes were worn full of holes. The same thing happened the second and third night ; so the king ordered his head to be cut off. After him came several others, but they had all the same luck, and all lost their lives in the same manner.

Now it chanced that an old soldier, who had been wounded in battle and could fight no longer, passed through the country where this king reigned, and as he was travelling through a wood, he met an old woman who asked him where he was going.

"I hardly know where I am going, or what I shall do," said the soldier, "but I think I should like very well to find out where it is that the princesses dance, and then in time I might be a king."

"Well!" said the old dame, "that is no very hard task, only take care not to drink any of the wine which one of the princesses will bring to you in the evening, and as soon as she leaves you, pretend to be fast asleep."

Then she gave him a cloak, and said:

"As soon as you put that on you will become invisible, and you will then be able to follow the princesses wherever they go."

When the soldier heard all this good counsel, he determined to try his luck; so he went to the king and said he was willing to undertake the trial. He was as well received as the others had been, and the king ordered fine royal robes to be given him, and when the evening came he was led to the outward chamber. Just as he was going to lie down, the eldest of the princesses brought him a cup of wine; but the soldier threw it all away secretly, taking care not to drink a drop.

Then he laid himself down on his bed, and in a little time began to snore very loud, as if he was fast asleep. When the twelve princesses heard this they laughed heartily, and the eldest said:

"This fellow too might have done a wiser thing than lose his life in this way!"

Then they rose up and opened their drawers and boxes, and took out all their fine clothes, and dressed themselves at the glass, and skipped about as if they were eager to begin dancing.

But the youngest said, "I don't know how it is, while you are so happy I feel very uneasy; I am sure some mischance will befall us."

"You simpleton," said the eldest, "you are always afraid; have you forgotten how many kings' sons have already watched us in vain? And as for this soldier, even if I had not given him his sleeping-draught he would have slept soundly enough."

When they were all ready they went and looked at the soldier; but he snored on and did not stir hand or foot; so they thought they were quite safe, and the eldest went up to her own bed and clapped her hands, and the bed sank into the floor and a trap-door flew open. The soldier saw them going down through the trap-door one after another, the eldest leading the way; and thinking he had no time to lose he jumped up and followed them; but in the middle of the stairs he trod on the gown of the youngest princess, and she cried out to her sisters:

"All is not right; some one took hold of my gown."

"You silly creature," said the eldest, "it is nothing but a nail in the wall."

Then down they all went, and at the bottom they found themselves in a most delightful grove of trees, and the leaves were all of silver, and glittered and sparkled beautifully. The soldier wished to take away some token of the place ; so he broke off a little branch, and there came a loud noise from the tree. Then the youngest daughter said again :

" I am sure all is not right ; did you not hear that noise ? That never happened before."

But the eldest said, " It is only our princes who are shouting for joy at our approach."

Then they came to another grove of trees, where all the leaves were of gold ; and afterwards to a third, where the leaves were all glittering diamonds. And the soldier broke a branch from each ; and every time there was a loud noise, which made the youngest sister tremble with fear ; but the eldest still said it was only the princes who were crying for joy. So they went on till they came to a great lake ; and at the side of the lake there lay twelve little boats with twelve handsome princes in them, who seemed to be waiting there for the princesses.

One of the princesses went into each boat, and the soldier stepped into the same boat with the youngest. As they were rowing over the lake, the prince who was in the boat with the youngest princess and the soldier said :

" I do not know why it is, but though I am rowing with all my might, we do not get on so fast as usual, and I am quite tired ; the boat seems very heavy to-day."

" It is only the heat of the weather," said the princess ; " I feel it very warm too."

On the other side of the lake stood a fine illuminated castle, from which came the merry music of horns and trumpets. There they all landed, and went into the castle, and each prince danced with his princess ; while the soldier, who was all the while invisible, danced with them too ; and when any of the princesses had a cup of wine set by her, he drank it all up, so that when she put the cup to her mouth it was empty.

At this, too, the youngest sister was terribly frightened, but the eldest always silenced her. They danced on till three o'clock in the morning, and then all their shoes were worn out, so that they were obliged to leave off. The princes rowed them back again over the lake ; but this time the soldier placed himself in the boat with the eldest princess, and on the opposite shore they took leave of each other ; the princesses promising to come again the next night.

When they came to the stairs, the soldier ran on before the princesses and laid himself down ; and as the twelve sisters slowly came up, very much tired, they heard him snoring in his bed, so they said, " Now all is quite safe " ; then they undressed themselves, put away their fine clothes, pulled off their shoes, and went to bed.

In the morning the soldier said nothing about what had happened, but determined to see more of this strange adventure, and went again the second and third night ; and everything happened just as before ; the princesses danced each time till their shoes were worn to pieces, and then returned home. However, on the third night the soldier carried away one of the gold cups as a token of where he had been.

As soon as the time came when he was to declare the secret, he was taken before the king with the three branches and the golden cup ; and the twelve princesses stood listening behind the door to hear what he would say. And when the king asked him, " Where do my twelve daughters dance at night ? " he answered, " With twelve princes in a castle underground."

And then he told the king all that had happened, and showed him the three branches and the golden cup which he had brought with him. Then the king called for the princesses, and asked them whether what the soldier said was true ; and when they saw that they were discovered, and that it was of no use to deny what had happened, they confessed it all. And the king asked the soldier which of them he would choose for his wife ; and he answered :

" I am not very young, so I think I will have the eldest."

And they were married that very day, and the soldier was chosen to be the king's heir.

THE TURNIP

Brothers Grimm

THERE were two brothers who were both soldiers ; the one was rich, the other poor. The poor man thought he would try to better himself ; so, pulling off his red coat, he became a gardener, and dug his ground well, and sowed turnips.

When the seed came up, there was one plant bigger than all the rest ; and it kept getting larger and larger, and seemed as if it would never cease growing ; so that it might have been called the prince of turnips, for there never was such a one seen before, and never will again. At last it was so big that it filled a cart, and two oxen could hardly draw it ; and the gardener knew not what in the world to do with it, nor whether it would be a blessing or a curse to him. One day he said to himself :

" What shall I do with it ? If I sell it, it will bring no more than another ; and for eating, the little turnips are better than this ; the best thing perhaps is to carry it and give it to the king as a mark of respect."

Then he yoked his oxen, and drew the turnip to the court, and gave it to the king.

" What a wonderful thing ! " said the king : " I have seen many strange things, but such a monster as this I never saw. Where did you get the seed ? or is it only your good luck ? If so, you are a true child of fortune."

" Ah, no ! " answered the gardener, " I am no child of fortune ; I am a poor soldier, who never could get enough to live upon ; so I laid aside my red coat, and set to work, tilling the ground. I have a brother, who is rich, and your majesty knows him well, and all the world knows him ; but because I am poor, everybody forgets me."

The king then took pity on him, and said, " You shall be poor no longer. I will give you so much that you shall be even richer than your brother."

Then he gave him gold and lands and flocks, and made him so rich that his brother's fortune could not at all be compared with his.

When the brother heard of all this, and how a turnip had made the gardener so rich, he envied him sorely, and bethought himself how he could contrive to get the same good fortune for himself. However, he determined to manage more cleverly than his brother, and got together a rich present of gold and fine horses for the king; and thought he must have a much larger gift in return: for if his brother had received so much for only a turnip, what must his present be worth?

The king took the gift very graciously, and said he knew not what to give in return more valuable and wonderful than the great turnip; so the soldier was forced to put it into a cart and drag it home with him. When he reached home he knew not upon whom to vent his rage and spite; and at length wicked thoughts came into his head, and he resolved to kill his brother.

So he hired some villains to murder him; and having shown them where to lie in ambush, he went to his brother and said, "Dear brother, I have found a hidden treasure; let us go and dig it up, and share it between us."

The other had no suspicions of his roguery; so they went out together, and as they were travelling along, the murderers rushed out upon him, bound him, and were going to hang him on a tree.

But whilst they were getting all ready, they heard the trampling of a horse at a distance, which so frightened them that they pushed their prisoner neck and shoulders together into a sack, and swung him up by a cord to the tree, where they left him dangling, and ran away. Meantime he worked and worked away, till he made a hole large enough to put out his head.

When the horseman came up he proved to be a student, a merry fellow, who was journeying along on his nag, and singing as he went. As soon as the man in the sack saw him passing under the tree, he cried out, "Good-morning! good-morning to thee, my friend!"

The student looked about everywhere, and seeing no one, and not knowing where the voice came from, cried out:

"Who calls me?"

Then the man in the tree answered:

"Lift up thine eyes, for behold here I sit in the sack of wisdom; here have I, in a short time, learned great and wondrous things. Compared to this seat, all the learning of the schools is as empty air. A little longer, and I shall know all that man can know, and shall come forth wiser than the wisest of mankind. Here I discern the signs and motions of the heavens and the stars, the laws that control the winds, the number of the sands on the sea-shore, the healing of the sick, the virtues of all simples, of birds, and of precious stones. Wert thou but once here, my friend, thou wouldst feel and own the power of knowledge."

The student listened to all this, and wondered much; at last he said:

"Blessed be the day and hour when I found you; cannot you contrive to let me into the sack for a little while?"

Then the other answered, as if very unwillingly, "A little space I may allow thee to sit here, if thou wilt reward me well and entreat me kindly; but thou must tarry yet an hour below, till I have learned some little matters that are yet unknown to me."

So the student sat himself down and waited a while; but the time hung heavy upon him, and he begged earnestly that he might ascend forthwith, for his thirst of knowledge was great. Then the other pretended to give way, and said:

"Thou must let the sack of wisdom descend, by untying yonder cord, and then thou shalt enter."

So the student let him down, opened the sack, and set him free.

"Now, then," cried he, "let me ascend quickly."

As he began to put himself into the sack, heels first, "Wait a while," said the gardener, "that is not the way."

Then he pushed him in head first, tied up the sack, and soon swung up the searcher after wisdom, dangling in the air.

"How is it with thee, friend?" said he, "dost thou not feel that wisdom comes unto thee? Rest there in peace till thou art a wiser man than thou wert."

So saying, he trotted off on the student's nag, and left the poor fellow to gather wisdom till somebody should come and let him down.

PEE-WIT

BROTHERS GRIMM

A POOR countryman whose name was Pee-wit lived with his wife in a very quiet way in the parish where he was born. One day, as he was ploughing with his two oxen in the field, he heard all on a sudden some one calling out his name. Turning round, he saw nothing but a bird that kept crying Pee-wit, Pee-wit!

Now this poor bird is called a Pee-wit, and like the cuckoo always keeps crying out its own name.

But the countryman thought it was mocking him, so he took up a huge stone and threw at it; the bird flew off safe and sound, but the stone fell upon the head of one of the oxen, and killed him on the spot.

"What is to be done with the odd one?" thought Pee-wit to himself as he looked at the ox that was left; so without more ado he killed him too, skinned them both, and set out for the neighbouring town to sell the hides to the tanner for as much as he could get.

He soon found out where the tanner lived, and knocked at the door. Before, however, the door was opened, he saw through the window that the mistress of the house was hiding in an old chest a friend of hers, whom she seemed to wish no one should see. By and by the door was opened.

"What do you want?" said the woman. Then he told her that he wanted to sell his hides; and it came out that the tanner was not at home, and that no one there ever made bargains but himself.

The countryman said he would sell cheap, and did not mind giving his hides for the old chest in the corner, meaning the one he had seen the good woman's friend get into. Of course, the wife would not agree to this, and they went on talking the matter over so long that at last in came the tanner and asked what it was all about.

Pee-wit told him the whole story, and asked him whether he would give the old chest for the hides.

"To be sure I will," said he; and scolded his wife for saying nay to such a bargain, which she ought to have been glad to make if the countryman was willing.

Then up he took the chest on his shoulders, and all the good woman could say mattered nothing; away it went into the countryman's cart and off he drove.

But when they had gone some way the young man within began to make himself heard, and to beg and pray to be let out.

Pee-wit, however, was not to be bought over, till at last after a long parley a thousand marks were bid and taken; the money was paid, and at the price the poor fellow was set free, and went about his business.

Then Pee-wit went home very happy, and built a new house and seemed so rich that his neighbours wondered, and said, "Pee-wit must have been where the golden snow falls." So they took him before the next Justice of the Peace, to give an account of himself, and show that he came honestly by his wealth; and then he told them that he had sold his hides for one thousand dollars.

When they heard it they all killed their oxen and would sell the hides to the same tanner; but the Justice said, "My maid shall have the first chance," so off she went, and when she came to the tanner, he laughed at them all, and said he had given their neighbour nothing but an old chest.

At this they were all very angry, and laid their heads together to work him some mischief, which they thought they could do while he was digging in his garden.

All this, however, came to the ears of the countryman, who was plagued with a sad scold for his wife; and he thought to himself, "If any one is to come into trouble, I don't see why it should not be my wife, rather than me"; so he said to her that he wished she would humour him in a whim he had taken into his head, and would put on his clothes, and dig the garden in his stead.

The wife did what was asked, and next morning began digging; but soon came some of the neighbours, and, thinking it was Pee-wit, threw a stone at her (harder perhaps than they meant), and killed her at once.

Poor Pee-wit was rather sorry at this, but still thought that he had had a lucky escape for himself, and that perhaps he might after all turn the death of his wife to some account: so he dressed her in her own clothes, put a basket with fine fruit (which was now scarce, it being winter) into her hand, and sat her by the roadside on a broad bench.

After a while came by a fine coach with six horses, servants, and outriders, and within sat a noble lord who lived not far off. When his lordship saw the beautiful fruit, he sent one of the servants to the woman to ask what was the price of her goods.

The man went and asked:

" What is the price of this fruit ? "

No answer.

He asked again.

No answer: and when this had happened three times, he became angry; and, thinking she was asleep, gave her a blow, and down she fell backwards into the pond that was behind the seat. Then up ran Pee-wit and cried and sorrowed because they had drowned his poor wife, and threatened to have the lord and his servants tried for what they had done.

His lordship begged him to be easy, and offered to give him the coach and horses, servants and all; so the countryman after a long time let himself be appeased a little, took what they gave, got into the coach and set off towards his own home again.

As he came near, the neighbours wondered much at the beautiful coach and horses, and still more when they stopped, and Pee-wit got out at his own door. Then he told them the whole story, which only vexed them still more; so they took him and fastened him up in a tub and were going to throw him into the lake that was hard by. Whilst they were rolling the tub on before them towards the water, they passed by an alehouse and stopped to refresh themselves a little before they put an end to Pee-wit; meantime they tied the tub to a tree and there left it while they were enjoying themselves within doors.

Pee-wit no sooner found himself alone than he began to turn over in his mind how he could get free. He listened, and soon heard Ba, ba! from a flock of sheep and lambs that were coming by.

Then he lifted up his voice, and shouted out:

" I will not be burgomaster, I say; I will not be made burgomaster."

The shepherd hearing this went up, and said:

" What is all this noise about ? "

" Oh ! " said Pee-wit, " my neighbours will make me burgomaster against my will; and when I told them I would not agree, they put me into a cask and are going to throw me into the lake."

" I should like very much to be burgomaster if I were you," said the shepherd.

"Open the cask then," said the other, "and let me out and get in yourself, and they will make you burgomaster instead of me." No sooner said than done, the shepherd was in, Pee-wit was out; and as there was nobody to take care of the shepherd's flock, he drove it off merrily towards his own house.

When the neighbours came out of the alehouse, they rolled the cask on, and the shepherd began to cry out, "I will be burgomaster now; I will be burgomaster now."

"I dare say you will, but you shall take a swim first," said a neighbour, as he gave the cask the last push over into the lake.

This done, away they went home merrily, leaving the shepherd to get out as well as he could.

But as they came in at one side of the village, who should they meet coming in the other way but Pee-wit driving a fine flock of sheep and lambs before him.

"How came you here?" cried all with one voice.

"Oh! the lake is enchanted," said he; "when you threw me in, I sunk deep and deep into the water, till at last I came to the bottom; there I knocked out the bottom of the cask and found myself in a beautiful meadow with fine flocks grazing upon it, so I chose a few for myself, and here I am."

"Cannot we have some too?" said they.

"Why not? There are hundreds and thousands left; you have nothing to do but jump in and fetch them out."

So all agreed they would dive for sheep; the Justice first, then the clerk, then the constables, and then the rest of the parish, one after the other.

When they came to the side of the lake, the blue sky was covered with little white clouds like flocks of sheep, and all were reflected in the clear water; so they called out, "There they are, there they are already"; and fearing lest the Justice should get everything, they jumped in all at once; and Pee-wit jogged home, and made himself happy with what he had got, leaving them to find their flocks by themselves as well as they could.

THE GOLDEN GOOSE

Brothers Grimm

THERE was a man who had three sons. The youngest was called Dummling, and was on all occasions despised and ill-treated by the whole family.

It happened that the eldest took it into his head one day to go into the wood to cut fuel; and his mother gave him a delicious pasty and a bottle of wine to take with him, that he might refresh himself at his work. As he went into the wood, a little old man bade him good day, and said:

"Give me a little piece of meat from your plate, and a little wine out of your bottle; I am very hungry and thirsty."

But this clever young man said, "Give you my meat and wine! No, I thank you; I should not have enough left for myself": and away he went. He soon began to cut down a tree; but he had not worked long before he missed his stroke, and cut himself, and was obliged to go home to have the wound dressed. Now it was the little old man that caused him this mischief.

Next went out the second son to work; and his mother gave him, too, a pasty and a bottle of wine. And the same little old man met him also, and asked him for something to eat and drink. But he, too, thought himself vastly clever, and said, "Whatever you get, I shall lose; so go your way!"

The little man took care that he should have his reward, and the second stroke that he aimed against a tree hit him on the leg, so that he too was forced to go home.

Then Dummling said, "Father, I should like to go and cut wood too."

But his father answered, "Your brothers have both lamed themselves; you had better stay at home, for you know nothing of the business."

But Dummling was very pressing; and at last his father said, "Go your way; you will be wiser when you have suffered for your folly."

And his mother gave him only some dry bread, and a bottle of sour beer; but when he went into the wood he met the little old man, who said, "Give me some meat and drink, for I am very hungry and thirsty."

Dummling said, "I have only dry bread and sour beer; if that will suit you, we will sit down and eat it together."

So they sat down, and when the lad pulled out his bread behold it was turned into a capital pasty, and his sour beer became delightful wine. They ate and drank heartily; and when they had done, the little man said, "As you have a kind heart, and have been willing to share everything with me, I will send a blessing upon you. There stands an old tree, cut it down and you will find something at the root."

Then he took his leave, and went his way.

Dummling set to work, and cut down the tree; and when it fell, he found in a hollow under the roots a goose with feathers of pure gold. He took it up and went on to an inn, where he proposed to sleep for the night. The landlord had three daughters, and when they saw the goose they were very curious to examine what this wonderful bird could be, and wished very much to pluck one of the feathers out of its tail.

At last the eldest said, "I must and will have a feather." So she waited till his back was turned, and then seized the goose by the wing; but to her great surprise there she stuck, for neither hand nor finger could she get away again.

Presently in came the second sister, and thought to have a feather too; but the moment she touched her sister, there she too hung fast.

At last came the third, and wanted a feather; but the other two cried out, "Keep away, for heaven's sake, keep away!"

However, she did not understand what they meant. "If they are there," thought she, "I may as well be there too." So she went up to them; but the moment she touched her sisters she stuck fast, and hung to the goose as they did. And so they kept company with the goose all night.

The next morning Dummling carried off the goose under his arm, and took no notice of the three girls, but went out with them sticking fast behind; and wherever he travelled they too were obliged to follow, whether they would or no, as fast as their legs could carry them.

In the middle of a field the parson met them; and when he saw the train, he said, "Are you not ashamed of yourselves, you bold girls, to run after the young man in that way over the fields? Is that proper behaviour?"

Then he took the youngest by the hand to lead her away; but the moment he touched her he too hung fast, and followed in the train.

Presently up came the clerk; and when he saw his master the parson running after the three girls, he wondered greatly, and said, "Hollo! Hollo! your reverence! whither so fast? there is a christening to-day." Then he ran up and took him by the gown, and in a moment he was fast too.

As the five were thus trudging along, one behind another, they met two labourers with their mattocks coming from work; and the parson cried out to them to set him free. But scarcely had they touched him when they too fell into the ranks, and so made seven all running after Dummling and his goose.

At last they arrived at a city where reigned a king who had an only daughter. The princess was of so thoughtful and serious a turn of mind that no one could make her laugh; and the king had proclaimed to all the world that whoever could make her laugh should have her for his wife.

When the young man heard this, he went to her with his goose and all its train; and as soon as she saw the seven all hanging together, and running about, treading on each other's heels, she could not help bursting into a long and loud laugh.

Then Dummling claimed her for his wife; the wedding was celebrated, and he was heir to the kingdom, and lived long and happily with his wife.

KARL GOTTLIEB PRAETZEL
1785–1861

A FATHER'S AUTHORITY

I

IN the afternoon of a hot summer's day a small crowd collected outside the house of Herr Helbrich, and in spite of all conjectures, and even though some of them mounted the piles of wooden planks that were stacked up there, they failed to solve the riddle presented to them.

That the Master Carpenter should be thrashing his thirteen-year-old son near the open window was not very startling, for such occurrences had been witnessed before ; but that with every blow he should shout, " Will you marry Fräulein Filterhof immediately ? You rascal ! Will you marry her this moment ? " and that the boy should always reply, " No, father, not if you kill me ! " was an adjunct incapable of explanation by even the most sagacious member of the crowd.

After giving such an indisputable proof of his strength and endurance the old man sank into his arm-chair thoroughly exhausted, while his son crawled behind the stove out of sight of the onlookers, who, seeing that no explanation of the cause of this extraordinary affair would be forthcoming, dispersed.

Though he had received the benefit of his father's opinions before in a similarly practical fashion, the boy had not expected that an innocent utterance would lead to such an utter defeat, and that those parts of his anatomy that primarily met the assault would give the good town fresh food for gossip.

" Father, have you heard that Fritz Hassling is going to marry that stout Susan Quermann ? She will look a guy in her bridal dress ! " he had called out as he returned from school.

" Well, and what concern is it of yours ? " said the old man, who had been indulging in his afternoon nap and now sat up crossly. " Old Herr Hassling is a very sensible man, and he knows what girl to choose for his son ! "

" But, father, I thought fellows chose their own wives ? How can other people know whom they like or dislike ? "

" Rubbish ! " shouted the old man, who was getting very cross ; " the father's wishes must be obeyed without question ; so don't talk !"

" But supposing they both think absolutely differently ? Say, for instance, you wanted me to marry that ugly Fräulein Filterhof across the——"

" Of course I should not think of her, you silly boy ; but presuming I did, what would you do then, ha ? "

" I should say, ' Excuse me, father, I am your obedient son in every way, but this one——' "

" What ? You would disobey my command, boy ? "

" Consider, father, to obey you in this matter would be impossible ; or——"

" I should like to see that," now cried out the old hothead, jumping up from his arm-chair and reaching down the cane from behind a picture. " Will you at once and without objections do as I tell you and marry Fräulein Filterhof ? " But not even the sight of the cane could influence the boy, and so occurred the incident we have just witnessed. Among those who saw and heard the incident was the old maid in question, Barbara Filterhof. Her parlour lying just opposite the scene of the tragedy, she had an uninterrupted view of the whole proceedings and was able to understand every word and to calculate to a nicety from the highest point of the Master's cane to the place where it would descend the rhythm of the swings, while she herself was screened by the white lace curtains. Annoyed by the emphatic words of the boy, she was in turn made happy by the equally decisive commands of the father, and finally sat down well pleased and smiling, reproving her twelve-year-old niece, an orphan who lived with her, for the sympathy she expressed for the youth.

II

The consequences of this somewhat theatrical exhibition were more far-reaching than could have been expected. The Master Carpenter rightly presumed that his reputation in the town as an upright, level-headed, well-balanced man would not be enhanced by this occurrence ; but instead of laying the blame for this at his own door he heaped it on the boy, who, in response to a peremptory summons, came out from his corner. " I have been much too indulgent with you up till now," he wound up his long reprimand ; " but all that will be changed, my boy. From now onward you will not have your own way in the very slightest matter ! Fancy you estranging me from Fräulein Filterhof by your insubordinate behaviour ! Away to bed this minute ! "

With troubled face Franz slunk from the room ; with a happy heart he hurried up the two staircases to his gabled attic. With the left hand he slipped the bolt while with the right he groped under the corner cupboard for his *Robinson Crusoe*, which lay hidden there, and which he would enjoy more than reading to his father, as had been his nightly duty, from the old book of home-sermons. Carefully he opened the little window to get the benefit of the last rays of the evening sun. He cast shy glances down to the windows of the cause of all his troubles, but only saw little Luise there. She immediately caught his eye, and soon afterwards a slight coughing at the little attic window opposite attracted his attention. As in consequence of the exposed position of the two attics even the softest conversation was extremely dangerous they had to make use of signs ; and before his whole story and all her sympathy could be fully exchanged, night fell and ended their happy interchange of confidences. In another ten minutes the fatherly command had at last been obeyed : Franz was in his bed.

III

" Before you go to school," called Herr Helbrich to his son in cold tones next morning, " you will call at Fräulein Filterhof's and ask her pardon for your execrable behaviour of yesterday." With the slightest encouragement Franz would have protested against this order ; but seeing the threatening mien of the old man, who by a good night's rest had thoroughly regained the necessary powers for administering a further chastisement, he did not wish to invite the same " dessert " after his breakfast as was handed to him after his supper the previous evening. He therefore made his way across the road followed to the gate of his enemy by the scowling look of his father. His heart rejoiced as on the stair he met Luise, who eyed him wonderingly. " Just think, Luise," he told her disgustedly, " my father has sent me to make my apologies to your aunt for refusing to marry her ! " and bursting into roars of laughter she preceded him into her aunt's room.

Fräulein Barbara received him most kindly and quickly interrupted his stammered words, spoken in utter humiliation. His courage, already awakened on the stairs, now quickly rose and so did this charming woman in his estimation.

"Oh, don't mention it, dear Franz," she called to him, "it was just all fun; and I'm only too sorry you've had to bear such a punishment! Come again soon and often, and you will be sure to like me. We shall be great friends yet!"

"Oh, please, dear lady, I will gladly do anything you wish me to!" replied Franz, and when pushed into a chair and offered a piece of cake by his magnanimous enemy he very soon promised to repeat his visit soon.

In high glee he rushed down the stairs; but why, on entering his father's presence, he made his features assume a solemn look, he hardly knew himself. "She has forgiven me everything," he answered in reply to his father's question, and added with wrinkled forehead and sour face, "even wants me to come again from time to time."

"And that you will without further ado!" his father roughly told him. Franz needed no such reminder, for Barbara's sweet friendliness, and still more her sweet cake, had completely captured him; but he never relaxed his features nor gave any sign of satisfaction, and shouldering his bag went off to school.

"The boy still seems obstinate!" the old man told himself when Franz had left. "I shall make it my sacred duty to knock all opposition out of him. In no matter however small will I let him have his own way. I will let him feel my fatherly hand."

And the Master Carpenter kept his word. That same day he proved his firm resolve. As Franz—as was customary after his evening meal—ran to fetch the book of homilies and without a word prepared to read to him, "Have you been asked for this? Or do you think that is unnecessary?" he queried.

"I've had to read to you every night out of the *postil*," he answered dejectedly, "therefore I wanted——"

"You must not want anything!" wrathfully interrupted his father. "Nothing at all! Off to your room you go this minute! Do you hear?"

Franz did not hesitate to carry out a careful retreat immediately, and was delighted at the success of his diplomatic manœuvre. Finding himself a few minutes later at his garret window he was delighted to see Luise opposite him already. They were happy to resume their pantomimic conversation of the previous evening, a conversation which was now less difficult, since the meeting in the morning at her aunt's had made so many of the happenings clearer to both of them.

IV

Gradually Franz had perfected the system by which he received from his father just those orders that corresponded to his own wishes ; and now the time approached when he would leave school and enter on a business career. " It had always been my intention," one evening began the Master Carpenter, " to apprentice you to my good friend the tallow chandler Quarz. However, circumstances have changed ; and although you have now for some time looked forward to going to him, I think after all he is too soft-hearted a man and would be unable properly to subdue your pig-headedness or to keep a firm enough hand on you. You will therefore remain here and assist me in my wood business ! "

Franz, who was overjoyed at this decision, yet managed to hide his delight simply by thinking of the awful fate that would have been his had he been sent to soap-boiler Quarz. So he postponed his expression of delight to a more suitable occasion. Presently he began to devote his careful attention to his father's business, which all along had seemed to him, everything considered, quite the most desirable of occupations.

Meanwhile Fräulein Barbara's endeavours to win the young fellow over to her began to show undeniable signs of success ; her kindness, her cakes, her sweets, and above all her motherly care of Luise, although she had not intended that this factor should influence him, all helped to draw Franz to her. She was too sensible a woman to take the father's words, " Will you marry her ! " emphasized as they were by the cane, seriously ; yet the boy's refusal had rather hurt her and certainly induced her to show him that she was not a woman to be despised out of hand. She succeeded admirably, and in time the boy grew really fond of her ; for the great kindness she showed him reminded him always of his mother's gentle care, which had been denied him early in his life.

V

But even between the Master Carpenter and his son's patroness an intimacy had sprung up since that famous summer's day. He often visited his neighbour of an evening to discourse to her on the political news contained in the daily paper, explaining to her the intricate points; and as he believed himself to be rather an expert in such matters he insisted that his son should always be there as a silent participant in the intellectual feast set before him. Franz neither liked the subject nor the way in which it was discussed and interpreted; but he was even then politician enough only to show his dislike when there was a likelihood of his father leaving him at home. One little word to that effect and the command would as surely go forth to him to get himself ready to accompany his father.

During those visits Franz's behaviour would have done honour to a young diplomat, if the love that gradually grew in his heart did not rather account for his demeanour. For hours he would sit quietly in the chair assigned to him, never taking any notice of Luise, who pursued the same tactics. Only his father's reproving look would induce him to pick up Luise's refractory ball of wool or hunt for one of the knitting needles for which she was looking. Strange to say, too, she seemed to accept his services very ungraciously; though she was ready enough to give Franz frequent opportunities of earning his father's scowls. "These two young people seem thoroughly to dislike one another," the old political expert thought to himself. "Well, all the better, then I needn't keep such a close watch over my young rascal." But the old man meant his boy to conform to the necessary standard of good manners anyway; so he saw to it that in future Franz and Luise took their places close together at the table. He little suspected that while he tried to enlighten Fräulein Barbara across the table on the political situation, two pairs of feet beneath it managed to understand each other perfectly.

One night Franz had got his foot too far to the right, and on the way home his father said to him: "Franz, you really are a young pup! I know that kick I got was meant for Luise. Now that I have stopped you making faces at her from your window you start kicking the girl under the table! Don't deny it, you stupid boy; and don't forget that if she should ever complain of you in the slightest, your height won't prevent me from exercising my right to give you as many more thrashings as I choose to hand out to you."

But the young boy soon outstripped his father in height and took good care that never should he read in Luise's eye any accusation against himself. Luise, too, had grown during these last few years and loved the happy evenings spent in Franz's company; while he, who so far had been perfectly happy in the many meetings under the supervision of the old people, now began, ever more attracted by her youthful charms and loveliness, to feel a keen desire for more intimate companionship and to dream of the undisputed possession of this lovely girl as the greatest happiness of his life.

VI

Just as his sky seemed so clear and bright, heavy clouds began to form, and soon threatened to overwhelm him. His father, through some unfortunate miscalculations and mistakes, suddenly found his prosperous business on the verge of ruin. Already the old man was being severely pressed by his creditors, and saw no way out of the terrible position he himself had brought about by his speculations.

Thus one evening, after he had just received some decisive bad news, he picked up his newspaper mechanically and made his way to Fräulein Barbara's across the road, intending to lead the conversation to his misfortune and to discuss with his old friend the ways and means of lightening the blow. There was no need for him to exercise any diplomacy, however; for the moment he entered she had seen that he was crushed down by some great misfortune. Luise had left the room at a sign from her aunt, who now kindly inquired about his affairs, and with judicious questions soon put him at his ease; so, quickly recovering his composure, he told her that he was face to face with complete financial ruin, informing her that in just two days the state of his affairs would be known to the world.

Deeply sympathising with her friend and assuring him that she would do anything in her power to tide him over his misfortunes, she took his hands in hers, and, begging him to believe in her earnest desire to help him, explained to him that circumstances made it absolutely impossible for her to lend him any financial assistance. This was not the kind of sympathy Herr Helbrich had expected; for well he knew that she would have but to touch a small part of her fortune to put an end to all his troubles. That was why he had set his last hope confidently on her.

"An advance of but a few hundred pounds would save me!" he cried with shaking voice and staring hard on the floor the while, as that often quoted saying about a friend in need flashed through his brain.

"I will return confidence for confidence, dear neighbour, and show you how circumstances prevent me from rendering you that assistance which I would otherwise not withhold!" said Barbara, who could follow his thoughts as if he had given utterance to them. "As far back as two years ago I transferred my fortune, of which considerably more than half was left me by her mother in trust for the girl, to Luise. Although I have not yet acquainted her with this fact, I shouldn't now like to take a step in regard to this money which at some future date I might have cause to regret. Only Franz could help in this difficulty, and, seeing how much I think of him, I certainly wouldn't withhold my consent if his desires should at all lie in Luise's direction."

"But, my dear Fräulein Barbara," here interrupted Herr Helbrich, "that seems out of the question; for I know those two young people simply hate the sight of one another! Have you never noticed how they go out of their way to hurt one another? How they keep apart and never voluntarily address one another? Of course in the case of Franz I could find means to make him obey our wishes; but whether you could use the same against Luise seems to me doubtful, in fact out of the question!"

"Of course in that case," continued Barbara, greatly tickled at his blindness, and smiling craftily, "he might feel even less inclined to carry out a certain proviso in the will, the existence of which has really kept me from speaking to Luise about the money so far."

"A proviso did you say? And may I know its significance?"

"That I am entitled to dispose again of my fortune as I like, if,—but don't look at me so intently, dear neighbour!—if sooner or later I myself may—may wish to marry!——"

"You spoke," stammered the Master Carpenter, "only a few moments ago so highly of my son—of Franz!"

"Certainly I did," whispered she, "and I don't know of any young man I like better than your son!"

"You are perfectly right, dear Fräulein Barbara: he is a good and fine fellow, and he has greatly improved since I took him seriously in hand. If he had a sensible, mature wife—you quite understand what I mean, dear Fräulein Barbara—a wife who could keep a firm hold over him, I am sure he would make quite a satisfactory husband. If, therefore, it was to be——"

"*I* should not decline the honour, dear neighbour."

"Nor shall my boy, dear lady. Of course he has outgrown the cane; but I will find ways and means."

"I have opened my heart to you, dear neighbour, and I think I am entitled to ask you not to hurt my maidenly feelings any further. If you can induce your boy without recourse to disciplinary punishment to propose to me, he will be able to satisfy himself that he need not regret taking the step."

VII

Hope sprang up again in the breast of Herr Helbrich, and no sooner had he got home than he summoned Franz, and, once more emphasising his hopeless position, went into all its details, finally winding up with the glorious news that to him, his only, his dear and devoted son, it was given to save his old father from want and disgrace by marrying Fräulein Filterhof.

"Father, what is it you demand of me?" asked Franz, whose blood ran cold at the idea. "You really seriously mean to ask me now, after eight years, to do what then, regarded merely as a joke, cost me so dear?"

"Upon my soul," cried the old man wrathfully, "this sounds like a refusal! However, I have made up my mind to arrange this affair with you in all kindness and also to give you time to think over it carefully. So take yourself off to bed and let me know to-morrow morning if you are going to save your old father or not."

Franz wanted to argue the matter out there and then; but as the old man covered up both his ears with his hands he ascended to his room, there to seek a solution of the problem.

Awaiting him there, wrapped around a stone that had been pitched in at the window—a stratagem that had been for some time adopted by the lovers—he found a letter from Luise that soon put him into a good humour:

"Agree to everything your father suggests, dear Franz, and be assured that from to-morrow we shall no longer be compelled to communicate with one another in this secret fashion. Rely entirely on my aunt's affection for us and trust your LUISE."

Next morning when he came downstairs Franz looked pale, for he had found but little sleep during the night, not, as his father thought, from considering the enormous sacrifice he was going to make, but from thinking of the fulfilment of all his dearest wishes. Quickly father and son dressed themselves in their Sunday best and made their way to their neighbour across the road. At the foot of her stairs the old man stopped and pressed his son's hand heartily in silence, a tear glistening in his eyes.

Fräulein Barbara, who received them alone, begged them to take their seats at the table and offered them a cup of tea. The Master Carpenter, however, realising the importance of the occasion, would not hear of this, and immediately assuming the correct attitude launched out into a proposal discourse which he had carefully thought out and learnt by heart during the previous night.

" This is against our arrangement," said Fräulein Barbara, interrupting him and gazing hard first at him and then at Franz. But when in response to a sign from his father Franz also made an attempt —a very unsuccessful one—she could contain herself no longer ; for these two looked so ludicrous. Running therefore to the door to another room and opening it she brought in Luise, saying, " If you find it so difficult to propose to me, just try your hand with this one. I think you'll manage better in this quarter."

But she was mistaken. Franz was quite incapable of regaining his self-possession or of uttering some even faintly coherent proposal. " Be careful," Fräulein Barbara continued, shaking her finger at him ; " all preparations for celebrating the engagement will at once be cancelled if you don't give Luise her betrothal kiss instantly ! " This produced the desired result. With boyish zeal he took the blushing girl in his arms and their lips met in a long tender kiss. The old man stood looking on as if turned to stone.

" You see, dear neighbour," Fräulein Barbara exclaimed, " that even though things have not turned out exactly as we arranged yesterday, we shall still in future be one happy family. I hope you will, just as I do, find great satisfaction in the happiness of these two young people."

The old man nodded his head and blessed with unbounded wonderment and satisfaction this alliance, which, even when he dandled its red-cheeked witnesses on his knees in later years, still remained an insoluble mystery to him.

"LOTHAR"
18TH CENTURY

THE ARCH ROGUE

THERE once lived years ago a man known only by the name of the Arch Rogue. By dint of skill in the black art and all arts of imposition he drove a more flourishing trade than all the rest of the sorcerers of his age. It was his delight to travel from one country to another merely to play upon mankind, and no living soul was secure either in house or field, nor could properly call them his own.

Now his great reputation for these speedy methods of possessing himself of others' property excited the envy of a certain king of a certain country, who considered them as no less than an invasion of his royal prerogative. He could not sleep a wink, and he despatched troops of soldiers, one after another, with strict orders to arrest him; but all their researches had been in vain. At length after long meditation the king said to himself, "Only wait a little, thou villain cut-purse; and yet I will have thee!"

So forthwith he issued a manifesto that the royal mercy would be extended to so light-fingered a genius, upon condition that he consented to appear at court and give specimens of his dexterity for his majesty's amusement.

One afternoon as the king was standing at his royal window, commanding a fine prospect of woods and dales, over which a tempest appeared to be just then gathering, some one suddenly clapped him upon the shoulder, and, on looking round, he saw a very tall, stout, dark-whiskered man close behind him, who said, "Here I am!"

"Who are you?" inquired the king.

"He whom you look for!"

The king uttered an exclamation of surprise, not unmixed with fear, at his amazing assurance, for he was quite alone, and he looked a little dashed.

The stranger observing this, said, "Don't be alarmed! only keep your word with me and I will prove myself quite obedient to your orders, and keep the peace."

This being agreed, the king acquainted his royal consort and the whole Court that the great sleight-of-hand genius had discovered himself; and soon in a full assembly his majesty proceeded to question him: " and mark what I say," he added, " nor venture to dispute one of my orders. To begin: do you see yon rustic not far from the wood, busy ploughing the field ? "

The conjuror nodded assent.

" Then go," continued the king; " go and rob him of his plough and oxen, without his knowing anything about it ! " At the same time he flattered himself that this was not possible, nor conceived how he could possibly set about it in the face of open day; in which case, thought he, I have him in my power, and will make him smart for it.

The conjuror proceeded to the spot; and as the storm appeared to increase, the rain beginning to pour down in torrents, the countryman, letting his oxen rest, ran under a tree for shelter until the rain should have ceased.

Just then he heard a jolly singing in the wood; such a glorious song he had never before heard in his life. In fact he felt wonderfully enlivened; and as the weather continued to look quite dull and sulky, he said to himself, " Well, where's the harm if I take a glass ? Yes, I must see what sport is stirring there "; and away he slipped into the wood, still farther and farther in search of the jovial songster, until he followed his nose so long that he could neither see nor hear anything of it at all.

In the meanwhile the conjuror, that wicked songster in the wood, was not idle. He changed places with the rustic, taking care of the oxen while their master went singing through the wood; and darting out of the thicket, in a few moments he had slashed off the oxen's ears and tails, and stuck them, half hid, in the ploughman's last furrow. He then drove off the beasts pretty sharply towards the palace. In a short time the rustic found his way out of the wood, looked towards the spot for his oxen, and could see nothing.

Then, searching on all sides in the utmost anxiety, he finally came to examine his last furrow, and beheld, oh horror ! the ears and tails of his poor beasts stretched upon the ground. Imagining that the thunderbolt must have struck, and the earth swallowed them up, he poured forth a most dismal lamentation over his lot, roaring aloud till the woods echoed to the sound. When he was tired he bethought himself of running home to find a pick and a spade to dig his unlucky oxen out of the earth again as quick as possible.

As he went he was met by the king and the conjuror, who inquired the occasion of his piteous lamentations. "My oxen, my poor oxen!" cried the boor, and then related all that had happened to him, entreating them to go with him to the place to witness the disaster.

The conjuror then said: "Why don't you try whether you can pull the oxen out again by the horns, or by the tail?"

With this the rustic, running back, seized one of the tails and pulling with all his might it gave way and he fell upon his back.

"Thou hast pulled thy beast's tail off," said the conjuror; "try if thou canst succeed better with his horns; if not, thou must even dig for them."

Again he pitched himself down in the attempt, while the king laughed very heartily at the sight. But as the worthy man now appeared excessively troubled at his misfortunes, the king promised him another pair of oxen; and the rustic was content.

"You have made good your boast," said the king to the conjuror, as they returned to the palace; "but now you will have to deal with a more difficult job, so muster your wit and courage. To-night you must steal my favourite charger out of his stable, and let nobody know who it is."

So, thought the king, I have trapped him at last, for he will never be able to outwit my master of the horse and all my grooms to boot. To make the matter sure the king ordered a strong guard under one of his most careful officers to be placed round the stable court. They were armed with stout battle-axes, and were enjoined every half-hour to give the word and pace alternately through the court. In the royal stables others had the like duty to perform; while the master of the horse himself was to ride the favourite steed the whole time, having been presented by the king with a gold snuff-box, from which he was to take ample pinches in order to keep himself awake, and to give signal by a loud sneeze that he was awake. He was also armed with a heavy sword with which he was to knock the thief upon the head when he approached.

The rogue first arrayed himself in the master of the bedchamber's clothes, without his leave. About midnight he proceeded to join the guards, furnished with different kinds of rich wine, saying that the king had sent him to thank them for their cheerful compliance with his orders, that the impostor was already secured, and that his master now permitted them to take a glass, and not to give the word quite so loudly as her majesty had not been able to close her eyes! He then marched into the stables, where he found the master of the horse still astride of the royal charger, busily taking snuff and sneezing every now and then.

The master of the bedchamber poured him out a sparkling glass, to drink to his majesty's health, who had sent it; and it looked quite too excellent to resist. Both master and guards then began to jest over the Arch Rogue's fate, taking, like good subjects, repeated draughts—all to his majesty's health. They soon began to experience the soporific effects; they gaped and stretched, sunk gradually upon the ground and fell asleep.

The master, by dint of fresh pinches, however, was the last to yield; but he too now blinked, stopped the horse, which he had kept upon a good walk, and said, "I am so confoundedly sleepy I can hold it no longer—take you care of the charger for a moment, bind him fast to his stall,—and just keep watch."

Having uttered these words he fell like a heavy sack of corn upon the floor, and snored aloud. The mighty conjuror took his place upon the horse, gave him whip and spur, and away he galloped through the slumbering guards, through the court gates, and whistled as he went.

Early in the morning the king, eager to learn the result, hastened to his royal mews, and was a little surprised to find the whole of his guards fast asleep upon the ground; but he saw nothing of his charger.

"What is to do here?" he cried in a loud voice. "Get up! Rouse, you idle varlets!"

At last one of them, opening his eyes, cried out, "The king! the king!"

"Aye, true enough, I am here," replied his majesty, "but my favourite horse is gone. Speak! answer, on the instant!"

While the affrighted wretches, calling one to another, rubbed their heavy eyes, the king was examining the stalls once more, and stumbling over his master of the horse, turned and gave him some pretty hearty cuffs about the ears. But he only turned upon the other side, and grumbled a little:

"Let me alone, you rascal, my royal master's horse is not for you."

"Rascal!" then exclaimed the insulted king. "Do you know who it is?" and he was just about to call his attendants when he heard hasty footsteps; and the conjuror stood before him.

He was laughing very heartily, and said, "My liege, I have just returned from an airing on your noble horse, he is indeed a fine animal; but once or so I was obliged to give him the switch."

The king felt excessively vexed at the rogue's success; yet he was the more resolved to hit upon something that should bring his fox's skin into jeopardy at last.

So he thought, and the next day addressed him thus: "Thy third trial is now about to take place, and if you are clever enough to carry it through you shall not only have your life and liberty, but a handsome allowance to boot. In the other case you know your fate: now listen! This very night I command you to rob my queen consort of her bridal ring, to steal it from her finger, and let no one know the thief or the way of thieving."

Thought the king to himself, "Now at last I have caught him; for this is not possible, for how can he devise any means? Well, we shall see."

When night approached his majesty caused all the doors in the palace to be fast closed, and a guard to be set at each. He himself, instead of retiring to rest, took his station, well armed, close to the queen's couch upon an easy chair.

It was a moonlight night; and about two in the morning the king plainly heard a ladder reared up against the window, and the soft step of a man mounting it, and just as he had reached the top and looked in, the king said, "Let fall!" and the next moment the outside shutter gave way, and something fell with a terrible crash to the ground!

"Wit!" exclaimed the king, and ran down into the court, telling his consort he was going to see whether the conjuror had died of the fall! No, he was not dead, but quite as whole and brisk as ever; for he had only dropped a dead body, which he had stolen from the gallows, into the court below.

The moment he heard the king's steps upon the staircase, he replaced the ladder, mounted, and going into the chamber said in the king's voice: "Yes, he is stone dead, so you may now go quietly to sleep, only hand me here your marriage ring, it is too costly and precious to trust it, while you are asleep, in bed."

The queen, imagining it was her royal consort, instantly gave her diamond ring without the least suspicion, and in a moment the conjuror was off through the window with it on his finger. Directly after the king came back. " At last," he said, " I have indeed carried the joke too far. I have repaid him ; he is lying there as dead as a door-nail ; he will plague us no more ! "

" I know that already ; you have told me exactly the same thing twice over, though I think it a little hard that you should have required me to give up my ring."

" How came you to know anything of that ? " inquired his majesty.

" How ? From yourself, to be sure," replied his consort. " You informed me the conjuror was dead, and then you asked me for my marriage ring."

" I ask for the ring ! " exclaimed the king. " Then I suppose you must have given it to him ! " continued his majesty in a tone of great indignation, " and is it even so at last ? By all the saints ! this is one of the most confounded unmanageable rascals in existence. I never knew anything equal to it " ; and he then informed the queen of the whole affair, though before he arrived at the conclusion of his narration he was fast asleep.

Soon after it was light in the morning, the wily conjuror made his appearance ; he bowed to the earth three times before the queen and presented her with the treasure he had purloined. The king, though excessively chagrined, could not refrain laughing at this sight, adding :

" Now hear, thou king of arch rogues ; I only caught a sight of you through my fingers as you were coming, or you would never have come off so well. As it is, however, let all old grudges be forgiven and forgotten. Only take up your residence for a time at my Court, taking care at the same time that you do not carry your jokes too far, in which case I might find myself compelled, if nothing worse, to withdraw my favour from you."

CASTLE CHRISTBURG

"LOTHAR"

IT was many years after the famous Tir-hill fight,[1] so fatal to the then existing order of German knighthood, when the magnificent and beautiful castle of Christburg, not far from the city of Danzig, was laid in a heap of ruins, and so many noble families were compelled to seek a foreign soil, that a poor mendicant, " all tattered and torn," sought refuge under its decayed walls from the bitter blasts.

Being unacquainted with the current reports, which bestowed a legion of spirits upon the old uninhabited vaults and other remnants of its former splendour, he built himself a little hut close upon the castle site, where he intended to close his earthly pilgrimage. Daily and duly, however, he continued to practise his old profession, begging alms in the neighbourhood, and frequently returning richly laden with bread-crusts to his solitary dwelling.

About a year had passed over his head when, in one of his evening rambles among the castle ruins, he remarked a light glimmering through the bushes which overspread its time-worn walls. Indulging no notions of a supernatural kind, he stood still and peeped through an opening into the vaults below.

There in a spacious and lofty cellar he saw a large table covered with well-filled pitchers, bumpers and bowls. His mouth watered at the delicious sight. " There is neither butler nor lackey that I see," said he to himself, " and who else is likely to refuse me a good draught ? "

So he quickly found out the door, which had a latch like any other door, and he opened it. Mounting a few steps he entered into the drinking-room, which was only just light enough for him to see. Other steps at the end of it led into the vaults, which were very dark, and made him a little uncomfortable ; but a row of vats stood before him, and he was content.

And behold ! he found he was not quite alone ; a respectable old man sat at a table in one corner, apparently employed in reckoning.

[1] The battle took place in the beginning of the eighteenth century.

Supposing he had now met with the owner, the intruder saluted him, entreating that he would afford him one glass of wine.

" Yes," answered the man, " drink! Take as much as will agree with you, and come again in the morning."

His mild manners took the fancy of his guest; he filled a glass of wine, which he four times repeated, and inquired as he went out if he might really venture there again.

" Yes," was the reply, " come when you please, seven times a week; but not twice a day. Be discreet and hold your tongue; you are a lucky fellow."

The beggar went and came again, regaled himself, and drank so much during the next seven days that he had cause to fear it was beginning to make inroads upon his constitution. He then bethought himself of taking only half of his daily allowance and keeping the rest for sale, with the proceeds of which he might buy fresh food and raiment.

A mendicant selling wine was rather a rare sight in the city. His purchasers laughed; all were eager to have a taste, and declaring that it was drink fit for the gods they showed him the way to the town-house, for it was too good for the palates of ordinary citizens, and the patricians could afford him a good price. So he willingly went; the alderman emptied his pitcher, and, requesting him to get more of the exact flavour, promised not to haggle with him about the price.

As often as he went with a fresh supply he obtained the same handsome reward; but towards the fifth day they began to inquire as to the source of so rich a spring. His vow of silence luckily occurred to the beggar; he began to invent a story, but as they threatened to chastise him if he did not reveal the whole truth he threw his pitcher at the alderman's head and ran as fast as his heels could carry him.

When he next paid a visit to the cellar it appeared that the old wine merchant who sat reckoning in the corner was acquainted with all that had passed.

" Look to yourself," he said to the beggar, " for they are in pursuit. In fact they have spied you out, but they will not come here again."

They had indeed caught a glimpse of him as he entered the ruins; they followed, but their reception was such that, half dead with fright, they had no inclination to proceed. For his pursuers, the moment they reached the awful precincts of the castle, beheld a solemn funeral procession, that rose like an exhalation from the ground, advancing before them, until, seized with an agony of fear, they turned back, reached the city with some difficulty, took to their beds and died.

This shocking occurrence, to which the voice of the people added fresh terrors, placed the beggar-man in perfect security. He lived unmolested in his hut, drank his wine, forgot that he was a poor mendicant, and by comparing old and new dates thought himself a very lucky fellow.

One day there joined his company just such another miserably clad wretch as he had once been. He had been equally roughly handled in the world, had nowhere to lay his head, and his good brother, uncorrupted by his late prosperity, humanely offered him a share of his own roof. In fact he took him into partnership; they beat up the neighbouring districts in different directions, made common stock of their net proceeds, and their firm continued for a considerable time. Nothing, however, was said to the new partner respecting the wine.

But one evening returning home earlier than usual with a well-filled scrip, he heard as he came nearer loud sounds of revelry and mirth; he thought a whole party must be assembled somewhere in the vicinity. One voice, at least, was in full key; he found the door and windows open, as he drew nigh; and all this loud jubilee came from within, as if intended to be heard through the country far and wide.

He entered and found no one besides his old friend; all the sounds of revelry were his; his countenance was lighted up with joy, his eyes sparkled, he sang, and two flasks stood between his knees, one empty, and the other full of wine.

"Welcome, old boy!" he cried, as his friend came in; "sit you down here!—drink, and sing a song for once in your life!—I am richer, man, than all the Red Cross Knights in Germany that ever flourished!"

In silent astonishment the old man seated himself, drank as he was bidden, and soon began to sing. The other flask was speedily emptied; and after this good drinking bout, both fell asleep. The new partner dreamed only of the oddity of finding so rich a beverage in so poor a place; and the first question he asked himself when he awaked was, where the deuce does he get it from? His friend being still asleep he searched his pockets and examined every article in the house, to get, if possible, into the secret. All in vain! yet the next day, the next, and the next, the flask was always full; he looked, he inquired from his friend, but could get no satisfactory answer, more than, "The butler has forbidden me to say a word about it; he gave it me."

But the curious old fellow was dying to know the secret, and determined to keep a sharp look-out. With this view he had recourse to an old stratagem: just as they were going to take a glass he suddenly fell down in a fit, began to kick and make mouths; till, getting under the table, he gave it such a hearty jog as quite upset the whole drinking apparatus, and every drop of wine was lost. During the continuance of his fit he took good heed of everything his friend did; who, thinking it a good opportunity to obtain a new supply before the old man recovered, took a key out of his pocket and went.

He was no sooner gone than up sprang his friend and glided softly after him. It was already dusk, and he had some difficulty to keep him in sight, till, with the help of the moon, he saw him enter the old castle and actually disappear down one of the vaults. He had now like to have fallen into a real fit; the ruins gleamed awfully upon his sight. Yet he had reached the entrance, his foot was upon the first step: he went on through the overhanging shrubs, and he saw his partner, nor far off, unlock a small door. He saw a light glimmering at a distance, and when the door opened it became still more visible; but he had scarcely gone a few steps farther towards the door when it slammed to, with a hideous noise, and not without catching the old inquisitive beggar a pretty sharp hit on the elbow.

At this he made a sad outcry, which echoed along the inner vaults; a figure was seen going up the steps, and the old man, in an agony of fear, leaving the skirt of his coat fast in the doorway, ran off quicker than he ever ran in his life, and only looking once round to see whether he was pursued, he at length reached the hut more dead than alive. Resuming a little courage with the return of light, and anxious for his friend's safety, the old beggar determined to visit the ruins, being now broad day, in search of him. He found the way and came to the bushes which he had passed the evening before; but he could nowhere discover the little door: the whole scene appeared to have been changed.

Thinking he must have missed the way, he wandered up and down the ruins; yet all his researches proved vain. Perceiving it was now near sunset he began to be alarmed, and set off home at full speed, the speed of an old beggar-man. He now came to the resolution of venturing no more near the fatal spot, but continued to beg honestly in the neighbourhood. A year had elapsed, and it was the eve of St. Martin's Day.

Once more, as formerly, seated upon the same spot where he had last been regaled by his lost partner, a victim to his fatal expedition, sat the old beggar-man. Twilight was already coming on, when lo! the door opened, and in walked a figure of which he had some faint recollection; he fixed his eyes upon him for a moment and ran towards him; it was his old friend.

"What, is it possible?" cried he. "Is it indeed you?"

"It is, sir, sure enough," replied the other; "the same who took you into partnership and gave you shelter here. And yet you were so very ungrateful and unreasonable as to upset all my wine in return—a plague upon your fits!—and thus compelled me to get into a horrid scrape by disobeying the butler's commands."

The strange beggar then related all he had seen, how he had spent a whole year with the spirits of the under-world, been initiated in all their secrets, and condemned to learn the most hard and frightful lessons of their power. At length, to his great relief, he was informed that the day of his release was at hand; that he must instantly depart and acquaint the upper world with the secrets he had seen.

ANONYMOUS

MARRIED OR NOT MARRIED?

THE Countess von Werbe became a widow very young. Her husband was old and rich when he asked her in marriage. She rejected his addresses, and wept in the arms of her father. Her father laughed at her tears. He did not conceive how it was possible to reject the count, and his daughter did conceive it. Her father reckoned the estates of the count, and she reckoned his years.

She had some time before become acquainted with Herr von Welt, who had fewer estates, and fewer years over his head, danced well, talked tenderly, and loved ardently. But the count was pressing—the father severe—the Herr von Welt was poor, and the count rich. She continued to love the Herr von Welt, and gave the count her hand.

The count had no children. The gout and a cough reminded him of temperance, and he retired in the arms of Hymen to one of his estates. The young countess lived in solitude; the count coughed worse, and remained without children. His old age and his infirmities increased every day; in two years he left the world and his estates, and the young wife was a widow.

She laid aside her white dresses and put on black. The countess was fair—the dark dress set off her complexion—mourning became her.

The count left her all his property: but old people are often fantastical! According to a singular condition of the will, if she married again the greatest part of the property reverted to one of his relations, living at the residence.

Herr von Welt hastened to comfort the widow. He found her beautiful, and she found him as amiable as before. He talked all day long without coughing, and she listened to him all day long without yawning. He could relate a thousand little anecdotes, and the countess was curious. He spoke of the torch of love and his own feelings, and the countess felt. He described the torments of separation, and the anxieties which had martyred him, and the countess was compassionate. He lay at her feet; protestations of his passion streamed from his lips, and his tears upon her hand, and the countess loved; but she thought with tears on the conditions of the will. She was melancholy. It was already six weeks since the count had bid adieu to his gout for ever, and grief appeared now for the first time on the countenance of the countess.

" My dear friend," said Herr von Welt to her in the morning, " you torment yourself with doubts, and it remains in your own power to put an end to them."

" How so ? " said the countess.

" You believe in the possibility," continued he, " of my ceasing to love you ; you consider the band of the feelings not strong enough to withstand time ; but, my dear friend, how easy it is for the hand of the priest to join ours together ; you will then be tranquillised."

" Have you then forgotten the will ? " said she, weeping.

" My love, the question now is only about making you easy. We will be married privately. You and I, the priest—and love will hear our oath."

" But you see, there must be a priest," said she, hastily.

" Let me manage that," said Herr von Welt. " Here in the neighbourhood lives an old man, who is borne down by poverty and close upon a century of years. He is as worthy as the times in which he was born, and as silent as the tomb which will soon receive him. He will carry our secret with him to the grave, and we will bury it in our bosoms."

The countess threw herself into his arms, and entreated him to hasten. Welt did so. The conscience of the priest was tranquillised ; twilight, and a distant summer-house, concealed them from the eye of suspicion, and Welt embraced with rapture—his wife.

A year passed away ; she no longer looked after him with inquietude when he rode out, and his eyes were no longer fixed on her window when he returned ; she could yawn when he related, and he sometimes felt *ennui* though she was sitting by him—but they lived together. The servants had observed familiarities not warranted by friendship ; yet their attachment did not appear to be ardent enough to account well for their being together. A year had made them feel secure, and they no longer paid that strict attention which they did at first to their conduct and conversation. People began to conjecture, to doubt, at last to believe, and after a time to impart their sentiments to each other.

The Count von Werbe, who was to inherit the property in default of the condition of the will being observed, was at this time out of favour with the prince, through the intrigues of his numerous creditors, and had left the residence with his wife to take refuge in the arms of nature. He had purchased the situation of grand chamberlain to the prince—had squandered his property by giving balls and *fêtes*, and destroying his health by dancing and dancers. His wife was formerly a lady of honour—people had formerly paid homage to her charms—she was formerly surrounded by a circle of admirers, but the boundaries of this circle grew smaller, and it was now many years since she had found the residence empty and tiresome, and the taste of the times quite spoiled.

Their estate joined that of the countess. The count attended with much interest to the suspicions which were imparted to him, and hastened to the castle of the countess to pay his respects to her as a relative, and to convince himself of the truth of the opinion of his neighbours ; but he did not convince himself. The countess was prepared for his visit. The Herr von Welt was tender and attentive—his eyes riveted on her. The countess showed all the cordiality of friendship and the attentions of a warmer affection. The count returned home sorrowful.

" Dear Augusta," said the count, as he entered the chamber of his wife, " our neighbours are not prudent. It is only necessary to see them both to give no credit to the tale they have amused us with. I was there two hours, and he had not the courage to come within three steps of her."

" But that proves for us," cried the countess ; " he would have sat at one end of the room and she at the other."

" Not so, my love," said the count ; " respect seemed to keep him at a distance. Their eyes sought each other—her countenance appeared to complain of my presence. Then the interest with which they spoke of each other ! No, my love, we see each other—we talk to each other, but believe me, on my word they are not married."

" But," said the countess, " our neighbours have eyes ; did you never, then, observe anything which can justify their opinion ? "

" My love," replied the count, " you may suppose that I observed everything very attentively. It is not my fault if our creditors are not paid."

" Trifles often betray us," said the countess. " Reflect a little ; did she not once drop her pocket-handkerchief ? "

"Her pocket-handkerchief?" said the count, and considered a little; "no, but her fan fell down."

"And she picked it up again?" said the countess, quickly.

"Truly yes, she picked it up," said the count, looking at her with astonishment.

"And he was there, and suffered it?" said the countess.

The count looked thoughtful—she struck him playfully on the shoulder: "Believe me, good count, our neighbours are in the right."

"When I consider well," said the count, "it appears to me probable; she was very well dressed; her toilette was certainly a few months behind the fashion, but we are in the country, and I was astonished at her taste."

"And he?" asked the countess.

"He held a long dissertation upon taste; he went through the whole history of fashions, from the fig-leaf of the first lady to the last gala-dress of the grand-duchess. He particularly admired the Grecian costume."

"And was she dressed like a Greek?" said the countess, quickly.

"Oh no," said the count: "she was true German—buried up to the chin."

"They are man and wife," said the countess, throwing herself into his arms.

"But her eyes," said the count, shaking his head.

"You are a keen observer," said the countess. "What proofs do you wish to have? The lover would have fallen to the ground with the fan, the husband remained quietly seated; the lover would have had eyes only to admire, the husband had time for a long conversation; the lover would have been delighted to see a German woman he admired dressed in the German fashion, and the husband praised the Greek women. My dear count, are you not aware of all that?"

The count laughed. "Well," said he, "we are invited to-morrow to our neighbour the chamberlain's; the Herr von Welt and the countess will likewise be there. In a large society we fancy ourselves less remarked, and give ourselves up more to our ease; we can therefore both observe them. You may be in the right, but her countenance, and her eyes. I have had the honour, during the last fifteen years, of presenting many married men to his royal highness, and I know mankind well! Matrimony has a peculiar look, something like despair—if you are right, my knowledge of mankind is good for nothing."

The next day all the company was assembled at the chamberlain's except the countess and Herr von Welt. The chamberlain was impatient, all eyes turned toward the road; at last a cloud of dust was observed, and then the carriage of the countess driving quickly up. She was looking out of the right window of the carriage. Welt, leaning on his arm, was looking out of the other. The lady of the grand chamberlain touched her husband and smiled; he turned round good-humouredly, and said in a low voice, "I believe you are right." The carriage stopped; Welt sprang out, the servants assisted the countess; he stood quietly by and brushed the dust from his coat. "They are man and wife," said the grand chamberlain's lady softly.

"Yes, yes, I begin to doubt my knowledge of mankind," said the count.

The countess made excuses for being so late; Welt knit his brow in vexation. Dinner was announced; the master of the house offered his arm to the lady of the grand chamberlain. The grand chamberlain and Welt, the countess and a strange lady remained. Welt offered his arm to the strange lady, and left the countess to the grand chamberlain. His wife looked back and smiled; the grand chamberlain nodded significantly. The society was gay. Welt sat between the countess and the strange lady. He conversed with the stranger on fashion and feeling, and left the countess to be amused by the grand chamberlain. The latter smiled, his wife looked at him good-humouredly. After dinner Welt approached the countess. He talked of the influence of the body over the mind, which occasioned satiety in everything. The countess yawned. "That is the body," said she. Welt continued calmly talking, and the body of the countess yawned again.

The grand chamberlain stole up to his lady. "They are man and wife," she whispered.

"It is certain," said the grand chamberlain.

The chamberlain proposed a walk in the garden, and the company went. A narrow plank led to a fine waterfall. The grand chamberlain had brought his vertigo with him from the residence; the chamberlain was too lusty to trust himself on the plank, and the ladies were timid. Welt sought to tranquillise them. He escorted them over the plank; but he offered his services last to the countess.

The grand chamberlain stood smiling on one side, and his wife stood smiling at him from the other. It was evening, and the company hastened back to the house. The countess was behind, Welt near her. He walked on thoughtfully ; she followed him fatigued.

The grand chamberlain pressed the hand of his wife. The carriages were ordered ; the party separated, and hastened home.

" You are a clever woman, my love," said the grand chamberlain ; " it is certain they are man and wife."

" Now, my dear," said the countess, " only take the pains to get certain proofs."

" Leave me alone," said the count. " The thing is clear, and when that is the case, there must be proofs." Accordingly he went round the neighbourhood to obtain more information ; but he wanted proof, and could only procure conjectures. People had heard this, and seen that ; one referred to another ; and when he wanted proofs, the one had said nothing, and the other had heard nothing. He came back sorrowful. " My dear," said he, " I return just as rich in conjectures, and as poor in proofs."

" Indeed ! " said the countess. " Can the people yet doubt that they are married ? "

" Alas ! no," said the count ; " but no one can prove it. However, I will try what I can do ; the day after to-morrow Herr von Welt has business in the residence ; I will send immediately to my lawyer. We must take advantage of the moment, for conjectures lead to nothing."

The lawyer was called ; they were shut up together, and on the second day he drove to the château of the countess.

" All alone ? " said the grand chamberlain, as he entered the room with an appearance of surprise.

" Herr von Welt is in town," said the countess ; " he will be sorry that he was not at home when he finds that you have been here."

The grand chamberlain took a seat near her ; he admired the arrangement of the house, and some pictures which were in the room.

" My husband was a connoisseur," said the countess. " The collection of paintings he has made proves his taste."

" Ah ! his taste proves other things still more," said the count, smiling ; and he kissed her hand. " But he was an extraordinary man ; he had caprices, which he showed even to the last ; his will proves that."

The countess looked at him surprised. The grand chamberlain appeared not to observe it, and continued, " So young as you are, to remain a widow can only be the caprice of an old jealous husband, who wishes to torment you after his death. The poor man forgot that the heart is very susceptible at your age."

The countess cast down her eyes and blushed.

"Herr von Welt is an old acquaintance, at least I think so," said the grand chamberlain.

"I have known him above four years," said the countess, embarrassed.

"He was remarked at Court for his talents and affability," continued the grand chamberlain, smiling, and his smile was expressive; "but the last year he has been quite lost to the Court and to the world. How is it possible for him not to forget the caprices of an old man who is dead?"

The countess was evidently more embarrassed.

"Why were you not sincere with me?" said he softly, and took her hand. "Your secret is known in the neighbourhood, why would you conceal it from me?"

The countess started up terrified. "Is it possible?" said she—and her voice faltered. "Can the old man have—Oh, count! what do you know—what is known?"

"Do you think," said the count, "that I watch my advantage so servilely?" and his tone was tender and sincere. "I will see and hear nothing. Enjoy in peace what you have dearly enough bought, by a sacrifice of two years. But, dear countess, I have children, who may hereafter complain of my pliability and indulgence. I must therefore do something to fulfil the duty of a father. Another in my place would here require—he would lay before you proofs on which to ground his claims, but I spare your heart, and respect your secret. The friend is silent—it is the father only entreats."

"Alas!" cried the countess, and tears streamed from her eyes, "what do you require of me?"

The grand chamberlain drew a paper out of his pocket. "You know," he continued calmly, "that my property is greatly embarrassed. Your husband left you large estates, and a great fortune; I am silent on his will, of which I make no use; but this wound which I give to my interest must not continue bleeding in my children. Sign, therefore, this writing, my dear friend. You undertake therein to discharge a part of my debts, which have been occasioned by my service in the State, and your secret will ever remain concealed."

He fetched a pen. The countess in the meantime recovered her presence of mind.

" Allow me," said she, more tranquilly, " to request that you will present me the proofs on which you ground your suspicions."

" Why so ? " said he, smiling, " the Government will perhaps soon communicate some to you."

" The Government ? " said the countess, terrified.

" You know," continued he, " the steady course of justice ; you will be cited. It is certainly only a form, but still unpleasant. You must appear and take your oath."

" Oh, heavens ! " cried the countess, and her voice faltered again.

" You take your oath," said the grand chamberlain, " and remain in possession of your property."

The countess seized the pen hastily. " Your children shall lose nothing," said she, and signed. The grand chamberlain kissed the hand which returned him the paper, and went gaily to his carriage.

Herr von Welt returned the next day. " We are betrayed," said the countess, and threw herself weeping into his arms.

" Betrayed ? " said he, astonished.

" The old priest must have chattered," said the countess.

" Indeed ! " says Welt, " he has not spoken these nine months, for he is dead."

The countess looked confounded. She related to him the visit of the grand chamberlain, his behaviour and her signature.

" That is a deception," cried Welt, " he has taken you by surprise ; but he shall not long enjoy his triumph." He hastened out of the room, ordered his horse, and rode to the grand chamberlain. The count came to meet him on the steps.

" I have a word to say to you, count," said Welt ; " but I should wish it to be in private."

" A word also with you, for it is time to sit down to dinner, and you must be our guest," said the grand chamberlain affably, and led him into the room.

" Count," said Welt, " you expressed a suspicion yesterday to the countess, in which I am concerned."

" Quite right," replied the count ; " people told me of these conjectures, and I repeated them to the countess."

" Count," said Welt, " by what can you prove your conjectures ? "

" We will talk about it after dinner," said the grand chamberlain ;

" it is already on the table. Our conversing longer may occasion surprise, and you do not, of course, wish that we should furnish the people with more materials for conjectures ? "

Welt bowed embarrassed. " After dinner, then," said he, and his tone was somewhat milder. The grand chamberlain opened the dining-room door, and introduced him to his wife.

Two sons of the count were at table with them. The youngest, the mother's darling, sat next her, and amused himself by getting under the table to pinch the calf of his father's leg. The count drew up his feet several times, making a wry face ; but the strength of the darling seemed to increase, for he clung like a crab to the calf. The grand chamberlain at last kicked him from him with an exclamation, and the darling fell screaming at his mother's feet.

" The child grows unbearable," cried the grand chamberlain, as he rubbed the calf of his leg, which was smarting with pain ; and the mother wiped the tears from the cheeks of the little one. " Poor child ! " said she, " has he hurt you ? "

" Go on spoiling him," said the count, " and he will one day give your heart as much pain as he has now done my calf."

" Only do not torment him," said the mother, stroking his cheeks ; " he must be allowed to grow like the tree of the field. It was so that Jean Jacques wished boys to be educated."

" But he is to be a gentleman of the chamber," said the father, " and you will at last make a Jean Jacques of the boy. He will then be good for nothing at most but to be a stable-boy."

" When the children are grown up," said she coldly, " you may present them at Court ; that you may understand, but do not interfere in their education. You do not wish the tender plants to wither before their time."

The grand chamberlain was silent, and looked vexed ; the countess expatiated on the virtues of her children, and the cruelties of certain fathers, who had no steady principle of education.

The storm subsided by degrees, and they rose from the table. Welt impatiently reminded the count of his promise, who conducted him into his room.

" Herr von Welt," said the grand chamberlain, as he begged him to be seated, " am I married ? "

Herr von Welt looked at him with astonishment.

" I do not know what this question means, count ? "

" You were not a witness at our marriage ; you did not accompany us to the altar ; may I be allowed to ask you by what means you know we are married ? "

" I think you must be joking," said Welt ; " how I know ?—people have told me so."

" You consider that as a proof, then ? " said the grand chamberlain quickly.

" You embarrass me," said Welt ; " I knew it before I had the honour of seeing you, and my eyes convinced me."

" What have you seen, then ? " asked the count.

" Oh ! " said Welt, " there are certain trifles which soon discover that connection. One is more familiar together, one is not so attentive to the choice of expressions when speaking together, and sometimes one differs about the mode of education."

" Precisely so," continued the grand chamberlain, " the ardour of first love is gone by, but we live together, we bestow our attention on strangers, and leave our wives to be entertained by others : we walk onwards lost in thought, and forget that a wife is following."

" Count," said Welt embarrassed, " you describe the most minute features of the picture. But we have digressed from the main point of our conversation."

" And I think we have been constantly discussing it," said the grand chamberlain ; he went to his bureau and took out a paper—" Will you have the kindness to deliver this to the countess ? You may read it, Herr von Welt ; it is the ratification of my promises. You see I therein renounce my claim according to the will."

" The countess will be astonished at your generosity," said Welt ; " but she delivered you a contract yesterday which she requires back."

" Indeed ! " said the grand chamberlain ; " then I beg you to return me my writing. But, Herr von Welt, you have withdrawn yourself entirely from Court. Do you know that people have made observations upon it ? Thence arise conjectures ; you must have rendered a few people jealous. I give you warning, my dear friend ; no one can hurt you, but they seek to revenge themselves on the countess."

" How is that possible ? " said Welt, astonished.

" I am entreated to ground a complaint on the conjectures I have heard : I have not done so, but have explained my apprehensions to the countess. The ecclesiastical court, which puts the consciences of his royal highness's subjects to proof, can put her upon her oath."

Welt looked over the paper much agitated. "I will give your renunciation to the countess," said he, getting up.

"And if she wishes her contract again," said the grand chamberlain, smiling, "it lies here amongst my papers."

"Count," said Welt, "the countess will not be behind you in generosity. Her property comes from her husband, who bore your name, and I am convinced she will be happy to appropriate a part of the property to support the splendour of his family."

He took a friendly leave of the count, who accompanied him to the hall door.

"Will you not soon travel?" said the grand chamberlain, as they descended the steps.

"Possibly very soon," said Welt; "I mean to accompany the countess, who is anxious to be in a warmer climate."

"Well, the observations you make on your journey cannot be otherwise than instructive," said the grand chamberlain. "But, my dear friend," he continued, "when in London or at Madrid you see a man sitting opposite a lady, and the lady lets fall her fan, and he does not stoop to pick it up, or when he speaks learnedly, and the lady yawns —and they yawn at Madrid as well as here—then believe me, they are man—and wife."

Herr von Welt threw himself on his horse.

"Ride fast," said the count, laughing; "make haste home; a gallop will confound the neighbours, who always walk their horses home to their wives."

Welt laughed, and spurred his animal. The grand chamberlain soon after satisfied his creditors, and returned to Court.

THE SENATOR OF BREMEN

A POPULAR TRADITION

Anonymous

ONE summer evening, in the year 1749, the family of Mr. Sebaldus Beerlein, senator of the free imperial city of Bremen, were seated together, whiling away the hour between eight and nine in conversation, and the juniors amusing themselves with various innocent games. The apartment which they were in was spacious, panelled, according to the custom of that time, with carved woodwork, and decorated with oil-paintings of some value, which Mr. Sebaldus had picked up in his travels in Holland. His aged grandmother was seated at the window, in a chair covered with leather, embossed with flowers of gold, looking, as usual, at the steeples of the distant churches, tinged with the radiance of sunset. She hummed at the same time to herself an old hymn of Paul Gerherd's, which treats of the repose of the godly after death, and the happiness of those who have fought the good fight, and are delivered from all the trials and tribulations of this mortal life. She numbered full eighty years, and so she had good reason to hum such a hymn. Catherine, the senator's wife, a still young and comely woman, of the most respectable family of Ruhberg of Hildesheim, sat not far from the window at a small table, playing a game at lansquenet with her nephew Ruhberg, copying-clerk to the senate, an almost boyish-looking young man. She mistook the cards in the twilight; the youth took advantage of this, and purposely cheated his aunt, and she reproved him with good-humoured severity for his knavish tricks. A group of children were sitting together in the middle of the room, and Sigismunda, the eldest daughter, twelve years old, was telling her brothers and sisters, in a low tone, a long story, to which they listened in silent attention. Theobald Ahlevert, an old and faithful servant of the family, was standing at the corner of the stove, calculating the last week's receipts from a little shop which his wife kept, and, as he had reason to apprehend, not to the best account. Thus each of the members of the family was engaged his own way, and not attending to what the others were about.

Mr. Sebaldus Beerlein himself was sitting on the sofa, with a hand in his waistcoat-pocket, and his head propped by the other; he looked straight before him, listening with pleasure to the playful tones of his wife and the soft whispering voice of his daughter, and now and then casting a glance at the dark form of his grandmother, whose shaking head and sharply-formed, noble features were defined upon the evening sky. Such moments are of great value to the father of a family. He takes a survey of his past life; he thinks of all the comforts and blessings that Providence has bestowed on him, and he forms plans for the further improvement of his circumstances, for the sake of those who are dearest to his heart.

The clock of the neighbouring church now struck nine. As the sound of the last stroke died away, the senator rose, took his hat and cane, and hastily left the room.

" Sebald," cried his wife, " art thou going to the counting-house? Shall a light be brought down to thee? "

The senator gave no answer. They heard him going down the stairs, and presently the house-door shutting heavily after him.

" Where can he be going to? " asked the grandmother.

" Indeed, I don't know," replied his wife. " He meant to spend the evening with us. Something must have suddenly occurred to him."

The old lady shook her head. A light was brought, and the family sat down at the round-table to their simple supper. A place was left for the master of the house, as everybody felt thoroughly convinced that he would presently return. The quarter chimed, then the half-hour, then three-quarters, and at last the clock struck ten, and still he had not come back. Theobald was sent to the vintner's over the way, to inquire whether the senator might not have turned in there and met with friends who had detained him; but he came back, saying that the vintner assured him he had not seen his master. Catherine joked about this sudden disappearance of her husband, but nobody joined in her mirth, especially as the venerable grandmother assumed so serious a look. For some days past she had felt unwell.

" It is not right of him to go just now," said she; " I am liable to be called from one moment to another; and it would grieve me much not to see him once more."

Catherine scolded the grandmother for this expression, and told her that she ought not to talk in that manner. The old lady said her prayers, and Catherine led her to her chamber.

The children were put to bed, too; young Ruhberg retired, and Catherine was left by herself. She took up some work, and seated herself near the candle, resolving not to go to bed till her husband came in.

It struck eleven, it struck twelve, and not a footfall was heard out of doors. The streets were deserted and silent: the watchman's horn was heard at a great distance; and from a curtained back-window of a neighbouring house sounded the low mournful tones of women singing while they watched with a corpse. The sky was overcast, and here and there a few solitary stars, so few, that Catherine could count them, peeped forth from between the clouds. She stood at the window, and she made sure that every shadow which glided along either side of the street was her husband coming home at last; but still he came not. When she returned to her work at the table, she was seized with despondency and alarm. She now bethought her that it was not Sebald's way to go out so suddenly without saying a word, and to stay out so late. If he had changed his mind, and been obliged to go out that evening, he would surely have said a word to that effect to his wife, who was sitting not far from him. Never did he go out for a single hour without acquainting her, and desiring her to save his supper for him; and now he was away the whole night! She turned over in her mind his behaviour during the day; uneasy as she was, she fancied that it had not been altogether as usual; but on closer reflection she could not adduce any particular circumstance. The anxious wife tried to recollect whether any petty jar had arisen between them, but she soon said to herself, "How could I forget a quarrel so serious as to drive a husband away from his wife? Besides, it was not Sebald's disposition to bear such a violent grudge."

Catherine's thoughts then turned to his circumstances; but, as far as she knew, these were prosperous: indeed, had they been ever so deranged, the senator, a man universally beloved and esteemed, would have had no need to abscond by night on that account, for he had friends and wealthy relations who took an interest in his welfare.

Amid these musings, day dawned, and Catherine extinguished her lamp. Weary as she was, sleep kept aloof from her eyes. By degrees the family began to stir, doors opened, and the short dry cough of the grandmother gave notice that she was awake. The children came, and Catherine said not a word to them or to the old lady about the absence of her husband. But she could not long conceal it. People came upon business; the messenger of the senate wanted him; friends asked to see him; and at last she was obliged to confess that she knew not where her husband was. A day was suffered to pass; and then it was publicly reported in the city that Senator Beerlein had disappeared, and nobody knew what had become of him. Some now pretended that a man's hat and stick had been found on the bank of the river; others declared that a report of fire-arms had been heard at night in a neighbouring wood, and it was whispered that the corpse of the suicide had been carried very early in the morning to the city by charcoal-burners, secretly hired for the purpose. Still more extraordinary rumours were circulated: it was alleged that Mr. Beerlein had been conducted by an escort over the frontier, to be punished for some crime suddenly discovered in a neighbouring country. It is easy to conceive what Catherine and her family must have suffered when they heard these reports. The poor forlorn woman still believed that her husband would come back daily, hourly—but she was disappointed. A month passed away, two months, three months, and not a trace of the senator was to be discovered. Advertisements in the newspapers proved fruitless; and private inquiries indefatigably prosecuted were equally unavailing. The man was as completely lost as if he had sunk into the earth. Nobody had seen him go out at the door, nobody had observed him in the street; minutely as his dress, face, and figure were described, nowhere had such a person been seen in any of the neighbouring places.

Three years had elapsed, and the lost senator had ceased to be talked of, when, late one evening, likewise in the middle of summer, a man knocked at the door of Beerlein's house. He looked pale and fatigued. He was asked what he wanted. The stranger was evidently astonished at this question.

"Who are you?" said he to the young man who opened the door. "What brings you into my house?"

"Your house!" exclaimed the youth, scrutinising the interrogator from head to foot. "This house belongs to Mr. Van Peters, the wine-merchant, and I am his clerk."

"Van Peters!" exclaimed the stranger. "What a silly oaf you must be to crack such a stupid joke! As if I did not know where the wine-merchant lives, and where my own house is!"

With these words he pushed the young fellow roughly aside, and ascended the well-known staircase. He went along the passage; here he saw furniture and pictures that were strange to him. He was about to open the door of the sitting-room, when bursts of obstreperous laughter, the clang of glasses, and voices of men in loud disputation met his ear.

"Is it possible?" said he to himself; "has Catherine company—and especially such noisy company as this?"

He opened the door gently, and was thrilled with horror on seeing a number of drunken faces around a public-house table. The apartment, which used to be kept so neat, so clean, and so comfortable, looked dirty, and was filled with tobacco-smoke. The wainscot was damaged, and here and there gone from the wall. The chair at the window, where his grandmother was accustomed to sit, was occupied by a sleeping "mountain of gross flesh." But the evening sun shone, as it did when he was there last, through the windows, and its golden radiance cut the returned senator to the heart like a dagger. He stood upon the threshold of his own room; he sought the dear objects whom he had left there but an hour before, as he thought, and how was all so frightfully changed, as in the wild vagaries of an extravagant dream! The poor man rubbed his forehead, he shut his eyes, and opened them again, to convince himself that he was not mistaken, and tottered like one who is on the point of swooning. The noisy revellers, on perceiving him, laughed aloud at the pale stranger for coming into a public-house when he seemed to be already intoxicated.

"Good Heavens!" all at once exclaimed the landlord; "why, it is the lost senator!"

At this exclamation the guests were seized with a panic, set down their glasses, and stared at the door, as though they had seen a spectre. The stranger advanced and seated himself at the end of one of the benches. Those who occupied it moved as far from him as they could. The landlord alone had the courage to go up to him.

"Mr. Senator," cried he, "where have you been? For these three years search has been made for you to no purpose."

"Three years!" repeated Beerlein, staring at the landlord.

"This house," continued the other, "is no longer yours. Your widow—your wife, I would say—I beg your pardon, I am talking to you as if you were dead—sold it to me in the second year, as you did not come back, and now lives in a small town in the neighbourhood."

"And my grandmother?" asked Beerlein.

"She died a few weeks after your disappearance."

"And my children?"

"Dead, too. A disease which made great havoc in our good city last year carried them off."

At these answers, the head of the unfortunate senator drooped lower and lower; no tone of horror or of grief escaped him; but his whole frame denoted heart-breaking and unutterable anguish. He left the room as quietly as he had entered it. The landlord followed him, stopped him on the stairs, and asked in a loud and sharp voice, "But where have you been all this time, neighbour?"

"Ask me not," replied the wretched man. "God has been pleased to try me in a wonderful way. I feel that I shall die."

With these words he fell into a deep swoon. Care was taken to convey him to his wife, and one may conceive the fright and joy of Catherine when she saw her long-lost husband return. She received him in her widow's weeds, which she put off immediately, but only to resume them in a few weeks, and this time with sufficient occasion, for Mr. Sebaldus Beerlein departed this life, as he had foretold, with pious resignation; but before he died he communicated to the clergyman who attended him the extraordinary circumstances of his absence, and this document is still preserved by the family. It is attested and signed by several witnesses living at the time, who were well acquainted with the senator before his disappearance, and who saw him return, and the seal of the city authorities was affixed to it. This narrative was, in substance, as follows:

"On Trinity Sunday, in the year 1749," relates the senator, "between eight and nine in the evening, I was sitting quietly, and occupied with the most pleasing thoughts about my family, which was collected around me, when I distinctly heard a rap at the door. I took no notice of it, concluding that Ahlevert, my servant, who was close to the door, would see who was there, or that the person who had knocked would come in, when he found his signal disregarded. Instead of that, however, the knocking was thrice repeated, and very loud. I was surprised that not a creature in the room seemed to hear it: all quietly kept their seats. All at once it was as if a voice said to me, 'Rise, take thy hat and cane and go.'

"I strove to silence this extraordinary inward injunction, but was seized with such an anxiety, oppression, and faintness of heart, as if I had been ever so ill. This painful sensation became at last so unbearable that I was forced to take up my hat and stick and to go to the door.

"When I was in the passage, I there found a man who eyed me with steadfast look, and again the words sounded in my ears, 'Come, follow me.'

"I knew not the man, neither did I know what he wanted with me; but I felt that from the moment I had crossed the threshold of my room he had power over me, and I followed him.

"We descended the back stairs and went through a passage in the next house, of the existence of which I had never before been aware. It was vaulted, and, as far as I can recollect, casks and empty chests were piled against its dark walls. It became lower and lower, so that at last I was obliged to advance stooping after my guide, who went just before me. We came to a dark water, which I took to be a covered canal: the water looked black and unnatural. A couple of crazy planks, which served for a bridge, swayed much as I was passing over them; but my guide moved light as a feather and without the slightest noise over this dangerous crossing.

"We got at last into the open air, and I saw the starry firmament above us. The evening red still glowed in the west, and I recollect that, on looking back, I distinctly saw the steeple of our principal church; everything else seemed to be enveloped, as it were, in mist. We now came to a plain, extending farther than the eye could reach, and which appeared absolutely strange to me. Not a tree, not a hut, not a road was to be seen. The ground was covered with dried or singed grass, as if a vast fire had lately raged there.

"I made this remark to my guide, asking at the same time whither he was leading me. Without answering, he signified, by a silent gesture, that we must proceed. Accordingly, without exchanging a word, we pursued our course together over the dead level of the heath. The last tinge of the evening red disappeared; a fog shrouded the face of heaven, so that earth and sky seemed to be covered with one uniform lead-coloured veil. I cannot describe to you the awful and soul-depressing effect of this solitude. How grateful to my ear would have been the slightest sound of life! We heard not even our own footfalls on the soft ground. From time to time a cool breeze blew over the plain, but it refreshed me not, for it wafted with it an intolerable smell of mould.

"Having proceeded in this manner for about half an hour, I perceived a house standing quite alone upon the plain, and the windows of which were brilliantly lighted up. It was in that sort of style in which palaces are built; pillars supported the roof, and the edifice was decorated with magnificent flights of steps, rich coats-of-arms, and gilt statues. My companion beckoned me to enter. I represented to him that I knew not either the house or its owner.

"'Thou wilt learn to know him,' he replied; 'but beware of putting a single question either to him or to those about him concerning what thou shalt there see. Silent as thou camest must thou go again, and impress upon thy memory what thou seest.'

"With these words he opened the door of a large magnificent saloon, along the sides of which I saw by the light of a thousand tapers a large company sitting in full dress. When I entered, every eye was turned upon me. The company consisted of gentlemen of quality and ladies of extraordinary beauty; but I knew none of them. They were faces which I had never seen in all my life. My companion, who stopped in a respectful attitude at the door, motioned me to approach the company. I did so, though I felt abashed, and they replied to my salutation with a formal but not unfriendly obeisance; for every one seemed to be wholly occupied with himself or his neighbour, and to take no further notice of me. I had time for observation, and I soon remarked that all these beautiful women had red cords round their necks, which were white as alabaster, and that the gentlemen wore the same mark over their cravats. Finding that I was permitted to walk about where I pleased, I went up to a card-table at the window, about which four grave gentlemen were assembled. They looked cold and indifferent; sleep seemed to weigh down their eyes: their clothes were most splendidly embroidered with gold, and broad ribbons of orders crossed their bosoms. They, too, had the distinctive red band round the neck; but what startled me more was to see that the cards with which they were playing were stained with blood.

"I turned shuddering away, and went into an adjoining apartment. It was fitted up still more superbly than the saloon, and hung with red velvet. On a sofa I saw a man who was taking a nap; his head drooped upon his bosom; but he, too, had the red band round his neck. Casting my eyes upon the floor, I perceived with horror a track of blood, which led to the next room. I followed it, and found a second apartment, but not a creature in it. The lights burned dimly, and a number of musical instruments huddled together in one corner indicated that they had been or were to be used to play to dancing. But not a musician was to be seen, and the profoundest silence prevailed. A door of immense magnitude occupied the farther side of this apartment. It was shut and surrounded with costly gilding. The traces of blood led to this door; but, in spite of all my efforts to open it, I could not stir the lock. Apprehensive lest the noise which I made might bring the company to me, I desisted from further attempts. Over the door was inscribed in large black figures '1789.' This number has deeply impressed itself upon my mind, as well as the track of blood which led to the mysterious apartment.

"I know that I fell into a reverie about these things, and a kind of stupor came over me, and made me sit down in a chair in a corner of the saloon. How long I might have sat there I cannot tell: when I woke up from my musing, I heard a clock strike one, and at the same time a great bustle in the saloon. I rose immediately and hastened through the apartments to look for my guide. He was still standing there waiting for me. We quitted the saloon and the house forthwith. I was again upon the solitary heath, and my companion walking mutely by my side. In this manner we arrived at the skirts of the city, where he took leave of me with a silent bow. I felt faint and ready to die. I had scarcely strength to reach the city, and I rejoiced to find myself again in the well-known streets. When I once more heard the noise usual in them, and human voices, my heart seemed to revive. The recollection of the ghostlike company, with its fearful mark, gradually became less vivid, but that prophetic number was constantly before my eyes, and will continue to haunt them as long as I live; for it is but too certain that the Lord hath caused me to see a wonderful vision."

Need we say that the import of this vision, or whatever it may be called, was fully explained by the French Revolution which broke out just forty years afterwards? About that time appeared a tract in German, with this title, "Wonderful and True History of the lost Senator of Bremen—how by the special permission of God he foresaw future Times and their Doings." Upon that publication the above tradition is founded.

UNCLE'S WILL

Anonymous

MR. HEIMAL, an old rich miser, and an odd fellow, felt that his hour was come, and therefore wrote to Adolphus, a very poor nephew, whom he always before neglected, to ask him to visit him, promising to make him heir to all his possessions. Adolphus lost no time, but travelled night and day, and reaching the little village, the residence of his uncle, early on the fifth morning, went to the Violet, the only inn of the place, in order to dress himself better, and to make inquiries about his uncle. The landlord answered, shrugging up his shoulders :

"According to all appearances Mr. Heimal was near his end. Since Wednesday he was sensible only for a few hours each day, and is likely, says Mr. Schneidab, the village barber and physician, to depart this evening. Since the peace, instead of the better times we hoped for, a pestilence rages here, which even destroys the child in the mother's womb. My cousin, the smith, who was so strong that he might have been used like a beam to force open the church door, is gone to God yesterday evening ; and Schneidab, who is not easily frightened, begins to lose courage. He believes it to be a *radical* pestilence, intended only for the benefit of the sexton, who, like an enchanted executioner, sees three dead bodies before him instead of one, and cannot heave in and out fast enough."

Adolphus asked more particulars of his uncle. "You will find with your uncle a faithful old housekeeper, and Albertina, an orphan, who lost her left eye by a ball entering the window in a skirmish, but who continues to set both young and old in a flame with the right, as if it were a burning-glass, and this without wishing it, for *Tinchen* is a perfect example."

With a heart beating so that it might be heard, Adolphus entered his uncle's house, and met Albertina. Her noble form, and her remaining burning-glass, caused the loss of the other to be overlooked. The gentle goodness of her spirit played about her face, and seemed independent of its form, though in truth it was, with the exception of the eye, beautiful. " Mr. Adolphus," repeated Albertina, as he named himself, " I will announce you immediately ; you are expected impatiently, and will be heartily welcome."

" Thank Heaven," said the deserving heir to himself. To her he said some flattering words as she disappeared, and then prayed that his uncle's heart might be favourably disposed towards him. Albertina opened the door and bade him enter. In a moment he was at the bedside.

Old Heimal was perfectly sensible : he thanked Adolphus in a friendly way ; praised his blooming appearance ; assured him he had inquired after him, and heard nothing of him but what was good, and therefore had made him his heir. Adolphus stammered forth his earnest thanks.

" Not too soon, not too soon," said the other ; " it is with conditions : hear them first. I am to be buried in the churchyard here, and you will receive the interest of eighty thousand thalers if you promise the magistrate to repeat piously the Lord's Prayer once a day over my grave till the end of your life. If you fail once, the informer is to receive a fourth part of the inheritance, and the remainder is to go to the hospital, the guardian of which will keep a good look-out that you perform your vow. Nothing but a serious disease, testified by two surgeons, is to excuse you from this duty. The testament lies ready with the magistrate ; take time, therefore, to think, for every condition is, early or late, a clog on the enjoyment of that good with which it is combined. 'Why did my uncle curse me,' you will say, 'with this condition ? Why did he poison to me the wine he was no longer able to drink himself ?' I answer, justice demands that my property should be expended for the benefit of the town in which I gained it—in which I went to school and grew up to manhood. On the boundary of the dominion of death you shall be at least reminded once a day to raise your thoughts to the Giver of all good ; and I wish to save the soul of my heir from the rock of worldly perdition. Go, my son ; I am weak."

Albertina had remained in the room by the command of the old man, and now accompanied Adolphus to the door. In the confusion of his feelings he seized her hand and asked what she advised. She blushed, and answered :

" I cannot believe that you will be guided in so important a matter by the advice of an ignorant girl."

"Oh yes!" answered he; "your situation here makes you a friend, and the good sense of your answer belies your pretended ignorance. The powers of fate announce their decrees with pleasure by the mouth of innocent maidens."

She replied, "Turn to our Father in heaven; prayer brings power and knowledge, and we then select, as if by inspiration, that which is best."

Adolphus left her with a grateful squeeze of the hand. He was disposed to follow her advice, but his wishes were earthly.

"Eighty thousand thalers," said he, "or rather the interest of this sum, is in truth a key to earth's heaven: but what is the price? The condition separates me for ever from all which can sweeten life or render it lovely. Suppose I might with swift horses reach the capital for a moment to strengthen my mind in the circle of beauty and intelligence, it can only be for a moment, and like a solitary moonbeam through the darkness of a wintry night; and I lose all if any accident happens to me on the road. Is there a bitterer cup than this eternal monotony—this seeing always the same faces, part expressing vulgarity, part signifying a mixture of rudeness and knowledge even more intolerable than vulgarity? Can anything be worse than to live with people who spy out every morning what I mean to nourish my body with at mid-day, and who treat every deviation from their own customs worse than the Inquisition treats heretics? Yet even here I may find friends, hearts allied to mine, though different in age, situation, and habits. But how soon is conversation exhausted! How does the daily return of the same materials diminish the charms of society! Whatever happens to the town falls on me as part of it. The inheritance makes me like one of its towers; and when I will fall sick, Mr. Schneidab, the village barber, will hasten, as accoucheur sent by the fates, to deliver me into another world."

In this manner, till late in the evening, did Adolphus weigh his situation; and as he was going to bed, Albertina came to announce the sudden death of his uncle. This news made him pass a sleepless night, and at times to be almost out of his senses. He imagined that the amiable Albertina glided into his chamber and begged earnestly of him to be pleased with the little town, that she delighted him very much, that she made his staying there the condition of obtaining her favour, and that she offered him her sweet mouth to seal the contract with a kiss. He then imagined himself, with her assistance, counting heaps of ducats, and he was full of gratitude for the golden shower and for the lovely bride. He embraced her with one arm and lifted a sack of thalers in the other. A cry of fire awoke him—the warm living image was fled, and the landlady burst into the room to save her wardrobe, which was safely stowed in the best chamber used for guests. The cry of fire ran through the house, for not one who could breathe but joined in the alarm.

Adolphus sprang out of bed, descended to the street, and saw the house of his departed uncle in flames. He reached it just as Albertina came out with a box of valuables, which she gave him as his property, and then hastened back to secure her own, and came not again. Adolphus felt how much he was indebted to her, and pressing through the burning house, found her in a courtyard clinging to a tree, which protected her for a moment from the flames.

"I am lost," said she; "save yourself."

He, however, sprang to her, the flames, as it were, following him, and making his retreat impossible. The hot air already made it difficult to breathe, when he discovered that, by climbing the tree, he might escape over the wall. With the arm of love strengthened by fear, he dragged the maiden up the stem and along one of the overhanging branches, and then dropped her safely on the opposite side of the wall and jumped after her. Here they stood in a neighbouring garden, and first thanked God for their escape. Albertina then extinguished the sparks on his waistcoat; he kissed her as he had done in his dream, and then led her to a place of safety.

When the fire was extinguished, which did not take place till the house was consumed, Adolphus returned to bed and slept nearly as sound as his uncle, whose corporeal part had been reduced by fire to a heap of ashes. Albertina had found it, and had secretly conveyed it away. In the morning his body was sought, for the will made it necessary to have it buried; but all in vain; not a bone was to be discovered. Albertina, however, sent in secret a casket to Adolphus, and wrote with it:

"If the accompanying casket serves, as I hope, to free my noble assistant from the heavy conditions which our departed friend imposed upon his heir, this latter will then only pray with more fervour over the ashes of his benefactor, which now lie in his hands."

Adolphus blessed in his heart her ingenuity, then went to the magistrate, who was full of thought, and knew not whom he could bury in Heimal's place—for a grave they must have, to fulfil the conditions of his will. Adolphus, however, said:

" You undoubtedly know beforehand what I mean to say to your worship. You know that a nonentity cannot be buried, and that I cannot be bound to pray over a grave where my uncle is not entombed; and, at the same time, his testament, making me his heir, remains perfectly valid. A process would evidently last longer than your life, and probably not be finished before the day of judgment. Far be it from me, however, to wish to injure this esteemed pleasant town, the cradle of my good fortune. I therefore resign in favour of its hospital a third part of the property left by my uncle. For this, however, you will give me permission to send to your good wife some of the newest fashions from the city, where I mean to take up my residence."

Seldom has a treaty been sooner ratified than this was; and the heir got away with difficulty from the gratitude of the magistrate, to seek out Albertina. She struggled against the embraces with which, in his joy, he overwhelmed her: they might be the mode in the city—here they were quite unheard of; but Adolphus spoke with a seducing tongue, and on a subject not usually ungrateful to a maiden's ear. She pretended, indeed, not to believe him, as if she regarded it as impossible, with the failure of her eye, to please a man who was so entirely without fault, and she concealed her wishes with maidenlike excuses. The gay people of the little town, however, were soon afterwards invited to Adolphus's marriage-feast. He placed, without the knowledge of the bride, the casket with the ashes of the now blessed uncle under the marriage-bed, and was thus enabled to offer the promised prayers daily with the greatest conveniency.

WHO COULD HAVE BELIEVED IT?

ANONYMOUS

THERE lived in Vienna a young man of rank and fortune, who bore a strong resemblance to many other young men of that and every city, for he was a dupe to all the follies of fashion and high life. He combined a flexible heart with a handsome person; it had cost his mother a great deal of trouble to make him what is called a *puppy*; but, by indefatigable diligence, she had at last effected her purpose. All the ladies, consequently, loved him, and he loved them all in return. It has been said that once or twice his attachments have been even of more than a month's duration, but never did he impose any constraint upon himself or the object of his affection by an irksome fidelity. He possessed the nicest powers of perception, whenever any word or look summoned him to victory; but he always had the good manners to pay every attention to the clock, when it announced the hour of parting.

With these qualifications he was certain of success with the ladies. He paid his devoirs to all, enjoyed all, and was at last tired of all. In one of his moments of torpid satiety our hero had returned home before supper. Happy is he who feels the time least oppressive when at home—he belongs to the better kind of men. Our young count threw himself upon the sofa, stretched his limbs, yawned, and so forth. Suddenly it occurred to him that he was married. No wonder that we should have forgotten it, since he himself only just now recollected it. "Apropos," said he, and rung the bell. A servant entered.

"Go to your mistress and ask if I may have the pleasure of seeing her."

The servant listened attentively, not believing the testimony of his own ears. The count repeated his orders, which the servant at length obeyed, shaking his head as he went. The countess was the amiable daughter of a country gentleman—she was a flower which, from the pressure of the Court atmosphere, drooped, but did not quite wither; to avoid *ennui* she had no resource but to swim with the tide of high life. She and her husband sometimes met—they never avoided, nor ever courted each other's society. Before marriage they had seen little of each other, and after it they had no time to devote to such an employment. There were people enough who spared the count the trouble of admiring his wife's perfections, and if they made no impression on her heart, they at least gratified her vanity.

Her husband's message was delivered to her at a moment when her state of mind was much the same as his. She knew not what to think of this unexpected visit; she replied, however, that she should be happy to see him. He entered—hoped he was not troublesome—took a chair—made remarks on the weather—and recounted the news of the day. The conversation, as far as related to the subjects of it, was quite common, but his vivacity and Amelia's genius inspired it with interest. The time passed they knew not how: the count looked at his watch—was surprised to find it so late, and requested permission to sup with his wife.

"With all my heart," replied Amelia, "if you can be content with my homely fare."

Supper was brought—they ate, and were merry, without being noisy. This calm pleasure possessed to them the charm of novelty; they were both pleasant without wishing to appear so, as is generally the case with most people. They were quite new acquaintances—the hours flew swiftly away, and the time for retiring to rest being arrived, the count took leave of the countess, highly pleased with his visit.

The next day he was invited to a concert, and did not learn till it was late that, one of the virtuosos being ill, the concert was deferred. How was he to pass the tedious evening? He inquired, as he passed, after his wife, and was informed she was somewhat indisposed.

"Well," thought he, "common civility requires that I should wait upon her, and ask her personally how she does."

He sent a message, requesting that he might be allowed to sit with her till supper, and was very politely received. He was cheerful, lively, and gallant. The supper hour arrived, and this time Amelia begged him to stay. He had been invited to a casino party after the concert, notwithstanding which he remained with his wife, and their conversation was quite as pleasant and less reserved than that of the preceding visit.

"Do you know," said Amelia, "that the party to which you were invited would find a little trouble in discovering *the cause* of your absence?"

He smiled, and paused for a few moments. "I must tell you something in confidence," began he at length, while he was playing with his fork, "something which you will perhaps think rather candid than gallant; you cannot imagine how much you are improved since your marriage."

"*My* marriage!" answered Amelia, in a jocose tone; "I believe it took place about the same time as your own."

"Very true, my lady," replied he, "but it is inconceivable how so happy an alteration can have taken place in you. At that time—pardon me—you had so much rustic bashfulness, it is scarce possible to recognise you. Your genius is no longer the same; even your features are much improved."

"Well, my lord," replied the countess, "without wishing to return the compliment, all that you have said of me I thought of you. But upon my word," added she, "it is well that no one hears us; for it almost seems as if we were making love."

The dialogue continued long in the same style, till Amelia at length looked at her watch, and in a fascinating tone remarked that it was late. The count arose unwillingly, slowly took his leave, and as slowly retired to the door—suddenly he again turned round.

"My lady," said he, "I find it very tedious to breakfast alone—may I be allowed to take my chocolate with you?"

"If you please," answered Amelia; and they parted, still more pleased with each other.

The next morning it occurred to the count that these frequent visits *to his wife* might give rise to scandalous reports. He therefore desired his valet not to mention the circumstance to any one. He then put on an elegant morning-gown, and went softly over to Amelia.

Amelia had just risen in the most cheerful humour. The bloom upon her cheek rivalled the blush of morning. She was animated and witty—in short, she was enchanting; and her husband, in an hour, discovered how much pleasanter it was to breakfast in company than to sit alone, and opposite a glass, gazing at his own person, and looking into his yawning mouth.

"Why don't you come here every day," said Amelia, "if my company is pleasant to you?" He answered that he feared his presence might prevent the visits of others.

"I shall miss no one," replied she, "as long as you indemnify me by your society."

" Upon my word," said the count, " I have more than once wished that I was not your ladyship's husband."

" Why so ? " demanded Amelia.

" That I might be allowed to tell you," returned he, " how much I love you."

" Oh ! tell me so, I beg," cried she, " if only for the sake of novelty."

" Fear not," answered the count ; " I hope, my lady, I shall never so far forget myself ; but we have had, I think, two very agreeable *tête-à-têtes* at supper—how if you were this evening to allow me a third? "

" With all my heart," answered the countess. The appointment was on both sides exactly adhered to. Their conversation was this time less lively, less brilliant—they gazed at each other oftener, and spoke less ; the heart began to assert its influence, and even arrived so far that they once, during a pause, involuntarily squeezed each other's hand across the table, although the servants were still in the room. *Who could have believed it ?*

Amelia very plainly perceived that it was late, but she did not look at her watch. Her husband made not the smallest effort to depart ; —he complained that he was somewhat tired, but not sleepy. In a word, from this day they parted in the morning instead of midnight, because they were then both ready to breakfast together.

The count, enchanted with his new conquest, eloped with Amelia into the country, where they, with astonishment, discovered that the theatre of nature, and the concert of the nightingales, surpassed all other theatres and concerts. They at first thought of staying only a few days—every morning they intended to depart, and every evening they changed their intentions. When autumn, however, approached, they returned to Vienna. The same evening they went to the play, and our hero had the courage to sit in the *same box* with Amelia.

Who could have believed it ? To such a dreadful extent may a man be led by one thoughtless step. Ye happy husbands in high life, take warning by the mournful example of our count !

FRANZ VON GAUDY
1800–1840

ANTONELLO THE GONDOLIER

IT is just half a century since I closed the eyes of my good father—the best of comrades, the fondest of husbands, the most honest Venetian of his time. Ah, if you had known my father you would have acknowledged him the hardiest, boldest fellow in the Republic, the cleverest mandoline-player, the best singer of Tasso, the smartest gondolier whose oars ever lashed to foam the waters of the Canalazzo. All this must be my excuse for rescuing from the oblivion of the fleeting years the fragment of his life I now relate.

My father felt his end approaching. With closed eyes he lay on a couch stuffed with maize-straw, a rosary in his wrinkled hands, and his pale lips moving in silent prayer. A death-like stillness filled the room, broken only by the sobs of wife and children. The rays of the evening sun burst through the vine-espalier that grew round our home; and over the face of the dying passed now patches of rosy light, and now the shadows of the broad leaves. Presently he opened the large, black, deeply-sunken eyes once more, looked slowly round as if to make sure that we were all there, and then began wearily and with difficulty to speak.

" For years, now," he said, " I have been wanting to make you the confidants of a strange, almost incredible, event which happened to me in my youth. I put it off from day to day for one reason or another, but I put it off too long. Now, I know not whether the time that is left me suffices for the telling of this long-guarded secret. Listen, however—but first swear on this dying hand that no word of the secret shall pass your lips till fifty years have gone. The heir of a great and powerful family has been involved in the destiny of so humble a man as myself—and the Tribunal of the Inquisition was compelled to intervene. An unguarded word may expose you to the vengeance of an undisciplined and powerful nobility, or to the severity of the legal authorities. Swear, therefore, a silence of fifty years! "

We obeyed the last command of our father; we laid our hands in his, and pronounced the binding oath. We have kept it faithfully—

my mother and sisters till their death ; I, the last surviving, till the period assigned has expired, and the time arrived when I have to fear neither the vengeance of the nobles nor the tyranny of the Council of Ten ; but to the point.

" It was at three o'clock on a sultry summer afternoon "—began my father—" that I sat myself down at the base of the granite pillar which supports the saintly Teodoro, and stretched my lazy limbs on the stone slabs below it. I fell to counting, with sleepy eyes, the pillars of the Doge's Palace, up and down, then down and up ; miscounted them, and tried again—feeling my eyelids becoming heavier with each number I told. The footsteps of the guard holding watch under the colonnade fell ever duller and fainter on my ears. Now and then one of the pigeons from the Place of St. Mark whirred past over my head, hastening to seek refuge from the glowing heat under the eaves of the church. It was so still that I could hear the little wavelets as they broke against the bows of the gondolas. All the world was having its siesta, and I was in a good way to follow suit, when the shout, ' Hi ! Antonello, up there ! A league's row on the canal ! ' startled me out of my doze.

" The shout proceeded from Count Orazio Memmo—the most amiable good-for-nothing in all Venice. Three-and-twenty years old, tall and slim, a well-cut pale face, with the blackest and most brilliant eyes in the world ; as clever as daring, as rich as generous, a bold gamester, a passionate worshipper of women—such was my patron.

" Mistrustful of the gondoliers of his uncle, the Councillor, in whom, not without ground, he suspected spies on his goings and comings, the young gallant needed on his adventures a quick-witted, fearless fellow, a silent, perfectly reliable assistant—and in me he had found his man. Ah, when I think of those old wild times, those brilliant Carnivals, those nightly revelries and serenades, those mysterious rendezvous in the gardens of the Giudecca ! Fathers and lovers cursed Orazio Memmo worse than the Grand Turk, and many a handful of silver coin has poured into my cap when my swift gondola has distanced the enraged pursuer, and I have landed the happy lover, undiscovered, on the marble steps of the Casa Memmo.

" Quick as thought did I spring to my legs at the sound of the well-known voice, then loosed the chain from the stake, and when his Excellency had seated himself on the luxurious cushions, pushed off vigorously from the land.

" The boat may have been gliding gently over the water for about half an hour. Inaudibly fell the oar into the green waves—but there was no hurry, and my patron had no aim but to dream away an hour in *dolce far niente.* Presently, however, a foreign gondola rushed up with hasty strokes of the oars behind us, and then shot quickly past. The deck was covered with a silver carpet streaked in red, and the heavy silk tassels that hung from the gunwales trailed along the surface of the water. The two rowers were clothed in a rich stuff of the same design. In front of the cabin sat on a brocaded cushion a Moorish boy, with a broad golden neck-band, a dagger hanging from glittering chains by his side, and balancing on his fist a shrill, rainbow-coloured parrot. The Venetian blinds were drawn up on both sides, and the eye could penetrate into the interior of the boat as she flew past.

" On the cushions reclined a divinely beautiful woman. A closely-fitting, gold-embroidered over-garment enveloped her dainty figure, and wide, open pantaloons of Eastern cut fell over her little slippers prettily worked in flowers. The long golden hair descended from the snowy whiteness of the brow, and fell in curly waves upon the shoulders and bosom. But how can I describe to you the sorcery of that lovely countenance, the moist glance of those black eyes, the smile that played around those pomegranate lips ? As the foreign boat floated past our own, the lady put down the long-necked guitar, on whose golden strings her fingers had been dallying, and, with a skilful throw, cast a lily into our cabin, calling out at the same time a few foreign-sounding words. The rowers at once began to ply their oars lustily, and in the twinkling of an eye were a hundred yards in front.

" ' Follow, follow, Antonello ! ' cried the patrician—' twenty sequins are thine if we overtake her, if we discover the home of this angelic stranger.'

" ' You may rely upon me, Excellenza ; so long as the oar does not break, and my arm retains its strength, the beautiful heathen shall not escape us.'

" And now to keep my word—to maintain my hard-won fame. Swift as the flight of doves fled the stranger before us, and like a bloodthirsty falcon we followed up behind. On the left they turned into one of the side streets, and there seemed to slacken their speed as if to make sure that we had not lost their track, as if they *wished* to be followed—and then once more started in wild haste through large and small canals—right and left, and then straight forward—

past San Nicolo—till at last both the gondolas were rocking on the waters of the lagoon that lies on the road to Fusina.

"Still onwards fled the enchanting boat. Sometimes it was as if a shooting star was before us, so gloriously did the sun stream down on the glittering deck, and I was obliged to close my eyes to shut out the glare, and cease for a moment to row. Then the Count would urge me on to still greater efforts, and I would fall on my knee, and drive the oar deep into the water till the foam swirled high to the iron-comb of the figure-head.

"From out of the pursued gondola sounded now and then the sharp cry of the parrot, and then again the notes of a lute, to which the Moorish boy answered with the rattle of the tambourine, and at intervals the bewitching enticing voice of the Eastern. She sang:

Where arcades of oleander,
Purple in the gloaming show,
Where in founts marmorean wander,
Fish that gold and silvern glow;
Where nightingales
Sigh out their wails,
To love-sick maidens murm'ring low—
There, there,
Shalt thou with me my secret share.

Where the darts from Phœbus' quiver
Never pierce the myrtle groves,
Where by many a lonely river
Birds trill out their happy loves;
Where the gushing
Streamlet rushing
Through the starlit dingle roves—
There, there,
Shalt thou with me my secret share.

Orazio Memmo, one of the cleverest improvisers of his time, seized my zither, and answered at once:

Where thou leadest I will follow,
Sweet enigma, after thee;
Heed I not if joy or sorrow
The guerdon of my quest shall be—
Yet on the strand,
Enchantress, land,
And if thy heart incline to me—
There, there,
Shall I with thee thy secret share.

"We were approaching nearer and nearer to the strange gondola. Our bow cut anew the waves before the track of theirs had disappeared on the water, and the foam that followed her was like a silver cord which she had thrown out to drag us, like prisoners, behind her. Thus we ran into the Brenta Canal, flew past the sumptuous villas and pleasure houses of the rich Venetians, and stopped before a high marble portal, through the gilt bars of which we could look into a spacious garden laid out with princely magnificence.

" The stranger stepped out. By San Marco ! a queenly form with witching grace in every movement. Slowly she turned her face, lighted with the sweetest smile, once more towards my master ; from the soft, black, gazelle-like eyes gleamed on him a friendly light, and then she moved forward from the spot. The little Moor, holding a gaudy sunshade over the head of his mistress, and the chattering bird on his fist, followed close at her heels. The gates flew open, shut clashing behind them ; the pair then slowly approached the castle through a lane formed of laurels and myrtles, and vanished.

" ' Beautiful as a dream ! ' cried Signor Memmo, rousing himself from his bewilderment ; ' and to whom does the garden, the castle, belong ? '

" ' I do not know at all, Excellenza ; I see them to-day for the first time ; and yet this is the Brenta Canal—a thousand times have I rowed over it ; I know every gate, every villa, every bush—but, by San Antonio, never have I seen a stone of this castle before. Ah, Illustrissimo, take my word for it, all is not as it should be here ! It is the delusion of the devil, nothing more. Utter but one " paternoster," and the whole phantasm will vanish like a streak of mist. Have you not heard of vampires ? You have only to ask the Grecian and Illyrian boatmen, and they will tell you how the wraiths of these child-murderers appear as young and beautiful women, and fill with love the brains of the young men, and suck out their hearts' blood as they slumber. And such a vampire is the Eastern princess there—I will take the sacrament on it ! Take my advice, Excellenza. Let us return, and that as quickly as possible. Here we stand on unholy ground.'

" I looked round now for the strange gondola ; she had vanished completely, as though swallowed by the Brenta. I pointed this out to my master ; he called me superstitious and a simpleton. I began to repeat an ' ave,' but the castle refused to vanish, and remained before my eyes a substantial and obstinate fact. Black cypresses looked with elongated necks over the wall, and fig-trees stretched gnarled branches like fingers towards us, as if to beckon us in. Glittering lizards crept up the parapets and looked at us with sparkling, spiteful eyes. On the cornices stood hideous figures in marble of the most repulsive ugliness—goat-footed satyrs that made faces at us, little hunchbacked creatures with three-cornered hats, crinolined dames with horses' heads, dragons, griffins, monsters with grins and leers and distortions that only *diabolus* could invent. Among the hateful masks walked a peacock with a long trailing tail, its blue neck shimmering in the sun.

" 'How to get into the garden ?' murmured Count Orazio, staring dreamily before him. 'The gate might be scaled—a bold spring, and——'

" 'What are you thinking of, Excellentissimo ?' said I, warningly. 'For the Madonna's sake, give up the thought. Your body and soul are alike at stake. Believe me, the devil walketh about like a roaring lion, seeking whom he may devour.'

" My warning sounded in deaf ears. He had already sprung from the gondola, when a wicket opened, and an old Moor stepped before him with a deep curtsey ; he brought a request from his mistress, the Signora Smeralda, for the honour of a visit in her garden. In vain did I hold back the blinded and intoxicated patrician by his black silk mantle ; in vain did I try to excuse myself from following him ; he rushed through the gate, dragging me with him, while the old slave remained to guard our gondola.

" Strange flowers, never seen before, such as can only be supposed to grow in the pleasure-gardens of the Great Mogul himself, nodded drowsily to us as we passed. Rainbow-coloured birds flew from branch to branch, twittering, singing, shouting with almost human voice, like a chorus of happy, chattering maidens. Once an ugly, long-tailed monkey swung himself down from a tree before us, holding on with his tail to a branch ; grinned spitefully at us, and then hurried off once more into the wilderness of foliage. From one of the side alleys stepped a purple-coloured stork, as gravely as a major-domo, before us, swayed his long neck hither and thither, as if bowing to us, and then walked forward as our guide, ever and anon looking round to see if we followed. For my part, I followed as in a dream, resisting, and yet drawn forward as by some inexplicable magic.

" Presently we stood before an immense, strange-looking tree, with broad shining leaves hung thick with silvery bell-shaped blossoms.

In the shade of its branches lay costly Persian carpets and cushions of crimson velvet embroidered in pearls, and on them the heathen Princess, surrounded by a bevy of beauteous maidens, was reclining with the utmost grace. The little Moor stood at her head, fanning her with a broad fan of bright peacock's feathers. The red stork, which had hitherto walked before us, now stood still, opened wide his legs, drove his long beak into the earth, and so, slightly raising its wings for cushions, formed a three-legged easy-chair, on which Count Orazio, at a sign from the lady, sat down.

"Lost in gazing at the fair Smeralda, the Count had sat down speechless before her, while she, calling for her lute, discoursed sweet music; I had stood beside his tripodal chair torn by many feelings, when the young Moor with a cunningly-worked golden goblet full of a dark-red foaming wine stepped up to my master. 'Drink not of this brew of hell, Signor!' I whispered, and at the same time felt myself embraced by the white arm of a lovely little witch, who offered me a similar draught.

"My first instinct was to spurn from me the beautiful little elf, to dash away the magic draught—but the wine gave out so sweet an aroma, sparkled so enticingly, so brightly, within the golden walls! The eyes of the elf glanced so entreatingly at me, her arms wound themselves so tenderly about me—ah, the spirit truly was willing, but the flesh was weak!

"Only one sip, thought I, only the wetting of the tip of my tongue—that will hardly cost me my neck. And then I sipped, I tasted, I sucked, I gulped down the liquid to the very last drop—then I fell on the neck of the pretty temptress, and on looking round saw my master on his knees before the seductive Smeralda. I touched with my own the lips of my charmer—my senses whirled in a transport of delight—when breathless from out the bush rushed the negro boy, crying, 'Fly! Fly! All is lost! Porporinazzo, our gracious master, is coming! He raves in his rage!'

"Ah, the warning voice had come too late; scarcely had it sounded when a short, globular creature, of the form and colour of a dark-red apple, rolled up to Smeralda and her *inamorato*. On close observation there might certainly be discovered some indications, at the extremities of the creature, of the existence of limbs, which you might or might not take to be head, arms, and legs; but of the depressions and bumps at the north pole of this globe, to construct in fancy eyes, nose and mouth, required a quite special faculty of which I was not the master.

"'Is this the thanks, serpent, for the trust reposed in you?' shrieked Porporinazzo to the pale Smeralda. 'Is this the reward of my true and constant love? You stoop to this unbelieving dog; and me, me, Don Porporinazzo, the Grand Master of the Wardrobe of the Sultan, thou desertest! Ha, by Mohammed's sacred cat, this cries aloud for bloody vengeance! Slaves, approach!'

"Six negroes, with diabolical physiognomies, with arms and sabres bare, started from the hedges, seized Orazio and myself, and tied our hands behind our backs. In vain did the Count plead his inviolability as a Venetian noble; in vain did he threaten with the wrath of the Doge and of the Senate. The little Grand Master made a sign with his little arm—a flash, a sabre-stroke—and our two heads were rolling on the ground!

"My fair one had long ago fled behind the myrtle hedge, and Signora Smeralda had taken the stereotyped step of ladies in desperate circumstances—she had fainted. The tyrant Porporinazzo, proud of his bloody deed, had now retired once more into the palace. I could see all, for my head was lying on the ground, with its nose turned skywards. Once or twice I made convulsive efforts with my arms to catch it, and fix it on my trunk again—but my hands clutched only empty air, and sank, nerveless, down. No words can describe my condition; only those who have found themselves in a like position, and felt their heads at so unreasonable a distance from their bodies, can at all appreciate my emotions at that moment.

"The spherical Grand Master of the Wardrobe had scarcely turned his back, when Smeralda awoke out of her faint, burst into a flood of tears, and despairingly wrung her hands. At the same moment my fugitive loved one emerged from her hiding-place, but lost no time in meaningless commonplaces, urging on her mistress to make the best of the precious moments.

"'For heaven's sake, Signora,' she said, 'send for a doctor, the cleverest there is to be had. Quick! With every second the blood grows colder and colder. In five minutes it will be too late. The magic doctor, Bartolinetto, of Padua, would be just the man—only quick, quick! Send Don Flamingo to Padua—for on his activity and fidelity we can safely rely.'

"'Happy thought, Libella,' answered the Princess; 'call the Don.'

"She clapped her hands thrice. The great red stork strode quickly up, and at a few whispered words from the elf, nodded as if in assent, and flew crowing into the air.

"Four pairs of eyes gazed now with anxious expectancy towards heaven. A horrid pause, during which the fair ladies dared not, and the Count and I could not, breathe, ensued. But before you could say a 'paternoster' there was once more a rushing noise high in the air, and the mighty bird stormed down, holding Doctor Bartolinetto, like a halfpenny doll, in his beak, and placed him, a little thin brown man, neat and well dressed, though a little out of breath, upon the ground.

"A glance sufficed to make the learned man acquainted with the state of affairs. He felt our pulse, then drew from his pocket the famous Perlimpimpino powder, his own infallible discovery, and turned up his coat sleeves. He was grumbling all the time at the indelicacy of his being interrupted in the middle of a lecture and dragged forcibly out of his college, to the scandal of his audience, and loudly bemoaned the derangement of his powdered wig, which had somewhat suffered in his aerial journey; then he seized my head by the nose, sprinkled some of the Perlimpimpino powder on the neck, dabbed it on to the defective part, took Orazio's head, did the same with that—we sneezed three times with some emphasis, sprang blithely up, shook ourselves, sneezed once more—the cure was complete!

"The fair ones flew joyfully to our arms; on my cheek burned the kiss of the beautiful Smeralda, while Libella hugged the Count—but to kiss, to tear away from the embrace, to utter a startled cry, was the work of an instant. Dreadful mistake! The doctor in his hurry had stuck my head on Orazio's shoulders, and that of the noble on the trunk of the poor gondolier!

"On recovering from the first shock at the discovery we turned to vent our wrath on the doctor. The nobleman promised him a hundred lashes, and I threatened still worse things, unless he restored to each his own. Poor Bartolinetto shrugged his shoulders till they reached his ears, made the most profuse apologies, and sought to pacify us with the sophism that 'after all, a head was a head.' But every one felt the hollowness of the plea; Smeralda called him a 'wretched old quack,' Libella threatened to make for his eyes. His reproaches of ingratitude were unheeded, his suggestion of a fee was rejected with scornful laughter. At a sign from Libella, he was again seized by the stork, and carried back thus ignominiously to Padua.

"We now directed our rage against each other. Our imprecations and threats would soon have developed into actual violence, had not each feared to do a part of himself some injury while belabouring his antagonist. Which was now Orazio, which Antonello? Which nobleman, and which gondolier? My old head pleaded its new and noble body as the most important half, maintaining that the hull of a ship alone determined its class, the flag which might happen to be hoisted at its stern being a mere secondary detail. My opponent, on the other hand, compared himself to a column in which the capital is the sole feature determining to what order it is to belong. The two fair ladies tried to settle our dispute—but they were themselves soon hopelessly confused, and ended by advising us to return to Venice and lay our case before the magistrates.

"Coldly we bade them farewell and departed. Antonello-Orazio, or the peasant head on the noble trunk, threw himself in a lazy and distinguished way on the cushions, and haughtily commanded Orazio-Antonello to row back. The latter was compelled to obey, for his plebeian arms alone could ply the oars and guide the helm—but he gnashed his teeth, and swore to take dreadful vengeance for this insult; and so we rowed back—the grandee with the coarse red gondolier's cap sitting on the cushions, and laughing to scorn the proud peasant in the bows with his feathered hat and faultlessly dainty wig.

"We landed at the *piazzetta*. Negligently I drew out the purse which I found in my new clothes, and tossed the rower a coin.

"'Give me back my money!' he cried; 'give me my rings, my watch, my head!'

"'Silence, wretched slave,' I cried; 'darest thou lay hands on my inviolate person? Help, help, against this crack-brained gondolier!'

"'Help, help,' he exclaimed, 'against this insolent boatman!"

"A crowd had by this time assembled, some taking my part and some his. The Doge, who was just then walking up and down the colonnade of his palace, heard the scandal, and ordered us to be placed in the inner dungeon of the Inquisition, and brought up for trial the same evening.

"The Public Prosecutor accused us, not only of the black art itself, but of being disturbers of the public peace and conspirators against the safety of the State. 'What have we come to,' he declaimed, 'when our senators and patricians begin to change their heads as often as their wigs? To lose the head is human. The history of the illustrious Republic is not poor in examples of senators and generals, aye, and Doges too, who have suffered this misfortune—but an exchange of heads, that is, indeed, an unparalleled proceeding! What endless upheavals of the Constitution may not be expected when noble and common blood begins to mingle in the same body? What endless confusion of aristocratic and democratic principles in the same man! A short-sighted leniency in this matter may mean the disruption of the State, the crumbling into atoms of the Republic. I decree therefore the death by beheadal of both the criminals.'

"The Secretary of the Inquisition informed us of our doom; at midnight we were to pay the penalty of the little doctor's mistake. Ah, what mortal has ever met a fate like ours? Who is there can boast of being, like us, beheaded twice within the space of four-and-twenty hours?

"The keeper of the prison was, as it happened, an old friend of mine, and a second cousin. The unspeakable pickle I was in moved him even to tears, and he tried to comfort me by the assurance that the pain of beheadal was nothing to speak of—a short electric shock—a tickling sensation made piquant with a dash of pain—that was all! But I shook my head sadly, and wept. Of all this I already knew somewhat more than he could tell me. Suddenly a glorious thought struck me. After our miraculous cure, as I now remembered, my fingers, guided either by the directing brain of Orazio or by the old instinct of Antonello, had picked up the remnants of the Perlimpimpino powder left by the doctor. 'Cousin!' I now exclaimed, 'you can save me yet; you can save the Count! Hasten to his cell, remind him of the remains of the powder in his pocket, and learn from him the way to use it, and all will yet be well!' He shook his head incredulously, pressed my hand, and went.

"Sadly passed the minutes away. The horrid doubt oppressed me, whether the powder would exercise its wondrous efficacy in the absence of the doctor; whether the mystic sentences he spoke over it had not everything to do with its power; whether the gaoler could exercise the necessary quickness and accuracy in its use. The lamp that half lit up my low vault burnt darkly and sadly, as if impatiently waiting my departure, so that it too might go to sleep. In despair I threw myself on the marble bench and shut my eyes, but the glitter of the dreadful axe shone through my fast-closed eyelids. Then a knock at the door sounded in my ears, and the words : 'Wake up, Antonello, the priest is waiting ; take thy beheading, cousin, and afterwards thou mayest sleep till the trump of doom !'

"The memory of what followed—of confession and absolution, of the executioner's block—has completely vanished from my brain. I only know that I sneezed violently, opened my eyes, and found myself once more in my usual dress, lying at the foot of the column under the shadow of the holy Teodoro ; that I saw standing at my feet the patrician Orazio Memmo, and that I heard him calling, 'Hi, wake up, Antonello ! A league's row on the canal !'

"'Excellenza !' I cried, 'and you will go again to the enchanted garden of Porporinazzo ? And we are both really alive and free, and the confusion with our heads is now happily disposed of ?'

"He measured me with his eye, shook his head as if at a loss to understand me, and asked if I was still dreaming, or if the cheap Vincentin wine was muddling my brain. Dejected and silent I loosed the chain and rowed the nobleman up and down. No trace of any strange red and silver gondola could be seen, far or near. Count Orazio dozed away the hour on the water with a composure that seemed inexplicable to me. When we landed, I implored him at least to tell me whether we had no further consequences to fear on the part of the Tribunal ; whether he had not saved a pinch or two of the Perlimpimpino powder for future contingencies. But he persisted in pretending surprise and called me a fool ; and I then concluded that a stony silence had been imposed on him by the Inquisition, and that he pretended ignorance with design.

"Since that day I have not breathed a word of the incident to any human being ; and you, my children, are the first to whom, under the seal of an oath, I entrust it. Had I not, since that day, suffered from a peculiar twitching sensation in the neck, at the place where the double wound was made—especially when the weather changes—I might have taken the whole for a dreadful dream. As it is, however, the plain facts remain, burned in, in vivid colours, on my brain."

With these words my father closed his story, the telling of which had used up all his remaining strength. We sent at once for the priest of San Moise. He came with the holy Viaticum, and anointed the forehead of my father, who soon after breathed out his last sigh. Peace be with the soul of the honest man !

WILHELM HAUFF
1802–1827

THE SEVERED HAND

I WAS born in Constantinople; my father was a dragoman at the Porte, and besides, carried on a fairly lucrative business in sweet-scented perfumes and silk goods. He gave me a good education; he partly instructed me himself, and also had me instructed by one of our priests. He at first intended me to succeed him in business one day, but as I showed greater aptitude than he had expected, he destined me, on the advice of his friends, to be a doctor; for if a doctor has learned a little more than the ordinary charlatan, he can make his fortune in Constantinople. Many Franks frequented our house, and one of them persuaded my father to allow me to travel to his native land to the city of Paris, where such things could be best acquired and free of charge. He wished, however, to take me with himself gratuitously on his journey home. My father, who had also travelled in his youth, agreed, and the Frank told me to hold myself in readiness three months hence. I was beside myself with joy at the idea of seeing foreign countries, and eagerly awaited the moment when we should embark. The Frank had at last concluded his business and prepared himself for the journey. On the evening before our departure my father led me into his little bedroom. There I saw splendid dresses and arms lying on the table. My looks were, however, chiefly attracted to an immense heap of gold, for I had never before seen so much collected together.

My father embraced me and said, "Behold, my son, I have procured for thee clothes for the journey. These weapons are thine; they are the same which thy grandfather hung around me when I went abroad. I know that thou canst use them aright; but only make use of them when thou art attacked; on such occasions, however, defend thyself bravely. My property is not large; behold I have divided it into three parts, one part for thee, another for my support and spare money, but the third is to me a sacred and untouched property, it is for thee in the hour of need." Thus spoke my old father, tears standing in his eyes, perhaps from some foreboding, for I never saw him again.

The journey passed off very well; we had soon reached the land of the Franks, and six days later we arrived in the large city of Paris. There my Frankish friend hired a room for me, and advised me to spend wisely my money, which amounted in all to two thousand dollars. I lived three years in this city, and learned what is necessary for a skilful doctor to know. I should not, however, be stating the truth if I said that I liked being there, for the customs of this nation displeased me; besides, I had only a few chosen friends there, and these were noble young men.

The longing after home at last possessed me mightily; during the whole of that time I had not heard anything from my father, and I therefore seized a favourable opportunity of reaching home. An embassy from France left for Turkey. I acted as surgeon to the suite of the Ambassador and arrived happily in Stamboul. My father's house was locked, and the neighbours, who were surprised on seeing me, told me my father had died two months ago. The priest who had instructed me in my youth brought me the key; alone and desolate I entered the empty house. All was still in the same position as my father had left it, only the gold which I was to inherit was gone. I questioned the priest about it, and he, bowing, said, "Your father died a saint, for he has bequeathed his gold to the Church." This was and remained inexplicable to me. However, what could I do? I had no witness against the priest, and had to be glad that he had not considered the house and the goods of my father as a bequest. This was the first misfortune that I encountered. Henceforth nothing but ill-luck attended me. My reputation as doctor would not spread at all, because I was ashamed to act the charlatan; and I felt everywhere the want of the recommendation of my father, who would have introduced me to the richest and most distinguished, but who now no longer thought of the poor Zaleukos! The goods of my father also had no sale, for his customers came no more after his death, and new ones are only to be got slowly.

Thus when I was one day meditating sadly over my position, it occurred to me that I had often seen in France men of my nation travelling through the country exhibiting their goods in the markets of the towns. I remembered that the people liked to buy of them, because they came from abroad, and that such a business would be most lucrative. Immediately I resolved what to do. I disposed of my father's house, gave part of the money to a trusty friend to keep for me, and with the rest I bought what are very rare in France, shawls, silk goods, ointments and oils, took a berth on board a ship, and thus entered upon my second journey to the land of the Franks. It seemed as if fortune had favoured me again as soon as I had turned my back upon the Castles of the Dardanelles. Our journey was short and successful. I travelled through the large and small towns of the Franks, and found everywhere willing buyers of my goods. My friend in Stamboul always sent me fresh stores, and my wealth increased day by day. When I had saved at last so much that I thought I might venture on a greater undertaking, I travelled with my goods to Italy. I must, however, confess to something, which brought me not a little money: I also employed my knowledge of physic. On reaching a town, I had it published that a Greek physician had arrived, who had already healed many; and in fact my balsam and medicine gained me many a sequin. Thus I had at length reached the city of Florence in Italy.

I resolved upon remaining in this town for some time, partly because I liked it so well, partly also because I wished to recruit myself from the exertions of my travels. I hired a vaulted shop, in that part of the town called Sta. Croce, and not far from this a couple of nice rooms at an inn, leading out upon a balcony. I immediately had my bills circulated, which announced me to be both physician and merchant. Scarcely had I opened my shop when I was besieged by buyers, and in spite of my high prices I sold more than any one else, because I was obliging and friendly towards my customers. Thus I had already lived four days happily in Florence, when one evening, as I was about to close my vaulted room, and on examining once more the contents of my ointment boxes, as I was in the habit of doing, I found in one of the small boxes a piece of paper, which I did not remember to have put into it.

I unfolded the paper, and found in it an invitation to be on the bridge which is called Ponte Vecchio that night exactly at midnight. I was thinking for a long time as to who it might be who had invited me there; and not knowing a single soul in Florence, I thought perhaps I should be secretly conducted to a patient, a thing which had already often occurred. I therefore determined to proceed thither, but took care to gird on the sword which my father had once presented to me.

When it was close upon midnight I set out on my journey, and soon reached the Ponte Vecchio. I found the bridge deserted, and determined to await the appearance of him who called me. It was a cold night; the moon shone brightly, and I looked down upon the waves of the Arno, which sparkled far away in the moonlight. It was now striking twelve o'clock from all the churches of the city, when I looked up and saw a tall man standing before me completely covered in a scarlet cloak, one end of which hid his face.

At first I was somewhat frightened, because he had made his appearance so suddenly; but was, however, myself again shortly afterwards, and said, "If it is you who have ordered me here, say what you want" The man dressed in scarlet turned round and said in an undertone, "Follow!" At this, however, I felt a little timid to go alone with this stranger. I stood still and said, "Not so, sir; kindly first tell me where; you might also let me see your countenance a little, in order to convince me that you wish me no harm." The red one, however, did not seem to pay any attention to this. "If thou art unwilling, Zaleukos, remain," he replied, and continued his way. I grew angry. "Do you think," I exclaimed, "a man like myself allows himself to be made a fool of, and to have waited on this cold night for nothing?"

In three bounds I had reached him, seized him by his cloak, and cried still louder, whilst laying hold of my sabre with my other hand. His cloak, however, remained in my hand, and the stranger had disappeared round the nearest corner. I became calmer by degrees. I had the cloak at any rate, and it was this which would give me the key to this remarkable adventure. I put it on and continued my way home. When I was at a distance of about a hundred paces from it, some one brushed very closely by me and whispered in the language of the Franks, "Take care, Count, nothing can be done to-night." Before I had time, however, to turn round, this somebody had passed, and I merely saw a shadow hovering along the houses. I perceived that these words did not concern me, but rather the cloak, yet it gave me no explanation concerning the affair. On the following morning I considered what was to be done. At first I had intended to have the cloak cried in the streets, as if I had found it. But then the stranger might send for it by a third person, and thus no light would be thrown upon the matter. Whilst I was thus thinking, I examined the cloak more closely. It was made of thick Genoese velvet, scarlet in colour, edged with astrakhan fur and richly embroidered with gold. The magnificent appearance of the cloak put a thought into my mind which I resolved to carry out.

I carried it into my shop and exposed it for sale, but placed such a high price upon it that I was sure nobody would buy it. My object in this was to scrutinise everybody sharply who might ask for the fur cloak; for the figure of the stranger, which I had seen but superficially though with some certainty, after the loss of the cloak, I should recognise amongst a thousand. There were many would-be purchasers for the cloak, the extraordinary beauty of which attracted everybody; but none resembled the stranger in the slightest degree, and nobody was willing to pay such a high price as two hundred sequins for it. What astonished me was that on asking somebody or other if there was not such a cloak in Florence, they all answered "No," and assured me they never had seen so precious and tasteful a piece of work.

Evening was drawing near, when at last a young man appeared, who had already been to my place, and who had also offered me a great deal for the cloak. He threw a purse with sequins upon the table, and exclaimed, "Of a truth, Zaleukos, I must have thy cloak, should I turn into a beggar over it!" He immediately began to count his pieces of gold. I was in a dangerous position: I had only exposed the cloak, in order merely to attract the attention of my stranger, and now a young fool came to pay an immense price for it. However, what could I do? I yielded; for on the other hand I was delighted at the idea of being so handsomely recompensed for my nocturnal adventure.

The young man put the cloak around him and went away, but on reaching the threshold he returned; whilst unfastening a piece of paper which had been tied to the cloak, and throwing it towards me, he exclaimed, "Here, Zaleukos, hangs something which I dare say does not belong to the cloak." I picked up the piece of paper carelessly, but behold, on it these words were written: "Bring the cloak at the appointed hour to-night to the Ponte Vecchio, four hundred sequins are thine." I stood thunderstruck. Thus I had lost my fortune and completely missed my aim! Yet I did not think long. I picked up the two hundred sequins, jumped after the one who had bought the cloak, and said, "Dear friend, take back your sequins, and give me the cloak; I cannot possibly part with it." He first regarded the matter as a joke; but when he saw that I was in earnest, he became angry at my demand, called me a fool, and finally it came to blows.

However, I was fortunate enough to wrench the cloak from him in the scuffle, and was about to run away with it, when the young man called the police to his assistance, and we both appeared before the judge. The latter was much surprised at the accusation, and adjudicated the cloak in favour of my adversary. I offered the young man twenty, fifty, eighty, even a hundred sequins in addition to his two hundred, if he would part with the cloak. What my entreaties could not do, my gold did. He accepted it. I, however, went away with the cloak triumphantly, and had to appear to the whole town of Florence as a madman. I did not care, however, about the opinion of the people; I knew better than they that I profited after all by the bargain.

Impatiently I awaited the night. At the same hour as before I went with the cloak under my arm towards the Ponte Vecchio. With the last stroke of twelve the figure appeared out of the darkness and came towards me. It was unmistakably the man whom I had seen yesterday. "Hast thou the cloak?" he asked me. "Yes, sir," I replied; "but it cost me a hundred sequins ready money." "I know it," replied the other. "Look here, here are four hundred." He went with me towards the wide balustrade of the bridge, and counted out the money. There were four hundred; they sparkled magnificently in the moonlight; their glitter rejoiced my heart. Alas, I did not anticipate that this would be its last joy. I put the money into my pocket, and was desirous of thoroughly looking at my kind and unknown stranger; but he wore a mask, through which dark eyes stared at me frightfully. "I thank you, sir, for your kindness," I said to him; "what else do you require of me? I tell you beforehand it must be an honourable transaction." "There is no occasion for alarm," he replied, whilst winding the cloak around his shoulders; "I require your assistance as surgeon, not for one alive, but dead."

"What do you mean?" I exclaimed, full of surprise. "I arrived with my sister from abroad," he said, and beckoned me at the same time to follow him. "I lived here with her at the house of a friend. My sister died yesterday suddenly of a disease, and my relatives wish to bury her to-morrow. According to an old custom of our family all are to be buried in the tomb of our ancestors; many, notwithstanding, who died in foreign countries are buried there and embalmed.

I do not grudge my relatives her body, but for my father I want at least the head of his daughter, in order that he may see her once more." This custom of severing the heads of beloved relatives appeared to me somewhat awful, yet I did not dare to object to it lest I should offend the stranger. I told him that I was acquainted with the embalming of the dead, and begged him to conduct me to the deceased. Yet I could not help asking him why all this must be done so mysteriously and at night. He answered me that his relatives, who considered his intention horrible, objected to it by daylight; if only the head were severed, then they could say no more about it; although he might have brought me the head, yet a natural feeling had prevented him from severing it himself.

In the meantime we had reached a large, splendid house. My companion pointed it out to me as the end of our nocturnal walk. We passed the principal entrance of the house, entered a little door, which the stranger carefully locked behind him, and then ascended in the dark a narrow spiral staircase. It led towards a dimly lighted passage, out of which we entered a room lighted by a lamp fastened to the ceiling.

In this room was a bed, on which the corpse lay. The stranger turned aside his face, evidently endeavouring to hide his tears. He pointed towards the bed, telling me to do my business well and quickly, and left the room.

I took my instruments, which I as surgeon always carried about with me, and approached the bed. Only the head of the corpse was visible, and it was so beautiful that I experienced involuntarily the deepest sympathy. Dark hair hung down in long plaits, the features were pale, the eyes closed. At first I made an incision into the skin, after the manner of surgeons when amputating a limb. I then took my sharpest knife, and with one stroke cut the throat. But oh, horror! The dead opened her eyes, but immediately closed them again, and with a deep sigh she now seemed to breathe her last. At the same moment a stream of hot blood shot towards me from the wound. I was convinced that the poor creature had been killed by me. That she was dead there was no doubt, for there was no recovery from this wound. I stood for some minutes in painful anguish at what had happened. Had the "red-cloak" deceived me, or had his sister perhaps merely been apparently dead? The latter seemed to me more likely. But I dare not tell the brother of the deceased that perhaps a little less deliberate cut might have awakened her without killing her; therefore I wished to sever the head completely; but once more the dying woman groaned, stretched herself out in painful movements, and died.

Fright overpowered me, and, shuddering, I hastened out of the room. But outside in the passage it was dark; for the light was out, no trace of my companion was to be seen, and I was obliged, haphazard, to feel my way in the dark along the wall, in order to reach the staircase. I discovered it at last and descended, partly falling and partly gliding. But there was not a soul downstairs. I merely found the door ajar, and breathed freer on reaching the street, for I had felt very strange inside the house. Urged on by terror, I rushed towards my dwelling-place, and buried myself in the cushions of my bed, in order to forget the terrible thing that I had done.

But sleep deserted me, and only the morning admonished me again to take courage. It seemed to me probable that the man who had induced me to commit this nefarious deed, as it now appeared to me, might not denounce me. I immediately resolved to set to work in my vaulted room, and if possible to assume an indifferent look. But alas! an additional circumstance, which I only now noticed, increased my anxiety still more. My cap and my girdle, as well as my instruments, were wanting, and I was uncertain as to whether I had left them in the room of the murdered girl, or whether I had lost them in my flight. The former seemed indeed the more likely, and thus I could easily be discovered as the murderer.

At the accustomed hour I opened my vaulted room. My neighbour came in, as was his wont every morning, for he was a talkative man. "Well," he said, "what do you say about the terrible affair which has occurred during the night?" I pretended not to know anything. "What, do you not know what is known all over the town? Are you not aware that the loveliest flower in Florence, Bianca, the Governor's daughter, was murdered last night? I saw her only yesterday driving through the streets in so cheerful a manner with her intended one, for to-day the marriage was to have taken place." I felt deeply wounded at each word of my neighbour. Many a time my torment was renewed, for every one of my customers told me of the affair, each one more ghastly than the other, and yet nobody could relate anything more terrible than that which I had seen myself.

About mid-day a police officer entered my shop and requested me to send the people away. " Signor Zaleukos," he said, producing the things which I had missed, " do these things belong to you ? " I was thinking as to whether I should not entirely repudiate them, but on seeing through the door, which stood ajar, my landlord and several acquaintances, I determined not to aggravate the affair by telling a lie, and acknowledged myself as the owner of the things. The police officer asked me to follow him, and led me towards a large building which I soon recognised as the prison. There he showed me into a room meanwhile.

My situation was terrible, as I thought of it in my solitude. The idea of having committed a murder, unintentionally, constantly presented itself to my mind. I also could not conceal from myself that the glitter of the gold had captivated my feelings, otherwise I should not have fallen blindly into the trap. Two hours after my arrest I was led out of my cell. I descended several steps until at last I reached a great hall. Around a long table draped in black were seated twelve men, mostly old men. There were benches along the sides of the hall, filled with the most distinguished of Florence. The galleries, which were above, were thickly crowded with spectators. When I had stepped towards the table covered with black cloth, a man with a gloomy and sad countenance rose ; it was the Governor. He said to the assembly that he as the father in this affair could not sentence, and that he resigned his place on this occasion to the eldest of the Senators. The eldest of the Senators was an old man at least ninety years of age. He stood in a bent attitude, and his temples were covered with thin white hair, but his eyes were as yet very fiery, and his voice powerful and weighty. He commenced by asking me whether I confessed to the murder. I requested him to allow me to speak, and related undauntedly and with a clear voice what I had done, and what I knew.

I noticed that the Governor, during my recital, at one time turned pale, and at another time red. When I had finished, he rose angrily : " What, wretch ! " he exclaimed, " dost thou even dare to impute a crime which thou hast committed from greediness to another ? " The Senator reprimanded him for his interruption, since he had voluntarily renounced his right ; besides it was not clear that I did the deed from greediness, for, according to his own statement, nothing had been stolen from the victim. He even went further. He told the Governor that he must give an account of the early life of his daughter, for then only it would be possible to decide whether I had spoken the truth or not. At the same time he adjourned the court for the day, in order, as he said, to consult the papers of the deceased, which the Governor would give him. I was again taken back to my prison, where I spent a wretched day, always fervently wishing that a link between the deceased and the "red-cloak" might be discovered. Full of hope, I entered the Court of Justice the next day. Several letters were lying upon the table. The old Senator asked me whether they were in my handwriting. I looked at them and noticed that they must have been written by the same hand as the other two papers which I had received. I communicated this to the Senators, but no attention was paid to it, and they told me that I might have written both, for the signature of the letters was undoubtedly a Z, the first letter of my name. The letters, however, contained threats against the deceased, and warnings against the marriage which she was about to contract.

The Governor seemed to have given extraordinary information concerning me, for I was treated with more suspicion and rigour on this day. I referred, to justify myself, to my papers which must be in my room, but was told they had been looked for without success. Thus at the conclusion of this sitting all hope vanished, and on being brought into the court the third day, judgment was pronounced on me. I was convicted of wilful murder and condemned to death. Things had come to such a pass! Deserted by all that was precious to me upon earth, far away from home, I was to die innocently in the bloom of my life.

On the evening of this terrible day which had decided my fate, I was sitting in my lonely cell, my hopes were gone, my thoughts steadfastly fixed upon death, when the door of my prison opened, and in came a man, who for a long time looked at me silently. "Is it thus I find you again, Zaleukos?" he said. I had not recognised him by the dim light of my lamp, but the sound of his voice roused in me old remembrances. It was Valetti, one of those few friends whose acquaintance I made in the city of Paris when I was studying there. He said that he had come to Florence accidentally, where his father, who was a distinguished man, lived. He had heard about my affair, and had come to see me once more, and to hear from my own lips how I could have committed such a crime. I related to him the whole affair. He seemed much surprised at it, and adjured me, as my only friend, to tell him all, in order not to leave the world with a lie behind me. I confirmed my assertions with an oath that I had spoken the truth, and that I was not guilty of anything, except that the glitter of the gold had dazzled me, and that I had not perceived the improbability of the story of the stranger. " Did you not know Bianca ? " he asked me. I assured him that I had never seen her. Valetti now related to me that a profound mystery rested on the affair, that the Governor had very much accelerated my condemnation, and now a report was spread that I had known Bianca for a long time, and had murdered her out of revenge for her marriage with some one else. I told him that all this coincided exactly with the " red-cloak," but that I was unable to prove his participation in the affair. Valetti embraced me weeping, and promised me to do all that was possible, at least to save my life.

I had little hope, though I knew that Valetti was a clever man, well versed in the law, and that he would do all in his power to save my life. For two long days I was in uncertainty ; at last Valetti appeared. " I bring consolation, though painful. You will live and be free with the loss of one hand." Affected, I thanked my friend for saving my life. He told me that the Governor had been inexorable in having the affair investigated a second time, but that he at last, in order not to appear unjust, had agreed that, if a similar case could be found in the law books of the history of Florence, my punishment should be the same as the one recorded in these books. He and his father had searched in the old books day and night, and at last found a case quite similar to mine. The sentence was : That his left hand be cut off, his property confiscated, and he himself banished for ever. This was my punishment also, and he asked me to prepare for the painful hour which awaited me. I will not describe to you that terrible hour, when I laid my hand upon the block in the public market-place and my own blood shot over me in broad streams.

Valetti took me to his house until I had recovered ; he then most generously supplied me with money for travelling, for all I had acquired with so much difficulty had fallen a prey to the law. I left Florence for Sicily and embarked on the first ship that I found for Constantinople. My hope was fixed upon the sum which I had entrusted to my friend. I also requested to be allowed to live with him. But how great was my astonishment on being asked why I did not wish to live in my own house. He told me that some unknown man had bought a house in the Greek Quarter in my name, and this very man had also told the neighbours of my early arrival. I immediately proceeded thither accompanied by my friend, and was received by all my old acquaintances joyfully. An old merchant gave me a letter, which the man who had bought the house for me had left behind. I read as follows: " Zaleukos! Two hands are prepared to work incessantly, in order that you may not feel the loss of one of yours. The house which you see and all its contents are yours, and every year you will receive enough to be counted amongst the rich of your people. Forgive him who is unhappier than yourself!" I could guess who had written it, and in answer to my question the merchant told me it had been a man, whom he took for a Frank, and who had worn a scarlet cloak. I knew enough to understand that the stranger was, after all, not entirely devoid of noble intentions. In my new house I found everything arranged in the best style, also a vaulted room stored with goods, more splendid than I had ever had. Ten years have passed since. I still continue my commercial travels, more from old custom than necessity, yet I have never again seen that country where I became so unfortunate. Every year since, I have received a thousand gold pieces; and although I rejoice to know that unfortunate man to be noble, yet he cannot relieve me of the sorrow of my soul, for the terrible picture of the murdered Bianca is continually on my mind.

JOHANN GABRIEL SEIDL
1804–1875

THE BLUE APRON

HARDLY had I rung the door-bell at my friend the doctor's house, when once again two bright black eyes looked out on me through the small grilled opening in the top panel of the massive street door. Again, as often before, a silvery voice put the question, " Who is there ? " And again the door swung back immediately I gave my name, and a dainty young woman told me in accents of regret, " Oh, dear sir, I am sorry you have called in vain ; the doctor has gone out to visit some friends in town."

How different this kindly information from the stupid answers often received on similar occasions from an ignorant domestic, or from the arrogant shoulder-shrug of an overbearing flunkey ! Very rarely, I must own, did the girl's polite regrets quite satisfy me ; I felt a desire to linger ; I questioned her about the details of the doctor's journey to town, as to when he was likely to return, and about other points sufficiently interesting to ensure an interesting answer. I always felt then as if I was speaking not to a poor servant girl, but to some young lady. With a feeling of tender shyness I glanced at her face, so dear to me, and so pallid—with always that look of deep pain just above the bright eyes. I noted her evasive replies to any question of mine, however discreetly worded, as to her position before she came into my friend's service.

I had meant to question the doctor long ago about this girl, who, as her dress and idiom proclaimed, had obviously come from some far-away district. But in spite of the unquestionable trust that I reposed both in him and in this dear girl, I had so far not found the courage necessary. You will admit there are certain situations which only become painful to those immediately concerned when they are made the subject of idle gossip and inquisitiveness, and I did not wish my curiosity to appear inquisitive. At last, on a certain evening of pleasant, intimate talk at my friend's, when we discussed the lazy uncertainty and tedium of bachelordom, the opportunity presented itself quite unsought.

"As far as my state of single blessedness goes," declared the doctor, "I have nothing whatever to complain of: I enjoy all its advantages; and as to its disadvantages, which overtake the unwary, the clumsy, and the inexperienced, in short, nearly every man, my—Jette protects me against these."

"Your Jette?" answered I, "that gentle and modest girl who always opens the door to me? She seems to be a very good-natured and domesticated person; one sees her excellent qualities in everything she does."

"She would do anything for me," replied the doctor; "I suppose I should not speak about it, but I really owe my good temper, as well as my broad views on certain matters of common prejudice, to her devotion to me. She hails from the Rhine; I came upon her quite by accident on my last journey there."

"I always thought she belonged to the Rhenish counties. Is she an orphan? I have often wondered what strange story her sadness hid, and her whole appearance has often curiously moved me."

I saw the doctor hesitate, and then, preparing to continue, he said, "I think I will tell you the story of this poor girl, in the hope that you will understand that my intentions are honest towards her. Just listen then. On my travels I arrived one day in a village upon the banks of the Rhine; the river bordered it on the one side, while the other three sides were shut in by hills rising to some considerable height. It was Sunday, and the church bells were calling the people to service. Fresh-complexioned and happy girls passed me, wishing me the time of day. Cleanliness and prosperity were apparent in both their bearing and their costumes. Girls and youths were making their way to church. I was particularly struck with the spotless whiteness of the apron that every girl was wearing, and in which they appeared to take especial delight, although these aprons seemed only an insignificant addition to the simple, tasteful dresses they were wearing. Just as I had turned the corner near the church, a strange sight met my eyes; a pretty, pale young girl, all alone—it was Jette—hurried along, wearing a glaring blue apron; she called out friendly merry greetings as she came up to the others, but they kept off from her as if she was a leper, and crying, 'The blue apron!' they left her by herself. Bursting into tears, Jette tottered backwards and found support against the village lime tree—I was almost behind it as I stood there watching —and sobbing loudly she wrung her hands in utter despair. The unhappy girl aroused my sympathy. I noticed how the girls in passing turned away from her, whispering scornfully; how proudly they straightened and surveyed their dazzling white aprons, while tears of desolate despair fell on the blue apron of the girl they despised.

" That the colour of the apron had some bearing on the display of public opinion I had gathered by now, without, however, guessing the reason. Then the remarks of some of the youths as they passed gave me the clue I had been seeking to find. The poor girl never moved under all the scorn that was heaped on her, and for a long time stood rooted to the spot. Suddenly, as if roused by some powerful impulse, she pulled herself together and feebly staggered away through a narrow alley. I followed. On the bank of the Rhine she stopped. I was immediately behind her, though unnoticed. I saw her clasp her hands and so stand in silent prayer, then tear the blue apron off, and raise herself to spring into the waves. . . . She awoke from a long, death-like swoon in my room in the village inn, where I had had her brought, careless of the remarks of the village people, whose scorn mattered nothing to me. When she revived, I told her who I was, and that at present she was just to look upon me as her doctor.

" She just did all I asked her, and, much to my joy, soon fell into a sound, strengthening sleep. This gave me time to make the necessary inquiries about her. My host of the village inn, who also was the girl's master, told me all her history, with much unnecessary embroidery and many a clumsy joke. It was not difficult for me to separate the truth from the unsavoury prejudice the man seemed to delight in, and the story of this poor girl may be told as follows.

" The village in which I had been able to save this human life was the girl's birthplace, a place which, in consequence of its solitary and isolated position, had fostered amongst its inhabitants some isolated and peculiar ideas and habits; so that—as it often happens—certain sayings, habits, and jokes were peculiar to just this particular secluded hamlet. The girl lost her parents, poor farming people, early, and was brought up as a daughter by an old novel-reading but good and dear lady of the manor in the neighbourhood, who wanted some one to cheer her in her old age. This old lady, with her novels, naturally influenced the girl to some extent, and Jette soon began to assimilate the slow poison of the mixed and cheap literature which, in her romantic loneliness, was all nature could feed on. Strict seclusion, a total lack of knowledge of the world, and want of every intellectual support helped further in the development of a lively imagination in the wrong direction. Suddenly Jette's benefactress died, before yet she had provided for her adopted daughter. For the second time Jette found herself an orphan, and this on the threshold of the most active development of her nature. Left to her fate, used to an atmosphere of culture and to kindly treatment, she now hired herself as waiting-maid to the small but well-ordered inn of the village where I had stopped. Here travellers descending the ancient river Rhine often stopped and stayed, and Jette, with her exceptional education, soon made herself popular with them, and also with mine host and his wife.

" One day there arrived—so she told me herself, after I had sufficiently assured her that all her story was well known to me—an artist, a painter—a young man, curly haired, with ' Vandyke ' moustache and beard, fiery eyes, high forehead over which the broad-brimmed hat sat recklessly on abundant locks, vivacious in his bearing, and sincere in his talk—a Viennese. It was a case of immediate, mutual attraction. As the artist was a companion to a rich nobleman, the length of his stay in the village did not lie within his inclination. However, it was long enough for two portraits to be painted, two rings to be exchanged, and a troth to be pledged hurriedly—a troth that was to poison the life's happiness of poor Jette. The painter left—against his will and broken-hearted as he said—yet he left, and was far away, far over hill and dale, when rumour first began to tell the world of poor deceived Jette's shame. Soon the anguish of her soul began to torture her. Then—afterwards—when weak and ill, for weeks only just able to creep about the house a broken creature, suffering many a slighting look and many a hard word, there came the day—it was the Sunday of my arrival in the village—when for the first time she was again to set her foot into the open. In the church close by the organ already invited the village folk to worship. A sweet longing seemed to impel her to make an effort to throw off her heart the burden of sin, to direct her first steps to holy ground, there to repent and to purify herself. She begged for her Sunday clothes. Silently the second serving-maid of the inn pushed towards her the chair whereon they lay. Already had she put the simple skirt upon her slender figure, already the neat head-dress graced her beautiful hair, already was her hand extended for the apron of dazzling whiteness, when she noticed, and shrank back terrified, that instead of an apron of pure white, one of glaring blue had been laid out for her. Now came to her the terrible meaning of an expression that she had heard referred to as a frightful insult, without understanding its true significance.

" There ruled in the village of her birth, as well as in Bavaria and several other German provinces, an old custom, that a girl who had been guilty of the same sin as poor Jette must never again wear a white, but, on the contrary, always a blue apron. The purport of this custom is to keep their guilt continually before their eyes : in church no one will admit these outcasts to their pew ; on festive occasions they will not find any companions ; at dances no partners will seek them out ; they have to put up with every coarse joke ; and should they attempt to complain of their lot people just turn away and say, ' Oh, let her be, she wears the blue apron.'

" Jette had to learn from bitter experience how terribly severe a simple article of dress, of an otherwise unimportant colour, could render her punishment. How retribution will use the apparently insignificant to chastise the more severely its victim ! No one listened to her entreaties and prayers for just the oldest, the worst apron to be found in the house, if only white, and so she needs had to put on—and she did so almost unconsciously—the dreaded blue cloth. After a while she appeared to take heart and stepped into the street to mix with the lasses now on their way to church, seemingly to try to smuggle herself, the unclean with the clean, into the place of worship. The village maidens in their aprons of splendid whiteness, mostly all of them Jette's playmates in early youth, sauntered along in happy pairs, in intimate companionship and solemn edification. She could not resist her longing further ; the knowledge of her convalescence after the long weary battle with death, the hope that her friends in the joy at beholding her once more would have no room left in their hearts for reproaches, led her to forget for the moment completely the outward and visible sign of her disgrace. How terribly and painfully she was reminded of it I myself witnessed, as I have told you already.

" While waking and sleeping this poor creature still battled with her painful and hard yet not undeserved punishment, I broke to her gently my intention of returning to Vienna, and taking her with me, to entrust to her care in all honour the management of my house.

" My simple nature, my unaffected pity, my sudden proposition—in short, everything decided her to come with me. I kept my word to her absolutely, so much I may say in my own praise ; she does not want for or miss anything here, with me—nothing—except——"

" Perhaps the chance to see him," I interrupted, " who is the cause of all her misfortune."

" This chance is given her more so here than anywhere else," rejoined the doctor. " The painter hailed from Vienna, and his heart, so she still insists to this day, was not bad. If I should be able to do more for her, dear friend, than I at first intended! What do you say to that ? "

" I say that it would be one of your most celebrated cases, doctor. To heal a broken heart, what a splendid triumph! I have never yet done any detective work, but if I could trace this young, curly-headed painter fellow of the fiery eyes and the 'Vandyke' beard I would try to cultivate his friendship. In an hour of mutual confidences I would touch his heart, and the tenderest place in his conscience, and try and recall to his memory the enormous debt of his past which he left unpaid, the betrayal of an innocent girl. If he then should tell me that his only wish in life was to atone for his error, how gladly I would extend to him a friendly hand and lead him to you, dear doctor. Such a balancing of the fates would be a heavenly thing! "

Silently the doctor and I shook hands; just then Jette entered the room. She may have noticed that our eyes were moist as we looked up at her.

FRITZ REUTER
1810–1874

HIS SERENITY AND THE THUNDER-STORM

ON his way to school the Konrektor felt so cheery and good-natured that his pupils might have expected to have a good day. As he stepped into the schoolroom he had the pleasant surprise of seeing a complete Roman battle before him, which his precious boys were carrying out in honour of Livy, and probably to give him an unexpected pleasure, and the noise they made was as natural as if the room were full of genuine Roman soldiers and genuine horses.

It was all very well for the boys, but it was not quite befitting the quiet which is supposed to reign in a schoolroom ; nor was it the best means of allaying the flushed spirits of a schoolmaster who had his own private troubles to contend with. The Herr Konrektor sat down on his platform, opened his Homer, and when the noise had somewhat subsided, he gave vent to his ire : " Now listen, you dunces ; first learn something, then you'll be better able to play heroes ! Last time we stopped just before the splendid passage where Hector said good-bye to his dear wife Andromache, and she exhorts him—

" *Δαιμόνιε*, says she ; *φθίσει σε τὸ σὸν μένος, οὐδ' ἐλεαίρεις*, says she ; but it's hardly worth while to read anything so fine to you scatterbrained dolts. *παῖδά τε νηπίαχον*, says she ; *καὶ ἔμ' ἄμμορον, ἣ τάχα χήρη*, says she. Karl Wendt, confound you, if you don't stop talking I'll stand you up by my platform, and then it'll be *my* turn to have a talk with you. *σεῦ ἔσομαι*, says she, *τάχα γάρ σε κατακτανέουσιν Ἀχαιοὶ πάντες ἐφορμηθέντες*, says she ; *ἐμοὶ δέ κε κέρδιον εἴη σεῦ ἀφαμαρτούσῃ*, and so on, says she.—Langnickel, you begin."

And Langnickel cleared his throat once or twice and nudged his neighbours right and left with his elbows, as much as to say : " Fellows, help me ; I'm in an awful fix."

" Well," said the Konrektor, " how long before you're ready ? *Δαιμόνιε*—what does that mean ? "

" *Oh, thou monster !* " said Langnickel, looking at the Herr Konrektor very doubtfully to see what he would say.

" It's more likely you are a monster. The next, go on," said the Konrektor, pointing to Karl Siemsen. " Well, Karl ! Eh ? the word's not easy ; how do we call a fellow that can do more than ordinary folks ? "

" A Tausendsasa," said Karl.

" Well, I never ! We may say that for a joke, but do you suppose Hector's wife felt much like joking just then ? Nay, she is scolding him. You madcap you, says she, bridle your pluck ! says she. Have you no pity for your little boy—she means her little Astyanax that she has on her arm—and for poor luckless me, says she, who will soon enough be a widow ? For how long will it be, says she, before the Achæans pitch in on you and kill you, and what is left to me but sorrow when I sit here without you ? says she. Well, here I am translating the whole of Homer for you. Go ahead, Karl Siemsen !" he exclaimed. Then the door was opened, and one of his Serene Highness's lackeys came in.

" Herr Konrektor, his Highness wants to know if you think we'll get a thunderstorm to-day."

Now this was the last straw for the Konrektor's patience. He turned upon the fellow in a mad choler and shouted, " Yes ! Go and tell his Highness we'll get seven."

" Seven ? " asked the lackey, looking blank and walking toward the door, and the Konrektor called after him : " Yes, seven ! Tell him we'll get seven ! "

The first lesson was over and the second had begun ; it was Latin, and there was Virgil's *Bucolica* to translate.

The Herr Konrektor had in the meantime taken a look at the weather, and now he was quite sure there was a storm coming up ; his pupils had taken a look at his face, and they also knew for sure that there was a storm brewing ; they were only doubtful where the lightning would strike. This question was about to be solved in a drastic manner when his Serenity sent the lackey once more :

" Herr Konrektor, his Highness wants you to come to him at once. The storm is coming mighty fast."

" Tell his Highness," cried the Konrektor in a rage, and was about to add, " to remember me to his grandmother," but he recalled himself and said : " First I must be through school, then I'll come."

At the palace things had gone on queerly enough for a while ; his most Serene Highness walked up and down in his apartments with pale cheeks, as if he were the walking ghost of the deceased Henry of the Three Oaks; the footmen stood in the corners and along the walls silent and fearful like the stage mimes when Dame Macbeth walks about washing her hands; the gentleman of the bedchamber, Von Knüppelsdörp, carefully bolted all the windows and doors, and looked as if he were gagged.

"Rand," called his Highness in an undertone, "smoke is a good conductor. Are all the fires put out?"

"Yes, your Highness, all except the kitchen—you know the dinner has to be cooked."

"We shall not dine to-day. Tell them to throw water on the fire."

"Dear me, your Highness," Rand began, for fast-days were not much to his taste, not even when there was a thunderstorm.

"Do you hear what I say?" cried his Highness with such alacrity that he frightened himself.

"And there shall be no bells pulled; the sound is a good conductor," he added in a lower tone.

"The sound, your Highness?"

"Confound you, fool! I—I say! It *might* draw, you know!" whispered his Highness snappishly.

"Humph," said Rand to himself, looking out of the window with one eye, "we can afford to be cross; the storm isn't high yet; later on we'll be more polite."

"Goodness me," said his Highness nervously, "why doesn't the Konrektor come?"

"Good gracious! what good is the Konrektor? He's no more able to——"

"He *must* be able to, he *must*! Here, get these buckles off from my shoes; metal is a good conductor. Is all in order in my cabinet?"

"Yes," growled Rand, looking at the floor while trying to take the buckles off, "we've put up all the mummery, and the carpenter says it looks for all the world like a bird-cage."

"Gracious goodness! Did you hear that? Did you hear it, I say? It's here already! Where can the Konrektor be? I am going into my cabinet. Send for the Konrektor. Don't go so fast! Don't go so fast! The lightning will catch. Oh, goodness me!" he said quite tremulously; "and here I am calling so loud!"

The lackey met the Konrektor on the market-place, the door was opened, just a trifle, according to the Duke's orders, so that there should be no draught, and the Konrektor crowded in with his fox-tail and the rest of it. He now entered his Highness's cabinet, and the sight he saw put him at first quite out of countenance. For a moment he stood bewildered in the door, and stared into the cabinet open-mouthed, then all at once he broke into a perfect roar of laughter.

"What the devil have we here? Begging your Grace's pardon! But what in the name of goodness can this mean?"

And Rand laughed too, and said, "Ay, you may well say so!"

I don't know but what I should have forgotten the dutiful respect I owed his most Serene Highness if I had been called upon to behold what the Konrektor beheld. Right in the middle of the room there was a small platform resting on the necks of bottles, on top of that a sort of pavilion made of glass that came down to the floor, and roofed over with a light-blue silk tent, that looked like a parasol for fifteen persons, and in this remarkable affair sat his Highness in his innocent terror, clothed in a yellow silk dressing-gown, with a green silk nightcap on his head, and with a pair of shoes on his feet varnished with red sealing-wax. He looked for all the world like a handsome canary with a green top-knot, that had been put in a cage to sing a sweet song; and he might have begun singing at any moment if only he had felt less down at the mouth.

In his quality as sovereign lord he would doubtless have sung a right testy little song at the Konrektor for laughing, the more so as he had a crow to pick with him anyway for his matrimonial intentions, had not a sudden stroke of lightning interrupted his Highness's sing-song. "What nonsense are you——?" and now came the lightning, and he clapped his silk handkerchief over his eyes—"Mercy on us!" and he peeped out from behind the handkerchief, listening for the thunder, and when it came he stopped up his ears and exclaimed again, "Mercy on us!"

The Konrektor had stopped laughing by this time, and examined the cage from before and behind, and his Highness looked at him in an uncertain way, and asked at last:

"Well, what do you say? Will it do? Glass, silk, and"—here he raised one of his legs—"here is sealing-wax; and I have had everything taken out that's made of metal."

"Ay," said the Konrektor, "I dare say it's all right, your Highness; what man can do has been done; but, begging your pardon, the gold ducal crown that's up on top of the throne you are sitting on you've forgotten."

"Didn't I tell you so? Didn't I tell you so? That ass, Rand. Oh, mercy on us!" for it lightened again.

"Sheep-headed fool, you! bring another chair! I don't want any ducal honours. When there's such a storm as this I'm no more than another man—mercy on us!" and he held his hands over his ears. "Eh, Konrektor?"

The Konrektor said he believed it; but the throne with the crown on it might stay there; they could wrap up the crown in a silk handkerchief.

After that his Highness ordered Rand to go out and take a look at the weather. Rand did it, and came back: "The storm is over, but there's another one all ready to burst, and it looks mighty grim."

"Rand, bring another chair in my weather-temple for the Konrektor."

"Oh, your Highness," said the Konrektor, "I don't need to come in."

"Ay, but *I* need you in here; but you can't come in like that; you'll drag in the lightning. Rand, another silk dressing-gown and nightcap, and the red-waxed shoes!"

Resistance was useless, he had to give in; and in a short time he stood there in a black nightcap and a bright orange bed-gown and red shoes; and he stood like a sorcerer in olden times, who might be supposed to have changed an unfortunate prince into a canary-bird, and put him into a glass box, where it was likely he would have to stay for ever, for naught but the sweet kiss of a beauteous fairy upon his beak could ransom him, and his Highness was possessed of a holy horror of kissing, and there was no beauteous fairy near, for Rand, who was the only other person about, could not possibly figure as such.

When the old sorcerer sat beside his enchanted victim, his Highness ordered Rand out, because the exhalations of so many persons might draw the lightning, but told him to put his head in at the door from time to time and give the news concerning the weather; and Rand was quite willing, for now he could run over to the baker's wife and have some talk.

"What say you, Konrektor? Is it safe now?" asked his Highness.

"Ay, so far as I can see."

"But is it *quite* safe?"

"Well, your Highness, what man can do has been done; but what are mortal measures against the will of our Lord God?"

"That's what I say," exclaimed his Highness; "that fool the carpenter was to have made it round, and he made it square. Corners always draw lightning."

"What good would that do? If our Lord God sees best He can blow away the whole of Neu-Brandenburg in a moment. Think of Sodom and Gomorrah."

"Goodness gracious! Yes, I know it, I——" Just here Rand put his head in at the door: "There's another one coming, and the baker's wife says——"

"Fool, I don't want to know what that impertinent woman says." Rand retired. "That woman has a lot to say; she says too—goodness gracious! she says you are going to get married, Konrektor. But I forbid you. I'll never set eyes on you again. I'd banish you from Court."

"I esteem your Highness as my liege lord," said the Konrektor, quietly getting up, "but whether I marry or don't marry ought to be all the same to you, and I won't brook interference from any man. If you want to banish me from Court you can do it, that's in your power; but I can also go of my own free will, that's in my power. I have the honour of bidding you farewell."

"Mercy on us! Do stay here; you're the only comfort I have. Oh, goodness gracious!"

Here Rand put his head in at the door.

"Your Highness, this one is going to be pretty bad; the storm can't come across the lake, and the baker's wife says——"

"You hare-brained dolt, I don't want to know what she says. Shut the door and bolt it on the outside, so that he can't get out."

"Well, your Highness," said the Konrektor, taking off his sorcerer's habit and donning his own honest coat, "you can hold me by force—that was a terrific clap!"

"Mercy on us!—yes, that it was. Do come in here again."

"Nay, your Highness, I'm not afraid of lightning," said the staunch old fellow, and gave his liege lord a quiet look. "I fear God, my judge, when I stand before Him as a miserable sinner, but I do not fear God, my father, for He knows what is good for me, and if He calls me to Himself by a stroke of lightning and without any suffering, then I know that it was an act of mercy, and I thank Him for it."

There was another awful clap, lightning and thunder falling almost simultaneously, and his Serene Highness screamed aloud.

"Konrektor, I'll grant ye a favour. What shall it be?"

"I need only God's favour; I don't need any man's favour, for all he may be a prince. Princely favour is the crutch that lame justice leans on, and when princes are gracious they are either trying to make up for past injustice and reap thanks for it, or they are about to commit some new injustice."

"You're growing mighty bold. I'll show you what princely disfavour is!" shouted his Highness in sore ire, for there had been no thunder for some time. "I'll show you——"

Then Rand put in his head. "Your Highness, the lightning struck a poplar on the embankment, the baker's wife says, and there's another storm coming up."

"Konrektor, do think upon something that will help us!"

"How can *I* think upon anything, your Highness? At such times when our Lord God is nearer than at others it is best to examine ourselves closely, and think of all the wrong one has done, and firmly resolve to undo it—that will give us courage and comfort."

"There is no man I have ever wronged," exclaimed his Highness hastily; but the storm was drawing nigh, and he covered his face with his handkerchief once more, and cried, "Goodness gracious!"

"Well, your Highness, I imagine it's much the same with you as it is with the rest of us; or is that no wrong when you imprison your courier Halsband for no fault of his?"

"My courier? He is my servant; how can a prince—mercy on us!—how can a prince be in the wrong against his own servant?" And again there was a flash of lightning, and his Highness disappeared behind his handkerchief. "Mercy on us! Let him go! Let the fellow go!"

"Ay, your Highness, that's all very good; but you must take the disgrace off from his shoulders as well."

"Mercy on us!" cried his Highness, stopping his ears because of the thunder. "I'm to ask his pardon, am I? No, no! The fellow——"

Rand appeared. "This will be a good one."

"Run and let Halsband out of prison," said his Highness.

"And," said the Konrektor, "give me pen and ink, and some paper."

"Here is paper and pen; but our ink is dried up. We're not much given to writing, except when the cashier is here."

"That's a fact," said his Highness. "Mercy on us! Go and buy some ink immediately." The ink came, and the Konrektor wrote.

"Good gracious," said his Highness to himself, "how can the fellow write in this storm!"

The Konrektor got him to sign it.

"Don't you feel a vast deal better," he said, "after this good deed?"

"Not a bit of it," said his Highness; "first the storm must be over."

The sky was clearing. Rand's head appeared again. "Now it's all over; the baker's wife says we had seven storms."

His Highness took breath once more, and said to himself, "Seven storms! And he knew it before, the insolent old fellow, with his confounded speeches! What becomes of the deference due to the prince from his subject, I'd like to know? But I can't do without him; he's too well posted about the weather."

BERTHOLD AUERBACH
1812–1882

TONELE

THREE girls are sitting in the shade of a cherry-tree in a meadow near the cross-roads leading to Muehringen and Ahldort. No cart is on the roads, no plough moves in the fields. The stillness of the Sabbath holds the country-side.

On a distant hill to the right, where the chapel of an ancient convent stands out against the siege of time, a bell rings home the good people who have been worshipping there. In a little dell, still to the right, yellow fields of rape lie amid stretches of corn, and beyond is the Jewish cemetery. But you can only see its four weeping willows, standing at the corner of the distant hill, under which sleep a grandmother, mother, and five children lost in a burning house.

A large cross, painted red and white, stands amid the flowery fruit-trees. On one side of the main road a pine forest rises sombre, with its ranges of red boles; on the other side is a higher glade of elm, oak, and beech.

The three girls sit chatting, and now and then one of them breaks into an old Black Forest country song, in which the others join with a fine feeling for harmony. In the cherry-tree above them a finch warbles at the top of his voice to their singing. When they stop or talk quietly, he becomes silent. Bang! A shot. Away flies the finch, and the startled country lasses look around.

In the dell, the forest ranger from Muehringen picks up a bird, pulls a feather from its tail, sticks the feather in his hat, and puts the bird in his game-bag. Calling his dog, he walks across the fields, the gun over his shoulder, looking a very manly, comely fellow.

"He might have spared the poor bird on a Sunday!" said Tonele.

"So I should think," Barbele remarked. "The rangers are not Christians. All they can do is to kill innocent animals and shut anybody in prison who takes any of their timber."

"Old Granny Ursul told me once," said Brigittle, the youngest of the girls, "that a ranger is compelled to kill some living thing every day."

Meanwhile the ranger had almost come up with them. With one accord the three girls began to sing quietly. They did not want to be spoken to.

"Good afternoon, girls! But why sing so quietly?" he said, stopping.

Tonele and Brigittle began to laugh; but Barbele, with ready wit, answered saucily, "Good afternoon, Ranger! We are singing only for our own pleasure, not for others. We hear ourselves quite well."

"Brr," said the ranger, "what a sharp tongue!"

"Sharp or blunt," answered the girl, "makes no difference. Those who don't like it need not listen." But Tonele nudged her and whispered to her not to be so rude.

The ranger heard, and looking down pleasantly said, "Oh, never mind! I can stand any amount of chaff."

The girls were a little embarrassed, and, getting up, linked arms and turned towards the village. But the ranger was not to be put off so easily.

"May I walk with you?"

Barbele again quickly took him up.

"This is the high road and it is wide enough," she exclaimed.

The young ranger was now half-inclined to leave the girls alone, but thought it a man's part to put up with woman's whimsies; he walked along with them without saying another word. Tonele, to put him at his ease again, asked, "Where are you off to on a Sunday?'

"I am on my way to Horb," he answered. "If you girls would care to come along with me, I should be delighted to treat you to some Horb wine and cakes."

Tonele blushingly refused, and Barbele, once more taking command, told him:

"We prefer to drink white wine from the spring, and that also costs us nothing." And having now reached the village, she added, "Ranger, your nearest way runs backward."

He had a sharp retort ready, but, suppressing it, answered, "I like to look an honest village and honest people in the face!" He could not resist turning his back on Barbele as he said that.

Walking along the village High Street he asked Tonele her name, but again Barbele interposed. "Whatever she was christened." And as the ranger now turned to her, saying she was very clever, and asking, "And what is your age?" he got the usual reply, "As old as my little finger." But Tonele softly whispered to him, " My name is Tonele. Why do you ask ? "

" Because I wanted very much to know."

Slowly they walked up the High Street. Then, on coming to a narrow branching lane, the three girls whispered to each other. In a moment they dispersed in different directions, and assembled again shortly afterwards near the stone pit outside the village. The ranger laughed to himself, whistled to his dog, gripped the strap of his gun, and quickened his pace.

The girls discussed the young man for some time. Tonele rather took his part, remonstrating with Barbele for snapping him up in that fashion, seeing he was such a decent fellow. Barbele, however, said that such forward fellows must be kept in their place. Just because he was the ranger to Baron Muehringen, that was no reason for making up to every girl he came across. Besides, what would their boys, Sepp and Kasper, say ?

Their lively chatter was interrupted by the appearance of those two sturdy lads, who had been looking for them in the meadow. Barbele related all that had happened and much besides—sharp repartees that only now occurred to her, and that she would not have had the courage to use had she thought of them before.

The lads agreed with all she said, and Sepp took Tonele's arm and Kasper that of Barbele, Brigittle linking herself by the side.

Sepp and Tonele made a fine couple. Both tall and slender, they looked striking when alone, and splendid when walking along arm in arm. Sepp held himself very straight, and his best clothes—short buck-skin breeches, long stockings, free knees, and fine green jacket—set off admirably his well-shaped figure.

After making their way towards the high ground above the village, they could see the ranger in the distance speaking to another forester of the Nordstetter district. Sepp even saw him pointing in their direction, and was about to shout a challenge towards him, but Tonele put her arms round his neck, and, kissing him, prevented it. Had Sepp heard what the ranger said, he would surely have carried out his intention and more, perhaps.

" Here she comes ; what a fine girl ! As handsome a lass as I have ever seen," he was telling his companion.

" Oh yes," was the reply, " it is Tonele right enough. A face like a Madonna, and wavy golden hair ! Our old minister knew what was what when he asked her father to let her come to him as his cook. He got a sharp answer from the old man, I guess ! "

As the others approached, the rangers separated and went away. The happy young people found a shady place at the edge of the clearing and spent the afternoon sweethearting. Only Brigittle, whose young man was away in the army, sat moodily by herself. But she made herself very useful towards the evening, by rearranging the hair and neckerchiefs of her friends, that had become rather tousled. Returning to the village, the girls and lads drew apart, and appeared, according to custom, with other friends, walking in long rows, each sex keeping to itself.

One row of girls had Tonele on the outside. Next to her strolled Marann, an unhappy maid whose face on one side was a deep blue from temple to chin. It is said that shortly before her birth her mother rushed out to see the burning house where the seven people died who lie under the willows, and received such a terrible shock that it communicated itself to the unborn baby. Unexpectedly the ranger passed through the village on his return from Horb. Coming up to Tonele, he cried, " Good-evening, girls ! Can't I now stroll along beside you ? "

" No, no ! " answered Tonele. " Please go in front with the boys. It would be wrong for you to come with us."

The ranger was pleased with her tone, and walked ahead with the lads. But near the Red Eagle they all stopped. For the convent bell rang out the evensong. All the fellows uncovered, and, like the girls, murmured a prayer, ending with the sign of the cross. This was hardly done when the ranger called out, "Good-night, everybody," and walked away.

The girls were chaffing Tonele about the ranger when Sepp came up. Hearing the talk he stopped dead, bit his pipe-stem savagely, and closed his fists tightly. He didn't say a word, but looked daggers at Tonele. As they all dispersed he walked with Tonele towards her house in utter silence.

" What is the ranger to you ? " he said sharply.

" Nothing."

" What were you two talking about, then ? "

" Whatever does one talk about ? "

" Then I ask you never to say another word to him."

" I don't allow anybody to dictate to me with whom I may speak."

" You stuck-up, false thing ! "

" If you think that, well and good, I don't mind."

Both kept silent during the rest of the walk. Then Tonele said good-night to him and went in. He did not answer, but remained outside her house till the end of the evening, thinking she would surely come out again to make it up. She did not.

All the following week they never spoke to each other. Indeed, Sepp avoided the girl. But returning from the fields one afternoon he met Barbele and offered her a lift home. She returned his kindness by giving him a good lecture about his silly behaviour towards Tonele. He took it to heart, and, waiting afterwards for Tonele at the village pump, helped her with the water, and made up the quarrel while seeing her home.

" But you must not speak to the ranger again," he told her.

" As often as I like," she answered. " I am not a child, and I know what I may do or not do."

" But," he insisted, " you need not speak to him unless you have to."

" That is quite right. But I will not be dictated to."

So peace was restored and the old delightful courtship was resumed. They loved each other more than ever. The ranger had no occasion to come to the village : the harvest was on ; and in the autumn Sepp was only called up for a short term of military service. After that they would get married.

Tonele had not met the ranger again since the Sunday in spring. But while she was cutting wheat with Sepp in the dell, a few days before her lover was to join the colours, the ranger passed the field. Seeing her, he called out, " Is it cutting well ? " Not having seen him approach, Tonele was rather startled and never answered. She kept on with her reaping, but Sepp, looking up, called out, " Yes, thanks ! " And kneeling on a shear, he twisted the straw rope especially tightly round it, biting his lips and wishing it was the ranger he had under his knee.

It only wanted then three days to Barbele's wedding ; and two days afterwards Sepp and Kasper had to depart for the manœuvres. During this time Sepp had resolved to be a model sweetheart and to enjoy life to the full. On the day of the wedding he was particularly boisterous, and engaged the band on the spot for his own wedding, with two trumpeters, for, being in the Guards, he was fond of brass instruments. In the evening, at the dance, the sudden appearance of the ranger somewhat upset his balance. His rival made straight for

Tonele to ask her for the first dance, and Sepp flared up, and not giving her time to answer, burst out, " Already engaged ! "

" I should think the lady can speak for herself," replied the ranger.

Tonele then interfered, and, taking Sepp's hand, turned to the ranger and said, " We will have the next dance together."

Sepp was furious ; and when he afterwards saw his girl and his rival dancing together, he swore to himself that neither he nor Tonele should dance another dance that night. However, Barbele, the bride, asked the angry, sullen lad to come and dance with her, and as it is impossible to refuse the bride, he had to do his duty. While they danced, Barbele gave him a good dressing-down for his stupid jealousy, telling him that it would serve him right if, in consequence of his boorish behaviour, Tonele got to love the ranger. " He at least behaves like a gentleman," said Barbele.

Sepp laughed and admitted she was right, and determined to behave properly in future and during the evening. As he sat with Tonele at the table he drank to the ranger's health and told Tonele to clink glasses with him. The ranger bowed low towards Tonele, but hardly nodded to Sepp, who, however, did not mind and rather fancied he had scored that time.

The party lasted far into the morning, and when at last it broke up Sepp saw his sweetheart home. They were both excited, and kissed and hugged each other, Tonele resting happily and closely in his strong arms. He began to talk of the ranger again, but she put her hand over his mouth, saying :

" Leave the ranger alone! You are everything in the world to me ; I love you, only you ! " Sepp was overjoyed, and pressing his lips to her cheeks told her, " I just could bite you."

" Then bite," said Tonele.

A scream ! Sepp had really bitten her, and blood was running down her cheeks. Putting her hands up to her face and feeling the wound, she gave Sepp a fierce push that sent him flying down backwards. Then she rushed into the house screaming, and soon every one was awake and running about. Old Ursul was fetched, and before putting on healing herbs, wanted to send for Sepp to suck out the wound. This, she said, was the only way to counteract any poison that might have entered the flesh. But Tonele swore she would rather die than let Sepp touch her again. The herbs were changed and Tonele groaned incessantly.

The next day everybody in the village crowded in. For the tale had soon spread, and from a mere bite, the attack had increased to something tremendous. Sepp also called, but Tonele at once began to rave, and would not see him, and insisted upon his leaving the house immediately. In despair he went to Barbele, who, after giving him a sound talking to, promised to do her best for him. But all her efforts were in vain. Tonele refused absolutely to see Sepp or to speak to him again in her life.

After a fortnight she left the house for the first time, and almost the first man she met was the ranger. It happened just outside the village, and he asked kindly after her wound. " How are you, dear Tonele ? " he said. " May I see the hurt place ? "

She blushed and felt quite hot, but pushed the bandage to one side to let him see the spot.

" It was unpardonable to disfigure a beautiful girl like you in this way," he said in astonishment. " But don't worry too much about it. To me you are still the loveliest girl I know, here or in any other village."

He spoke very sincerely and kindly, and Tonele was touched and deeply grateful. " Oh, you must not say those things," she told him.

" But I mean every word," he said, adding in an impressive voice, " I would marry you right off now." She blushed again, and walking quickly away over the fields, called out, " You must not say any more if you wish us to remain good friends."

The ranger was well content to remain her good friend—for the present. Shortly afterwards he heard to his delight that Tonele was coming to Muehringen to the wedding of her cousin. He got his sister to be particularly friendly with the young girl, and they quickly took to each other. Tonele appeared for the first time without her bandage, and the scar seemed to make her face only more interesting without spoiling its beauty. At the dance the ranger looked after the charming girl in a very attentive way, and in the evening he took her to the castle of the Baron, his master, where a theatrical performance had been arranged in the Baron's private theatre. It was the first play the country lass had ever seen, and she was overawed by what was really a crude performance, and by the fine people of the castle who attended it.

On the way home Tonele leant closely on her companion. She felt very grateful towards him for giving her such a splendid and wonderful treat. It seemed to her as if he had arranged everything solely for her, and she was happy. But the ranger too was very happy, for she promised to meet him next Sunday in the little beech glade near the old church.

In his manœuvres the ranger was certainly happier than Sepp was in his military operations in a distant garrison town. Before Sepp obtained his discharge there he received a letter of dismissal from Tonele's hands.

His first step, on his return home, was to Tonele's house. He found her sitting by her spinning-wheel in the parlour with her parents. But she never even looked at him, or came to the table when he proudly spread on it his army discharge.

He soon left and went to Barbele to hear all the news. Barbele told him that she had quarrelled with Tonele on account of the girl's friendliness with the ranger. Unable to control his feelings he tore up his discharge and dashed in a terrible rage out of the house.

Aimlessly he wandered about until the evening. Then, finding himself near the meadow where we first saw the three girls, he sat down under the cherry-tree, leafless now and swaying in the wind, put his bare head into his hands, and was lost in his anguish, neither hearing nor seeing anything. Suddenly he looked up, icy cold and shivering, and as he rose stiffly his eye caught in the distance two figures, and he also heard the low barking of a dog. Yes, it was the ranger coming from the village, and beside him he saw a white apron—it was the two of them—Tonele and her new sweetheart. She had seen him to the end of the village. They stood for a while, then the girl went back.

As the ranger drew up with him Sepp called out roughly, "Good-evening."

"Good-evening to you," replied he.

"I have an account to settle with you," said Sepp sharply.

"Ah! Master Sepp," the ranger exclaimed, "when did you come back?"

"Too soon for you anyway! Let us draw straws for Tonele, to see who of us is to have her, and if I lose I must have the loan of your gun."

The ranger calmly told him he would not draw straws.

Sepp jumped at him, and, gripping his throat with one hand and his gun with the other, cried, "Then I'll draw the soul out of your body, you thief."

"Seize him, boy!" screamed the ranger with half-choked voice to his dog. But the young giant of a farmer landed the dog such a kick that it flew yelping into the ditch. A mighty struggle went on for the gun. The ranger freed himself slightly while Sepp kicked at the dog, and now they held each other by the throat, exerting all their strength for the possession of the gun. Suddenly it went off, and the ranger staggered backwards into the ditch. He groaned twice and then was quiet. Sepp bent over him to see if he was still breathing.

The shot had been heard by Tonele. She came running up the road with a frightened face.

" There ! there ! " called Sepp to her. " There lies your fine new lover ! Now marry him ! "

Tonele stood terrified. She could not utter a word. She did not know what to say or do. Then she said quietly, " Sepp, you have ruined yourself as well as me."

" What is it to me ? " he said ; " I am done with the world," and he slowly walked towards the sombre pine forest. Nobody in the village ever heard of him again.

On the way to Muehringen, near the fruit-tree plantation, stands a rude stone cross to the memory of the ranger from Muehringen who there lost his life. Poor Tonele, after a long period of sorrow and illness, died also.

CLUMSY

Berthold Auerbach

I CAN still see you, dear old Clumsy, with your short fair hair, your broad heavy features, large blue eyes, and that mouth of yours which was always more or less open. I also vividly remember your scant, queer get-up—white shirt, red braces, and short black linen breeches, useful if quaint. On Sundays, of course, you held your own with the best of them—fur cap, blue jacket with large buttons, scarlet waistcoat, short yellow leather breeches, white stockings and black shoes, and sometimes even a scarlet carnation behind the ear.

Clumsy was not his right name, although everybody called him so, except his mother, Maria, and a few of the children. He lived close to us, and as the village kiddies were generally split up into several bands waging war on one another, this was an advantage. For since Clumsy was our great friend and ally, we were usually quite safe from attack at our end of the village when Aloys—that is Clumsy—was about.

Aloys was of an age when he, together with the other village lads of his years, began to be a power. Every evening they would gather by the Eagle Inn and chaff the passing country girls, or stroll through the High Street singing and whistling. Most of them had already bought one of those short pipes with large china-head bowls, and though they generally held them unlit between their teeth, now and then one lad occasionally ventured to light up, and proudly and smilingly puffed away, however bad he felt.

Aloys, too, had begun to smoke, but only at home in his bedroom. One Sunday evening, however, he took his pipe out with him, and was unmercifully chaffed by his friends. One of them snatched it away, and in passing round it somehow got lost in the crowd. Aloys did not argue the matter, but snatched at his nearest friend's fur cap, and dashed away with that into the house of his aunt, Mistress Bomueller, whom he generally visited of an evening. There his hatless friend soon brought the wandering pipe.

He was greatly attached to his aunt, and more so to her eldest daughter Marannele. Neither used his nickname in addressing him; they always called him Aloys. In the morning when he had seen to his own two cows and calves he always walked over to his aunt's. Marannele would open the gate to him with a simple "Good-morning," and he would walk straight to the stables and prepare fresh fodder for her two cows and her two oxen. As he went about his work of straightening and cleaning up he would talk to the cattle, and they knew him so well that they would watch him and look round at him. Particularly friendly was the fine pie-bald, long-horned cow in the corner, whom he had reared from a calf. As he rubbed her down she would turn round and lick his hand, and look at him as long as he was in the byre. Next Aloys pumped the trough in the yard full of fresh, clear water, and while the cattle came out to drink he cleaned the stable, so as to have everything ready when Marannele came to milk.

She would say, "Aloys, you are a dear boy." He never looked at her, but only brushed the floor all the harder; for he was very shy.

After that he went to the outhouse to cut enough fodder to last for the rest of the day, did various other odd jobs, and at last went into the house to fill the kitchen buckets at the pump in the yard, and to split wood if any was required. Finally he appeared in the parlour, where Marannele brought in the large dish with soup, set it in the middle of the table, folded her hands and said grace. They all ate from the big dish, and sometimes Aloys would help himself at the place where Marannele ladled. Meantime not a word was spoken, and when the dish was emptied and grace said once more he made his way home.

Thus the years passed and Aloys was now nineteen. At his last birthday Marannele gave him a shirt, not only cut and sewn by herself, but made from hemp which she herself had spun and woven. Aloys was delighted, and in spite of the winter cold he would have gone about the streets in his shirt sleeves had he not been afraid of being chaffed. Recently he had got very touchy about the least thing.

This was largely due to the chipping he got from the mayor's new coachman. Joergli was a fine straight fellow who had been in the cavalry. On Sundays when he swaggered through the village in his spurs, his forage cap, and his leather-seated, cloth riding-breeches all the girls looked after him, and Aloys had often seen Marannele with her face glued to the curtains admiring the ex-cavalryman.

Aloys had many a bad hour over this, and often wished that he, too, had been a soldier, or at least that he, too, had the handling of horses like Joergli. In his mind there existed only three social classes: those who, like himself, were cow-keeping peasants, those who kept oxen only, and those who kept horses.

It was New Year's Day, and Joergli showed his superiority by being required to take the mayor's daughter with her friend Marannele for a sleigh ride. Though he was in despair Aloys managed to look cheerful as he assisted in the harnessing of the horses to the sleigh; but after they had driven off and the crowd that had collected dispersed he slunk back home and tears of anger welled up in his eyes. The village seemed deserted without Marannele, and he did not know what to do with himself all that day.

For some time now Aloys had felt very miserable. In his mother's house, where the young girls of the village often assembled of an evening to spin and talk—they were all very fond of his mother, his father was dead long since—he had felt very much out of it; for when the village youths came in later in the evenings he seemed to be very much left to himself, while the others, and particularly Joergli, who could sing and "jodel" and tell stories to perfection, made all the running. After a few of these sociable nights at home and at other houses he began to tell himself, "Aloys! Buck up! You are now nineteen, and it is time you put yourself a little more forward; you must try to beat Joergli at his own game!"

Shortly after this at his own house he took the first big step forward. Marannele came with her new spinning-wheel, a beauty, inlaid with polished metal, and while the girls sat round in a circle, each one with her wheel, the hemp tied up with coloured ribbons, he brought in the usual dish of apples for the girls, to prevent their mouths getting too dry—they moistened the thread occasionally in their mouths—and seeing the new wheel immediately put his hand on the gilded ball at the top of the hemp-stick and recited the old piece of poetry in accordance with the custom. At first Marannele cast down her eyes in fear lest in his shyness he might stick in the middle of his recitation; but though he faltered and floundered he got safely through, and she gave him a resounding kiss, the usual ransom for the release of the hemp-stick. Aloys was overjoyed and proudly took his seat amongst the other youths. His peace of mind, however, did not last long, for Joergli had envied him that kiss and now asked Marannele to sing the ballad of the "Black-eyed Maid." She began at once, and though at first she faltered she soon recovered, and then Joergli fell in singing second part, and very finely too. Marannele now grew bolder and her voice became full and sweet, the support of Joergli's voice helping her, and they sang right through the six verses.

After the girls had spun five or six spindles the wheels were cleared out of the room, the chairs ranged round the wall; and they started a little dance. Joergli immediately danced with Marannele, and Aloys could only look on with set teeth, for he had never yet attempted dancing. However, Marannele came straight to him as soon as Joergli released her and said :

" Come along, Aloys, it is time you learned to dance ! "

" But I can't, Marannele," he answered sulkily ; " you know I can't ! "

" Oh, Clum . . ., you silly boy," she said, " you will easily manage, and you must learn some time, so come along."

She dragged him up and they danced, and Aloys flung his legs about in such a comical way that everybody roared with laughter.

" Never mind, Aloys," she whispered, " I'll teach you when we are quite alone ! "

The girls now took their lanterns which the boys had lit up for them; and they all made their way home. Aloys went with them and was pleased that Marannele avoided Joergli. When the boys had seen all the girls home they stopped for a parting chat, and, as Aloys turned to leave them, Joergli called after him, " You ought to have stopped with Marannele to-night, Clumsy ! "

" You rascal ! " Aloys called back, and the others laughed loudly as he went on his way.

The next morning as he watched Marannele at her milking he told her that she would have to be careful with Joergli, as he was a bad lot. She promised she would be, but told him that he ought to smarten himself up more and try to be as quick as Joergli, that he must not quarrel with him, but remain good friends. He promised her that, not without reluctance, however, and that was the reason why he had helped Joergli on New Year's Day to harness the horses.

Aloys was now in his twentieth year and liable to be called up for military service. He had long ago made up his mind to become a soldier, for he meant to outshine Joergli the cavalryman. So when the time came and the eligible young men of the village went up before the commission then sitting in the neighbouring town, he set out on his way delighted. He was—as we know—not a particularly brainy youth, but he had acquired plenty of acuteness, and having set his mind on the army he was quite saucy to the examining officers and surgeons. " Don't bother yourselves with punching me and listening to my breathing," he told them as he stood there in his nudity, " I shall pass all right ; I'm thoroughly sound and healthy." The officials were annoyed at his sauciness ; but the doctor quickly overlooked a slight defect in his sight, and he was enrolled.

As he returned home his mother met him and wept when she saw by the favours he wore that he had been taken. He ran up to her and soothed her, saying, " The year will soon be over, and our Xaver is quite able to look after our few fields and the cattle until my return. Don't cry, mother, for I wanted to be a soldier, and I tried hard to be taken on."

Aloys now set out with his companions, pipes alight, favours flowing in the breeze, singing through the village, and at the Eagle the celebrations lasted until late into the night.

Then his last day at home, the third, dawned. Early in the morning he went to old Jacob's—his uncle's house—and there found Marannele, who now had to do all the work herself, busy in the byre. " Give me your hand, Marannele," he told her, " and promise me you'll not get married before I return." " Surely I'll do that," she exclaimed, and he bent down to her for his last kiss ; the oxen and cows looked round at them as if they understood that something out of the way was going on, and Aloys went round and gave each one a parting pat.

Joergli had received permission from his master to take out the big cart and to drive all the recruits a good way towards Stuttgart, where they had to report themselves. So they left the village singing and shouting amidst the good wishes of the villagers. Food and drink were still being passed up to them as they went along the High Street ; but finally the village was left behind, and they settled down on their way. Aloys had become very quiet. As they passed the well-known fields and meadows, each one made almost doubly dear by some remembrance of his youth or by his walks here and there with his dear Marannele, he sat in his place deep in thought. As they drove through the little county town the singing and " jodelling " started afresh, and after they gained the heights on the other side he began to look cheerful again ; for there in the distance, not an hour away, lay his beloved Nordstetten. It looked so near in the beautifully clear air that he could see the yellow smithy with its green shutters, and he knew that two houses farther up the street stood Marannele's home. He waved his cap in the fulness of his heart.

Joergli took the party as far as Herrenberg, two hours' journey ; the remaining distance they had to walk.

" Have you got a message to send back to Marannele ? " he asked Aloys. " No ! " he snapped. " And take care you don't talk to her, for she can't stand you ! " He had rapped this out almost viciously, for had not Joergli just interrupted his most sacred thoughts, and had not he just been debating with himself whether he should send a message ?

On their way the recruits fell in with a carter coming towards them andforced him to turn back andto take them some wayon their journey. Aloys had been the ringleader in this matter out of sheer bravado, and we must give him this credit, he was the first to take out his purse to reward the carter as the latter was finally allowed to retrace his steps.

At last they arrived at the Tuebinger gate at Stuttgart, and there were met by a number of soldiers hailing from Nordstetten and the surrounding villages. " How are you, Clumsy ? " several of them called out to Aloys, and amidst great laughter and merriment they were escorted to the barracks. To his great regret Aloys was refused for the cavalry and put into the infantry ; but he proved himself quite a good recruit and soon got into his stride. He made friends everywhere, and particularly with a painter in his company, who, poor himself, laid himself out to please this young farmer's son who often received well-assorted parcels from home, which he freely shared with his friend. He, in turn, showed his gratitude by painting Aloys in his full uniform, with the colours of the regiment in his hands, and though the picture looked very effective, yet the face might have done for any one in the regiment.

This picture Aloys had framed and sent home, asking his mother to show it to Marannele and to give it her if she thought proper. He also asked his mother to send him a nice parcel with butter, cakes, and meat, as they all delighted in the beautiful country fare, and not to forget to enclose a few yards of home-spun linen as a present for his colour-sergeant's wife. He told her, too, that he had learned to dance, and was becoming quite one of the smartest fellows in the regiment.

Then he received his parcel and a letter : " Mathes has sent five pounds for you from America, and writes that he could set you up on some of his land as soon as you would care to come out to him. Be a good fellow, don't get into any scrapes, and do your duty well. I showed Marannele your picture, but she said it wasn't you at all, and somehow she sulks with me and calls in but rarely." When he read this Aloys smiled and told himself, " I knew it, she doesn't even recognise me; that shows I have improved and am quite a different man now."

Then came the day when he received his first leave; he knew the fair was on at Nordstetten, and by giving various small presents to his sergeant he had succeeded in inducing that all-important person to procure him four days' leave. He left Stuttgart in full war paint and arrived at his home after darkness had fallen. His mother's house was the first he came to; there was a light, he knocked; and his mother called out, " Good gracious, a policeman!" He quickly allayed the fears of his mother by making himself known; she was delighted with the unexpected visit and with her fine soldier boy; and quickly busied herself with getting him some eggs for supper. While she went about the kitchen he stood by the fireplace and told her everything that had happened since he left. He also asked after Marannele; and why his picture was still in the parlour.

" My dear boy, please put her out of your mind; she is not worthy of your love," she told him hesitatingly.

" Mother, don't say things like that!" he cried, and the red light from the fire showed up his strong, determined face. " I know she is a good girl, and I love her!"

His mother then carried his supper into the parlour, and only then saw what a great change had taken place in her boy, what a really handsome man he had grown; she lifted up his heavy helmet and almost cried over its cruel weight.

Next morning Aloys rubbed up his buttons, helmet and sword, and when the bells rang for the first time he stood ready for church and left the house when the second ringing started.

" Isn't this Clumsy?" he heard two boys whispering as he passed.

" Oh no; that's not him."

" But yes; it is he!" again exclaimed the first one.

Aloys threw them one of his severest looks and they immediately ran off. Everywhere he was greeted and welcomed; but he walked straight on, and as he passed Marannele's house no one was to be seen. He entered the church as the final bell rang, took off his leather gloves, and dipped his finger-tips into the holy water. He looked about anxiously, stopped at the door and looked amongst the newcomers, but saw no sign of his Marannele. The service started, her voice was not amongst the singers, he would have known it among a thousand. What was the good of all the admiring glances that were thrown at him if she, she for whom he had come, was not present, she for whom he had worked so hard, and for whom he now stood there so erect, as firm as a statue ? Then after he had sat listlessly through the sermon, what was that ? The parson called the banns of Marianne Bomueller, his Marannele, and Georg Melzer, his rival Joergli. Aloys was the first out of the church ; his knees trembling and his teeth chattering, he almost ran home. Throwing his helmet and sword on the floor, he hurried into the outhouse and buried himself in the hay, sobbing and crying like a little child.

At last his mother came to him there, wept with him, and soothed and comforted him as when he was a little boy. He now heard that Joergli had seduced Marannele and that it was high time they were married. He wept again, and following his mother tore his picture from the parlour wall and smashed it into a thousand pieces. Some hours later, when at last he had to some extent fought down his sorrow and eaten some dinner, he smartened up his uniform and went out. He passed Marannele's house with downcast eye and made his way to the Eagle, whistling the while, and finally entered the public rooms and the hall where the dancing had already begun. He looked round for Marannele and was glad she was not there ; at that moment Joergli came up to him and held out his hand, saying, " How are you, comrade ? " Aloys stared at him as if he would like to poison him with a look, and then deliberately turned his back on him without a word.

He took a seat at one of the tables, and ordering a bottle of the best he made merry with his friends, who all crowded round him. They drank to him and he to them, and the girls vied with one another in showing him how pleased they were to have him amongst them again. Mechtilde, the daughter of his cousin, sat next to him, and smiling at her almost happily, he asked her, " Wouldn't you care to dance ? " " Certainly I would," she cried. " Come along, then," he replied, and they sailed away.

Aloys kept his eyes on Joergli all the time. He heard some one ask him, " Where is Marannele to-day ? " and he also took note of the coachman's reply, " Oh, she's not very well ! " a reply accompanied by a leer and a coarse laugh. Aloys could hardly restrain himself : he longed to get at the foul fellow's throat and to squeeze the insolence out of him.

As time went on the company's boisterousness increased, and it was well on midnight when Aloys prepared to leave. As he was passing out with some of his friends, Joergli and his clique began to jeer and boo ; so they sat down again and struck up some jolly song and ordered some more wine. Then Joergli called across, " Shut up there, Clumsy ! " adding some vulgar term of abuse.

Aloys got furious at this, and throwing a glass at his rival followed up this insult by jumping over the chairs and table between them and grabbing hold of Joergli. The music stopped, glasses rolled to the floor, and after a moment's breathless silence the whole company yelled and shouted. The enemies fought like madmen, Aloys pummelling the other man soundly with all the fury of an insulted and cheated lover. Then the friends of either party joined in the attack, until the whole room was one mass of fighting humanity. Only when the village policeman appeared and separated the two principal offenders was the affair stopped.

Next morning found Aloys on his way back to his garrison town, although his leave had still one day more to run. He was utterly dispirited and dejected, and knew he would be heavily punished on his arrival at the barracks ; for his share in the brawl at the Eagle had been duly entered on his papers by the mayor. As he arrived at the cross-roads, one of which leads off towards Strassburg, he hesitated, and would have deserted and crossed the frontier had not a lonely wanderer just then joined him and accompanied him to Stuttgart. After he had served his six weeks' incarceration, he wished for nothing so much as that his time was up, and when he received a letter from his mother in which she told him that his cousin Mathes from America had sent twenty pounds and asked him to come out to him as soon as he had served his time, he was overjoyed.

In the autumn, then, he started on his voyage to the United States, and with him went Mechtilde, the daughter of the farmer up on the hill. As later on he wrote to his mother that Mechtilde was a good worker, but not like Marannele, there seems a likelihood that his old wound is now healed, and that he has found in the new land what was denied him at home.

HERMANN KURZ
1813–1873

MY GRANDFATHER'S WEDDING

I WAS thirty—my grandfather said—well into the thirties, and though the eldest among my already married brothers and sisters, still without a wife. The reason for this was my shyness; I could not look a girl in the face, and since I did not dance had few opportunities for so doing.

This upset my father very much, and he often told mother, "It is a crying shame; all his brothers and sisters are hitched up, and he, the heir, still roams the world."

But mother used to soothe him with words something like these: "Don't hustle him, father, everything comes to him who waits; he will yet find the girl who is waiting for him somewhere."

And this happened sure enough. One Sunday as I was strolling along the old town moat—alone as usual, for all my school friends were long since married and out with their wives—quietly enjoying the sunshine, a parrot of wonderful hue sitting in one of the lettuce beds in an allotment attracted my attention. I was sure I recognised him—yes, it was Miss Rieber's, the county doctor's daughter's bird.

Old Dr. Rieber was a very clever physician, but something of a crank; one could not help putting him down as such, for he would insist on the Prussian way of speaking, and this was quite out of place in a jovial south German. He had been through the Seven Years' War, and copied in all his mannerisms, and in the ordering of his household—this to the quiet amusement of his daughter—the famous King Frederick the Great, "Our Fritz," as he was commonly called by his armies. He did this in spite of the fact that he had no special liking for his old King, the result of a piece of rank bad luck at the battle of Zorndorf. There a cannon-ball had approached him sideways, and glancing off, wounded him in a way that made sitting and walking for some time, and riding for all time, impossible for our doctor. The army surgeon had replaced the loss by a piece of veal, but of course our friend had to be invalided from the service, and that with only a small bonus. "I've no money for you foreigners" (Rieber hailed from

Baden), said the King, who happened to be in a temper; "why didn't he dodge the shot?"

This the doctor could not forgive his hero for the rest of his days, and whenever any conversation veered round to the famous King, he let out:

"A famous tyrant, that's what he was, and he did me out of my well-earned pension just because I couldn't think of such a witty answer as that grenadier who, in reply to his query, 'In which alehouse did you get those scratches?' told him, 'By *Kolin*, Sire, where Your Majesty paid the bill'—one of the few battles that 'Our Fritz' lost!"

Of course the King could not have asked him that question, as his wound was not in his face.

Now this Dr. Rieber had a daughter Salome, whose figure was second to none of any girls in the town. People called her proud because she did not mix with them frequently; and though she did not speak "Prussian," like her dad, yet her speech sounded more elegant than that of other girls. Miss Rieber's parrot caused an enormous sensation, for it was a very rare bird to be seen in such an old-world place as ours. It was a present from a seafaring cousin, who, instead of the promised boxes of gold and treasure, had brought her the parrot; luck had not been with him, and he had not liked to come back quite empty-handed. She was delighted with the bird, and spent hours and days in teaching him to talk. Soon the parrot had acquired quite a vocabulary, and also picked up some Latin words from the doctor. Salome generally sat at the window with the cage on the sill, and every passer-by stopped to listen to the wonderful bird's chatter. So did I. No girl could have been annoyed at this, though Salome might have thought that I gazed at her. I often saw her smile roguishly as I stood there, or when I passed by, and gradually thoughts came to me, thoughts on which I used to dwell very pleasantly.

Therefore as I spied the parrot in the lettuce I said to myself, "How unhappy she will be over the loss of her bird. I must catch it, even at the expense of some beds of lettuce!"

"Salome!" shrieked the bird. "Where in thunder are you?"

I stalked him carefully; he spat and croaked, "Manum de tabula!" But to no purpose did he use the doctor's favourite expletive. I got him, though he also got me a deep gash into my thumb, and while he shrieked and scolded loudly all the way, I delivered him safely into his owner's hands. Salome, intensely pleased, called to her father. He thanked me, and told me I was a brave fellow to tackle this little brute, who might have hacked me about pretty badly.

Then Salome, seeing my handkerchief round my hand, cried out :

" O papa ! he is hurt ! "

" Let me see," commanded the doctor. " You silly fellow, why try to hide it ? "

I begged him not to bother, but he insisted, and as he was getting cross I let him have his way.

" Pretty badly damaged ! This must be seen to at once. 'Manum de tabula.' Get away, Salome, what do you know about a wound ? Get me my wound balsam, you know the glass. Salome ! " he cried as she did not return immediately. " Where in thunder are you ? " At last she brought the ointment. " The deuce ! girl, you have been crying ? Why ? "

She hesitated.

" Your eyes are red ; what has happened ? What are you blubbering about ? "

" Because the parrot has——" she stopped.

" Yes, has—has what ? "

" Has——" she looked at me.

" 'Has hacked his hand about,' do you mean ? " added the doctor.

" Yes," she sobbed, and again her tears started.

" Silly girl," growled the doctor, " hand me the ointment again ; that'll do more good than all your tears. It won't hurt, my lad," he added, " only burn a little. There you are, Salome, now you may bandage his hand."

I felt quite strange as her little fingers touched my hand. When she had finished, the doctor said :

" Call in to-morrow, do you hear, so that I can look at the wound again and wash it out. Now then, Salome, are you not going to thank him ? "

She thanked me sweetly and added, " You'll call in to-morrow, won't you ? "

Now, all my brothers and sisters with their belongings assembled every Sunday evening for supper in our house. When I came in and they saw my bandaged hand I had to own up to everything, and did so with many blushes. Mother smilingly rested her hand on father's, and all the others laughed heartily and nicknamed me from that day " the Fowler."

The next day saw me again at the doctor's, so did the next, and the day after that, and every following day until my wound was completely healed. By that time we had become such friends that I was asked to continue my visits, which I had resolved not to give up in any case. Often the doctor was out, and then I had some happy times with Salome and the parrot, the latter forming the connecting link between us. She liked me to tease him, and I would pretend to be hurt, when she would hold my hand and sympathise with me.

One day she played a joke on me. When I entered the room Salome was not to be seen, and the parrot was hopping about his cage, yelling, " Silly Hans ! Silly Hans ! "—something new she had taught him. I pretended to be annoyed, and went up to the cage and tapped the bird on its beak. Thereupon he shrieked, " Help ! Help ! Salome, where in thunder are you ? " And at this from a big box in the corner of the room came the cry, " Silly Hans ! " No sooner had I opened the lid of this box than I received two or three of the old doctor's powdered wigs full in my face, and Salome jumped out. At once, all covered with powder as I was, I gave chase, the parrot meanwhile screaming and shrieking. I had just caught her, when behind us I heard, " Manum de tabula ! " But this time it was not the parrot, it was the doctor, who, having entered the house, had been attracted to our room by the noise.

" What in thunder does this mean ? What sort of behaviour is this for a respectable young bachelor in a strange house ? "

I felt like a pat of butter in the heat of the sun.

" Silly Hans ! " called out the bird.

" Who taught the parrot that ? " continued the doctor.

Salome dropped her head.

" Ah, I thought as much. And you wanted to take satisfaction, isn't that it, young man ? "

" Yes," stammered I, " I wanted——"

" What you wanted you need not tell me, I can guess that. But tell me—do you love her ? "

" To be sure ! "

" Do you want to marry her ? "

" If Salome has no objection ! "

" Now, girl, what do you say to that ? Will you have him ? "

Salome was too bashful to speak.

"Listen; if you won't answer you won't get him. If you don't want him then say 'No.'"

Salome answered with a laugh, "Not at all; I wouldn't say 'No' for anything in the world!"

"Well, then, take her," said Dr. Rieber, "hold her tight and well, she is my only child. Don't let her indulge in self-will; she requires discipline, but let it be tempered with love and gentleness."

I promised to take every care of her, and added, "Now I must run off to get my parents' consent."

"You have that, my boy," called out the doctor. "I have talked this over with them long ago; you don't suppose you would have been allowed to come here so freely otherwise? I'll just send for them now, to celebrate the engagement."

Four weeks to our wedding-day! I was in ecstasy. Yet those four weeks were to be a miserable time, had I but known it. As soon almost as we were engaged, Salome seemed to change entirely towards me. I could not do anything to please her, she found fault continually; my clothes, my walk, my coming, my going, in short everything in turn was adversely criticised. She was frightfully jealous. After every walk she would take me to task for having looked at this girl or that, and then she began to cry and scold, and alternately to forgive me.

I was often very much upset, but the old doctor advised me to let her be now, and to hold the reins very tightly once we were married. As his only child, he said, he had spoilt her, and she had known quite well that his continual storming and strong language were mere make-believe.

Shortly before our wedding-day we had a really serious quarrel. Salome insisted upon being married in a crinoline frock—for the crinoline was still worn at that time—a costume which I with equal persistence ridiculed. She seemed to think it suited her particular style, and when I played what I thought my trump card by saying, "You in a crinoline! Why, they are going out of fashion" (this was true enough), "and you, who are supposed to be a leader of fashion, must not be so backward," she blazed up. "Fancy you talking about fashions! What do you know about them, you silly Hans?"

Immediately the parrot chimed in with his infernal shrieks: "Silly Hans! Silly Hans!"

I threatened to kill that interfering bird, and while we were having a tussle for the possession of the cage one of us—I do not know to this day which it was—knocked it over, the door flew open, and before I could shut the window the parrot had flown out.

Imagine my consternation and her temper! She accused me of having engineered the whole thing. I alternately begged, scolded, and implored; all in vain—she would not believe me, and the final result was that she told me she would not become my wife until I had recovered her pet.

Miserable and sad I left her. She had been so nice and sweet to me that day until the quarrel arose, and now my joy was dashed to pieces!

I hunted everywhere for that parrot. One clue I followed up and found—the man who had captured the bird; but he had been scratched and bitten so badly, and had been so frightened by its almost human voice and epithets, that he got scared and let it go. I told Salome about this, and she seemed somewhat mollified, but still treated me with coldness. This spurred me on to further efforts, and soon I heard that the parrot had been caught in a neighbouring village.

On my way there I met a peasant girl, who, in reply to my question, told me that she was from that very village. Eagerly I asked her if she had heard anything of my friend, the parrot, and was delighted when she told me she had.

"I will reward you well," I told her, "if you will help me to get him back."

"That will be rather difficult!" was her reply.

"Why difficult? Hasn't he been caught, then?"

"Oh, he has been caught right enough, caught and buried."

"Good gracious!" I cried, "and how did that happen?"

"Well, some few days back a boy captured a strange and savage bird, that pecked him horribly; he took it to my cousin the schoolmaster, but even he did not know what kind of animal it was, and could only suggest that it must have been painted those colours. Soon the whole village had gathered to see the strange bird, and as we wanted to know what colour it really was, we first washed it in cold water, and when this did not remove the stains we soaked it in hot water, and washed it with soap and soda afterwards once more in cold water. This still did not remove the paint, nor seemingly do the bird any good, as afterwards it would not even eat; and it died the same day."

I was dumbfoundered, and yet could have shrieked with laughter.

"You are stupid people, upon my soul," I told her, "and particularly your schoolmaster. Fancy steaming a parrot! This beats everything. That was a bird from the tropics and its colours were natural. It belonged to my bride and was very valuable." Again I burst into uproarious laughter, and the girl, who had been gazing at me open-mouthed, then went off annoyed, muttering uncomplimentary remarks.

I stood wondering, deep in thought, and just as I had decided what to do, between the trees in the opening of the little forest path I caught a glimpse of what looked to me like a white straw hat with a green ribbon. Salome was the proud possessor of just such a hat, so I hastened towards the clearing, calling her name. But I must have been mistaken, for I found nobody there.

I hurried back home, and called at the doctor's presently, telling Salome the result of my search. She seemed to look at me rather peculiarly, neither scolding nor praising, and was neither unfriendly nor sweet. However, I bore in mind the doctor's well-meant words, and resolved to let her be until we were married.

Our wedding-day came at last. I only saw my bride for a few moments, and was glad she looked so calm, though she had put on that crinoline The doctor, noticing my glance, caught hold of me, saying:

"Never mind, Hans, let her have her way for the last time; to-night you can make her take it off and hang it up never to be used again!"

The bells were ringing, and we started on our way to the church, walking silently side by side. Large crowds had turned out to see the procession, for the doctor, at least, was a popular public man. The minister stepped to the altar before us and the ceremony began. As he asked me if I would have this woman Salome Rieber for my wedded wife I called out with loud joyful voice, "Yes," and was wondering in my heart if she would also give her reply in a loud voice, or in the usual trembling low tones. But as the minister put the question to her I was astounded to hear a very loud and hearty "No."

I was speechless with astonishment, and meanwhile the clergyman asked her kindly and quietly what she meant by her most unusual and unseemly behaviour.

"I shall explain afterwards," replied Salome, who now looked pale and frightened. The ceremony was at an end, the company dispersed wonderingly, and I arrived home almost distracted with anger and shame. I had been unable to utter one word.

My parents were equally upset and deeply resented this insult. We were discussing the matter when Dr. Rieber, leaning on his crutch, entered unceremoniously, and began at once:

"Friends, I could not have faced you here if after what my daughter has just told me I did not consider it my duty to try and clear up this terrible affair. I am far from believing what she tells me; yet there must be something at the bottom of all this trouble, for she tells me she wilfully caused it to punish Hans for his infidelity. His honour no less than mine demands an inquiry."

I merely said, "Please proceed, my conscience is clear."

"She affirms," he then continued, "that you have an affair with a peasant girl whom you met in the woods a few days ago; that you have laughed and joked with her, and have made the parrot an excuse for your meetings with her!"

"Then it was she," I said, and told them all that had happened that day in the wood. As luck would have it, at that very moment there came a knock at the front door, and the same peasant girl appeared selling butter and eggs. She had no sooner seen me than she cried out, "You again! If I had known this was your house I would not have come within miles of it."

"What has he done to you, my girl?" Dr. Rieber at once said to her.

"He insulted me; called me a stupid goose, and laughed at me after I had answered his questions about that silly bird."

"Then he has not made love to you?"

"Made love to me! What next? I would soon have knocked that out of him. He was rude to me, very rude, and you are getting rude too. If you don't want my eggs or butter why not say so? Why keep me here answering stupid questions?" and with that she slammed the door and was gone.

"This is satisfactory," cried the doctor, joyfully, shaking me by the hand. "Now you shall have your satisfaction. To-morrow there shall be another wedding ceremony, and you will just do to her as she did to you. Now, no refusal, you simply must. There is no other alternative, or you shan't have her at all. I have insisted upon her making amends to you, and now she has had her way she is quite ready to marry you. I have seen the minister and after a great deal of trouble induced him, and he has promised to ask her first this time, so I take no refusal from you."

Here I interrupted him. "No! No!" I cried, "not for anything——" But the doctor would not let me finish, breaking out into a fresh exposition of the whole case and telling me my honour and my future happiness with his daughter were at stake, for how could I ever look my wife and children in the face with such an insult unavenged? Finally I consented to say "No" after she had said "Yes." My father also had joined in and thought some sort of satisfaction was due to us, and although my mother was with me and pitied Salome, we had to give in. My only hope was that the old people would find some other way to gratify their desire to punish my dear girl. However, that was not to be.

I went to the church at the appointed hour. Again a large crowd of people had collected and the church was packed. Dr. Rieber had seen to that, for he said the atonement must be as public as the outrage. My relatives accompanied me to church, and there Dr. Rieber gave the bride to me. She was as pale as death, her cheeks showed traces of much weeping, and she did not raise her eyes to mine. I seemed to see something else besides humiliation on her face, I seemed to feel a joyful pressure on my arm as we walked slowly down the aisle. The minister had no book before him, nor again did he read the marriage service, but simply and solemnly said:

"Two of our community have appeared here before me, to express before God and this Christian congregation their will and intention towards each other." He then approached closer to us, and asked Salome first if she would have me for her husband. I had to look at my dear bride stealthily; she spoke her "Yes" with humble submission, not too low, and not too loudly. It was then that a great wave of pity for her—for both of us—surged over me, and as the pastor spoke to me and asked me if I would have her for my wife, I spoke with a firm voice a trustful "Yes."

This "Yes" ran through the congregation like some electric current, for I felt rather than heard behind me a sudden stir, as of a breeze running through the trees. But I only had eyes then for my wife. She looked thunderstruck, and would have fallen had I not quickly clasped her in my arms. I gazed anxiously into her eyes; however, she quickly opened them, and seeing no reproach, nothing but quiet happiness in them, I held her still and whispered, "Hold fast to me, Salome, I shall never again leave you."

The parson seemed astonished also, but quickly recovering himself he now gave us his blessing, adding, " Young friend, you have chosen the right path ! "

Is it necessary to tell you the rest ? My father found it difficult to make the best of the bad bargain as he put it, but with the help of my mother we soon got him to welcome Salome and make her feel at ease. My mother of course was delighted with the turn that I had given the whole affair, and the more so as, and these were her very words, " The wedding-cake and wedding-breakfast will not now be spoiled, and we can all do justice to the good things and rejoice over the happy ending."

The last one to be pacified was Dr. Rieber. He called me a coward, said I had played fast and loose with his honour and so forth, but finally he allowed himself to be appeased, and I am sure that in his innermost heart he was glad that his only child had been let off so handsomely, and that he esteemed me more for disobeying him.

Salome afterwards confessed to me that she could have bitten off her tongue after her " No," but she had felt as if in a fever ; and anyhow, she repaid me my " Yes " with the most unselfish love and devotion during all her life.

THEODOR W. STORM
1817–1888

IN THE GREAT HALL

THERE had been a christening in the afternoon; now it was near dusk. The parents of the infant sat with their guests in the great hall, among them the grandmother of the man. The others, too, were near relatives, young and old; but the grandmother was older by a whole generation than the oldest of these. After her the child had been named Barbara; but it had been given another, prettier name, for Barbara alone sounded so very old-fashioned for the sweet little babe. Yet this was to be the name by which it should be called. Both parents would have it so, however much their friends might object. But the old grandmother never heard a syllable that the worth of her old-proven name had been called in question.

Soon after the performance of his office the clergyman had left the family party to itself. Now old, dear, oft-told tales were brought to light, and, not for the last time, told again. Each knew the other; the old had seen the young grow up, the oldest seen the old grow grey. All told the merriest, the most charming tales of childhood; if no one else knew them, grandmother took her turn. Of her alone no one could tell a tale; the days of her childhood lay beyond the birth of all the others; to have known it one must have exceeded all human age. Amid this talk it had become evening. The hall faced towards the west; a glowing light fell through the windows upon the plaster roses on the white stuccoed walls; then this faded too. It had grown still, and from afar there sounded a hollow monotonous murmur. Some of the guests listened.

"That is the sea," said the young wife.

"Yea," said the grandmother, "I have often heard it; it has long been so."

Again no one spoke. Without, before the windows, in the narrow paved yard there stood a great lime-tree, and there the sparrows could be heard going to rest under the leaves. The host had taken the hand of his wife, who sat by his side in silence, and fixed his gaze upon the bossy old-fashioned plaster ceiling.

"What is it?" asked the grandmother.

"The ceiling is cracked," said he; "the cornice, too, has sunk. The hall grows old, grandmother; we must rebuild it."

"Nay, the hall is not so old," she made reply, "I mind me well when it was built."

"Built? What was here before?"

"Before?" the grandmother repeated. Then she fell silent for a while and sat there a lifeless image; her eyes gazed beyond into the time that was past, her thoughts dwelt among the shadows of things long vanished. At last she spoke: "It is eighty years now; your grandfather and I, many a time have we recounted the story—in those days the hall-door led not into a chamber, but out of the house into a little pleasure-garden. But this is not the door; the old door had panes of glass; through them one could see into the garden as soon as one entered at the street-door. A flight of three steps with a gaily coloured Chinese hand-rail on either side led down into the garden. Between two borders with low box-edging lay a broad white shell-strewn path to a lime-tree arbour, and before this, slung between two cherry-trees, was a swing. On either side of the arbour against the high garden wall stood carefully tended apricot-trees. At noon-tide of a summer's day your great-grandfather could be seen punctually walking up and down this path tidying the auriculas and Dutch tulips in the borders or tying them with bass to little white sticks. A severe, precise man he was, of military bearing, and his black eyebrows, with his white powdered wig, gave him a very distinguished appearance.

"Now it befell one fine August afternoon that your grandfather descended the little garden stairs; but at that time he was far from being a grandfather. My old eyes can still see him approaching your great-grandfather with a light step. From a neatly embroidered pocket-book he drew a letter which he presented with a graceful bow. He was a refined young man, with gentle engaging eyes, and his black bob-wig contrasted pleasantly with his bright complexion and pearly-grey cloth coat. Having read the letter your great-grandfather nodded and shook your grandfather by the hand. He must have liked him; it was not often he did that. Then he was called into the house and your grandfather walked down the garden.

"On the swing before the arbour there sat a young maiden of eight; she had a picture-book upon her lap wherein she read busily; bright golden curls hung down over her hot little face, gleaming in the scorching sunshine. 'What is your name?' the young man demanded.

"Tossing back her hair, she replied: 'Barbara.'

"'Have a care, Barbara, your curls will melt in the sun.'

"Swiftly she passed her hand over her hot hair; the young man smiled—it was a very gentle smile. 'Never fear,' he said, 'come, let us swing.'

"Down she jumped. 'Wait, I must first see that my book is safe.' She placed it in the arbour. When she returned he offered to lift her up. 'No,' she said, 'I can get up alone.' Then, standing upon the swing, she cried, 'Now, away!' And your grandfather pulled till his wig danced about his shoulders, now to the right, now to the left of him; the swing, with the little maiden, rose and fell in the glare of the sun, and her bright curls blew out gaily. But yet she could not mount high enough! Now the swing rushed into the linden branches, that the birds darted from the espaliers on either side, making the over-ripe apricots to roll upon the ground.

"'What was that?' said he, and held the swing.

"She laughed that he should have put such a question. 'That was the robin; he is not usually so timid.'

"He lifted her from the swing and together they went to the espaliers; the golden fruit lay among the shrubs. 'Your bird has treated you,' he said. Shaking her head she placed a lovely apricot into his hand. 'For you,' she murmured very softly.

"And then your great-grandfather returned into the garden. 'Beware, beware,' he said, with a smile, 'you will never be rid of her.' Then he spoke about their affairs and they both entered the house.

"That evening little Barbara was permitted to sit at table. The kindly young man had begged for her. Not quite as she had wished it, did things fall out; for the guest sat by her father's side at the head of the table; but she was only a very little maiden and must sit at the other end by the youngest of the clerks. Therefore she quickly finished her meal and crept stealthily to her father's chair. But he talked so earnestly of accounts and discounts that the young man had never an eye for poor little Barbara. Yes, yes, that was eighty years ago; but the old grandmother minds her well, how little Barbara grew very impatient upon that evening and was none too well disposed towards her good parent. The clock struck ten and she had to say good-night. When she came to say it to your grandfather, he asked her: 'Shall we swing to-morrow?' And then little Barbara was quite happy again. . . . 'What an old dandler you are, to be sure,' said the great-grandfather; but he was himself really quite unreasonably in love with his little maiden. And the next day, towards evening, your grandfather left us again.

"Eight years passed by. Often in the winter time little Barbara would stand by the glass-door and breathe on the frozen panes; then she would peer through the peep-hole down into the snow-covered garden and dream of the beautiful summer, the gleaming leaves and the warm bright sun, of the robin that built in the espaliers, of ripe apricots that once upon a time did roll on the ground; then of a summer's day, and, at last, of none but this one summer's day whenever her thoughts dwelt on summer. Thus the years passed. Little Barbara was twice as old and was really no little Barbara at all; but that one day of summer stood out radiant in her memory. Then one fine day he actually returned."

"Who? The summer's day?" and her grandson smiled.

"Yes, yes," she said, "your grandfather. It was a proper summer's day." "And then?" he asked again.

"And then," said the grandmother, "then there was a wedding, and little Barbara became your grandmother, just as she is, sitting among you now and telling the old tales. But it had not come to that yet. First there was a wedding, and for that wedding it was that your great-grandfather built this hall. Well, there was an end to the garden and the flowers; but that mattered little, for there soon came living flowers to cheer his noon-day rest. As soon as the hall was built, the wedding took place. It was a merry wedding, and many a day did the guests speak of it. None of you were there, you who must be in everything nowadays; but your fathers were there and your grandfathers, your mothers and grandmothers, all people who might well speak for themselves. They were quiet and modest times then, to be sure. We did not pretend to know everything better than our rulers and their ministers; and if any one thrust his nose into politics, we called him a tinker, and if he was a cobbler we went to his neighbour for our boots. The maids were plain Sarah and Jane; and we were dressed according to our station. And to-day you even wear moustachios like squires and cavaliers. What would you? Do you all want to rule?"

"Of course," said the grandson.

" And what of the people of rank, and the nobles, that are born to it ? What shall become of them ? "

" Oh . . . nobles . . ." said the young mother, looking up at her husband with proud, loving eyes. He only said, with a smile, " Wipe them out, grandmother ; or let us all be noblemen, all Germany, every man Jack of us. I see nothing else for it."

The old dame made no reply to this ; she merely said : " There was no talk of State affairs at my wedding ; the entertainment pursued its even course, and we were just as merry as you with your new-fangled parties. At table a jesting riddle, a doggerel rhyme, and when they served the sweets we sang all the pretty songs that have long been forgotten ; and your grandfather's clear tenor voice could be heard above them all. Ah, folk were more polite to one another ; shouting and arguing were not held to be seemly in elegant company. It is all changed now ; but your grandfather was a gentle, peaceable man. It is a long while since he left us ; he has preceded me far ; it is about time that I should follow."

The grandmother was silent for a moment, and nobody spoke. But she could feel them grasp her hands ; they all wanted to keep her with them. A peaceful smile lit up the dear old face ; and gazing on her grandson she said : " His body lay here too, in this hall ; and you were but a six-year-old, and you stood by the coffin to weep. Your father was a hard, ruthless man. 'Don't howl, lad,' he said, and took you on his arm. 'See here, that's what an honest man looks like when he is dead.' And brushed a secret tear from his eye. He had always held your grandfather in great reverence. They have all passed over now ; and to-day I have held my great-granddaughter at the font in this hall, and you have given her the name of your old grandmother. May the good God let her come to my years just as happily and contentedly ! " The young mother sank on her knees before the grandmother and kissed her delicate hands.

The grandson said : " Grandmother, we will pull down the old hall altogether and plant a new pleasure-garden ; little Barbara is come back again. The women all say that she is the image of you ; she shall sit again in the swing and the sun shall shine once more on the golden childish curls ; and then, perhaps, one summer afternoon grandfather will come down the little Chinese stairs ; perhaps——"

" Go to," said the grandmother, with a smile ; "you are a dreamer," she said, " and so was your grandfather."

THEODOR FONTANE
1819–1898

WHITHER?

"YES, my dear Leontine, you must decide now, decide whither we are to go! I don't want to have to do it always; I don't want to ponder over the divisions of the earth in so far as they concern baths and spas, and then to find the expected heaven in an attic!"

"'Whenever you come, your place will be ready for you.'"

"That may be good enough for the poets, but not for us. Do you remember Kissingen, and our first night in that hencoop? With everything so dear and always trusting to luck! I've had enough; so I ask you, Leontine, whither?"

"My dear James, I wish you would not worry me with that eternal word 'whither'! It makes me quite nervous to hear it. We are only at the end of May, and have at least six weeks before us to consider it in. Besides, what do you mean by 'hencoop,' 'heaven,' and 'attic'? Mere words. What you describe in that way was only a temporary shelter for a day, but we got a nice room afterwards. There is no need to hurry; no one remains for ever without decent lodgings, especially such a generous person as you are."

"No compliments, Leontine; make suggestions."

"What do you say to Misdroi?"

"Do you know Misdroi?"

"No. If I did . . ."

"You would be sure at least not to commence your suggestions with it. Let me enlighten you about Misdroi. It contains more Berliners than Berlin, and, moreover, a thing you would object to still further, more invalids than Berlin, besides Russians and negroes And above all, Leontine, my principal reason for going to a spa is to get away from the dear old faces."

"In which I quite agree with you," laughed Leontine; "so let us drop Misdroi and consider Norderney."

"Good; it is worth consideration, but, on the other hand, you must remember that it is not much more accessible than Heligoland.

You board ship at Emden, and then four hours of sea, and the four hours generally mean six. The ship will heave, the sea will be rough, and you will be sea-sick."

"I shall not be sea-sick. At any rate I shall always be presentable. I assure you, James, will goes a long way in these matters. Besides, it is a matter of good breeding. The sea would not frighten me if I wanted to go, for, frankly, Norderney has pleasant memories for me. I have been married long enough and happily enough, but still, I should like to refresh such poetic memories."

"Leontine, please!"

"Yes, James, poetic memories, in spite of, or perhaps because of the fact that I was still almost a child at the time, not much older than our Lulu. Do you remember how we played skittles every afternoon?"

"We did the same at Wilmersdorf and Holensee. . . ."

"Not at all, for, firstly, we played among the dunes in the wrack and thistle. . . ."

"It was very nice!"

"And, secondly, ours was no ordinary Berlin skittle-alley, with a board and groove from which you get splinters if you are not careful. At Norderney the ball hung from a curious old Frisian ship's-hawser, and was thrown among the skittles in the same way that at home we used to throw the brass ring attached to a green cord on to a peg stuck into a pear-tree. But it had to be done skilfully. I remember how Alfred Meyer—an active youth then, barely seventeen, with the down just beginning to show on his cheeks—knocked down all nine skittles three times in succession."

"Quite possibly, Leontine. Most probably, in fact. But later, to be sure, he went bankrupt and escaped to America, and being such a marvel at skittles as you say, he might have set up a public-house out there. At Niagara perhaps, near the great falls."

"Now, James, you know I don't like such jibes, especially against people who were dear to me in my youth. I don't pretend to get my own way—one learns to do without that—but you asked me to make suggestions, and that led to what I was saying. But really, what have you against Norderney?"

"Nothing. Let it be Norderney, if you like. It's not quite a savage island; the wild tribes in the shape of native as well as immigrant hotel-keepers, as far as I remember, are keener on money than blood. So why not, Leontine? But though your description of the skittles was so vivid, I should find it too little to occupy the whole five weeks with, especially as I am fully convinced that I shall never be able to overthrow all nine of them three times in succession."

"No," she said, with that peculiar sarcasm which women know how to use so much better than men; "no, James; you will never be able to do that!"

And in her sudden burst of good humour she was about to extract a new arrow from her quiver and complete her triumph with another excellent shot, when a servant entered and announced Herr Markaner, King's Counsel.

James rose to meet the visitor, who gave him a slight greeting, while he approached the beautiful hostess and kissed her hand.

"Business?" queried James.

"No."

"Good; then we'll lunch together. My wife has just been raving about Norderney. I have nothing against it, though, I must confess, I have nothing to say for it. I must tell you, however, that memories of youth have been invoked, which always indicates a weak position, and makes the thing doubtful. You, Markaner, know all the spas of Western Europe, and others too. You shall decide for us. Maybe you will raise my consent (given merely in the interests of peace) to a higher level. It all depends on you. What is to be the decision? Do you remember this island, rich in memories of youth?"

While speaking, James pushed the two decanters across the table to his guest.

"Port or sherry, Markaner? Or perhaps you would prefer some Rhenish wine, or Steinwine, or perhaps some old German? We have only to look at ourselves in the glass in order to recognise our special privilege."

Both laughed, but Leontine, who was very sensitive on the point, and was at bottom rather anti-Semite, went to the open piano and began toying with the keys.

"Well, what about Norderney?" James insisted, pouring out some wine for Markaner. "Do you know the place?"

"I've been there three times. In '64, when it was still Hanoverian, in '80, and in '81."

"Now bear in mind, my friend," said Leontine, walking over

from the piano to the table, "that I can correct you if you make mistakes; so proceed, please, without prejudice."

"Why, of course, dear friend! But shall I be pardoned if I speak the truth?"

"The truth by all means. Truth is almost a passion with me; the passion of my maturer years."

"Of which you must not speak in connection with that comforting word."

James laughed, and Markaner continued:

"Now, to return to Norderney. We will begin with the soil. We find the dune-sand, together with a recent stercoral deposit, in all three states, or to speak more plainly, guano. Norderney ought to be converted into a fruit-garden at all costs. It would be a valuable enterprise from the agricultural point of view, but very questionable as a means of purifying the air. One hears a lot about pure air out there, but from my own personal experience their so-called pure air, the breeze descending from heaven and playing over the island, is in no way connected with the relatively modern aristocracy of ozone, but rather to the—by all accounts—effete family of sulphuretted hydrogen. I think this last remark can pass without contradiction, since, if I am not mistaken, hell is older than heaven."

"We won't go into that. It is too difficult a question even for you, Markaner."

"And, perhaps," the lawyer continued, "there is an unconscious connection between these penetrating hygienic breezes of Norderney and the huge hotel on the seashore that bears the startling name of 'The Dram Shop.' There is also a music salon of which *Lohengrin* and *Tannhäuser* form the entire repertoire. There are two flower-beds containing mignonette and wallflowers, and add to that the excitement of a seal being found either dead or alive about every third day, and you have the whole of Norderney as it is. There are steamers, too, that go to Borkum, Juist, and Spiekeroog; pleasure-steamers, supposed to be, and may appear to be such at a casual glance, but obeying the old law of choosing the lesser of two evils, I would counsel any one who is keen on his pleasure to remain on Norderney Beach. And then the eternal sea! It must be rather boring to be surrounded by it all the time. Personally, I prefer hills; the Alps; if not Rigi, then the Brocken, and if not the Brocken, then at least the Oybin."

"The Oybin? In Zittau, isn't it?" Leontine put in.

"Yes; do you know it?"

"No, but Lulu does. She stayed last autumn with her Aunt Sarah in Zittau, for ten days only, because the Michaelmas holidays would not allow of more, but when she came back she talked of nothing but the Oybin. And so you know it too?"

"To speak truthfully, I don't, in spite of the modern craze to know everything. I merely mentioned it as an example."

"We had better call in Lulu," James broke in. "I remember we wouldn't listen to her at the time, but then, who will suffer the description of scenery and landscapes? She will triumph over us now."

And walking over to the telephone he called up to the nursery for Lulu to come down, and soon she was heard singing and warbling as she walked down the iron staircase leading into the room, and a moment later appeared through the curtained door. She was a girl of thirteen, with a thick auburn plait. She shook hands with the lawyer, and went up to her father, whom she saw for the first time that day.

"Good-morning, father. Fräulein Oberlein is still upstairs, but she is so dull that I was glad when you called me." With these words she seated herself on the arm of her father's chair and began tugging at his moustache.

"Now, don't do that, Lulu! Don't destroy the only sound thing I have left. Each hair is sacred to me. I know you can't appreciate that with your thick plait! I bade you come, not to destroy, but to create. We are sitting in solemn council and you must give the decision."

"I know what it's about!"

"What?"

"I know what I have to decide!"

"Well, what is it?"

"Whether we are going to the Cingalese Show."

All three laughed, but Lulu was unperturbed, her gaze fixed on a basket of red cherries that stood among the dishes on the table. She walked over to them and began to eat them, dropping the stones unceremoniously into her hand.

The lawyer screwed up his little beady eyes and said, with a kind of gravity:

"The Cingalese, the Zoological Gardens, that is to say? Hm! I wonder if there is some higher wisdom lurking in this child's words? I almost believe there is, though it may be difficult to explain. The child has hit the nail on the head. Oybin! pooh! Oybin is too far!

The memorable word ' Cingalese ' our Lulu has so unwittingly uttered contains not only the whole truth, even though it be hidden, but coincides with the intuitive knowledge of my dead friend Meddelhammer."

At this stage, the lawyer naturally wished to proceed to tell a story about this knowledge of Meddelhammer's, but James, who was a universal genius in a small way, and dabbled in every subject, from the turf to painting and lyrical poetry, and had a passion for etymology, and in particular for proper names, forgetting all his plans for the holiday, forgetting even Oybin and Lulu, suddenly interrupted the lawyer with an almost professional solemnity.

" Meddelhammer ! What a curious name ! Dutch, I suppose ! "

" Quite possibly," the lawyer remarked, who, as one can imagine, would far rather have come to his story than to discuss anything so trivial as the derivation of Meddelhammer's name. But James was insistent.

" Very curious ! Meddelhammer ! Hammer, of course, means nothing, it is so commonly met with ; but Meddelhammer ! What is meddel ? Is it the English ' middle,' or a corruption of the German ' mädel ' ? I must ask a German scholar. Middlehammer is more likely, but Mädelhammer is more amusing. What do you say to Mädelhammer ? "

" Now, James, please don't begin your researches in the matter, and show some consideration for the rest of us. And Lulu is so engrossed in eating cherries that she has not even heard a word."

" Not at all," said Lulu ; " I've heard everything, and I hope father will never say anything worse ! I've heard him say such heaps of things ! "

" I can see," said James, with a grateful glance at his pet, " that it is useless to go on before your unscientific attitude. I will drop etymological research. Come, Markaner, tell us about Meddelhammer and his peculiar knowledge of travel. Will it bear hearing ? "

" Oh yes ! particularly when you hear who he was. He was, in fact, a schoolmaster, and though I dislike schoolmasters in general, because they go to extremes and are either dreary pedants or superficial cynics (the doings of one of them made me blush the other day), still, I liked Meddelhammer—at least, at the time. Why ? you may ask. Because in a quite unpedantic way he had his lighter moments."

" How remarkable ! "

" It was. And now listen. One day I went to the Museum to see some old statuary (I confess they are too contorted for my taste), and just as I had finished and had gone into the entrance hall for my umbrella, at the very moment when I was about to put a twenty-pfennig piece into the box (I never give more or less), I turned, to find Meddelhammer confronting me. But in such a guise! and in such circumstances! He was wearing a loud pepper-and-salt travelling suit, a Tyrolese hat, and had a field-glass by his side. A *Baedeker* was in his hand, and, last but not least, there was his wife in a remarkably fashionable Rembrandt hat. 'Heavens, Meddelhammer!' I exclaimed. 'What are you doing here? Won't you introduce me to your wife?' 'Delighted, I am sure.' 'In Berlin, in this July weather! It must be about 100° in the shade! I thought you were in Ostend. . . .' "

" Too high a flight financially, I should think," James broke in.

" Possibly, but Meddelhammer made no objection to my remark. Instead he took my arm (a thing he had not done for years, because, owing to our development, we had had to drift apart), and said, while his wife kept pace with us, 'Before I satisfy your curiosity, my dear friend, let us cross the Frederick's Bridge to a capital lunch house I know, where we have lunched for the last three days. That is the exact time we have been wandering about. It is certainly tiring, in spite of the thrills we get over each new discovery. We have done the old Museum, the new one remains for to-morrow, and then for the National Gallery. A pleasing prospect. We shall wind up with the collection of engravings. The " Dante " of Botticelli should be very fine. Do you remember, Markaner, how you and I used to read Dante together? It was when we were in the upper second at Joachimsthal, and your great desire was to be a poet.' Yes, my dear friends, he said that in the hearing of the two Museum attendants and I couldn't contradict him, for it was the truth."

Lulu burst out laughing. " Fancy Uncle Markaner a poet Uncle Markaner a poet! how funny! "

" Do you hear that, my friend? For the second time observe th child's wisdom."

" Rudeness," the mother said reprovingly, and would have con tinued, but James intervened.

" No interruptions, Leontine. Markaner must finish his story Well? "

"Well, we got safely to the restaurant, and seated ourselves in a corner, which, to my utter astonishment, Meddelhammer described as 'a cosy corner,' in a 'man of the world way.' He had already tried it, and, I must confess, it was cosy. It was in a deep niche near a large window and a mirror. We could see everything that was going on in the street through the curtains, though we ourselves were unseen."

"Listen, Markaner, I am beginning to be impressed by your Meddelhammer. Did you say he was a schoolmaster?"

"Just a schoolmaster. But let me finish; the best is yet to come. I was very hungry; I generally am when I work hard for an hour or so. I called the waiter and ordered soup, eggs, roast beef, and a half-bottle of Larosse, and then I noticed that my schoolmaster was giving his orders, as though I had said, 'My dear Meddelhammer, it is now your turn!' Meddelhammer understood me perfectly, but he did not order anything more than two glasses of port wine and a couple of rolls and cheese, which took me doubly by surprise."

"Why?"

"I will permit myself a little digression on that point, provided that the child, who was so needlessly called in to give her opinions about Oybin, does not mind."

"Not in the least," said Lulu, putting down her large collection of cherry stones and wiping her hand on a serviette.

"Well, then, the reason I was so impressed by their order was, in the first place, its peculiarly English or cosmopolitan character; it showed a knowledge and experience of travelling. In the second place, I was impressed by its lightness. I can hardly think of a more appropriate example for a light lunch than 'a roll and cheese,' especially since, owing to the rise in the price of wheat, the rolls continue to diminish in size."

"Quite true. The poor bakers have nothing but trouble and worry."

Markaner continued:

"I could see at once that Meddelhammer read my soul like an open book (schoolmasters always seem to get a deeper knowledge of men), for when my half-bottle of Larosse and their two glasses of wine arrived, he clinked glasses with me and without so much as a question on my part said, 'My wife and I, Markaner, have to be very circumspect and curb our appetites, though, for my part, I confess that three hours at a Museum with new things to see and references to make is no light matter, and I envy you your soup and roast beef. But we must face matters squarely, especially since I am a schoolmaster. We dine at five, and if we took a full lunch at half-past two, we could not do justice to our dinner.' "

" But five is rather late, isn't it ? " interrupted James, who believed in putting schoolmasters into a different class of men from bankers.

" So it is," said Markaner, " and I told him so."

" What did he say ? Most people are very sensitive on that point nowadays."

" Not Meddelhammer. He was too sensible for that. He merely laughed and said, ' Five o'clock is late, certainly, and when we are at home, like good citizens, we always dine at two. I dislike innovations when they are not necessary.' On my part, of course, I was anxious to smooth things over and return to the original subject, but he repeated, ' When we are at home. . . . But now, we are not at home ; we are travellers, sightseers, if you like, in Berlin. When the holidays commenced we began to consider whither we were going. After three days of deliberation, during which time we discussed no less than fifty places, we decided to remain here and get to know Berlin as though we were foreigners. Yes, real foreigners. For, actually, we folk born in Berlin only live here, and do not know our capital. To put an end to this unpatriotic state of affairs, and perhaps to set an example to others (as a schoolmaster should), we packed our trunks, and at ten o'clock that same evening, about the time when the Paris express arrives, we drove up to the Hôtel de Paris, and just like travellers—Russian or English, perhaps—we had our tea brought to our own room, and sat for an hour and a half looking out of the window. The sight was enthralling. Over the Linden Avenue—which not one of us really knows—the lights were twinkling from behind the balconies—everything seemed so romantic, just like a scene in Spain. This is our third day of it. It will take us two or three weeks to do it all.' Thus Meddelhammer spoke as we sat in our corner, until he recalled us to fresh activities by drawing out his watch. ' We ought to be at Krautzler's from three to four,' he said, ' for an ice or a glass of soda-water, and in that spirit of pedantry into which circumstances have forced us,' he added, with a laugh, ' we must make no exception to-day.' And to be sure, half an hour later, we were all seated at Krautzler's, each with an ice in front of us. As good luck would have it, a flower-girl happened to come along, and I was able to present his wife (who, by the way, looked more like a duchess than a schoolmaster's wife) with a bunch of flowers. She accepted it prettily, and said she would wear the flowers at table. From Krautzler's we went to the Hôtel de Rome, and there we parted. And now, my dear Madame, what do you think of my schoolmaster and of his method of travelling?"

Leontine was silent, but James burst forth:

"I vote we erect a memorial to your schoolmaster, an obelisk, let us say, with an inscription above the figures round the plinth!"

"What figures?"

"Meddelhammer in front, of course, and above him Krautzler and Mühling!"

"Why?"

"It is necessary to emulate him, to follow his example. Lulu, fill Uncle Markaner's glass! Now for a toast! Long live Meddelhammer!"

"Meddelhammer and a summer in Berlin!"

THE BARROWMAN OF GRIFFELSBRUNN

THEODOR FONTANE

SUMMER had taken me to Norderney, not so much for the pleasure of bathing, as that of beholding the sea once more, and at the same time to seize the opportunity of meeting a couple of old friends, who regularly spent their holidays in that fairly attractive though not exactly beautiful North Sea island. Their regularity of visit had brought about the finding of a permanent lodging in a suitably sequestered inn quite by the sea. From our rooms we could easily have cast our goblets into the ocean like the King of Thule, but we preferred instead to sit and gossip about things old and new. One evening the suggestion was made that each of us should in turn tell a story to the best of our ability, the story to be taken from real life. This was a necessary condition. The last to contribute a tale was Oldermann, an architect.

" There is a story I could tell you," he began, " of a barrowman, and in order to give the story a name I shall call it ' The Barrowman of Griffelsbrunn.'

" Now Griffelsbrunn, which at one time was not altogether unknown as a health resort, developed towards the beginning of the century quite a reputation as a coffee-garden among the people of the neighbouring town of L——, and when the latter town began—as you know—to expand during the 'seventies, and to absorb all the neighbouring tourists' centres and villages, Griffelsbrunn was among the doomed. It had to go as a matter of course; all the pavilions, booths, maples—everything had to go to make room for a big hotel with a bazaar on the ground floor.

" My plans being approved of, I was entrusted with the work. As soon as the excavations were begun, I was convinced from the boggy nature of the soil that a firm foundation would be absolutely essential, so I gave the necessary instructions to the builder and his old foreman, both of whom, as natives of the place, showed promise of serving us faithfully.

" A long stretch of board was put across the excavation, and a couple of dozen labourers were taken on to shovel into barrows the necessary gravel and sand—whole mountains of it—and tip it into the foundations from above. I inspected the work twice a day to see that all was going well, as I wanted, if possible, to get the building roofed in before the harvest. Everything went smoothly, without a hitch ; all the men worked well, but the best of them all was a swarthy, rather handsome man of about five-and-thirty. Without holding himself aloof from the others, or any sort of nonsense, he seemed quite obviously to differ from the rest. He was bigger and stronger, had a well-kept beard and slightly reddened eyelids. He wore a tight-fitting jacket instead of a coat ; a cap of military cut, and thick boots that must have belonged to and done service for a traveller in the Alps. All his garments were in a lamentable condition, and showed signs of having been patched and darned by his own hand, but the cut of them, as well as the man himself, were impressive. In every movement of his there was a certain ' chic,' to borrow a word from the world of fashion, it being especially noticeable in the way he handled the barrow. Grasping the handles tightly, he trundled the barrow along with its wheel exactly in the centre of the plank as though it were a trick at a circus. But the most triumphant moment of all was when, with a quick, dexterous jerk, he tipped the contents of the barrow down into the pit.

" He had been working thus for about a week and a half, when I took the occasion of speaking to the foreman in order to get some information about the man who stood out so conspicuously from his surroundings. The foreman, however, was unable to satisfy my curiosity, having seen him only for the first time when he applied for work some ten or twelve days before.

" ' And I took him on, for any fool can wheel a barrow. It is easy to see he is not one of us ; you have only to look at his hands ; they are sunburnt, it is true, but not the hands of a workman.'

" That was all I could learn. It was little enough, and did not lead me any further. One day my curiosity, or, I should say, my sympathy, urged me to approach the man and say to him, ' Would you care to come and see me at my house next Sunday ? I am always in between nine and eleven.'

" And he came. His garments, in a woeful condition, were the same as he had worn every day ; the same coat, the same boots, but everything was brushed and scrupulously clean. He gave me the impression of a man who had seen better days, of a man of education and breeding. He stopped by the door and said: 'At your service.' I asked him to come in, but he did not move, and stood waiting until I should address him again, which I did.

"'I daresay you have guessed why I wanted to see you. I can see that you belong to a different class than the one you appear in just now; you were not marked out for barrow-wheeling at your birth. You come from a good stock, and have had a good education. Some time or other you came to grief, through your own fault or not, who can say? but probably through your own fault. Cards, women, bills, perhaps dishonoured ones. It was too much for your people; their patience had reached a limit, and you had a family no more. And what happened . . . happened. . . .'

"He followed each of my sentences with a little nod, and when, on finishing, I asked, 'Am I right?' he answered:

"'Yes. There were nine of us—six went into the schools, and the rest into the army. My father could do no more.'

"'Yes . . . I understand. I know enough, and have no desire to pry into your secrets. And now listen. I am not rich, but I have connections, and think I can help you if you want help.'

"He was silent, and I went on. 'I shall speak to the foreman, or better still, to the builder; he will give you some other work on the building, and I will see to your clothes. Where there's a will there's a way. You are big and strong (I hope morally too), and you can pull yourself out of the mire. It all depends on whether you have the strength to take my hand.' He stepped towards me, and I saw that his eyelids had reddened. Shortly and abruptly he thanked me, and I felt a tear on my hand. I was as moved as he was, and then, with repeated assurances on my side, we parted. That same day I spoke to the builder, who, as usual on a Sunday, was my guest. He agreed to everything, and promised to do his best, but thought it would be difficult to make any change until the end of the week. Thus it was agreed, and the same evening I set off on a little visit to Dresden, which kept me away three days. The first thing I did on my return was to inquire about my barrowman. But he was no longer there.

"'But where is he, foreman? You know the man I mean!'

"'I know. He never came back.'

"I grew anxious and set inquiries afoot, in which the authorities helped considerably. But in vain. No trace of him could be found.

"Where had he gone? To the new world . . . or further?"

HERMANN LINGG
1820–1905

NIKISA

FOR many long years after Christianity was officially established in the Eastern Roman Empire, the old Greek philosophy and mathematics and the pagan books of Homer still supplied the standard works in the schools for women, no less than for men.

True, of first importance was it to learn the creeds, and the interpretation of mystical chapters in the Bible, and to study the writings of the Fathers of the Church; yet even to this end the rhetoric and dialectics of the philosophers were of the greatest assistance.

In splendid palaces and mansions the daughters of the highest families spent their youth studying music and the arts. They rarely caught a glimpse of the great outer world, though spacious gardens surrounded by lofty walls adjoined their dwellings, and allowed them every relaxation and splendid scope for entertainments. The delicate skin for which the Byzantine women were famous is commonly ascribed to this mode of living, and their continuous study of philosophy and the fine arts must surely have intensified and made yet more attractive the natural fire of their wonderfully spiritual eyes.

Nikisa, the daughter of an important official at the Court, excelled as much in her beauty as in her culture and her knowledge. To the most learned questions she would find a quick reply; she spoke several foreign languages, could solve mathematical problems with ease, and was an adept in explaining the meaning of religious mysteries. She was her parents' pride, and they had no wish to give her hand in marriage to any of her many suitors, while she herself seemed equally loath to give her heart; so perfectly happy was Nikisa with her books, her music, and her drawings. One day there came a summons from the Imperial palace, an invitation to the noblest ladies in the capital to present at Court their marriageable daughters. For the Empress had decided that her son, the youthful Emperor, Theophilus, was now to choose a consort from the beauties of his land. As the arrangements for this competition had been made in utter secrecy the invitation caused much private speculation.

At the appointed hour the beauties of the capital, together with their mothers, assembled in the glorious Pearl Room, a spacious hall duly prepared for the function. The floor, walls, and ceiling gleamed with wonderful mosaics; gold, and precious stones, so set by skilful hands as to outshine their own magnificence, sent brilliant shafts of light in all directions, and made all the ladies, accustomed though they were to magnificent splendour in their own homes, open wide their eyes. Soon the Emperor appeared, an apple in his hand, the prize of beauty. He advanced, visibly astonished at the array of wondrously lovely women, each one of whom appeared to merit his reward. Yet quickly his eyes descended on Nikisa, and lit up joyously. Striding forward he thus addressed the sweet maidenly figure:

" Ah, if only the beauty of woman had not brought so much misery into the world already!" He spoke as if he could thus appease the Fates, for the choice so quickly made.

Nikisa, happiness stirring in her youthful heart, made reply:

" But through the devotion of one woman, all evil was redeemed!"

The young Emperor looked displeased at this unexpected answer; he thought it inappropriate, even impertinent, and, disliking theological references of any sort, he felt rebuffed.

" She babbles like the noisy starling," he told himself, and turned away to another maid, Feodora, the beautiful daughter of a dowager lady-in-waiting. A simple girlish blush was here the only answer to his question. Delighted, he handed her the apple with exquisite grace; then, taking her hand, he led her to his mother.

Nikisa, realising her mistake, yet felt deeply the affront put upon her. Pride and shame fought within her youthful bosom, but with head erect and smiling she returned the proud looks of her rival, the sneering laughter of the company. Arriving home, in the solitude of her chamber, she gave full rein to her great grief. She knew that in those moments in her Emperor's presence her heart went out to him, that her love was fully given to be but trampled on. The days went by and her restlessness only increased; she could find no more pleasure in her arts or in her talents; a great emptiness seized her, and in her sorrow she decided to take the veil. Her parents could not finally withhold their consent, and just to show the world a finer path had been chosen than the one she might have trodden, her entrance into the convent was made the occasion for great festivities and rejoicings. The Emperor heard of this with much displeasure.

The wedding of Feodora was not long delayed. Theophilus, her husband, returned to the Palace with his newly wedded wife and overwhelmed her with costly presents, and all the splendour that his Court could give. Festivities followed festivities, and Feodora always accepted modestly the homage that was showered upon her. In public she would show her husband a dignified respect, while by his side she tenderly abandoned herself to his love. Thus weeks and months passed in undisturbed happiness. Feodora, without possessing the high culture of Nikisa, lacked nothing in diplomacy, and made herself well loved and popular by carefully considering all her actions.

Brought up in prosperity, but not in affluence, she found ways and means to profit by her good fortune, and at the same time saw that all her relatives had a good share of it. Through her influence, one of her cousins had been made a captain in the Imperial fleet that voyaged to the East in search of treasures for the Court.

This greedy man, encouraged by success, thought out a scheme whereby he might smuggle in, under the Imperial seal, big loads of merchandise ; and so, avoiding the custom dues, sell them again with huge profit in the bazaars of Constantinople. To this end he craved his cousin's permission to bring her on his next voyage some presents as a slight return for favours shown to him. Innocently was this permission given. Another greedy kinsman, who by Feodora's efforts had been made Treasurer to the Emperor, shared in the enterprise by advancing all the necessary funds from the Imperial treasury. Favoured by wind and weather the venture succeeded so far that in a few weeks the galley was safely back in the shelter of the Golden Horn. Now on that same day the Emperor attended the church of the convent where Nikisa had retired. Here for the first time again he heard her name. One of the hymns, through its noble words, its sublime conception, and the sincerity of its pious melody, aroused his curiosity, and on inquiry he was told that Nikisa, the new sister, had composed it and others equally fine.

" What ! " cried he in accents of displeasure, " is it not forbidden that poems by women are admitted into the hymnody of our holy church ? This girl, this presumptuous fool, thus permitted to force herself into the company of saints and kings ! Hear, then, the renewal of my Imperial decree that no such verses are to be sung in any church." And with these angry words he left. Nikisa in her lonely cell was told of this occurrence. She had found some measure of consolation in her devotion to the church, and, deeply wounded, now resolved to retire far away from the capital to some monastery up in the inaccessible mountains, or on the borders of the great desert.

The Emperor in angry mood had gone to pace the gardens near the shore. There his trading galley was pointed out to him on the offing, and he gladly welcomed the diversion of boarding her with all his suite. At once he was struck with the great bulk of goods all bearing his Imperial seal, and asking what they were, and if all were his, was told that part were presents for his wife, the Empress. "Impossible," he cried. "Open them!" This was done, and certain articles were seen that could not possibly be presents for the Empress. Several of his suite encouraged his suspicions, and, pressed to explain, the Captain finally confessed his guilt, but shifted all the blame on Feodora.

"Has a Roman emperor or his wife been ever known to engage in trade?" he thundered. "Land the cargo and burn the lot! The Captain and his ship remain under arrest till further orders!"

On his return to the Palace the Empress was immediately examined, and, utterly cast down by the weight of her misfortune, was unable to utter one word in self-defence. Condemned out of hand to exile in a distant castle, the poor woman in her sorrow yet saved her kinsman from immediate death by her silence, and bore her cross in fortitude. One more evil overtook Theophilus. Enormous crowds had gathered on the quay to save some plunder from the burning stacks of merchandise, and through their carelessness the smouldering piles they dragged away set fire to some dwellings, which, bursting out in one huge conflagration, destroyed the oldest wing of the Imperial Palace.

Theophilus, raving wrathfully at this, cried out: "Oh! Nikisa, that miserable woman who has brought all this misfortune on my house through her silly answer; her evil spirit seems to haunt me; let her go forth to the farthest corner of my empire; cast her out!"

When Nikisa was handed this peremptory decree, tears flooded her sad eyes, and again her love for him who had scorned her welled up within her youthful bosom. But quickly she composed herself, and hurrying to the shore she boarded the galley lying there, the Emperor's trading boat; the Captain, seeing the Imperial parchment, was overjoyed at his good fortune, and immediately gave orders to set sail. Midnight saw him out upon the open sea.

As in the case of Feodora, small causes have often momentous effects. The guilt that really rested on her was minute and yet dishonouring. It could easily be forgiven, yet never forgotten. She had heard of her husband's grief at the fresh disaster, and that no man had yet been found in all his dominions to undertake the rebuilding of the burned wing. It was then she wrote and opened out her heart to him, telling faithfully of the little share she had in her kinsman's treachery, and praying him to take her back to his heart.

Theophilus, deeply touched by the eloquent appeal, went to her and found the little pathetic figure with her beautiful face more desirable than the day he first saw her. "In all truth I feel my happiness has returned!" he called to her, and whispered his forgiveness.

"Consider me the culprit, but also know that I honestly repent!' she replied. "Oh, what terrible havoc my stupidity has wrought; would that I could give my life to have the beauty of your Palace restored." Passionately he pressed her to his heart, assuring her that no treasure on this earth could replace her life, and happily she begged him to use her every jewel, every gift, to find an artist to rebuild the wondrous wing.

Again he pressed her to his heart, and tenderly continued:

"There is no master in my empire who can restore that glorious monument of Eastern splendour; an exact duplicate of the great Caliph's palace, its plans and their execution are secrets of the wise men of the East, and as the Court of Bagdad is unfriendly to us, not one of them could be got to do us service."

"Then why not approach the Sultan personally?" exclaimed Feodora enthusiastically. "If he refuse, then punish him with war, and our arms shall be victorious against the infidels."

"A holy war against the infidels!" And Theophilus, young and brave, gave orders to despatch the messenger.

For some time all went well and the Imperial couple seemed more devoted to each other than ever before. However, in the heart of Theophilus there rankled continually that old sore. On every hand he seemed to stumble on some word which, although innocent, did not ring true. His ministers, his servants, even his hunchbacked spy and jester seemed to him to whisper things when unobserved, and he knew positively that the Greeks in the bazaars retailed that trading story of his wife's in a thousand different versions. Just then another incident upset Feodora's master, who was a sworn enemy of idolatry. Feodora in secret was still an idolater, and the dwarf, the Emperor's spy, circulated a tale to that effect about the Empress.

"Who has accused me?" she asked indignantly, and when the Emperor declared it was the dwarf, she replied ingeniously:

"Oh, the atrocious monster! Early this morning, impudent fellow that he is, he entered my room while I was dressing and molested me. I angrily ordered him away and hence his accusation!"

"Yet he swears he saw you before a picture!"

"What he saw was the picture of myself in the mirror, nothing else!"

"The picture of an angel," laughingly cried the Emperor, mollified, and promised dire punishment for the dwarf. Feodora, however, was much disturbed, for well she knew that this tale also would now spread in Court and capital.

Shortly after this the messenger returned from Bagdad bringing an absolute refusal, and immediately the fullest preparations for war were made. The first army had left, and already the Emperor and all the nobles were about to follow with the Empress when there appeared a Greek from Asia Minor, who, so he said, had been a prisoner in the hands of the Turks for many years, had learned the secrets of the Moorish palace, and would undertake to draw the plans and to rebuild the ancient glories of the old gutted wing. Theophilus and his wife gladly welcomed this young Greek.

Feodora seemed particularly attracted by the young artist, and frequently received him, that she might have his plans shown and explained to her. Often she would listen to his stories of suffering and privation at the hands of the Turks, and her glorious eyes, tear-stained, would dwell upon the beautiful features of the stranger. Continually she made opportunities for having the Greek near her, until her affection for him gradually ripened into a love only intensified by the great deference and restraint the artist showed her. Then the news of a reverse to the Imperial arms reached the capital. The Greek was suspected of being a spy, and even brought before a tribunal, where, however, he was released on the direct intervention of the Empress. Nevertheless some slight suspicion still remained, and particularly in the mind of Theophilus, who marvelled at the vigorous defence made on the artist's behalf by the Empress.

One evening as she wandered aimlessly alone within the Palace gardens, she found herself quite suddenly before the gutted wing. A shiver shook her as she gazed upon the desolate walls, and sorrowfully thought of the cause of this destruction and the part she was accused of playing in it. She had never been able to forget the cruel treatment she had suffered at the hands of her husband, and her love for him had never stirred again since that time of her expulsion.

While thus lost in contemplation she saw a figure in the gloom ; it was the stranger ! He also stood in meditation near the ruins. It was plain he had seen her, and he quickly approached in a way which previously she had not observed in him. With a free, almost imperious bearing he offered her his escort. She felt embarrassed, strange, and unable to refuse his offer, the more so as the quickly gathering darkness oppressed her. He led her through the ruins and explained to her his plans and how there would arise again a building the like of which would not be found in any land. Her admiration for the stranger grew as he led her away by his flights of imagination.

" I envy you," she said, " your heavenly genius that can create marvels only to be compared with the wonders of nature."

" And rightly so," replied the Greek ; " for our masterpieces are founded on the laws of nature, our art follows the teachings of the stars and of the heavens, and enables us so to create the wonderful, the marvellous."

" And surely this is the reason," she responded, " why, in the contemplation of some great palace, we feel the harmony of the Almighty, just as the beauty of the human form excites our admiration and inspires us with love."

Their eyes met as she looked up, but as he bent his head to kiss her forehead a cry of terror rang from her lips ; he held her fast or she would have slipped down the passage that yawned before them. A malicious laugh was heard, and now he saw the cause of all her terror. A hunchbacked figure stood before them in the gloom, pointing a shaking finger to a group of Cupid and Psyche that lay half covered with dust beside them.

" It is Denderim, the Emperor's dwarf ; we are lost ; I shall be guilty in my husband's eyes, guilty before the world. Oh, what can I say in my defence ? "

" Have no fear," answered the artist, " your affection is blameless ! "

" Oh," she continued, " but you are already under suspicion, and I, yes, I could not save you again ! "

" Save me again ? But how is that ? "

" I spoke up for you the last time ; I, who have now been seen in your arms ! They are coming ! Listen ! They are hunting for us ! "

A number of Palace troops could now be seen moving towards them; as if going in their direction, these two now descended the passage before them, and finally sprang into the centre of a huge creeping plant, which entirely covered an opening in the side of a grotto. This opening led into a maze of passages and finally brought them out upon the shores of the sea. The Greek alone knew of this way, which he had discovered while exploring the foundations.

"Here we are safe," the Greek assured her, "and as I was not unprepared for what has happened, we shall soon be able to escape on board a vessel which is kept in readiness for me. Follow me and fear not."

"How can I answer for this before God, and before my conscience?"

"Well," answered her deliverer, "did you not tell me that accident only had bound you to your husband, that he repaid your love by harshness? Accident and boyish caprice raised you to be Empress—your slight mistake was punished by callous severity—how can you hesitate? No justice, no reconciliation lies before you, if you stay—only death, inglorious death!"

"What you say is true, only too true! Know then, O stranger, that I love you, that I will flee with you!" He pressed her tear-stained face to his breast, and so they set out on their voyage.

A few days later Theophilus, who had been absent on business of war, returned to his capital. The terrible news awaiting him there he met with stony indifference; no angry words escaped him, no orders were given to pursue the fugitives. Deeply he plunged into the affairs of his army, into the relentless prosecution of the war, and strove with superhuman might to avenge the defeat inflicted upon one of his generals by the enemy. He, who up till then had only taken a passive interest in the affairs of his empire, now discovered that within his realms lay latent powers which, with capable leadership, would overwhelm any foe. Inspired by his sovereign duties he now became really great. The war obsessed him. Weeks and months passed before finally the opposing main armies were ranged against each other. Then a messenger under a flag of truce brought a parchment from the Caliph offering the Emperor of the Romans peace, and as a proof of his goodwill the immediate surrender of a prisoner, a traitor, the Greek, who had so shamefully betrayed his confidence. Theophilus was too astonished at the offer to refuse it, and burned with eagerness to take heavy vengeance on the treacherous artist.

A truce was proclaimed, and a troop of Mohammedan horsemen brought in the prisoner next morning. The Emperor had him brought into his presence immediately. In his rage, pale with wrath, he had already drawn his sword to run it through the traitor, when the figure before him throwing off its cloak revealed itself as that of a woman; quickly raising the veil, he saw confronting him a face of such calm and intent beauty that he was struck with awe and wonder—it was Nikisa!

"You, Nikisa?" came at last from his lips. "What means this? What do you want with me?"

"Your forgiveness."

Overwhelmed by her wonderful beauty, her sweetly caressing voice, Theophilus dropped his sword, and, forgetting all the past, said:

"Dear Nikisa, I have done you much injustice; I do not think it is my forgiveness you need!"

"Only this once," she answered, smiling; and bending her head to one side and covering her face with the veil, added, "Do you know me now?"

Utterly taken aback was the Emperor, for now he saw before him the features of the treacherous Greek. Astounded, hardly able to trust his eyes, so complete was the deception—"But explain," he cried, still incredulous.

Nikisa then told her story.

"After you, exalted master, had condemned my poor songs, my sorrow drove me out of your dominions. Could you but know what misfortunes, what dangers and what sufferings I encountered, your pity would assuredly outweigh your condemnation. The ship had hardly left the Golden Horn when, to my horror, and that of my companions—nuns who wished to share my exile—the infamous character of the captain was apparent. He did not even hide his intentions—for we were absolutely in his power—to sell us into slavery to the Turks. The days of danger and distress, however, sharpened my wits and I planned to save myself from that terrible fate. By playing on that dissolute captain's religious superstition, by bribing him with rubies which I had managed to conceal in my bosom, but more still by his hope of further gain, if he could sell me as a youth of exceptional learning and position, I prevailed upon him to provide me with a boy's suit of clothes. After great hardship and privations we were finally landed in a small town in Syria, and there sold as slaves. Happily my master was a venerable old man of high position at the Mohammedan Court, who, finding that I spoke his language to perfection and could both draw and solve mathematical problems, employed me in his work as master of the Sultan's Palaces, and soon put me in charge of several important undertakings. I quickly gained renown and finally became one of the principal architects at the Caliph's court. It was then that I was able to lay at your feet, O Theophilus, a plan of that great piece of architecture of which the burnt wing of your Palace was a copy."

A mild smile here flitted over the Emperor's face, and Nikisa continued :

" I came, and neither you nor Feodora knew me. My strange costume, my hair, the change in my features, and in my figure, the results of my long stay in a different country and climate, would not let you connect this youth with the old Nikisa. Then—fate changed your consort's sisterly affection for me into a strange delirium of love ; and, as if I was that which I seemed, her love went out to me. And who could condemn her ? With this love she repaid a debt to me, for had not she in turn deprived me of your love ?—not knowingly, true ; yet see how I have suffered all this time ; the desire to punish you, when the opportunity arose in yonder gardens of your Palace, overwhelmed me and I fell. No harm has come to Feodora by my side, she is still faithful, and still your wife ; though she fled from your Imperial wrath she did not mean to leave you thus for ever. Therefore, O Theophilus, forgive—forgive her and me."

The scowl on the Emperor's face had gradually deepened.

" Where is she ? that I may judge her ! But you, Nikisa, go, for I have already given you my Imperial pardon ! "

At this moment the curtains of the tent moved to one side and Feodora entered. She took a few steps forward towards her husband, but, deathly pale and trembling, she stopped, her outstretched hands falling to her side. A wave of pity, then of love swept over Theophilus. His earnest gaze fell on the saintly, beautiful face of his wife, and pointing at Nikisa he spoke :

" Since I have pardoned the greater sinner—the seducer—I needs must now extend my clemency to the seduced ! "

And reading in his eyes the confirmation of these generous words, Feodora, with a cry of gladness, threw herself into his arms, to be held in fond embrace.

W. HEINRICH VON RIEHL
1823–1897

WOOING THE GALLOWS

IN the year 1594 the town-scribent of Nördlingen had an extraordinary visitor. A herculean lad of about twenty, unkempt and ragged, came to the court-room one morning, planted himself squarely before the scribent, and stared at him in silence.

Unto the gruffly put question, "What do you want?" he answered no less gruffly, "A rope!"

The town-scribent told him he had come to the wrong door, the rope-maker lived round the corner. But the fellow replied to the effect that he did not need the rope-maker, but the hangman; he wanted to be hanged. The town-scribent shivered, for he thought the stranger was crazy. He therefore called a vigorous servant before entering further into this extraordinary conversation.

The stranger now confessed himself to be a homeless tramp, called by his companions Jörg Muckenhuber, and his language being pieced together out of as many rags of dialect as his coat was of rags of cloth, there was no further certificate required to make it evident that he was at home everywhere and nowhere.

He then proceeded to relate briefly and coldly how several weeks ago he had murdered a travelling pedlar in the precincts of Nördlingen, and also between Augsburg and Kaufbeuern a foreign Jew. Both the Jew and the pedlar gave him no peace at night, so he wanted to be hanged, and as the last murder had been perpetrated on the ground of Nördlingen, so the senate of that town could not refuse to hang him on the Nördlingen gallows.

The town-scribent swore furiously, and said it wasn't every fool could have that for the asking, the town of Nördlingen had built its gallows for its own citizens and not for villainous vagrants; at the same time Muckenhuber was taken into custody, and the scribent presented the affair to the senate.

The senators put their heads together without coming to any definite conclusion as to whether the lad was a fool or a desperate villain. As it was customary, however, in those days to cast the insane into the same dungeon as thieves and murderers, Jörg Muckenhuber was put in safe keeping in the tower, and the business was getting under way in a most correct manner, whatever further details might be brought to light.

The executioner, the parson, and the barber, who went in turn to visit the prisoner and sound him each in his own way, declared with one voice that the fellow was rough and uncared for, but that his mind was very clear, and that there was no gainsaying him in his confession.

Meanwhile the news was scattered through the town, and the good citizens had lively quarrels as to whether a person could be hanged upon the strength of his mere confession and urgent demand, even though there was no further proof of the deed of which he accused himself; for nowhere was there to be found a trace of the travelling pedlar and the murder perpetrated on him.

And when Muckenhuber was taken out, well guarded and followed by a curious crowd, to show them the exact spot where he had murdered the pedlar and buried his corpse, he managed to confuse and puzzle his judges by fine-spun evasions and equivocations, but there was no actual evidence of the crime to be found. The prisoner, however, clung with tenacity to his previous declaration, that he had murdered the pedlar in the precincts of Nördlingen, and must therefore be hanged on the Nördlingen gallows.

Although German burghers of provincial towns were as well accustomed to highly spiced criminal dramas in those days as they were to their daily bread, the sensation about this unusual case grew from day to day; especially was the reply of the Augsburg and Kaufbeuern magistrates anxiously looked forward to, to whom the acts had been submitted with a neighbourly request to have inquiries made concerning the murder said to have been perpetrated between those two towns upon a foreign Jew. But here too there was not a vestige of a Jew or a murder to be found.

But in the scrupulous proceedings of the sixteenth century, confession of crime was considered a proof by far superior to any other, and so the judges refused to be satisfied, the more so as the prisoner continued to bring forth reasons to explain the absence of all testimony.

It was deemed best to fall back upon that most unrelenting test of truth, the rack. How often had people who objected to being criminals been tortured into a confession; why should it not be possible to reverse the method and torture a man, who had set his mind on being a criminal, into a confession of his innocence?

But in the torturing-chamber the senate of Nördlingen got out of the frying-pan into the fire. For when the thumb-screws were applied Jörg Muckenhuber persisted in piping his old song, and when the effect was heightened by forcing him into the Spanish boots, he proceeded at once to add to his original offence by confessing a list of robberies, each of which alone would have brought him to the gallows. The inquisitor had also a ride upon the sharp-edged ass upon his programme, but fearing lest the invincible Jörg should add two or three cases of arson into the bargain he did not press the point, and the triumphant rogue was conducted back into his dungeon, while the senate was writhing in an agony of impotent rage.

To the more sagacious it became more and more evident that Jörg Muckenhuber was making game of the town authorities, but at the same time a joke of such ghastly grimness was unprecedented. Then, too, no one could hit upon a possible motive why the churlish fellow should subject his neck to the rope and his limbs to the rack with an amount of courage and power of will that was worthy of a better cause. This seemed too much for the most vicious facetiousness. Moreover, not only the acknowledged crime but the whole person of this Muckenhuber seemed to have sprung up out of the ground overnight as it were. For his sudden appearance in Nördlingen was surrounded with as much mystery as his crime. There were some who confidentially affirmed that he was the devil, who was out for a lark and had chosen this method of twitting the whole of Nördlingen by the nose.

However, this did not help to solve the difficult question of what was to be done with the vagabond.

Public opinion in those days generally inclined to the assumption that where the case was doubtful it was better to hang three innocent men than let one guilty one get away. And, moreover, Jörg Muckenhuber was guilty any way you might look at it. For if he had committed the murder in question, then he deserved the gallows, and if he had not committed it, then he deserved the gallows more than ever, because by reason of his iniquity the senate of the town had made a confounded fool of itself. But as there was no unanimity in court in which of these two ways he had deserved the gallows, he was left for the present quietly in the dungeon.

It was not exactly attractive there. The cell was half above ground and half below, in a small tower, which upon three sides faced a swampy bog; there was no surplus of light, but a narrow little window let in a bit of chiaroscuro, which would have enabled one to distinguish a chair from a table on a sunny noon-day—that is, if there had been any such objects of luxury at hand. There was more pleasure to be derived from outside. Under the window the frogs sang in a varied and full chorus. At one side there was another dungeon, occupied by an old hag, who obstinately refused to confess to being a witch. Her so-called window also faced the bog, and when the two neighbours looked out of the window they could converse with facility, although it was without seeing each other, and no one excepting the frogs overheard their conferences.

Jörg had received the first intimation of his neighbour's presence by hearing her pray aloud one day. It was no soft, humble prayer; it was passionate, almost as if the old woman were storming the Almighty with commands rather than petitions. Jörg had never learned to pray, and at first the devotions of the old woman struck him as very odd; gradually it came to look very grand to him that an old hag should venture to address herself to God with such vehemence, and he came to the conclusion she must be a giant in strength and able to hold her own against ten men.

He did not open the conversation, but waited until his neighbour should discover his proximity and address him. Even heroic women like to talk. Soon an intimacy sprang up between these two comrades in distress who had never seen each other. At first Jörg often interrupted his neighbour's kind words with many a scornful and dogged remark, but she always answered him so mildly, and at the same time with so much quiet superiority, that Jörg's insolence was soon tamed.

In the course of a few days Jörg knew the history of his neighbour by heart, but he obstinately kept silence about his own.

The old woman was the well-to-do, childless widow of an innkeeper. In her sixtieth year she had the misfortune to be accused of witchcraft. A wealthy witch is a rarity. But it so happened that during the last five years all ugly poor women had been burned up in Nördlingen, and as every witch was called upon to name accomplices, and as the zeal of the judges increased with each execution, at last it came to be the turn of young, handsome, and rich women as well. There were enough of these unfortunate women, but none was so unfortunate, and at the same time so heroic, as Maria Hollin. She had been on the rack fifty-eight times, and had confessed nothing. She was indeed, as Jörg had rightly judged from her prayer, able to hold her own against ten men. The judges were in despair; it was out of the question to acquit a person who had been tortured fifty-eight times, and it was equally so to condemn her without a confession.

Moreover, the rumour of her firmness had gone among the populace, and there was much sympathy with her, and a threatening murmur of displeasure against the much-feared judges. Up to now everything had gone smoothly and comfortably. Thirty-two women had been accused, put on the rack, convicted, and burned; not one of them had made any trouble. At the worst, the one or the other had to be left hanging with weights on her feet until the judges had had some refreshments. But when they came back from lunch the fullest confession had always rewarded them. And now, through the obstinacy of this woman, the smooth course of events had been most aggravatingly interrupted.

And then, too, there was that provoking affair with Muckenhuber. The one would not confess her guilt, while they were hankering to condemn her; the other they would have been only too happy to let go, but even the rack was powerless to extract the confession of his innocence. The town-scribent thought if Jörg Muckenhuber were only a woman, then by a bold strategy he might be burned, as it were by mistake, instead of Maria Hollin, and she might be dismissed in his stead, so that each should have his heart's desire, and the court should preserve its authority.

But the worst of all for the senate was the prospect of a diplomatic storm that was brewing at the horizon in the direction of Regensburg. Maria Hollin had well-to-do relatives at Ulm, and the magistrate of that town, convinced of her innocence, had applied for her release. But that did her little good. The town-scribent thought it would endanger the reputation of a court to put a person on the rack for fifty-eight times and then not even to have the satisfaction of singeing her a little, not to speak of burning. But the burghers of Ulm would not be silenced. At Regensburg there was an important Reichstag that year, and the Emperor, Rudolph II., was present in person. The ambassador from Ulm received orders from his town to intercede for the accused, and as he was not given a hearing he threatened to set the Emperor and the Reich against the law-court of Nördlingen.

The history of Maria Hollin made a deep impression upon Jörg Muckenhuber. Until now he had looked upon himself as a hero before his judges, but by the side of this true heroine he appeared to himself to be playing the part of a bad boy. Out of stubbornness and pride he had kept silent about his true history before his judges; before this woman he kept silent for shame. But finally he could not resist the firm, sympathetic voice of his invisible companion.

So he was tame at last, and began to confess his tale to the old woman. At first he asked her if she had ever seen a pair of fighting dogs that had locked teeth, and so held each other as in a vice, for all the cuffs they got to make them let go. He and his judge, he said, were like such dogs. From a child he had led a bold vagabond life; he had enjoyed all the pleasures of a restless, adventurous rover, and had suffered all the deprivations and distress and shame of such. He had never murdered or robbed, only taken along what he needed. He was tired of the whole business. Life was a burden to him, but to take his own life, and be found later in the water or in the woods like a beast, was not to his taste.

He had often heard death on the gallows lauded as the best, and when his companions spoke of their "heroes," it was always of such persons as had reached the highest point of their career on the upper round of the ladder leading to the gallows.

To put a showy end to life, which had lost its attraction for him, Jörg went to Nördlingen, a town which was then notorious for its hasty justice.

Dame Hollin thereupon gave Jörg a most terrific lecture. To judge by the tone of her voice, he thought of her as standing in her dark cell like the angel with the flaming sword. For all that her sermon did not touch him specially. He was much more deeply contrite when in the silent night he compared her heroic courage and disdain of death with his own sorry tale, making his invincible obstinacy look like the caricature of her bravery. He admitted the justice of everything she said when with a firm hand she shook his conscience; but he did not admit the justice of what the others said. And when Dame Hollin condemned him it frightened him as much as damnation at the last judgment might; but before that day came he was determined to play his joke upon the senate of Nördlingen, and hang on their gallows.

Months passed. The two neighbours grew to be more and more to each other. The alleged witch succeeded in implanting a little bit of Christianity upon him, at least as much as could be crowded through the narrow-barred window. Jörg accepted her dogmas willingly enough, but would not let go of his own dogma, that he must be hanged on Nördlingen ground.

Jörg had locked teeth with the senate, but the senators had also locked teeth with each other because of this same Jörg.

Two parties formed and quarrelled so heartily that they quite forgot the object of their quarrel. One side, as before mentioned, wished to hang him because he had committed murder; the other, because he had not committed murder. Only the town-scribent constituted, in silence and all by himself, a third party of mediation. He wanted to let Jörg get away. For, he said to himself, if he had been put on the rack the first day, the truth would most likely have come to light; now it is too late. If we wait until both parties agree as to which offence Muckenhuber shall be hanged for, he may meanwhile die of old age in the tower. This would be a clear loss to the town, which supplies the vagabond with food and lodging all for nothing. The town-scribent further concluding with subtle psychological insight that Jörg would probably by this time be mellow and tired of the poor fare of prison, it seemed to him to be the best plan to leave the door open by accident, so that the fellow could run away.

So he gave orders to have the door of his cell left unbolted from time to time. Jörg noticed it, but did not stir; he was determined to be hanged on Nördlingen ground.

But when he told his neighbour of the growing carelessness of his gaoler, things took a new turn. With the knowledge of the open door, though it was not that of her cell, the mighty love of freedom awoke in Dame Hollin. "If I could get out!" she cried, "it would not be to escape; I should but go to come back—go to tell my friends at Ulm of the disgrace I have suffered, and come back with witnesses and testimonials of my innocence. I do not want freedom; I want my honour and reputation——!" She did not finish what she wanted to say, but Jörg understood her.

For some time he had been at work breaking through the thin partition between the two cells. His only tool was a small piece of iron, and the work progressed but slowly. After these words of Dame Hollin he worked day and night with the utmost exertion of his strength, and in the third night he could manage to crawl through the small hole.

There was no time to be lost. This same night Jörg's door was left unbolted again, so there were a few hasty words of farewell spoken. Dame Hollin crept through into her neighbour's cell. Thus Jörg, trembling from head to foot, threw his arms about the old woman's knees, and, as if he wanted to throw the fulness of his obedience and gratitude into one word, he cried, " Mother ! " and she passed her hands gently over his face, feeling his features in the darkness, and crying, " My poor, unhappy son ! "

Dame Hollin hid in the house of a faithful friend, to escape to Ulm the next day. Jörg slipped over into the deserted cell, and when his gaoler came to the door in the morning to push in a dish of humble fare, he crouched down in a corner, wrapped in the cloak of the old woman, and when the man passed on to his cell, he slipped nimbly through the hole in the wall, and in the garb of Jörg Muckenhuber received his own ration. He kept this up for about a week with much skill and secret delight, if sorrow for the loss of his faithful comrade had not choked his pleasure.

But one day the door was opened wide enough to admit the town-scribent, together with the gaoler, the former ordering Dame Hollin to follow him to the court-room. Jörg played his rôle as long as he could, crouched down in terror in the darkest corners, and repelled his tormentors with silent gestures. But when the town-scribent cried reassuringly, " Woman, come boldly forth ; I lead thee not to the rack, but to freedom," then Muckenhuber forgot his mask, threw his cloak from his shoulders in impotent rage, started up indignantly and cried, with his clenched hands in his side, " You will do no such thing ; I want to be hanged, and I won't let you off ! "

The town-scribent tore his hair in despair and rage when he perceived that the witch was gone and the vagabond was left. He had intended to conduct Dame Hollin to freedom, but it was to have been freedom under weighty conditions ; and now she had disappeared without any conditions whatsoever. Jörg, however, who was to have disappeared and no questions asked, sat once more firmly upon the neck of the senate. " Fellow, there's no putting an end to you ! " cried the town-scribent, foaming at the mouth. But Muckenhuber replied coldly, " It is this I complain of, that you won't even try ! "

The senators poured bitter reproaches upon each other, at first in a low tone, then louder, until the storm grew, and there was a wild confusion of voices. Then the town-scribent silenced them all with his deep bass, and united the disputants with a word. He cried, " The cause of all this trouble is only Jörg Muckenhuber. Hang him at once if he does not recant his old confessions ! " Jörg replied, " I do *not* recant ! " and when the town-scribent asked him for the second time, " Now, I certainly shan't recant," and the third time . . .

There stood old Dame Hollin as if she had grown out of the ground, conducted by two of the most respectable burghers of Nördlingen and Ulm. She looked sharply at Muckenhuber, and said in a firm tone, " Jörg, you will recant your false confession ! " The voice struck the insolent fellow like a peal of thunder. He was silent and lowered his eyes. There was no sound, one could hear the laboured breathings ; then he spoke : " No other power on earth could have made me recant, but I cannot lie in the face of this woman ;—I recant ! "

Meanwhile the tumult of the populace without was increasing. The air was filled with wild threats, and with demands for the immediate release of Dame Hollin. The gentlemen saw that there was danger in delay. After a short, whispered debate the town-scribent read aloud the writ the old woman was to swear to. But Dame Hollin replied that she did not want mercy but demanded her right. The gentlemen of the senate made very wry faces and began to try persuasion, but they had learned ere this that there was little to be gained in that way with Dame Hollin.

After a moment's thought, she said to her judges, " You have tried to make a bargain with me. Having done so, you are no longer my judges, and cannot give me my right. Well, then, I too am ready to offer you a bargain. Release that wicked lad yonder, I will adopt him in child's stead, and take him to Ulm with me, and see if I can do better by him than you have done. My property has lain dead while you kept me in the tower. You should refund the usury I have lost ; instead of that give me this wicked lad. On this condition will I sign your writ."

Already the populace clamoured outside the door. The senate would have had no choice, even though she had demanded much more than this.

As she signed the writ, she found a bill appended for her fare during the time of her custody. She returned the leaf with a courteous smile to the town-scribent, and as the rabble was knocking at the door he plucked the interesting document into bits as fast as possible, and strewed the pieces under the table.

Meanwhile the chains had been removed from Jörg; he looked about him as in a dream. Dame Hollin took his hand, and went to the door with him, where both were received by the gratified shouts of the shuffling crowd.

. . . .

The old woman kept her word. In her house Jörg became an honest, valiant man, who in the Thirty Years' War did great service to Ulm, the town of his adoption, and his name was never spoken but in honour and gratitude. But the witch's counsel was forced to resign office, and after those five years of terror followed a better decade, during which law and justice reigned once more in the old Reichstadt.

BARONESS VON EBNER-ESCHENBACH

B. 1830

AN ORIGINAL

IF the assertion be just that originals have ceased to exist, then all who have met Herr Gabriel Teufenberg may boast to have seen something that does not exist.

His appearance excites neither interest nor antipathy. His height is six feet,—breadth to match; he has the complexion of a rosy, well-fed child, and a large face with small features, a fine straight nose, a well-cut mouth under a thin, almost white moustache with the sheen of silk. His eyebrows and lashes, too, are almost white, his eyes round and blue and expressive of nothing.

Alas, how cold and mute the boy's eyes are, his mother would think whenever she looked at him, even colder than those of his poor dead father.

Her own were brown and warm, and her six-and-forty years notwithstanding she was still a charming and pretty woman. Her married life with a lumpish husband, not her equal in intellect, had brought her no happiness. Though flattered and courted on all sides, she had never been touched by scandal. Her indolent spouse had left the management of his estates and property in her hands and her son followed his example. He could not have done better. His mother reigned willingly and successfully and was, besides, a charming hostess in town and country. Her house was graced by three young orphaned nieces, any one of whom she would have welcomed as a daughter-in-law. But Gabriel paid no more heed to his cousins than to waxen dolls, that is to say, to the immovable variety, for the moving dolls would at once have excited his lively interest. Any mechanism, —engines, large and small,—were his hobby. As an infant he constructed pumps, mills, and dredgers of cardboard and tin, and they really worked if one pulled a string or turned a handle. Later in life he was less fortunate; the great agricultural machines which he furnished with all sorts of improvements would not work.

His life was placid enough. Early to bed and late to rise, he took a couple of hours to dress, ate much and slowly and without the least culinary understanding. Had he been asked whether he preferred potatoes or Perigord-truffles, he would have replied: "It is all the same to me." His evenings in town in the winter he spent either in the theatre or playing whist in his club, and it was all the same to him what they played in the theatre or whether he won his rubber or lost. In the country he spent most of his time in the workshop which he had fitted up in the castle. The ladies called it "Vulcan's stithy." Thence he had to be fetched for every excursion into the country if his company was desired. And during the loveliest rides or walks, attended by three pretty jolly young girls, he dreamed of engines.

"Look here, Gabriel," his mother said to him one day, "you ought to marry one of your cousins."

"Gladly," he answered.

Then she was happy. "May I tell one of them?"

"Certainly."

"But which one?"

"It's all the same to me."

And there was an end to her joy.

One after another the pretty cousins married away, and soon after Teufenberg had acted as groomsman to the last he lost his mother.

She had been nursing the sick in the village during an epidemic, caught the disease herself, and died within a few days. Gabriel neither wept nor complained; there was not the least trace of sadness about him, but everybody sought to comfort him in his loneliness and to hearten him. Friends and relatives were naturally agreed that now he must marry, and when they pointed out to him that it was merely a question of choosing aright, he said: "Exactly." In the end he did not choose, but was chosen by a charming young widow, the picture of a woman, with black eyes, black hair; delicate and slender as he was strong-jointed and bulky. She did not fall in love with him, but she liked him, valued his tranquillity, his refined and dignified bearing, his moral soundness. She would have it that he was nothing like the indifferent phlegmatic that people took him for. A warmth of feeling lay dormant within him that only wanted rousing.

Her friends mocked her: "Will you do the rousing? We notice no change. He is the same as ever."

She was not to be put out. "You wait," she said, "it will come."

Cecilia Teufenberg was looking forward to the birth of her first child and longing for a son. "What do you wish for?" she asked her husband, "a son or a daughter?"

"It's all the same to me," he said, and she would not believe it, and urged: "You darling, that is just your delicacy, that I should not be grieved if I were to present you with a daughter."

But she bore him a son, and another the year after, and these children grew up splendid boys. They had the honest heart, the clear intellect, the beautiful eyes and features of their mother and the father's fine figure. They were ten and nine respectively when another happy event occurred in the house of Teufenberg. The head of the house had been away for some weeks on a visit to a friend in England, the owner of a large engineering works who had invited him to see an improved Alliance engine in working. A telegram announcing the birth of a daughter and that mother and child were doing well was brought to him as he stood before the model of a travelling crane which excited his admiration. He could not tear himself away, and begged his host to wire his congratulations to his wife.

He stayed another month in England and then returned with a waggon-load of presents: bicycles, tandems, telephones, gramophones, typewriters and sewing-machines, and a precious naphtha-launch. But his most valued acquisition was a transformer. This new and dangerous inmate was set up, well guarded and with every conceivable precaution, in the workshop, there, fed by an adjacent mill, to supply power to the whole of the machinery.

Gabriel had found everything at home in perfect order, his wife and the boys in flourishing health. He never inquired after the new arrival, his daughter, and Cecilia was determined to make no mention of the baby while the father ignored her. But the boys could not suffer to have their sister passed over in silence. After dinner they each took an arm and led their father in to the nursery. Frau Teufenberg followed. Entering the spacious, lofty, bright apartment, they were met at the door by a healthy nurse, and an even more goodly foster-mother. Within the shadows of a deep recess there was what appeared to be a rosy cloud floating over a frame-work of gold. On approaching, this cloud resolved itself into a dainty arrangement of chiffons and ribbons and lace, and buried in the midst of it was some tiny thing, a human miniature with a little round face, large blue eyes which had an amazingly firm and steady gaze, a delicate tiny nose, and slightly open mouth, the mouth of a cherub just ready to sing.

And a pair of dainty hands were raised, and fought wildly and absurdly through the air.

Teufenberg regarded this little thing attentively. He could not have regarded the most complicated machine more attentively. Slowly and carefully he laid a finger in one of the little hands, which clutched him at once. And this moment wrought a transformation in Gabriel Teufenberg. His voice became soft as it had never sounded before, and he exclaimed: " A girl, just see, a girl."

" Your daughter Gabrielle," said his wife, amazed at the impression.

From the little fingers which still clung to the father there seemed to issue a current, some vivifying rousing force which flowed from the crown to the soles of the tall broad man. It was as if a flame had been lit within him and spread a genial warmth through all his veins. He stooped to kiss the face and the hands of the infant, and then he turned to his wife.

" I thank you," he said, " that you have given me so dear a daughter." His glance fell on his sons and dwelt on them a long while with joyous pride. Then he added: " and two such dear boys." He had a few kind words for the nurses too; then he turned to contemplate anew his daughter, who had now fallen asleep.

After this there were whole days when he never set foot in the workshop. The development of the little being by his side filled him with joy. All harshness in his nature was softened and vanished. His dull eyes were opened to the wealth of happiness which had so long been his without his knowledge.

He has always been a good and comfortable man, thought his wife, but now he actually grows attentive and tender, and she really feared that, after their twelve years of married life, she might fall in love with him. But another, more serious care beset her. It seemed as though all the happy change might be called in question by the creator herself. For at a time when other children show repugnance to anything like learning and serious study, this young person displayed an astonishing thirst of knowledge and spirit of inquiry. Especially in mechanics. She gave early proof of rare skill and, like her father, made little pumps and mills and things. They were, however, much daintier and neater, and they worked more accurately. She would hollow out the wooden beasts of her Ark and the family of Noah, and fill them with primitive clockworks and wheels and make them move automatically.

And her favourite resort was the workshop. In the woods, in the garden she would long for the workshop and the machinery; instead of dolls she would play with models of steam engines, pumps, and winches, which she learned to handle with remarkable cleverness. If some mechanism had broken down and her father tried in vain to discover the cause, she would detect it at once and never rest until she had devised a remedy. Her ingenious brain was crowded with ideas, some of which were actually approved by experts and put into practice.

Her father went about in the purple of pride for this wonder-child. Her mother was vexed with the successes of a talent so wholly unnatural in a young girl.

"My daughter—the engine-man," said the mother, when Gabrielle came from the workshop with horribly soiled hands, the pretty face all aglow with eagerness, streaked with soot, and her frock stained all over with oil. "No more dresses for you, my dear: you shall have overalls and nothing else. And beware! If you drag father back into the clutches of the engine-demon, you shall see. . . ." And she cleaned her, and changed her frock, and hugged and kissed her, thinking: "Only to have you, you little fairy-godmother, that hast really given life to your father."

Nor did it seem as though he should lose it again. His pleasure in the triumphs of his little daughter had made a dear, affectionate man of him, an excellent head of his household, and cured him completely of his own hopeless passion for mechanics. She reigned as queen in the realm wherein he could never have risen to eminence. His sole ambition was to serve her in the execution of the ingenious works which she created with ever-increasing skill and brilliance.

The fame of the young inventor began to travel abroad. She received an invitation to exhibit the model of an electro-magnetic motor, which had attracted attention in England, at a technical exhibition in London. It was to be packed up next day. Gabrielle coaxed a promise from her parents to journey with her in the spring to the promised land of machines. Before going to bed she laughed and jested and frolicked like the child she still was, in spite of her wits and her fifteen years.

At dawn she suddenly awoke, her heart beating, bathed in perspiration. In a nightmare she had seen her motor immovable, defying all effort to start it. It seemed to possess a will of its own, mocked her anxious nervous endeavours, stared at her. . . .

Cold shivers ran over her; she could not rid herself of the terror which closed in upon her. Then she felt the irresistible desire to be satisfied of the existence of her work, her idea!

Rising stealthily, she donned her soft slippers and bath-gown, and crept cautiously from her room so as to wake no one. Noiselessly she hurried along the heavily carpeted passage, down the stairs to the third door on the left, and entered the workshop.

The windows were curtained, there was an uncanny gloom. The young girl, usually the embodiment of caution and composure, shook with a fever of flurry and excitement. She did not wish to be discovered, to be reproached by her parents. Swiftly to switch on the current, to see her work in motion, to hear the breath of its power, the smooth running of the metal wheels!

She stretched out her arm to the source of power . . . and she, whose fingers seemed to be gifted with sight, she who had hardly done a hasty thing in her life, mistakes, touches the wrong, the live wire. . . .

Frau Teufenberg was an early riser. Day by day she was wont to go betimes into her daughter's adjoining room, to sit by her bedside and gaze on her and wait for her waking. When Gabrielle opened her eyes her first glance met her mother's look; the first word she heard and uttered was a word of love.

Entering this morning, Cecilia found the bed empty, and called back into the bedroom: "Dear me, gone already; Gabriel, only imagine, she is already up."

"She must be in the workshop," he answered; "I will follow her at once." And he dressed and hurried down.

It was a dull March morning. As Teufenberg stepped out on to the landing, he noticed the servants moving about quickly like shadows, in manifest terror, sobbing and wringing their hands and passing in and out of the workshop door. "The master, the master!" they whispered as they caught sight of him.

He shudders, a deadly fear seizes him. What ails them? What dreadful thing is it they see? For one instant he pauses. Then he rushes down the stairs to the workshop door.

"Do not enter, for heaven's sake!" they cry, and crowd into his way.

He pushes them aside and enters, the servants following timidly at a distance.

Everything in the great smoke-stained apartment is still and motionless, everything that used to puff and whirl and swing and turn at the bidding of the little mistress. She, too, is still and motionless, lies dead at the foot of her masterpiece.

Teufenberg, in helpless horror, stares at the white lifeless form. Suddenly he utters a piercing cry of despair: "Gabrielle! . . . child! . . ."

But the child makes no reply.

No one dared to touch her. He bore her upstairs, laid her on her couch, and two days later into her coffin, which he never left until it was taken up, nor withdrew his gaze for one moment at the solemn funeral. His wife leaned upon his arm; he was not conscious of her presence, nor saw his sons who, at their mother's wish, had hastened home, whence their professions had long since taken them.

The priest had spoken the benediction, the notes of the funeral hymn died away; amid clouds of incense the coffin was lowered into the depth. He was handed a spade with the first clod that should follow the pilgrim into the pit. As he let it glide down softly, his wife thought: "Poor wretch, there goes thy life down with it."

She had borne herself bravely all this time. When she returned to the house from which the soul had fled, her anguish overpowered her, and she said, with just a shadow of reproach: "Gabriel, I too have lost my child," and moved towards him and held out her hand. But he avoided her. Her sons took her in their arms, and the elder asked: "May I stay with you? I will stay gladly. Shall I go or stay, father?"

Teufenberg shrugged his shoulders. The old chill light was in his eyes.

"What shall I do, father?" the son asked again; "shall I go or stay?"

"It is all the same to me."

He is in flourishing health, eats and drinks, dresses with care, reads the papers, occasionally even a book, he takes his wife out for walks or to the theatre or a concert, but impression he receives none. Nothing excites his sympathy. The flame that illumined and warmed him is extinguished.

Everything in existence is all the same to him.

RICHARD VOLKMANN
1830–1891

THE SAD TALE OF SEVEN KISSES

IT is quite a while ago, I think, since one day the dear God called the angel Gabriel to Him, as He often does, and said, "Thou, Gabriel, go and open the slide and look down! Methinks I hear some crying!" Gabriel went and did as the dear God said, put his hand up to his eyes because the sunlight dazzled him, looked all around, and finally said, "Down there is a long green meadow; at one end sits Barbelie pasturing her geese, at the other sits Christoph pasturing his pigs, and both of them are weeping to melt a heart of stone."

"Indeed!" said the dear God. "Go away, you tall fellow, and let Me see."

When He had looked He found it was just as Gabriel had said.

And this was how it came that Christoph and Barbelie were weeping so pitifully. Christoph and Barbelie loved each other dearly; one of them took care of the geese and the other took care of the pigs, and so it was a very suitable match, there being no disparity of rank. They made up their minds to be married, and they thought being fond of each other was a good enough reason. But here their employers differed from them. So they were obliged to be content with a betrothal. Now, as it is well to be methodical in all things, and as kissing plays an important part in betrothals, they had come to an agreement to the effect that seven kisses in the morning and seven kisses in the evening would be quite the proper thing. For a while all went well, the seven kisses being duly given and received at the appointed time. But, on the morning of the day when this story occurred, it came about that, just as the seventh kiss was coming around, Barbelie's pet goose and Christoph's pet pig had a falling-out over their breakfast, threatening to end in a serious *mêlée*. To settle this difficulty it was necessary for the two to stop short of the proper number. Later, when they were sitting lonely and far apart by the edge of the meadow, it occurred to them how very bad a thing this was, and they both began to weep, and were still weeping when the dear God looked down.

The dear God thought at first that in the course of time their sorrow would subside of itself; but when the sound of weeping waxed louder and louder, and Christoph's pet pig and Barbelie's pet goose began to grow sad for sympathy, and to make woebegone faces, He said, "I will help them! Whatever they wish for this day shall come true."

But as it was the two had but one thought; as each looked in the direction where the other one sat, and neither could see the other, for the meadow was long and there was a bush in the middle, Christoph thought, "If I were but over where the geese are!" and Barbelie sighed, "Oh, could I but be near the pigs!"

All at once Christoph found himself sitting by the geese, and Barbelie was with the pigs; but for all that they were not together, and there was still no possibility of correcting that wrong number.

Then thought Christoph: "Barbelie very likely wanted to make me a little visit"; and Barbelie thought, "No doubt Christoph has gone around to see me!" "Oh, if I could but be with my geese!" "Oh, if I could but be with my pigs!"

So Barbelie sat once more beside her geese, and Christoph sat beside his pigs, and so it went turn and turn about all day, because they always wished past each other. And so to this day they are short of that seventh morning kiss. Christoph, to be sure, was all for making it up that same evening when they both came home tired to death with wishing, but Barbelie assured him it wouldn't do a bit of good, and that there was no possibility of getting things straightened out again.

And when the dear God saw how the two had been wishing themselves away from each other, He said: "Well, this is a nice kettle of fish. But what I have once said I *have* said! There is no help for it!" He made up His mind then and there never to grant lovers' wishes rashly in future, before having made careful inquiries as to what it was they wanted. Later, I am told, He once told Gabriel confidentially that it was really a great pity that their wishes were so very rarely of a kind that He could grant them; and a long, long time ago, when I applied to Him in a similar affair, He did not so much as give me a hearing. Later Gabriel told me this story, and then I ceased to wonder.

PAUL VON HEYSE
1830–1914

THE FURY

(L' ARRABIATA)

THE day had scarcely dawned. Over Vesuvius hung one broad grey stripe of mist, stretching across as far as Naples, and darkening all the small towns along the coast. The sea lay calm. Along the shore of the narrow creek that lies beneath the Sorrento cliffs, fishermen and their wives were at work already, some with giant cables drawing their boats to land, with the nets that had been cast the night before, while others were rigging their craft, trimming the sails, or fetching out oars and masts from the great grated vaults that have been built deep into the rocks for shelter to the tackle overnight. Nowhere an idle hand; even the very aged, who had long given up going to sea, fell into the long chain of those who were hauling in the nets. Here and there, on some flat housetop, an old woman stood and spun, or busied herself about her grandchildren, whom their mother had left to help her husband.

"Do you see, Rachela? yonder is our padre curato," said one to a little thing of ten, who brandished a small spindle by her side; "Antonio is to row him over to Capri. Madre Santissima! but the reverend signore's eyes are dull with sleep!" and she waved her hand to a benevolent-looking little priest, who was settling himself in the boat, and spreading out upon the bench his carefully tucked-up skirts.

The men upon the quay had dropped their work to see their pastor off, who bowed and nodded kindly, right and left.

"What for must he go to Capri, granny?" asked the child. "Have the people there no priest of their own, that they must borrow ours?"

"Silly thing!" returned the granny. "Priests they have in plenty—and the most beautiful of churches, and a hermit too, which is more than we have. But there lives a great signora, who once lived here; she was so very ill! Many's the time our padre had to go and take the Most Holy to her, when they thought she could not live the night. But with the Blessed Virgin's help she got strong and well, and was able to bathe every day in the sea. When she went away, she left a fine heap of ducats behind her for our church, and for the poor; and she would not go, they say, until our padre promised to go and see her over there, that she might confess to him as before. It is quite wonderful, the store she lays by him! Indeed, and we have cause to bless ourselves for having a curato who has gifts enough for an archbishop, and is in such request with all the great folks. The Madonna be with him!" she cried, and waved her hand again, as the boat was about to put from shore.

"Are we to have fair weather, my son?" inquired the little priest, with an anxious look toward Naples.

"The sun is not yet up," the young man answered; "when he comes, he will easily do for that small trifle of mist."

"Off with you, then! that we may arrive before the heat."

Antonio was just reaching for his long oar to shove away the boat, when suddenly he paused, and fixed his eyes upon the summit of the steep path that leads down from Sorrento to the water. A tall and slender girlish figure had become visible upon the heights, and was now hastily stepping down the stones, waving her handkerchief. She had a small bundle under her arm, and her dress was mean and poor. Yet she had a distinguished if somewhat savage way of throwing back her head, and the dark tress wreathed around it was like a diadem.

"What have we to wait for?" inquired the curato.

"There is some one coming who wants to go to Capri—with your permission, padre. We shall not go a whit the slower. It is a slight young thing, but just eighteen."

At that moment the young girl appeared from behind the wall that bounds the winding path.

"Laurella!" cried the priest; "and what has she to do in Capri?"

Antonio shrugged his shoulders. She came up with hasty steps, her eyes fixed straight before her.

"Ha! l' Arrabiata! good-morning!" shouted one or two of the young boatmen. But for the curato's presence, they might have added more; the look of mute defiance with which the young girl received their welcome appeared to tempt the more mischievous among them.

"Good-day, Laurella!" now said the priest; "how are you? Are you coming with us to Capri?"

"If I may, padre."

"Ask Antonio there; the boat is his. Every man is master of his own, I say, as God is master of us all."

" There is half a carlino, if I may go for that ? " said Laurella, without looking at the young boatman.

" You need it more than I," he muttered, and pushed aside some orange-baskets to make room : he was to sell the oranges in Capri, which little isle of rocks has never been able to grow enough for all its visitors.

" I do not choose to go for nothing," said the girl, with a slight frown of her dark eyebrows.

" Come, child," said the priest ; " he is a good lad, and had rather not enrich himself with that little morsel of your poverty. Come now, and step in," and he stretched out his hand to help her, " and sit you down by me. See, now, he has spread his jacket for you, that you may sit the softer. Young folks are all alike ; for one little maiden of eighteen they will do more than for ten of us reverend fathers. Nay, no excuse, Tonino. It is the Lord's own doing, that like and like should hold together."

Meantime Laurella had stepped in, and seated herself beside the padre, first putting away Antonio's jacket without a word. The young fellow let it lie, and, muttering between his teeth, he gave one vigorous push against the pier, and the little boat flew out into the open bay.

" What are you carrying there in that little bundle ? " inquired the padre, as they were floating on over a calm sea, now just beginning to be lighted up with the earliest rays of the rising sun.

" Silk, thread, and a loaf, padre. The silk is to be sold at Anacapri, to a woman who makes ribbons, and the thread to another."

" Spun by yourself ? "

" Yes, sir."

" You once learned to weave ribbons yourself, if I remember right ? "

" I did, sir ; but mother has been much worse, and I cannot stay so long from home ; and a loom to ourselves we are not rich enough to buy."

" Worse, is she ? Ah ! dear, dear ! when I was with you last, at Easter, she was up."

" The spring is always her worst time. Ever since those last great storms and the earthquakes she has been forced to keep her bed from pain."

" Pray, my child. Never slacken your prayers and petitions that the Blessed Virgin may intercede for you; and be industrious and good, that your prayers may find a hearing."

After a pause: "When you were coming toward the shore, I heard them calling after you. 'Good-morning, l' Arrabiata!' they said. What made them call you so? It is not a nice name for a young Christian maiden, who should be meek and mild."

The young girl's brown face glowed all over, while her eyes flashed fire.

"They always mock me so, because I do not dance and sing, and stand about to chatter, as other girls do. I might be left in peace, I think; I do *them* no harm."

"Nay, but you might be civil. Let others dance and sing, on whom this life sits lighter; but a kind word now and then is seemly even from the most afflicted."

Her dark eyes fell, and she drew her eyebrows closer over them, as if she would have hidden them.

They went on a while in silence. The sun now stood resplendent above the mountain chain; only the tip of Mount Vesuvius towered beyond the group of clouds that had gathered about its base; and on the Sorrento plains the houses were gleaming white from the dark green of their orange-gardens.

"Have you heard no more of that painter, Laurella?" asked the curato—"that Neapolitan, who wished so much to marry you?" She shook her head. "He came to make a picture of you. Why would you not let him?"

"What did he want it for? There are handsomer girls than I. Who knows what he would have done with it? He might have bewitched me with it, or hurt my soul, or even killed me, mother says."

"Never believe such sinful things!" said the little curato very earnestly. "Are not you ever in God's keeping, without whose will not one hair of your head can fall? And is one poor mortal with an image in his hand to prevail against the Lord? Besides, you might have seen that he was fond of you, else why should he want to marry you?"

She said nothing.

"And wherefore did you refuse him? He was an honest man, they say, and comely; and he would have kept you and your mother far better than you ever can yourself, for all your spinning and silk-winding."

"We are so poor!" she said passionately; "and mother has been ill so long, we should have become a burden to him. And then I never should have done for a signora. When his friends came to see him, he would only have been ashamed of me."

"How can you say so? I tell you the man was good and kind; he would even have been willing to settle in Sorrento. It will not be so easy to find another, sent straight from heaven to be the saving of you, as this man, indeed, appeared to be."

"I want no husband—I never shall," she said, very stubbornly, half to herself.

"Is this a vow? or do you mean to be a nun?"

She shook her head.

"The people are not so wrong who call you wilful, although the name they give you is not kind. Have you ever considered that you stand alone in the world, and that your perverseness must make your sick mother's illness worse to bear, her life more bitter? And what sound reason can you have to give for rejecting an honest hand, stretched out to help you and your mother? Answer me, Laurella."

"I have a reason," she said reluctantly, and speaking low; "but it is one I cannot give."

"Not give! not give to me? not to your confessor, whom you surely know to be your friend—or is he not?"

Laurella nodded.

"Then, child, unburden your heart. If your reason be a good one, I shall be the very first to uphold you in it. Only you are young, and know so little of the world. A time may come when you will find cause to regret a chance of happiness thrown away for some foolish fancy now."

Shyly she threw a furtive glance over to the other end of the boat where the young boatman sat, rowing fast. His woollen cap was pulled deep down over his eyes; he was gazing far across the water, with averted head, sunk, as it appeared, in his own meditations.

The priest observed her look, and bent his ear down closer.

"You did not know my father?" she whispered, while a dark look gathered in her eyes.

"Your father, child! Why, your father died when you were ten years old. What can your father (Heaven rest his soul in paradise!) have to do with this present perversity of yours?"

" You did not know him, padre ; you did not know that mother's illness was caused by him alone."

" And how ? "

" By his ill-treatment of her ; he beat her and trampled upon her. I well remember the nights when he came home in his fits of frenzy. She never said a word, and did everything he bade her. Yet he would beat her so, my heart felt ready to break. I used to cover up my head and pretend to be asleep, but I cried all night. And then, when he saw her lying on the floor, quite suddenly he would change, and lift her up and kiss her, till she screamed and said he smothered her. Mother forbade me ever to say a word of this ; but it wore her out. And in all these long years since father died, she has never been able to get well again. And if she should soon die—which God forbid !—I know who it was that killed her."

The little curato's head wagged slowly to and fro ; he seemed uncertain how far to acquiesce in the young girl's reasons. At length he said : " Forgive him, as your mother has forgiven ! And turn your thoughts from such distressing pictures, Laurella ; there may be better days in store for you, which will make you forget the past."

" Never shall I forget that ! " she said, and shuddered. " And you must know, padre, it is the reason why I have resolved to remain unmarried. I never will be subject to a man who may beat and then caress me. Were a man now to want to beat or kiss me, I could defend myself ; but mother could not—neither from his blows nor kisses—because she loved him. Now, I will never so love a man as to be made ill and wretched by him."

" You are but a child, and you talk like one who knows nothing at all of life. Are all men like that poor father of yours ? Do all ill-treat their wives, and give vent to every whim and gust of passion ? Have you never seen a good man yet ? or known good wives, who live in peace and harmony with their husbands ? "

" But nobody ever knew how father was to mother ; she would have died sooner than complain or tell of him, and all because she loved him. If this be love—if love can close our lips when they should cry out for help—if it is to make us suffer without resistance, worse than even our worst enemy could make us suffer—then, I say, I never will be fond of mortal man."

" I tell you you are childish ; you know not what you are saying.

When your time comes, you are not likely to be consulted whether you choose to fall in love or not." After a pause, he added, " And that painter: did you think he could have been cruel ? "

" He made those eyes I have seen my father make when he begged my mother's pardon and took her in his arms to make it up. I know those eyes. A man may make such eyes, and yet find it in his heart to beat a wife who never did a thing to vex him ! It made my flesh creep to see those eyes again."

After this she would not say another word. The curato also remained silent. He bethought himself of more than one wise saying, wherewith the maiden might have been admonished ; but he refrained, in consideration of the young boatman, who had been growing rather restless toward the close of this confession.

When, after two hours' rowing, they reached the little bay of Capri, Antonio took the padre in his arms, and carried him through the last few ripples of shallow water, to set him reverently down upon his legs on dry land. But Laurella did not wait for him to wade back and fetch her. Gathering up her little petticoat, holding in one hand her wooden shoes and in the other her little bundle, with one splashing step or two she had reached the shore. " I have some time to stay at Capri," said the priest. " You need not wait—I may not perhaps return before to-morrow. When you get home, Laurella, remember me to your mother ; I will come and see her within the week. You mean to go back before it gets dark ? "

" If I find an opportunity," answered the girl, turning all her attention to her skirts.

" I must return, you know," said Antonio, in a tone which he believed to be one of great indifference. " I shall wait here till the Ave Maria. If you should not come, it is the same to me."

" You must come," interposed the little priest ; " you never can leave your mother all alone at night. Is it far you have to go ? "

" To a vineyard by Anacapri."

" And I to Capri. So now God bless you, child—and you, my son."

Laurella kissed his hand, and let one farewell drop, for the padre and Antonio to divide between them. Antonio, however, appropriated no part of it to himself ; he pulled off his cap exclusively to the padre, without even looking at Laurella. But after they had turned their backs, he let his eyes travel but a short way with the padre, as he went toiling over the deep bed of small, loose stones ; he soon sent them after the maiden, who, turning to the right, had begun to climb the heights, holding one hand above her eyes to protect them from the scorching sun. Just before the path disappeared behind high walls, she stopped, as if to gather breath, and looked behind her. At her feet lay the marina; the rugged rocks rose high around her; the sea was shining in the rarest of its deep-blue splendour. The scene was surely worth a moment's pause. But, as chance would have it, her eyes, in glancing past Antonio's boat, met Antonio's own, which had been following her as she climbed.

Each made a slight movement, as persons do who would excuse themselves for some mistake; and then, with her darkest look, the maiden went her way.

Hardly one hour had passed since noon, and yet for the last two Antonio had been sitting waiting on the bench before the fishers' tavern. He must have been very much preoccupied with something, for he jumped up every moment to step out into the sunshine, and look carefully up and down the roads, which, parting right and left, lead to the only two little towns upon the island. He did not altogether trust the weather, he then said to the hostess of the osteria; to be sure, it was clear enough, but he did not quite like that tint of sea and sky. Just so it had looked, he said, before the last awful storm, when the English family had been so nearly lost; surely she must remember it?

No, indeed, she said, she didn't.

Well, if the weather should happen to change before night, she was to think of him, he said.

"Have you many fine folk over there?" she asked him, after a while.

"They are only just beginning; as yet, the season has been bad enough; those who came to bathe came late."

"The spring came late. Have you not been earning more than we at Capri?"

"Not enough to give me macaroni twice a week, if I had had nothing but the boat—only a letter now and then to take to Naples, or a gentleman to row out into the open sea, that he might fish. But you know I have an uncle who is rich; he owns more than one fine orange-garden; and, 'Tonino,' says he to me, 'while I live you shall not suffer want; and when I am gone you will find that I have taken care of you.' And so, with God's help, I got through the winter."

" Has he children, this uncle who is rich ? "

" No, he never married ; he was long in foreign parts, and many a good piastre he has laid together. He is going to set up a great fishing business and set me oveı it, to see the rights of it."

" Why, then, you are a made man, Tonino ! "

The young boatman shrugged his shoulders. " Every man has his own burden," said he, starting up again to have another look at the weather, turning his eyes right and left, although he must have known that there can be no weather side but one.

" Let me fetch you another bottle," said the hostess ; " your uncle can well afford to pay for it."

" Not more than one glass ; it is a fiery wine you have in Capri, and my head is hot already."

" It does not heat the blood ; you may drink as much of it as you like. And here is my husband coming ; so you must sit a while and talk to him."

And in fact, with his nets over his shoulder, and his red cap upon his curly head, down came the comely padrone of the osteria. He had been taking a dish of fish to that great lady, to set before the little curato. As soon as he caught sight of the young boatman, he began waving him a most cordial welcome ; and he came to sit beside him on the bench, chattering and asking questions. Just as his wife was bringing her second bottle of pure unadulterated Capri, they heard the crisp sand crunch, and Laurella was seen approaching from the left-hand road to Anacapri. She nodded slightly in salutation ; then stopped, and hesitated.

Antonio sprang from his seat. " I must go," he said. " It is a young Sorrento girl, who came over with the signor curato in the morning. She has to get back to her sick mother before night."

" Well, well, time enough yet before night," observed the fisherman ; " time enough to take a glass of wine. Wife, I say, another glass ! "

" I thank you ; I had rather not " ; and Laurella kept her distance.

" Fill the glasses, wife ; fill them both, I say ; she only wants a little pressing."

" Don't," interposed the lad. " It is a wilful head of her own she has ; a saint could not persuade her to do what she does not choose." And, taking a hasty leave, he ran down to the boat, loosened the rope, and stood waiting for Laurella. Again she bent her head to the hostess, and slowly approached the water, with lingering steps. She looked around on every side, as if in hopes of seeing some other passenger. But the marina was deserted. The fishermen were asleep, or rowing about the coast with rods or nets ; a few women and children sat before their doors, spinning or sleeping ; such strangers as had come over in the morning were waiting for the cool of the evening to return. She had not time to look about her long ; before she could prevent him, Antonio had seized her in his arms and carried her to the boat, as if she had been an infant. He leaped in after her, and with a stroke or two of his oar they were in deep water.

She had seated herself at the end of the boat, half turning her back to him, so that he could only see her profile. She wore a sterner look than ever ; the low, straight brow was shaded by her hair ; the rounded lips were firmly closed ; only the delicate nostril occasionally gave a wilful quiver. After they had gone on a while in silence, she began to feel the scorching of the sun ; and, unloosening her bundle, she threw the handkerchief over her head, and began to make her dinner of the bread ; for in Capri she had eaten nothing.

Antonio did not stand this long ; he fetched out a couple of the oranges with which the baskets had been filled in the morning. " Here is something to eat to your bread, Laurella," he said. " Don't think I kept them for you ; they had rolled out of the basket, and I only found them when I brought the baskets back to the boat."

" Eat them yourself ; bread is enough for me."

" They are refreshing in this heat, and you have had to walk so far."

" They gave me a drink of water, and that refreshed me."

" As you please," he said, and let them drop into the basket.

Silence again. The sea was smooth as glass. Not a ripple was heard against the prow. Even the white sea-birds that roost among the caves of Capri pursued their prey with soundless flight.

" You might take the oranges to your mother," again commenced Tonino.

" We have oranges at home, and when they are gone I can go and buy some more."

" Nay, take these to her, and give them to her with my compliments."

" She does not know you."

"You could tell her who I am."

"I do not know you either."

It was not the first time that she had denied him thus. One Sunday of last year, when that painter had first come to Sorrento, Antonio had chanced to be playing *boccia* with some other young fellows in the little piazza by the chief street.

There, for the first time, had the painter caught sight of Laurella, who, with her pitcher on her head, had passed by without taking any notice of him. The Neapolitan, struck by her appearance, stood still and gazed after her, not heeding that he was standing in the very midst of the game, which, with two steps, he might have cleared. A very ungentle ball came knocking against his shins, as a reminder that this was not the spot to choose for meditation. He looked round, as if in expectation of some excuse. But the young boatman who had thrown the ball stood silent among his friends, in such an attitude of defiance that the stranger had found it more advisable to go his ways and avoid discussion. Still, this little encounter had been spoken of, particularly at the time when the painter had been pressing his suit to Laurella. "I do not even know him," she said indignantly, when the painter asked her whether it was for the sake of that uncourteous lad she now refused him. But she had heard that piece of gossip, and known Antonio well enough when she had met him since.

And now they sat together in this boat, like two most deadly enemies, while their hearts were beating fit to kill them. Antonio's usually so good-humoured face was heated to scarlet; he struck the oars so sharply that the foam flew over to where Laurella sat, while his lips moved as if muttering angry words. She pretended not to notice, wearing her most unconscious look, bending over the edge of the boat, and letting the cool water pass between her fingers. Then she threw off her handkerchief again, and began to smooth her hair, as though she had been alone. Only her eyebrows twitched, and she held up her wet hands in vain attempts to cool her burning cheeks.

Now they were well out in the open sea. The island was far behind, and the coast before them lay yet distant in the hot haze. Not a sail was within sight, far or near—not even a passing gull to break the stillness. Antonio looked all round, evidently ripening some hasty resolution. The colour faded suddenly from his cheek, and he dropped his oars. Laurella looked round involuntarily—fearless, yet attentive.

" I must make an end of this," the young fellow burst forth. " It has lasted too long already! I only wonder that it has not killed me! You say you do not know me? And all this time you must have seen me pass you like a madman, my whole heart full of what I had to tell you; and then you only made your crossest mouth, and turned your back upon me."

" What had I to say to you?" she curtly replied. " I may have seen that you were inclined to meddle with me, but I do not choose to be on people's wicked tongues for nothing. I do not mean to have you for a husband—neither you nor any other."

" Nor any other? So you will not always say! You say so now, because you would not have that painter. Bah! you were but a child! You will feel lonely enough yet, some day; and then, wild as you are, you will take the next best who comes to hand."

" Who knows? Which of us can see the future? It may be that I will change my mind. What is that to you?"

" What is it to me?" he flew out, starting to his feet, while the small boat leaped and danced; " what is it to me, you say? You know well enough! I tell you that man shall perish miserably to whom you shall prove kinder than you have been to me!"

" And to you, what did I ever promise? Am I to blame if you be mad? What right have you to me?"

" Ah! I know," he cried, " my right is written nowhere. It has not been put in Latin by any lawyer, nor stamped with any seal. But this I feel: I have just the right to you that I have to heaven, if I die an honest Christian. Do you think I could look on and see you go to church with another man, and see the girls go by and shrug their shoulders at me?"

" You can do as you please. I am not going to let myself be frightened by all those threats. I also mean to do as I please."

" You shall not say so long!" and his whole frame shook with passion. " I am not the man to let my whole life be spoiled by a stubborn wench like you! You are in my power here, remember, and may be made to do my bidding."

She could not repress a start, but her eyes flashed bravely on him.

" You may kill me if you dare," she said slowly.

" I do nothing by halves," he said, and his voice sounded choked and hoarse. " There is room for us both in the sea. I cannot help thee, child"—he spoke the last words dreamily, almost pitifully—

"but we must both go down together—both at once—and now!" he shouted, and snatched her in his arms. But at the same moment he drew back his right hand; the blood gushed out; she had bitten him fiercely.

"Ha! can I be made to do your bidding?" she cried, and thrust him from her, with one sudden movement; "am I here in your power?" and she leaped into the sea, and sank.

She rose again directly; her scanty skirts clung close; her long hair, loosened by the waves, hung heavy about her neck. She struck out valiantly, and, without uttering a sound, she began to swim steadily from the boat toward the shore.

With senses benumbed by sudden terror, he stood, with outstretched neck, looking after her, his eyes fixed as though they had just been witness to a miracle. Then, giving himself a shake, he seized his oars, and began rowing after her with all the strength he had, while all the time the bottom of the boat was reddening fast with the blood that kept streaming from his hand.

Rapidly as she swam, he was at her side in a moment. "For the love of our most Holy Virgin," he cried, "get into the boat! I have been a madman! God alone can tell what so suddenly darkened my brain. It came upon me like a flash of lightning, and set me all on fire. I knew not what I did or said. I do not even ask you to forgive me, Laurella, only to come into the boat again, and not to risk your life!"

She swam on as though she had not heard him.

"You can never swim to land, I tell you, it is two miles off. Think of your mother! If you should come to grief, I should die of horror."

She measured the distance with her eye, and then, without answering him one word, she swam up to the boat, and laid her hands upon the edge; he rose to help her in. As the boat tilted over to one side with the girl's weight, his jacket that was lying on the bench slipped into the water. Agile as she was, she swung herself on board without assistance, and gained her former seat. As soon as he saw that she was safe, he took to his oars again, while she began quietly wringing out her dripping clothes, and shaking the water from her hair. As her eyes fell upon the bottom of the boat, and saw the blood, she gave a quick look at the hand which held the oar as if it had been unhurt.

"Take this," she said, and held out her handkerchief. He shook his head, and went on rowing. After a time she rose, and, stepping up to him, bound the handkerchief firmly round the wound, which was very deep. Then, heedless of his endeavours to prevent her, she took an oar, and, seating herself opposite him, began to row with steady strokes, keeping her eyes from looking toward him—fixed upon the oar that was scarlet with his blood. Both were pale and silent. As they drew near land, such fishermen as they met began shouting after Antonio and gibing at Laurella; but neither of them moved an eyelid, or spoke one word.

The sun stood yet high over Procida when they landed at the marina. Laurella shook out her petticoat, now nearly dry, and jumped on shore. The old spinning woman, who in the morning had seen them start, was still upon her terrace. She called down, "What is that upon your hand, Tonino? My God! the boat is full of blood!"

"It is nothing, comare," the young fellow replied. "I tore my hand against a nail that was sticking out too far; it will be well to-morrow. It is only this confounded ready blood of mine that always makes a thing look worse than it is."

"Let me come and bind it up, comparello. Stop one moment; I will go and fetch the herbs, and come to you directly."

"Never trouble yourself, comare. It has been dressed already; to-morrow morning it will be all over and forgotten. I have a healthy skin that heals directly."

"Addio!" said Laurella, turning to the path that goes winding up the cliffs. "Good-night!" he answered, without looking at her; and then taking his oars and baskets from the boat, and climbing up the small stone stairs, he went into his own hut.

He was alone in his two little rooms, and began to pace them up and down. Cooler than upon the dead calm sea, the breeze blew fresh through the small unglazed windows, which could only be closed with wooden shutters. The solitude was soothing to him. He stooped before the little image of the Virgin, devoutly gazing upon the glory round the head (made of stars cut out in silver paper). But he did not want to pray. What reason had he to pray, now that he had lost all he had ever hoped for?

And this day appeared to last for ever. He did so long for night! for he was weary, and more exhausted by the loss of blood than he would have cared to own. His hand was very sore. Seating himself upon a little stool, he untied the handkerchief that bound it; the blood, so long repressed, gushed out again; all round the wound the hand was swollen high.

He washed it carefully, cooling it in the water; then he clearly saw the marks of Laurella's teeth.

"She was right," he said; "I was a brute, and deserved no better. I will send her back the handkerchief by Giuseppe to-morrow. Never shall she set eyes on me again." And he washed the handkerchief with the greatest care, and spread it out in the sun to dry.

And having bound up his hand again, as well as he could manage with his teeth and his left hand, he threw himself upon his bed and closed his eyes.

He was soon waked up from a sort of slumber by the rays of the bright moonlight, and also by the pain of his hand; he had just risen for more cold water to soothe its throbbings when he heard the sound of some one at the door. Laurella stood before him.

She came in without a question, took off the handkerchief she had tied over her head, and placed her little basket upon the table; then she drew a deep breath.

"You are come to fetch your handkerchief," he said. "You need not have taken that trouble. In the morning I would have asked Giuseppe to take it to you."

"It is not the handkerchief," she said quickly. "I have been up among the hills to gather herbs to stop the blood; see here." And she lifted the lid of her little basket.

"Too much trouble," he said, not in bitterness—"far too much trouble. I am better, much better; but if I were worse, it would be no more than I deserve. Why did you come at such a time? If any one should see you? You know how they talk, even when they don't know what they are saying."

"I care for no one's talk," she said passionately. "I came to see your hand, and put the herbs upon it; you cannot do it with your left."

"It is not worth while, I tell you."

"Let me see it then, if I am to believe you."

She took his hand, that was not able to prevent her, and unbound the linen. When she saw the swelling, she shuddered, and gave a cry: "Jesus Maria!"

"It is a little swollen," he said; "it will be over in four-and-twenty hours."

She shook her head. " It will certainly be a week before you can go to sea."

" More likely a day or two ; and, if not, what matters ? "

She had fetched a basin, and began carefully washing out the wound, which he suffered passively, like a child. She then laid on the healing leaves, which at once relieved the burning pain, and finally bound it up with the linen she had brought with her.

When it was done : " I thank you," he said. " And now, if you would do me one more kindness, forgive the madness that came over me ; forget all I said and did. I cannot tell how it came to pass ; certainly it was not your fault—not yours. And never shall you hear from me again one word to vex you."

She interrupted him. " It is I who have to beg your pardon. I should have spoken differently. I might have explained it better, and not enraged you with my sullen ways. And now that bite——"

" It was in self-defence ; it was high time to bring me to my senses. As I said before, it is nothing at all to signify. Do not talk of being forgiven ; you only did me good, and I thank you for it. And now, here is your handkerchief ; take it with you."

He held it to her, but yet she lingered, hesitated, and appeared to have some inward struggle. At length she said : " You have lost your jacket, and by my fault ; and I know that all the money for the oranges was in it. I did not think of this till afterward. I cannot replace it now ; we have not so much at home—or, if we had, it would be mother's. But this I have—this silver cross. That painter left it on the table the day he came for the last time. I have never looked at it all this while, and do not care to keep it in my box ; if you were to sell it ? It must be worth a few piastres, mother says. It might make up the money you have lost ; and if not quite, I could earn the rest by spinning at night when mother is asleep."

" Nothing will make me take it," he said shortly, pushing away the bright new cross, which she had taken from her pocket.

" You must," she said ; " how can you tell how long your hand may keep you from your work ? There it lies ; and nothing can make me so much as look at it again."

" Drop it in the sea, then."

" It is no present I want to make you ; it is no more than is your due ; it is only fair."

" Nothing from you can be due to me ; and hereafter when we

chance to meet, if you would do me a kindness, I beg you not to look my way. It would make me feel you were thinking of what I have done. And now good-night; and let this be the last word said."

She laid the handkerchief in the basket, and also the cross, and closed the lid. But when he looked into her face, he started. Great heavy drops were rolling down her cheeks; she let them flow unheeded.

"Maria Santissima!" he cried. "Are you ill? You are trembling from head to foot!"

"It is nothing," she said; "I must go home"; and with unsteady steps she was moving to the door, when suddenly she leaned her brow against the wall, and gave way to a fit of bitter sobbing. Before he could go to her she turned upon him suddenly, and fell upon his neck.

"I cannot bear it!" she cried, clinging to him as a dying thing to life—"I cannot bear it! I cannot let you speak so kindly, and bid me go, with all this on my conscience. Beat me! trample on me! curse me! Or if it can be that you love me still, after all I have done to you, take me and keep me, and do with me as you please; only do not send me away so!" She could say no more for sobbing.

Speechless, he held her a while in his arms. "If I can love you still!" he cried at last. "Holy Mother of God! Do you think that all my best heart's blood has gone from me through that little wound? Don't you hear it hammering now, as though it would burst my breast and go to you? But if you say this to try me, or because you pity me, I can forget it. You are not to think you owe me this, because you know what I have suffered for you."

"No!" she said very resolutely, looking up from his shoulder into his face, with her tearful eyes; "it is because I love you; and let me tell you, it was because I always feared to love you that I was so cross. I will be so different now. I never could bear again to pass you in the street without one look! And lest you should ever feel a doubt, I will kiss you, that you may say, 'She kissed me'; and Laurella kisses no man but her husband."

She kissed him thrice, and, escaping from his arms, "And now good-night, amor mio, cara vita mia!" she said. "Lie down to sleep, and let your hand get well. Do not come with me; I am afraid of no man, save of you alone."

And so she slipped out, and soon disappeared in the shadow of the wall.

He remained standing by the window, gazing far out over the calm sea, while all the stars in heáven appeared to flit before his eyes.

The next time the little curato sat in his confessional, he sat smiling to himself. Laurella had just risen from her knees after a very long confession.

" Who would have thought it ? " he said musingly—" that the Lord would so soon have taken pity upon that wayward little heart ? And I had been reproaching myself for not having adjured more sternly that ill demon of perversity. Our eyes are but short-sighted to see the ways of Heaven ! Well, may God bless her, I say, and let me live to go to sea with Laurella's eldest born, rowing me in his father's place ! Ah ! well, indeed ! l' Arrabiata ! "

THE HUNGARIAN COUNTESS

Paul von Heyse

IN the first quarter of the last century a countess, who through her great beauty and cleverness was famed far beyond the frontiers of her country, and whose tragic end was talked of for many years, lived in a fine castle on the western border of Hungary.

Countess Helene S—— was a member of an old Austrian noble family, and although she could have chosen a husband from amongst a host of young and brilliant aristocrats, she accepted the oldest and least attractive of her many admirers, the fifty-year-old Count N——y, and followed him far from her home to his Hungarian estates. Her husband, who had left the army on account of a serious fall from his horse, seemed the most unlikely man to attract this beautiful girl, nor could his fortune, which hardly equalled her own, explain her strange choice. Only her immediate relatives, who knew her seriousness and depth of character, realised that for years she had wished to enter a convent, and that she had now chosen the still heavier burden of acting as companion and attendant to an ageing husband. Her mother warned her in vain. Even when a child she would accept nobody's counsel, and only followed the dictates of her heart, keeping them secret from every one. Nobody knew then if in the five years of her marriage she had found cause to regret her choice. At her husband's death she wore no excessive mourning; people would have thought it hypocritical if she had, though the dead man had been held in high esteem. Yet when the young widow of twenty-three, even after the year of mourning, still persisted in her lonely life at the castle, and only visited her parents for a few weeks at rare intervals, people concluded that her sorrow was deeper than they had expected her to feel.

The boy, who had been born to her a year before her husband's death, was a very delicate child, and had been spared to her only through the unselfish mothering she lavished on him. When he reached the years of childhood in which the mental faculties begin to develop, it was found that his brain remained unresponsive, and it was only with the greatest difficulty and the most untiring patience that the unfortunate boy could be taught a few simple words. Otherwise he developed into a fine good-looking youth, and his misfortune was not at all stamped on his face ; on the contrary, he possessed the beauty of his mother, and only his eyes looked dreamy and somewhat sad, like those of an over-indulged child that needed waking up. There were times when the boy was afflicted with fits of melancholy, and then his condition was apparent to any one ; then only his mother could rouse him to a faint smile, in which, however, all the sweetness and nobility of his dormant mind seemed to peep out like the petals from a bursting bud. The people in the castle, the villagers, and particularly the domestic servants, were devoted to the boy.

The Countess had consulted every doctor and man of science about him. None had been able to do anything for him except to lighten the affliction by careful physical treatment, and as he reached his teens it was apparent that he would never be able to go through life unaided. His mother had been the last to give up all hope ; but she finally reconciled herself to this great misfortune, and having so far borne it outwardly at least in all fortitude, she now seemed to have composed herself also inwardly and to have accepted the inevitable. She began to visit and to invite to her castle the neighbours of the surrounding estates, and when her friends pitied her she used to insist that she was far happier with her boy than many a mother with a son who in full possession of his mental as well as his physical powers seems to delight in employing them only to indulge in excesses and to bring dishonour upon himself and his family.

When, on her return from one of these visits, and they were never long, she heard from afar the violin-playing of her son, who had come out to meet her in the company of his old servant ; when she saw his fine head against the instrument, his long fair curls reaching to his shoulders, his eyes lighting up with joy as he looked at her, she did not in the least feel an unhappy mother, and one could understand the reply she gave to the friends who pitied her.

Music was the only language the young Count ever mastered. Unfortunately Countess Helene had never taken any interest in music herself, and therefore could not help her son, and as his instructor, the old village schoolmaster, had been transferred to a new post and his successor was unmusical, she had advertised for a music-teacher. Of the great number of replies received only one seemed promising. The letter came from a small town in Silesia ; it was simply and well written in a style which made an immediate appeal to the Countess; and though no testimonials were enclosed, she wrote engaging the applicant, whose name was Georg Lindner, sending him a substantial sum for his travelling expenses, and bidding him start immediately if he felt inclined to accept the offer after he had read the exact description she gave him of her son's state.

A couple of weeks passed without bringing the new music-master. The Countess had given him up, when one evening there arrived a dust-covered weary wanderer. He was a pale, slender young man, who, in spite of his dilapidated appearance and melancholy aspect, bore himself well and seemed to flash intellect from his piercing dark eyes. He told her in simple language that he had left the money she had sent him with his mother, and had done most of the journey on foot, carrying everything for his immediate needs in his knapsack, and that his box would follow.

The Countess had him shown to his room, which lay next the apartments of the young Count. She felt somewhat disappointed, yet could not say why. The young man was what she had expected from his letter. He had not denied his poverty, and had borne himself confidently. Yet she had expected that she herself, whose beauty and rank had flustered many a high-born nobleman, would make a great impression on this unimportant youth. Not once had he cast down his gaze, and only one quick flash, as he first entered her presence and had looked on the proud stately mistress of the castle, had told her that the blood of manhood coursed through his veins.

She was astonished once more, when, on entering the dining-room a few hours later, she saw him with his arm round the shoulders of her son, as if he meant to show her what good use he had made of his time, and what a suitable companion he would be for her son in spite of his poor attire. The young Count appeared to be in high spirits, and during the meal stroked his neighbour's arm now and again, always a sign of his attachment.

After dinner the Candidate—as the young man was called in the castle—opened the piano, and by his masterly accompaniment of his pupil soon roused the Countess out of her mood, and presently his wonderful playing attracted to the corridor outside almost every servant in the castle, who came up to hear "the German" play. The Countess had never anywhere heard such playing, and the young Count had long since put aside his violin and sat enthralled, listening to some quaint

Hungarian folk-songs which were now the theme of the Candidate's extemporising. "Happy! Happy!" was all he could whisper to his mother.

The two young fellows became inseparable companions. When Georg worked or composed Count Stephan would lie on his divan watching his friend, and jump up immediately he had finished, asking his tutor in clumsily-uttered disjointed words, more like a servant than a master, what they should do next. Every one soon remarked how much better the Count looked, how his eyes had brightened, his speech improved, and how much happier he seemed to be—all brought about by the original scheme for the boy's treatment which the clever German carried out.

Only when his pupil was confined to his room would Georg go out by himself, roaming about the forest and countryside for hours. He was still dressed in his old suit; yet all the womenfolk about the castle and in the village spoke about him, said what a fine fellow he was, and wondered why he had no eye for their charms and would not respond to their encouraging glances. They told each other that he must have left a sweetheart at home, that the Germans were more constant than the Hungarians, and yet that it was a pity; for he could have such a fine time if only he would use his eyes and look about him.

The Countess's maid, who was particularly enamoured of the young German, told her mistress of all the talk that went on about him; but the Countess seemed to interest herself in none of the Candidate's doings save those which immediately concerned her boy's welfare. A few weeks after Georg's arrival she had thanked him for the good influence he exercised over her son, and inquired kindly and in a motherly fashion about his people and his circumstances; but Georg had received her expressions of solicitude rather passively, told her that his quietness and shyness were inborn in him, that his father, a minor official of good repute, had, in a fit of melancholy, drowned himself, and that he himself only found life bearable through his love of music.

After this, finding that she had no influence over him, she found it incompatible with her position to treat the Candidate otherwise than with an even politeness. Georg appeared in his old shabby suit even when company arrived at the castle and he was bidden to play; on these occasions politics were frequently discussed, and he expressed his opinions fearlessly and bore himself always with his old assurance, often rousing the temper of the Countess's friends, but quickly appeasing them by his wonderful playing.

Thus months passed without the mutual relationship of the inmates of the castle changing in the slightest. Only Georg seemed different. He had grown paler, quieter, and more restless; his play had become wilder and less joyous. On some days he kept carefully out of the Countess's way, excused himself from taking his meals with the family, and disappeared for hours in the country around the castle. To Count Stephan he was always the kind, considerate, guiding friend. Boriska, the maid, again spoke to her mistress; but she told her that the spring weather often affected melancholy-inclined persons, and that this phase would pass off.

As summer came and Georg's condition, instead of improving became ever stranger, Countess Helene resolved, though she had not forgotten the previous rebuff, to speak to the young man again; she thought it her duty not only to him who had done so much for her son, but also to his mother who had allowed her son to come so far away to Hungary.

However, just then an incident occurred which drove the matter from her mind for some time.

At Christmas the owner of a neighbouring estate, Count Sandor, had returned from years of travel abroad, and already, at his first meeting with Countess Helene, who was now thirty-seven, and had arrived at the zenith of her beauty, he had shown unmistakable signs of having fallen in love with her. The Count had not taken the first friendly refusal that he received seriously, and continued to lay siege to the heart of this fine woman. The social gaieties of the winter afforded him plenty of opportunity, and almost every morning he rode into the castle on his thoroughbred to spend the day in the company of the woman he loved. She had told him of her firm resolve not to marry again, that immediately after her husband's death she had made up her mind on this point and had determined to devote the rest of her life to her poor son. Besides, any third party might after a time find the presence of this unfortunate boy an encumbrance, and sooner or later torture her by treating him with indifference. "Don't let us talk any more about the impossible," she had concluded.

Count Alexander appeared to be satisfied with her offer of a sincere and honest friendship; but after a time, his forty summers sitting but lightly upon him, his blood still rushing hotly through his veins, there came a day when, on a cross-country ride, he took the bit between his teeth and made another impetuous and ardent proposal.

She allowed him to finish, stopped her horse, and then said, " I am so sorry, Count, that you have held my wishes so lightly as your own promise. In these circumstances I must discontinue a friendship which has been very dear to me; but my mind is made up, I shall never give you another answer. *Sans rancune*, dear Count; if in a year or so's time a change of air has helped you to forget, I shall be glad to see you again."

With a flick of her whip she started off at a gentle gallop, and commenced to talk of ordinary things in her quiet way.

The Count was deeply moved; he had great difficulty in retaining his composure; and when they returned to the castle he wished to take his leave immediately. She, however, would not hear of it, and told him everything must remain that day as before; reluctantly he stayed, and a strangely silent dinner was followed by an equally uncomfortable hour in the music-room. The Countess had greeted her son and his tutor more kindly than usual; she seemed happy that the air had cleared, that she would again be left to herself with the other two.

Georg had never taken to the splendid Hungarian nobleman, and when he asked him to which piece he would treat them that evening, showing plainly that the answer he would receive was a matter of perfect indifference to him, Georg, turning away, said, "I shall not play to-night."

" Aren't you well ? " the Count asked, " or is the audience too small ? "

" My reasons, Count, I may perhaps be permitted to keep to myself."

" Just as you like, Herr Lindner," quietly replied the Count, and then added pointedly, " particularly as the tone of your speech leads one to suppose that you might also strike some discords in your playing."

The young man flashed a meaning look at the Count, and exclaimed in a vibrating voice, " I know what I owe the house in which I live; at any other place I should have a different reply for you, Count." Bowing slightly he left the room.

" What have you been doing to my Musicus ? " asked the Countess, who just then entered. " You must have hurt his feelings to judge by his expression. I can read his face."

" Really, Countess, it was quite inadvertently that I offended him.

But this is one of my bad days ; I have only to open my mouth seemingly to be rebuffed. But I must protest to you, Countess, against your partiality. You have forbidden me your door as from to-morrow, while you allow a man who has burned his wings much more badly than I have to remain in your immediate company daily."

She gazed at him bewildered.

"Indeed, I don't understand you, Count Sandor."

"Extraordinary! And you asserted only a few moments ago that you could read this young German's face."

"Your joke is in very bad taste, Count."

"Bad taste? I don't know. Yet don't take this matter too jocularly. I have only lost my heart here ; but this young man looks as if he was about to lose his reason as well. However, I have your forgiveness already ; so I shall be glad to have your permission to leave now, it is getting late."

He pressed her hand lightly to his lips. "Then *au revoir*, in a year's time, and a complete convalescence!" she told him, with an absent-minded expression on her fine features. Her thoughts had settled on a graver issue than the departure of the Count.

She retired to her boudoir immediately her other guests had left. Boriska had to open all the windows after she had lit the candles ; her mistress felt hot and uneasy, and sat lost in thought. At ten o'clock she rang for her maid and asked her to request Herr Lindner to come to her, as she wished to speak to him. Five minutes later he knocked and entered.

"You wished to see me, Countess," he said quietly.

She did not answer at once and looked at him partly astonished, partly perplexed, as if she had only just discovered some new trait in his character. He held her gaze unflinchingly.

"I asked you here, dear Georg," she said slowly, without asking him to be seated, "because I have something of importance to say to you, and this is better said before going to bed. You know I esteem you greatly, and am thankful for all you have done for my son. I hoped you, too, were happy in my house, and satisfied and pleased with your position. I am grieved to think I have been mistaken." She stopped here for a moment. He had turned his face away and was looking on the floor. "What makes you think that, Countess?" he asked, in a voice in which only her watchful ear could have discerned his agitation.

"You are becoming more taciturn, more misanthropic ; you are getting paler and thinner, and your eyes are dull ; in short, you must be suffering from some secret illness or from some great sorrow. I know your goodness of heart, your devotion to my son, perhaps you think you ought to subordinate your personal desires, your dearest wishes to his welfare ; I cannot accept such a sacrifice ; neither my religion nor my regard for you would allow me to take, much less to ask it, from you." Again she was silent, to give him time to think over her words, and paced to and fro over the heavy carpets. His eyes followed her, the fine womanly figure seemed to have cast a spell over him.

" And yourself, Countess ? " he said at last. " Aren't you sacrificing yourself ? Haven't you given up more than I can ever sacrifice to my duty ? "

She stopped before him. " How can you draw comparisons ! I am his mother. Besides—I have no future to think of. Let us be sensible, Georg ; you are not in your right place, you are secretly straining to get away. I will write to my cousin, the Duchess D—— (you remember the lady who was here last autumn, and who wanted so much to take you away to teach her children at Vienna), and I will ask her to let you lead her house orchestra. You will be received there with open arms ; I'll write to-night."

His gaze again rested on the carpet ; his pale features worked in great agitation ; with difficulty he composed himself as he strode to the open window. At last his answer fell tonelessly from his lips.

" Don't write that letter, Countess. Leave me to my fate, which brought me under your roof because it wished me well. If, through my unfortunate disposition, I should destroy my happiness here, you, at any rate, will be blameless : to you I am indebted to all eternity."

She looked at him sorrowfully, pityingly. " I knew it," she said. " I am not surprised ; yet I wonder that I did not see it coming on long ago. Georg, you want to put me off, to keep me in the dark. You don't wish to speak of it ; yet this thing must be cleared up between us, much as I dread to speak of it. You love me, Georg ! And you see yourself how mad, how hopeless it is, and that it makes it impossible for you to stay on here. But you'd rather ruin yourself than fight against this passion. Isn't it so ? "

He looked into her eyes, and as if it were some inconvertible law of nature affirmed, " It is so ! "

She gazed on him in wonder. Never had any man—and many had sworn they loved her—told her the secret of his heart in this manner.

" And as it is so, what—are you hoping—or expecting ? "

" Nothing. What could I hope ? I know it—I knew it from the first day I came, it was my fate."

" Fate ! Don't use the word in this frivolous way. Don't be a coward, face the facts, I might almost be your mother. I certainly thought you more level-headed, braver, Georg."

" Unfortunately, I am neither the one nor the other, though I have vainly tried to be both. I have fought against this for months. At last I had to acknowledge defeat, I had to surrender. But why talk of it any longer, it cannot interest you, and it is over."

" You are now twenty-three ; you say you have never loved before, not since your childhood ; yet you don't seem to have overcome your inclination to childish jealousy. Your behaviour this evening towards Count Alexander——"

" I beg your forgiveness," he interrupted. " I forgot myself for a moment, it shall never happen again." He had flushed scarlet. " I shall keep out of his way."

" You won't have to do that, for he is not coming here again ; he has proposed to me several times, and I have refused him. You see I'm quite serious when I tell you that in the interests of my boy I want to have everything going on here smoothly as usual. But you'll have to be sensible, Georg, or it will be necessary for us to part. Think over what I have said and let me have your answer in a week, when I hope you will come to me and tell me with a smile that you have completely got over your infatuation. And now—good-night and happy thoughts ! "

He made as if to say something, his head had dropped again, and without seeing her outstretched hand he left the room with faltering steps.

" I shall lose him, I see it coming," she told herself. Then she quickly undressed and went to bed. For hours she lay sleepless ; but it was not flattered vanity, womanly weakness, or excitement that kept her awake, although the figure of the strange young man who had confessed openly the innermost thoughts of his soul stood continuously before her. She harboured no glowing sparks of passion that the breath of a stammering and infatuated lover might have fanned into flame. She could read Georg's face, as she had told Count Alexander, and realised that their talk had been fruitless.

The sun shone into her bedroom as the sudden entrance of her maid unbidden frightened her out of her short sleep. "What has happened?" she exclaimed in apprehension.

The Candidate had suddenly been taken ill, and the groom was already on his way to fetch the doctor; but the fever had increased so alarmingly that they were hardly able to hold the young man to his bed. Quickly Countess Helene dressed and hurried to Georg's room, where she found her son in tears and in a pitiable condition by the bedside of his friend. Georg was unconscious, but as she called him by name a happy smile seemed to illuminate his features. The doctor came and looked very serious, but pronounced the case not hopeless. The illness was a long and anxious one, and the Countess ceased her personal ministrations only after the patient became conscious, thinking it better that he should not see her, and that he should be left in the hands of the nurse. He never asked for the Countess, who received daily reports of his condition from the doctor as well as from Boriska; the latter told her that the Candidate seemed quite changed, whistled all sorts of tunes, and was bright and happy.

As he went out for his first drive, the Countess stood by the open window and called down to him friendly words of congratulation, which he acknowledged, colouring slightly. He seemed taller and looser, his long hair and beard gave his features a new soft expression which was pleasing, and when he returned after an hour, a healthy red in his cheeks, greeting her gaily and thanking her for the flowers she had sent to his room, they found no difficulty in entering again upon the friendly relationship that had previously existed.

He had evidently resolved to fight down his passion, and what the Countess thought of it all it was impossible to say.

In this way the time went by and the summer was drawing to a close. On a fine mild afternoon the Countess with her son and his tutor had driven to a neighbouring village to attend the wedding of a young peasant girl who had been in service at the castle. After the ceremony, when everybody had left the church, and the strains of the village band had died down in the distance, Georg had expressed a wish to play on the organ, which seemed a particularly fine instrument, and the young Count had scrambled up beside him on the seat. Under the masterly touch of the German a Praeludium by Bach filled the old church with wonderful chords, and its walls seemed to tremble to the glorious music. The Countess sat alone in the castle pew, her large veil drawn closely around her. Twilight fell as Georg finished his inspiring playing with a grand finale, and they made their way carefully down from the organ-loft into the nave now almost lost in darkness. There the Countess met them; she did not say a word, but softly pressed the player's hand. As he assisted her into the carriage he saw that her eyes were wet. He had never seen her cry. Why these tears should make him happy he could not say. On the way home he sat opposite her lost in happy wonderment. Nobody spoke. He could not see her face, over which her veil was closely drawn.

She was very quiet during the evening meal, and retiring early to her rooms left the two friends together. Ringing for her maid she had several trunks quickly packed, wrote several letters, gave the girl various orders, and at ten o'clock dismissed her, saying, "I shall now just go and look at my son before I retire, I expect he will have a bad night after this exciting day and the close night. You go to bed, Boriska, for you will have to be up early in the morning." The maid kissed her hand and went upstairs to her room. The Countess sat for a while in her dressing-gown, then got up and paced the room restlessly, "How my face burns!" she said. "Is it with the wind or——"

Excitedly she brushed her hair back over her shoulders and extinguished all the candles except one; this she took up, and went along the long dark corridor that led to her son's rooms. A luxurious sitting-room separated the two bedrooms. She crossed the empty salon and softly entered her son's bedroom, sitting down beside him, and placing her hand on his forehead as she had so often done before. He slept soundly. As she left she heard a noise in the other bedroom. Georg was pacing restlessly up and down, sleepless as usual. She thought perhaps he was composing.

Suddenly he heard a soft knocking.

"Come in!" he called out in astonishment.

The door opened noiselessly; in the red half-light of his lamp he saw the woman he adored on the threshold of his room.

"Helene!" he exclaimed. "You! What has happened? Is Stephan ill?"

"Sh!" she whispered, a mysterious wonderful smile overspreading her features but vanishing quickly, "he is asleep. Don't let us waken him! Georg, I have come to you—I couldn't sleep to-night until I had seen you once more—God be merciful! I surrender——!"

. . . .

Late next morning, late as usual, for he lay awake half the night,

Georg awoke from his dreams. He lay still now for another hour with eyes closed, thinking over the wonders of the past night, looking about him in the room where every article, every picture on the walls, the carpet that had borne her feet, the glass that had moistened her fevered lips testified to the unexpected, the heavenly happiness that had dawned for him. As he lay there the unusual silence that prevailed in the castle struck him ; Stephan usually came to him at this time, perhaps he had found him asleep and gone out ; he missed Boriska's tuneful voice singing her folk-songs as she went about her work ; and presently he rang for the servant.

On his breakfast tray was a letter. "From the Countess," the old man said in a queer voice. "They left early this morning, and Count Stephan, who did not know as he entered the carriage that they were going to Vienna, will be very much cut up and miss you, sir. They have gone to visit Countess Szilagyi, and I hope they will soon return."

Georg could not utter a word. As the old man left the room he gazed at the letter as if he knew every word it contained, then opened it slowly and read the few lines.

"I have gone with my son for a few weeks or months to my parents, to lighten for him that blow of parting from you which is now inevitable. We shall not return until I know that you have left the castle. Don't try to cross me in this, my absolute determination ; but stay on until you have quite recovered or found another home. Believe me, this parting cannot be more painful to you than it is to me ; I shall never forget what you have been to and done for my son. Fate is more powerful than our desires. Farewell! HELENE."

He sat down at once and wrote a long letter to Vienna, and waited, at first happily, and then restlessly, feverishly, and gloomily for a reply that never came. Suddenly he left without a word to anybody.

Summer and autumn had gone by and a severe winter had covered the vast Hungarian plain with snow when orders came from the Countess, who had been informed of the Candidate's departure long since, that two sleighs were to meet them at the nearest station.

They arrived that afternoon, and the Countess had seen her son, who had a slight cold, to his room and his bed, and was busy unpacking her personal belongings, when there came a knock at her door. She unlocked it, thinking her maid wished to speak to her, when a figure closely muffled and covered with snow burst in upon her.

"Good gracious!" she called out, "Georg! What does this mean?"

"Yes, it is I," he said. "Perhaps I have come at an awkward moment; but when one has waited months it's at last impossible to wait minutes."

She remained speechless. With one look she saw the state of his mind and her own awful position. "Georg!" she cried imperiously, "how dared you come to this house again—have you forgotten what you owe me, or rather—what you should owe your honour and the honour of a woman?"

"Honour?" he mumbled after her. "Excuse me if I can't see what you mean. I must sit down after my three hours' tramp through the snow. Wonderful how beautiful you have grown, more beautiful than I remembered." He rambled on, sometimes addressing her and gazing at her, but mostly talking to himself.

"What do you want here?" she managed to say at last. Her voice trembled, and her large blue eyes were fixed intently on the man.

"What do I want here?" he answered in a far-off voice. "I am just here as you see. If you knew what I have suffered, what I am suffering now, no sleep, no work, only one longing, one single wish like that of a thirsty man in the desert. You must let me remain here, otherwise you are heartless, a monster. And I know you have a heart —and what a heart!"

"Must I? And as what must I let you remain here? And how long? Come, Georg, collect yourself, you are ill, tired, worn out; let me speak to you quietly, let me try to cure you. I have tried once already—yes—and failed miserably—and I call our good God to witness my deep humiliation and terrible suffering. This time I must be strong. You can't live here with me as my lover and as tutor to my boy, and to make you my husband is impossible. Think of it! I who have refused the highest in the land to give my hand to one Georg Lindner, a man of no position, of no name to be the master of this house! It is unthinkable, and would mean endless misery, endless shame. Dear friend," she continued hesitatingly, "in this hour I must be honest with you—I don't love you—I—have never loved you —it would go against my heart—against my nature to make the slightest response to your passion."

"Even if you want to be honest with *me*," he spoke softly now, "you are now dishonest with *yourself*. Think—I am neither beautiful nor noble, not even agreeable. What else can it be then, than that mysterious power—love—that has brought us together—a power that it would be foolish to resist. That night when you came to me you spoke differently—you spoke the truth then! Shall I repeat your words to you, not one of which I have forgotten?"

While he spoke she fought a violent battle, the struggle was visible in her face, intolerable pain convulsed her features; then they became still and hard.

"I deceived you," she said. "I have never loved you, and," hesitatingly and falteringly she added, "I know now that I could not live with you. Compose yourself, Georg, think of me what you will, but tear your love for me from your heart, for it is not returned. And now go, and know that you have yourself to blame that we must part in this way!" Her voice failed her, and she had to turn from him to hide the tears that had welled up into her eyes.

As she turned again and looked at him, a terrible change had come over him. He had got up from the couch and stood by the table opposite her, his left hand clutching his throat, his right fingering the revolver that her aunt had pressed upon her before she started on her journey as a weapon against possible prowling wolves that penetrate deeply into the plains of Hungary in winter. "What is it?" she cried. "Calm yourself—wait—I will ring for some wine—you are worn out—your nerves——"

Quickly he interposed between her and the bell-rope. "Stop!" he cried, "I want nothing but the truth—nothing. There is only one truth—either you lied to me then or now! You have robbed me of my trust in you, I have lost my self-respect, I am done for—I have lost everything that makes life worth living, and I had better use this toy to put an end to all my sufferings before the little brain that is left to me deserts me."

"You are raving!" she cried, freeing her arm from his grasp with a violent wrench. "You forfeit the last shred of pity that I feel for you by making this scene; you must leave this house at once. Besides, I have consented to marry Count Alexander, and in three weeks' time the wedding will take place. I have found that a lonely woman must have some protector, and this behaviour of yours has confirmed me in my decision. Georg . . .! Dear God—Georg . . .!"

Boriska tore open the door just as two shots rang out. She saw the Countess sink to the floor and the Candidate stand staring down on her, blood streaming from his forehead. With a cry she rushed to her mistress and raised her up in her arms; the Countess opened her eyes, and, gazing at the unhappy man opposite to her, managed to utter a few disjointed words.

"You are—a fool! What have you—done now? About Count Alexander—did you think it was true? It's all right, Boriska—look how Herr Georg bleeds—I was playing with the revolver—the silly thing—but go, Georg, get yourself bound up. Forget what I said—they were white lies—nothing was true—forgive me—a thousand times—I loved you only too well—Boriska—a glass of water—my son——!"

She then closed her eyes and expired. The girl's cries for help were soon answered, and presently everybody in the castle was assembled. The young Count tottered into the room in his nightdress; but as he saw Georg, who still stood there as in a trance, he rushed to him and threw himself on his neck. Only then Georg seemed to come to his senses, and, supporting his pupil, went with him to his rooms, where by the light of the lamp they spent the night.

Georg was taken to gaol next morning. At his examination he never uttered a word, and on the sixth day he was found dead in his cell, having refused to touch any food ever since his arrest.

Count Stephan survived his mother and friend for some years. At first he inquired now and again after them; but gradually his reason seemed to go, and finally only his playing of the violin was heard in the deserted castle, sounding like a death-dirge for lost life and lost love.

THE HUNTSMAN

PAUL VON HEYSE

ON the western shore of the Königssee, opposite to the steep wall of the Watzmann, which descends precipitously into the deep, a wild footpath leads straight through the wood. The wood-cutters and hunters know it, the cow-girls climb on to the Alm by it, the deer run across it. Twice it passes through grassy wood-clearings, where stand solitary Sennhütten, and blockhouses in which the wood-cutters spend the winter. The nearer it approaches the edge of the mountain, the fewer are the stems, until at length the ridge rises bare from out the firs and larches, and looks down freely into the beautiful valleys round about Berchtesgaden, into the dark lake at its feet, and on to the gay hunting-castle Bartholomä, encircled by lofty maples, which beckon to the wanderer from out this rocky wilderness.

In autumn, when it is the stag's rutting-time, a youth, accompanied by a young huntsman, ascended the steep path, and often looked down admiringly into the deep. He wore the customary hunter's dress, but it was evident the hand of a city tailor had tried his art on it. The fine cloth jacket was bound with green velvet; he wore a green waistcoat of quilted silk, chamois-leather breeches to the naked knees, green stockings, whose strings were fastened by gold buttons, mountain shoes that, in spite of the heavy nails, were as bright as possible, and were daintily fastened by yellow laces. On the brand-new pointed hunting-cap were a chamois beard and a blackcock feather; but these were fastened at the wrong place, which had long been troubling the boy of fifteen years, who bore beneath his coarse jacket the heart of an able and complete hunter, only he did not dare to tell the grand gentleman of it. He carried the beautiful double-barrelled gun meditatively after the young baron, and noticed with satisfaction that the sharp edges of the stones which seemed sown around left many a mark on the shining polish.

But we by no means wish to rouse any prejudice against the gentleman with the fine shoes. He was a tolerable hunter in the forests of his own estates, but unaccustomed to the mountain chase, and new to the customs of the country. The higher he mounted the more cheerfully he looked about him. The autumn air made every sound from the lake distinctly audible: he heard the oarswomen, who were going to Bartholomä, singing far below, the pistol-shots fired off opposite to the echoing wall, and the rolling roar of the echo; and, when silence reigned once more, the song of the titmice in the wood, and the murmur of the little brooks. He stood still, raised his hat, and looked attentively into the woods around.

"It is beautiful here in your country, Phrygius," said he to the boy, who bore into the romantic wood this classical name, bequeathed him by his ancestors, a long line of worthy schoolmasters.

"I should think so, sir," exclaimed the youth. "There are many chamois over there in Warteck, and higher up marmots, if your honour would like to shoot one once."

Here the conversation stopped; for Phrygius spoke the purest mountain dialect, and the baron, a Franconian, scarcely understood a word of it, and feared to forfeit respect by questions. His desire was for a mighty stag, that was to be found up on the Regenalm, and of which he had heard from the ranger. Phrygius knew its beat; and after spending the night in the Sennhütte, they meant to go out next day to stalk it. So he continued his way in silence.

They had been several hours on the road, when a strong daring-looking fellow came towards them from above, stood still suddenly, and examined them with an angry gaze. He could scarcely have been twenty-four years of age, wore a very faded old jacket, a weather-beaten little hat with a long cock's-feather; the strong bare knees showed their brownness as they looked out from the leather breeches and woollen socks, and his coarse shirt left neck and chest uncovered. He stood now leaning on his tall mountain stick in the middle of the way with almost sarcastic obstinacy, as though he were ruler here, and did not turn a step aside when the dandy stranger approached. The bold fellow pleased him. He looked confidingly at him, nodded, and said:

"God greet you! How far is it from here to the Regenalm?"

The youth's sharp-cut mouth fell, he bit his lips together as though he preferred to swallow the answer.

"To the Regenalm?" he repeated at length, with a scornful glance at the stranger's costume. "Do you suppose it is carnival up there?"

He raised his stick, and struck it against a stone, as if to test the power of the sharp iron point.

"Seppi," said the hunter-boy, "stand aside at once, or I will tell the ranger you know what!"

The other laughed.

"Talk what stuff you please," said he. "I fear no devil, least of all such a creature as you, who carries the gun for such a monkey. God be with you, Phrygius!"

And with another laugh he struck aside among the firs, and disappeared in a hollow. The other two looked after him.

"Who is that rude fellow?" asked the baron.

"Seppi from Thiereck, your honour," answered the boy, staring down into the hollow, as if a wounded deer had escaped that way. "The ranger has had his eye on him for some time; for he poaches about dangerously, just as he feels inclined. Formerly, when his mother still lived, he kept quieter; now he carries on in broad daylight. Resei on the Regenalm is his sweetheart. That is why he pricked up his ears when your honour asked the way there. And another thing that did not please him was that you wear the blackcock feather in front instead of behind. When any of the people wear it so, it means he wants to pick a quarrel, and every one is ready to fall upon him. I will not answer for it that Seppi may not want to pick a quarrel with your honour, although he has gone out of your way now."

"What can he do to me?" said the young man calmly. "He has not even a gun."

"Oh, yes, he has, sir; only you did not see it. He has one to screw. He carries the butt end in his pouch, and the barrel, which is quite short, in his jacket pocket. When he wants to shoot, he can put it together in a second. But if the gamekeeper gets hold of him he must give it up, and then he will be locked up for several weeks."

"And what did you threaten to tell the ranger about him, Phrygius?"

"I saw him last Saturday with a chamois in the Ofenthal, just by the place where the king shoots. He was going down to the Hintersee. If his mother were not my godmother, I believe he would have shot me, he was so furious at my meeting him. I promised him to keep silence. But he has no peace in his conscience."

"Is he poor, that he must go poaching?"

"He might live quite comfortably if he did not gamble and act the grand gentleman at every kermess and shooting-match. But he thinks it must be so; and for that his box-making does not bring him in enough. His mother, who kept things together a bit, is no longer there; he has sold his cows, is in debt for his house. Where is he to get something from? Resei does not care about him any more either; I heard myself how she said to her friend that she would not take a good-for-nothing and poacher. That makes him twice as fierce and furious, and he would like to shoot down every one. But your honour need not be afraid. I will take care, with the gun behind you. In another hour we shall be at the huts."

After this conversation they were silent again, and the more persistently since the last steep bit of road required firm breath. When they passed out of the shade of the wood, and now looked up at the free green slopes of the last height, the baron again stood still, and fixed his eyes on a spot high up on the hill, where something dark was moving backwards and forwards before the clear sky. The boy told him that it was a seesaw, on which the cow-girls sometimes amused themselves. Continuing his way, he soon heard the shrill cry with which the quick-sighted girls welcomed him from a distance. But when he reached the top, had climbed the highest ridge, and approached the seesaw, he felt a cold shudder at the sight of this dangerous game. Hard by the steep precipice a stake of about a man's height had been driven into the ground, and over it lay the long board of the seesaw, and moved backwards and forwards. At each end, holding on to a short peg, sat one of the Sennerinnen astride, with her legs crossed. Up and down they flew, while the ends of their black head-dresses fluttered, and the ground shook when they struck on it with all their weight, to fly up next moment high over the precipice, into which the least swerve of the pole must have thrown them. As they hung in mid-air, nodding and laughing welcome to the strange hunter, and waving their hands high in the air, while their white teeth shone, the spectator forgot all his fear, and enjoyed the sight of the fresh youth that smiled on him here in the wilderness, like a bunch of Alpine roses on the steep rocky wall.

At last the two girls grew tired of their game, and stopped. In an instant they were off the swing, for Phrygius helped them, and greeted the new arrival kindly, who asked for their hospitality. Now, for the first time, he was able to look around from the height on which he stood, and thought himself well repaid for his troublesome ascent.

On the crest of the Watzmann fresh snow had fallen ; the "Stony Sea" shone softly in the evening red, and the glittering ice-mantle of the Alm sparkled in it like a large diamond among the crown jewels of the vast Alpine domain. The Alm descended to the south in a gentle slope ; here and there a large rocky fragment overgrown with Alpine roses looked out from the depth, or a thicket of dark-green dwarf-pines, between which the cows were grazing. Lower down towards the Regenalm firs and some larches reappeared.

The four wended their way in this direction, in such conversation as hunters, in coarse or fine shoes, generally carry on with Sennerinnen. The taller and handsomer of the girls was that Resei whom Phrygius had mentioned in connection with the poacher. The other, Genoveva, or Vefa, was inferior to her companion in beauty, but by no means in good humour. They both wore close-fitting bodices, and over them tight brown woollen jackets trimmed with red stripes and a number of coloured glass buttons. They had woollen socks from their ankle to the knee. Resei was barefooted, and Vefa wore heavy wooden shoes. Both inhabited a large Sennhütte by the Regen, divided by a partition-wall into two equal parts, so that each of the girls had her own domain of dairy, cellar, hearth, and stable for the cattle. There they had already spent several weeks, and the time was approaching when they were to drive off with the well-fed herds back to the peasants who had entrusted them with their cattle.

All this they told the baron on the way from the seesaw to their hut. Meantime the twilight was beginning to envelop them, and it was growing cold on this exposed height. The "Stony Sea" shimmered grey, the snowy crest of the Watzmann stood out in spectral paleness in the colourless air, and beyond, from the invisible basin of the Obersee, a white mist rose slowly. Scarcely a quarter of an hour later, although moving with apparent slowness, it had covered the whole horizon, and hung like a tough spider's web even round the firs and dwarf-pines on the Alm, so that the hunters and girls reached the hut only just in time.

Within they already found a fire on the ground opposite the door. An old wood-cutter sat there cooking his evening meal in Resei's frying-pan. Two Sennerinnen and a cow-boy from the neighbouring Alm had also looked in to have an hour's chat.

There were rather close quarters round the blackened hearth, and the two little seats were not sufficient. Phrygius crouched down next the cow-boy on the threshold of the dairy; the baron had a warm seat between Vefa and one of the strange girls; Resei was going backwards and forwards, preparing in haste a real mountain *Schmarren* for her guests. But close quarters are no hindrance to cosiness. Soon laughing and giggling began in the merry circle. The tin spoons clattered; the baron did justice to a wooden bowl full of sweet milk, into which Vefa threw large bits of bread. Phrygius smoked a cigar that the baron had given him with all a novice's satisfaction. The old wood-cutter, who at first had also been somewhat mistrustful of the stranger, became so cheerful from the effects of the hunting-flask out of which he was allowed to drink, that he began to turn out his endless store of ancient songs, accompanied by the monotonous music of an old zither; while the cow-girls often joined in, laughing and jogging each other's elbows.

The baron slung his gun across his shoulder, and stepped after Resei out into the morning mist. She wanted to show him his way as far as the beat which Phrygius had described to her. From the Regenalm a gentle beautifully-rounded slope descends between the mountain peaks to the west, until it sinks in steeper craggy cliffs into the lake. The ground is covered with soft grass, tolerably free from stones; a sparse copse of beautiful maples extends through the whole length of the hollow, which is called, after it, the Maple Valley. Here the stag driven by Phrygius was to pass between the trees.

"Hunter's luck to you!" said the girl, as she stood still at the entrance to the Maple Valley.

He also stood still and looked back. There lay the huts peacefully in the first light of the rising sun, while it was only just dawn in the hollow. The cows had dispersed. Vefa's form could be distinguished on a piece of rock, and she sent a strong *jodel* cry across to them.

"That will not drive the game away," said Resei. "They are accustomed to it. Sometimes the stags come to us so trustfully that we could touch them. But then there must be no hunter near, or they would soon scent him."

She seemed to have something else on her mind, for she hesitated to go.

"Listen," said she at length. "It may be that Seppi will try to play a trick to spoil your hunt. He will scarcely dare do more. But if you meet him, do not speak an angry word to him, whatever he may do, or he will do what he might repent. And now, once more, hunter's luck to you!"

She left him standing, and again returned to her hut, and he gazed after her strong and yet graceful form. He did not fear Seppi, for he bore his protecting weapon, and knew himself to be quick and strong. Besides, in this late season the maple wood was scarcely dense enough for an ambush, nor did he fear one much from this very straightforward fellow. So he loaded his gun, and now began creeping cautiously among the stems to seek a convenient station. A young deer crossed his path, a few chamois hastened past in quick flight on the top of the ridge, and sent down stones into the valley. This showed him that his Phrygius must be approaching. But still the hero of the day—the stag—kept him waiting. The hunter could plainly distinguish his track on the dry leaves; and as he came to an open space which it crossed, he took up his station between two little fir trees, on whose roots lay a mossy stone. There he crouched down behind the stems, between which he could see and aim very well. All around him not a creature stirred, except the birds, who now and then buzzed out from the branches, and always made the watcher's heart beat faster, as though they proclaimed the approach of the expected stag.

Gradually, amid watching and listening, he sank into a pleasant day-dream. He planned out for himself how he would set to work this evening to please Resei. He laid his gun down beside him, and removed the traces of his hay bed from his clothing. Meantime the sun was slowly rising behind the ridge, and pouring a full light into the Maple Valley. The hunter wore a ruby on his finger; he let it play in the sun, and felt, as he looked at his image in the bright blade of his new hunting-knife, that he was completely irresistible, the handsomest, most distinguished, and richest man for many miles around. How could he fail in anything?

Just as he had finished his toilette, he heard a rustling of dead branches close by, and saw the stag breaking forth on a side to which the track had not pointed. He was not running, but looking round wildly—a strong royal stag, quite black, with shaggy breast, and spreading sharp-pointed branches. One moment he stood in the clearing, scenting, with head erect, and emitting a low murmuring noise. The next moment he became aware of the man behind the fir; his black eye gave the hunter one hasty glance, then he turned round with a mighty spring, and stormed into the wood up the slope. But behind him sounded two reports one after another, and the certain tokens of a hasty flight showed the startled hunter that he had had more luck than prudence, and had certainly hit the animal. Eagerly he sprang up, and rushed after the fugitive into the forest, intent now only on discovering the stag's blood. With strong steps he followed in that direction, and a cry of joy escaped from him when he perceived on a piece of bare rock the red track, although it was almost immediately after lost among grass and tall ferns. He stood still for one moment and considered whether he should wait for Phrygius. But after his contemptible beginning, he felt the desire doubly strong to seek the stag alone, whom he expected to find dead. So he carefully reloaded both barrels of his gun, and continued to climb the difficult path between cliffs, bushes, and underwood, from time to time encouraged by meeting the bloody track.

He had soon climbed so far up the mountain that he could look down on to the trees in the Maple Valley, and see along the whole length of the hollow. Two or three times he thought he saw his hunting-boy's grey jacket appear between the branches; and now he also heard a whistle, but farther in the distance. Without letting himself be detained, he climbed on along the wild slope, up which the wounded stag had hurried, following the track which shone plainly in bright red drops on the grey rock, and the perspiration stood on his forehead from the difficult pursuit. For still the warm south wind was blowing up from the valley, which, even had the sun not been rising higher in the heavens, would have increased a wanderer's difficulties. Now he had climbed the ridge of the mountains, and the view opened out on to the blue lake below and the walls of the giant Watzmann. But close by the huntsman's feet lay another craggy wilderness of immense blocks, here and there overgrown with Alpine roses. A novice could not be blamed for stopping here to take breath and consider what he should do next. Now he did repent that he had not first waited for his able hunting companion. He listened to hear whether he might not have climbed after him of his own accord; and in truth he fancied he heard, at no great distance, the sound of nailed boots on the hard rock.

"Phrygius!" he called three times. Not a sound in answer. But should he turn back now, while there in the bright sun lay the red track, whose drops were getting bigger and bigger? "Forward!"

exclaimed he, with determination, and again began to pursue the uncertain zigzag course of the fugitive over the loose stones that rolled beneath his steps fast and noisily down into the abyss.

Suddenly he saw a mighty vulture flying from the lake, shooting through the steel-blue air. Now it stopped just above the cliff, its glance firmly fixed on one spot. There could be no doubt, there, only fifty paces from the baron, behind the sheltering rock that rose sheer from among the stones, the stag had stopped, and was perhaps already dead. While the huntsman rejoiced in the auspicious omen, its motionless hovering roused him to attempt a new aim. The barrel of his gun was loaded with a bullet. But the bird was as still as the black spot in the target, and, if the one ball failed, there still remained the other for the stag. He calmly took aim, shot, and with convulsive wings the vulture fell out of the air. At the same moment the mighty head of the stag rose from behind the rock, and the wounded creature stood opposite its enemy, in the wild mountain solitude, prepared for a last struggle. He felt his heart beating. Next him he saw the precipice, where there was no escape either up or down. He knew by the animal's proud bearing that the shot had only wounded its thigh, but had not reached the seat of life. The savage creature had already bent its antlers for the attack ; everything depended on one last bullet ; but with cool hand the hunter raised the gun to his cheek, aimed just as the stag was storming against him, and would have been sure of his shot, when his gun treacherously failed him, and only the cap went off. A sudden shudder overcame the defenceless man. He saw the raging beast springing towards him, and had only sufficient consciousness to commend his soul to God and throw himself down, so that the enemy might possibly rush over him, when—hark !—behind him sounded a shot ; and when he started up and looked round he saw, twenty paces from him, the falling stag, who struck down the low dwarf pines, and in his death struggle threw down sand and stones into the abyss with the points of his antlers.

Instantly the baron sprang to his feet saved, and turned towards the ridge of the mountain, whence help in need had come. "Phrygius!" exclaimed he, for his eyes were dazzled, and he did not immediately recognise the form that stood calmly among the crags. Now it moved. The marksman opposite threw the discharged blunderbuss over his shoulder and turned round, slowly reascending the height. Not till then did the baron see that it was no other than Seppi from Thiereck.

But before he could realise how it had all come about, his suspicious deliverer had disappeared on the other side of the ridge, and he was left alone with the dead stag.

A quarter of an hour later, when Phrygius came breathlessly to the spot, he found the baron plunged in reverie and mentally exhausted, sitting on a stone and staring into the animal's breast-wound, so that he at first thought the gentleman must be asleep with his eyes open. He had to call him several times before he stirred.

" I am glad," said the honest fellow, " that your honour has all your limbs left you. For I heard Seppi's shot, that sounds different from your twin barrels. I turned hot all over ; for I know well enough that when Seppi is in a passion, he could aim at the Lord himself ; and directly after, when I met him there where the trees begin, he looked at me so strangely, that I could say nothing to him but " Seppi, have you seen the baron ? " Then he pointed back over the ridge with his hand, and said, ' He has shot a stag and a vulture.' And with that he went his way. But, sir, it is a glorious stag, and a beautiful shot. And where is the vulture ? "

The baron pointed to the rock, from which Phrygius soon brought the stately bird. He tied it on to the gun, threw it across his back, and said :

" We will fetch the stag this afternoon ; he will never get up any more. But what was that about Seppi, sir ? What did he shoot at ? And how is it that I only heard you shoot once up here ? "

" I will tell you some other time," said the hunter, rising. " Where is Seppi gone ? "

" I cannot tell. No one knows his ways."

FERDINAND VON SAAR
1833–1906

THE TOILERS OF THE ROCKS

I

ONE of the most remarkable railways in the world is that which crosses the Semmering—a ridge belonging to the Noric Alps which marks the frontier between Austria and Styria the Green.

The traveller who makes this journey for the first time receives a deep and lasting impression. In truth, what can be more terrible, more striking, than the narrow track running at infinite heights between beetling walls and yawning precipices?—what more impressive than the carriages rolling with a crash like thunder over viaducts elevated to fabulous heights, or burying themselves to the shrill scream of the locomotive in the deep night of the long tunnels?

The air is cold—freezing. The train is swept along as by a whirlwind. The earth below is so far away that it can hardly be distinguished through the half-transparent mists. In the midst of scenes and works of such sublimity man realises his own insignificance. But little thought is given to the thousands of poor people who, amidst the greatest dangers, have spent their strength in hauling the enormous rocks and blocks of stone, in spanning the gigantic gulfs with bridges, and in bringing their titanic task to a successful issue.

It is the story of two of these poor creatures that I propose to tell. Not that my intention is to excite the public pity for their fate, or to idealise their lives. I shall simply strive to shed a little light upon the immense mass of the suffering poor who, after a life of struggle, of privations, and of rude labour, sink, despised and unremembered, into the common tomb. I shall speak of the human heart, of its joys and its sorrows, and of the great tragedy of life which is renewed for ever amongst the humblest as among the most powerful of the earth.

The Semmering railway was almost finished. The hubbub of the labourers, the thunder of the blasting had ceased. The swarm of workpeople who had come from Bohemia, from Moravia, from sterile

Karst and fertile Frioul, had dispersed, and had pushed on farther south in search of work.

Reassured by the tranquillity of the place, the wild animals began to come forth again from the depths of the forest. Only here and there were still seen some of the little wooden huts which the wandering labourers had inhabited, most of which they had pulled down before they left.

These scattered cabins served as a shelter to a small number of workers who still remained to finish the railway; for still, at certain places, rails had to be fixed, telegraph poles to be placed, and the pointsmen's boxes to be completed, under the roofs of which the swallows had already made their nests.

One Sunday afternoon a woman was sitting upon the threshold of one of these little huts, which stood against the rock, near the line. Her hair was hidden by a coarse scarf twisted round it; her face was worn and old-looking, and contrasted with her girlish figure. Deep lines crossed her forehead, and drew down with a mournful expression the corners of her lips.

The sun was sinking at the horizon. Great shadows already wrapped the highest summits, but a flood of living light bathed the valley and the forest pines. A cloud of flies, of butterflies and bees, whirled dizzily in the sunlight. The solitary girl saw nothing of this charming landscape. Her eyes were fixed upon a man's shabby jacket which she was darning. This work appeared to be particularly difficult to her, for if the coarse and horny hand that awkwardly held the needle was examined, it was easy to see that it was accustomed to handle the hoe and spade.

Suddenly the young woman's attention was attracted by the sound of footsteps. She lifted her head, and perceived a man of miserable aspect advancing towards the cabin.

He was slight and insignificant in figure, and was clothed in an old military coat with flapping skirts, too loose and too long for him. A soldier's cap, blue and greasy, was pulled down over his forehead to his eyes. He staggered as he walked, though to sustain himself he leant upon a knotty stick, and though the little sack which he carried slung across his back appeared almost empty. He approached timidly, and looked helplessly at the young girl out of his weak eyes.

"Is this hut Number 7?" he asked in a faltering tone.

"Yes, this is it," she replied with the harsh accent peculiar to the Germans of Central Bohemia. "What do you want?"

"I have been sent here to work." And as he spoke he showed her a paper which he held in his hand.

The young girl scrutinised the strange costume of her questioner and his thin white face with its straggling beard.

"The overseer is not here at present," she said at last. "He has gone down to the tavern at Schottwein with the men. Rest yourself whilst you wait, if you are tired." She cast a last glance upon the poor creature, who appeared to be in suffering, and then returned to her interrupted work, drawing the needle with renewed haste.

The soldier did not reply. He dragged himself a little farther away, and let himself fall upon the grass with a great sigh of weariness. He lay there at full length, whilst the sun sank more and more at the horizon, pouring over the whole scene its liquid golden light. A deep silence reigned. Far above in the azure sky a solitary vulture wheeled, uttering its piercing cry. Very soon from the distance came the bellowing of drunken voices. The girl trembled.

"Heavens!" she murmured, speaking to herself. "They are already returning, and the jacket is not done!"

The voices became more and more distinct, the howlings stronger, and in a few minutes a band of individuals of savage aspect burst upon the scene. In the midst of them, and rather better clothed than his companions, a man of herculean figure caught the eye. He was about fifty years of age. His big face was red and swollen by drink, and from under his straw hat, which was tilted backwards on his head, escaped a tangled mass of greyish hair. On his left shoulder was slung his coat, which he had taken off; his right arm, with its powerful muscles displayed by the turned-up sleeve, carried a great pannier filled with provisions. Two of his companions were loaded with heavy sacks full of potatoes, which were hoisted on their shoulders.

"Halloa, Tertschka!" cried the man with the basket in a hoarse voice; "give us a light, so that we can put our provisions in the cellar."

As she stood before him his eye fell upon the unfinished jacket, which she held timidly against her breast.

"Well, is it done?" he asked abruptly.

"Not quite," she replied, in some confusion.

"What, not done yet?" he cried, so fiercely that his face grew purple. "Did I not tell you that I should want it to-morrow?"

"I have worked at it all the afternoon. But I cannot darn it as quickly as some one who has learnt to sew."

The reproach contained in these plaintive words appeared to increase his irritation.

"You have always an answer ready," he cried. "But if at daybreak to-morrow my jacket is not finished, take care of yourself!"

He put down his basket of provisions and strode towards her, menacing her with a terrible gesture. She shrank back from the blow, and at that moment he caught sight of the man in the soldier's coat, who had timidly drawn near.

"Who is this?" he demanded, letting his hand fall.

"He has been sent here to work," replied Tertschka breathlessly.

The overseer, for it was he, drew himself up to his full height and advanced towards the wretched little creature, measuring him from head to foot.

"Bah! to work! The rascal cannot even stand upon his legs."

"I have come a long journey," said the stranger, hesitating. "I have walked here from Otterthal."

"That is a feat, no doubt," sneered the overseer, scanning in the twilight the paper which the young man held out with a shaking hand. "You are called Huber?" he asked, after a pause.

"Yes, George Huber."

"And why do you wear a soldier's uniform?"

"I have been in the army and have been discharged."

"What, you have been in the army?"

"Seven years in the 12th Regiment. I have been dismissed now because I cannot get rid of a bad fever which I caught during the siege of Venice."

"Good Heavens! Fever! This is the last straw! The devil must be in the Government that sends us such fellows. We get nothing but invalids to make stone-breakers of. And then people are astonished that no work is done. As for you," he added, with another threatening gesture, "take care, for if you fail to do your two cart-loads of gravel daily, I shall send you packing. This is not a hospital, remember!"

Thereupon he picked up his basket and, followed by his companions, entered the cabin. Tertschka led the way, holding in her hand a brand lighted at the fire. A door barred with iron led into a sort of grotto hollowed in the rock, in which the provisions were stored. The overseer then retired to rest in an adjacent room; upon which the labourers stretched themselves, yawning, here and there upon the floor, and without troubling themselves about their new comrade, prepared to sleep upon the old straw mattresses which were ranged against the walls.

George all this time stood irresolute by the door. In a few minutes Tertschka came towards him.

"You can sleep there," she said, pointing with her hand to a vacant place.

He obeyed her awkwardly, screwing himself together so as to take up as little space as possible. After making a pillow of his sack and covering himself with his old coat, which he had taken off, he uttered a great sigh of weariness and composed himself to sleep. Tertschka lighted a little lamp and, crouching down by the fire, began to sew with feverish haste. When she had finished her work she extinguished the smoky flame, and stretched herself, dressed as she was, in a corner near the chimney.

Outside the night was blue and balmy—a summer's night in all its splendour. A cool wind blew. From the interior of the hut, whence could be heard the deep breathing of the sleepers, myriads of stars sparkled through the disjointed planks and crannies of the roof.

II

The dawn was already beginning to whiten the horizon when George awoke from his deep sleep. He watched the workmen quit their meagre couches, rise and pass out, furnishing themselves as they did so with all sorts of tools which were hanging on the walls of the cabin. He followed their example, and, after putting on his coat, stood hesitating in what direction to proceed in search of his work, when Tertschka came up to him, carrying on her shoulder a long-handled hammer.

"The overseer is still asleep," she said, "but I know what you have to do. Take this hammer and come with me."

He obeyed her, and they went out together.

Outside all was cool and peaceful. Only now and then a bird twittered in the bushes. The grass was heavy with clear dew.

They walked silently along. After some distance they came upon a stone quarry, where several of the men were at work, whilst the rest were busy upon the line, with wheelbarrows and spades. Tertschka, followed by George, passed these groups and paused at a heap of stones.

"This is my place," she said, seating herself on the middle of a pile of stones. "I never care to remain near the men. They are coarse and wicked; but if you like, you can work here."

He made no reply, but sat down at her side.

"See, these great fragments of rock must be broken into tiny pieces. There," she added, pointing to a great heap of fine gravel, "is my last week's work."

He took a piece of limestone, and struck it with his hammer, but the stone remained unbroken.

"Strike harder," cried Tertschka. This time she struck it in her turn, and the rock flew into fragments. He watched her in amazement, and after making a second attempt was rewarded with success. Then, without saying a word, both devoted themselves to their task.

All around them lay stretched a wild but charming scene of hill and valley. But the workpeople did not pause in their labour to admire its beauties. With stooping shoulders they struck and broke their stones, whilst the sun, now mounting in the heavens, beat down with scorching heat upon their unsheltered heads. The strokes of George's hammer became fainter and fainter, and at last the tool fell from his hand. He began to fan himself with his cap, and to dry the moisture which streamed down his face. Tertschka stopped also.

"Are you tired already?" she asked, surveying him compassionately.

"Ah! Heaven only knows how tired," he replied in a dreary voice. "It is only now that I begin to feel how low the fever has brought me."

"Feeble and ill as you are, how could you accept work so hard and rude as ours?"

"What else remained for me to do? To beg? Not that, at any rate. I had learnt no trade. In my nineteenth year I was placed in the army. Now I am ill, they send me here to break stones. Yes, now I am a stone-breaker," he said, with a smile frightful in its bitterness. He picked up his hammer.

Tertschka stood silent with drooping head.

"But you will never be able to stand it," she said at last in a low voice.

"Oh yes, perhaps, when I get food to eat; these last days have been very hard for me. I have eaten nothing since yesterday morning."

She made no reply, but slowly unwrapped and took out of her apron a piece of black bread, which she broke into two parts. She held out to him the larger of the two pieces.

"Eat," she said.

He glanced timidly at the piece she offered him.

"But—it is your bread," he replied in confusion. And he made a gesture of refusal.

"That does not matter. I have quite enough for myself."

As he made no movement to accept it, she placed the bread by his side.

"You must be thirsty also," she continued. "I will go and fetch you some water; there is a stream hard by."

She rose, took a small pitcher fixed among a heap of stones, and ascended the quarry towards the pine forest, where a tiny rill of limpid water trickled between tufts of green moss. She filled the pitcher and drank, and then filled it again, and returned with it. The piece of bread was still untouched.

He accepted the cool draught with gratitude.

"Thank you very much—very much," he said in a broken voice when he had finished drinking.

"It was done willingly; there is nothing to thank me for."

She sat down again.

"Eat," she continued in a tone of sweet persuasion. "You can surely accept that of me."

The blood rushed to his face, and he took up the bread.

"Surely you, who are so kind-hearted, must also have been unhappy," he said, without looking at her, and breaking off a piece of bread.

"Yes, I know what it is to be unhappy; and I am often hungry myself."

A lump rose in his throat, and he felt as if he were choking.

"Is this work so badly paid then?" he asked, after a pause.

"I do not get paid at all."

"What—you receive no wages?"

"No; the overseer takes charge of them."

"The overseer?"

"He is my stepfather."

"Your stepfather?" he repeated mechanically.

"Yes; my father was killed when I was quite little. Then my mother married the overseer, who at that time was simply a labourer. We all came hither from Bohemia."

"Then you are a native of Bohemia? and that is why you speak such a strange dialect, and why you have such a singular name? Tert——I cannot pronounce it."

"Tertschka," she repeated. "In German it is the same as Theresa; for short I am called Resi."

"But," he continued, "if the overseer receives your wages, it is his duty to maintain you."

"Oh, he gives me just enough to keep me from starvation. He is a bad man. He beats me continually. You saw him, how he threatened me yesterday about his jacket?"

She paused, plunged in mournful remembrances.

"But if he ill-treats you like that, why do you stay here?"

"I know that he would never let me go," she replied. "Some poor, defenceless being is always necessary to him, to torment with impunity. For he is a coward, though always ready to quarrel. And then, where should I go?" she continued with a sigh. "Everywhere life is sad. Everywhere there is suffering."

So saying, she picked up her hammer, and George, feeling a little more revived, followed her example. Silently they returned to their work.

The hours rolled on; the heat of noon spread into the valley and upon the mountain. All was quiet, except for the regular heavy strokes of the hammers and the tapping of the woodpecker in the branches. From time to time the hoarse voices of the men occupied on the line were heard, bursting into some brief refrain.

Suddenly the shrill tinkle of a bell rang out.

"What is that?" asked George, seeing the workpeople leaving their work and proceeding in the direction of the cabin.

"It is the dinner-bell," replied Tertschka. "Come, let us go."

He rose and followed her in silence. After finishing their meagre meal they returned together to the quarry, where they continued their hard toil until night fell.

III

Thus days followed days, and they worked together side by side. George began to pick up his strength with amazing rapidity. The wretchedness in which he had hitherto lived was overcome. The vivifying mountain air swept away the fever which was consuming him. Already he handled his hammer with real vigour, whilst at the same time recounting to his companion the perils and adventures of his military life. There were many things which Tertschka only understood intuitively—others not at all. They were all so alien to her monotonous life, passed amidst the solitude of the great mountains. One thing she seized clearly, and that was that George had suffered. She began to tell him in return her own sad life and all its unhappiness. These long days of toil, passed side by side under the high scorching sun, became very sweet to them both. They started each morning at daybreak to the quarry, and when the bell rang at meal-time they were loth to be torn from their solitude and pleasant companionship, to endure the coarse jests and savage humour of the other occupants of the hut.

But, alas! these days, when mutual friendship was beginning to heal their wounds, and to soothe their poor bruised hearts, were not to last.

Whether the overseer had been informed of their intimacy by some vindictive companion, or his own evil nature made him divine the pleasure they took in each other's society, they never knew. But suddenly one day they perceived him standing behind them.

"What are you always doing here together, like two toads?" he bellowed. "Begone to your proper place, you famished scarecrow," he cried, turning to George, and pointing to another part of the quarry.

"As for you, you hypocrite," he continued to Tertschka, whilst George crept silently away, "I should like to know what plots you are contriving with that wretched dwarf. Listen: if I see you speaking to him again I will kick the vagabond out of the place, and that day will be your last; you understand?"

Thus were the two poor creatures brutally separated.

On the following day George received an order to work farther away, near the line. It was only at meal-times, or in the evening after the sun had set, that they saw each other; and then they dared not give a glance of recognition. Harder still, they could not speak a single word, for the overseer's eye was ever on them, and they were under the constant surveillance of their companions, who watched them with mocking smiles.

It was Saturday evening, and the overseer, accompanied by some of the labourers, had gone to the tavern. Those who remained sat down to a game of cards, and soon became absorbed in handling the greasy pack. Presently they began to quarrel. Now was his time. George stepped softly over to Tertschka. The young girl was sitting in a corner on an old box, lost in thought.

"Why has he separated us like this?" he asked. "Surely it cannot matter to him if we sit together, as long as we do our work?"

She looked straight before her with a mournful expression.

"He is a wicked man," she said at last. "He cannot bear to see any one happy. He would like to deprive every one of every pleasure."

She rose and, lifting up the lid of the box, began to take out some articles of clothing.

"What are you going to do?" George asked, watching her.

"I have a great desire to go to-morrow to the church at Schottwein. There is no doubt I shall have great difficulty in obtaining permission from him. But let him say what he likes, I must not forget my religion in the midst of creatures who do nothing but drink and gamble."

George stood musing, with bowed head.

"It is a very long time since I went to church also," he said. "How delightful it would be if I could come with you."

"But it is impossible."

"Why? The overseer will know nothing. Let us each start separately and meet afterwards."

She reflected for an instant.

"It might be managed. In that case you must start before I do. Listen! On issuing from this cabin, there is a little pathway to the right which leads into the valley, and at the bottom of the path a wooden cross. Wait for me there. Now go," she added in an imploring voice, "or we shall be observed."

George went back and threw himself upon his couch, whilst the players roared and squabbled over their cards. He felt quite lighthearted and joyous in thinking of the morrow, and, absorbed in pleasant anticipations, he soon fell asleep.

The next day was magnificent. A bright sun glittered through the pine trees as George descended the narrow green path that Tertschka had pointed out to him. He peered about for the cross which he was to find at the entrance to the valley. Soon he caught sight of its brown, worm-eaten wood among the young beech leaves. As he was there in good time, he sat down upon a large, mossy stone which served as a *prie-dieu.*

A deep silence reigned; the stillness of a Sabbath day. Even the bees, which were plundering the many-coloured petals of the flowers, seemed to restrain their drowsy hum. The moss was starred with blue gentians. At length he started up impatiently and began to walk up and down. He gathered some of the gentians, and also some white and some yellow flowers which gleamed amid the grass.

"I will give them to Tertschka," he murmured, casting a complacent glance at his improvised bouquet.

At last he caught the gleam of a light dress upon the hill. Some seconds after he saw Tertschka descending the pathway. He hastened to meet her. "Here I am," she said, out of breath. "I have been able to get away this time without hindrance."

George stood gazing at her.

Her head was bare; the scarf which she habitually wore was gone, and her thick hair was parted simply on her forehead. A crimson kerchief which she wore around her neck cast a soft flush upon her pale cheeks, and her sober-coloured bodice, though too large for her, and her striped petticoat of muslin, were not unbecoming.

"How pretty you look!" he said at last.

She cast down her eyes and blushed.

"Take these flowers," George continued. "I plucked them whilst I was waiting for you."

She took the bouquet, which he had until then held behind his back, and tried to fasten it in her bodice, but it was too large, and so she continued to hold it in her hand, together with her rosary. They went on together down the mossy path and on through the cornfields, where the newly-reaped wheat stood in great sheaves of burnished gold.

At length they reached the hamlet of Schottwein. They found it in a state of great animation. It was Mass day; the long, wide street which composed the village was thronged with all sorts of vehicles and with peasants clothed in their holiday garb. Opposite the church stalls were standing, crammed with every kind of goods for sale in rich variety—shawls of gay colours, cotton handkerchiefs, pipes, knives, glass bead necklaces, imitation coral ornaments were piled side by side with cooking utensils, gingerbread, and children's toys.

They paused in ecstasy before the grandeur of the sight. George longed for a pipe. He used to smoke when a soldier. Now that he gained a living, and neither drank nor gambled with his comrades, he could well afford the luxury. He asked Tertschka's advice, and she encouraged him to buy one. Whilst he made his purchase Tertschka strolled on in advance.

George elbowed his way through the crowd of loafers who pressed around the stall, and bought a pretty porcelain pipe embellished with tassels and a silken cord.

A brilliant necklace of amber beads caught his fancy. He imagined how pretty it would look on Tertschka's neck. The stall-keeper asking him but a moderate sum, it was soon wrapped in paper and in his pocket. And next, out of the change of the florin which he had given in payment, George bought at a neighbouring stall a gingerbread cake in the shape of a heart. He finally purchased some tobacco, and hastened on to join Tertschka.

He began by showing her the pipe, which she admired exceedingly.

"This is for you," he added, holding out the gingerbread heart. The heart was stamped in the centre with another heart, red, thrust with an arrow, and encircled with a garland of flowers.

She slipped it with a pleased smile of gratification between her bouquet and her rosary.

"I have something else for you," he continued presently, drawing the little packet slowly from his pocket, half opening it, and letting her see the gleaming of the yellow beads. She cast a rapid glance upon it.

"How could you spend so much money on me?" she cried. But her face was all rosy with pleasure, and her eyes sparkled with innocent joy.

"If I could only give you all that I desire!" he replied with emotion. "But put it on and see how it looks."

She gave him her things to hold whilst she put on the necklace. But she could not succeed in fastening it.

" Let me do it," said George, and lifting gently the heavy masses of hair which clustered on her neck, he brought the two little ends of the snap together.

" There ! " he said, examining her with a look of satisfaction.

They continued their route and soon came in sight of the little chapel standing in a cluster of lime trees.

Tertschka knelt down in the last row of benches, and placed her flowers and gingerbread before her. George stood erect behind her. He was much affected by that scene, so calm, so still. A mellow light streamed down through the lofty arched windows. But he could not pray. His eyes were fixed constantly upon that kneeling figure with bowed head and murmuring lips before him.

The Mass ended. The priest blessed the congregation as they passed out, but still she knelt. At length she rose, and, followed by George, advanced to the door where the impatient verger was shaking his bunch of keys. Outside the sun was glittering through the green foliage.

" Come," said Tertschka, " let us go and sit down."

They proceeded towards a forest of young pine trees which fringed the meadows. A little hill, carpeted with soft moss, provided them with a seat, from which they looked down upon the village inn at their feet. They gazed with interest. The little inn was *en fête*. A merry wedding party were celebrating their happiness before the entrance, under a great beech tree, which spread its branches above their heads. Strains of music, softened by the distance, presently stole upon their ears. They saw the bridal pair advance and begin dancing upon the greensward to the music.

" How gaily they dance," cried Tertschka. " Do look at them."

" Yes, they are happy," he replied dreamily. " If only we could celebrate our marriage too ! "

" Oh ! what are you saying ? " she murmured almost inaudibly ; and, stooping down, she plucked a red flower in the grass at her feet.

" Resi ! " he whispered—he called her by this name for the first time—and at the same moment he passed his arm timidly about the young girl's waist. " Resi, if you knew how much I love you ! "

She made no answer, but she raised her eyes and fixed them upon his. In the lovelight of their depths he read his happiness. He drew her gently to his heart, and their lips met for the first time in one long kiss of love.

IV

Since I have undertaken the task of narrating this simple story as faithfully as possible, must I describe to you the dream of happiness in which our lovers lived from that day? I think it will be wise for me to pass it by in silence. What words can render the exquisite joys of a passion so pure as theirs?

It is true that they were compelled to conceal their happiness from all eyes, trembling with fear lest it should be discovered, as if they had been guilty of a crime. But in their secret hearts their passion throve and flourished.

The fear that the overseer should learn of their visit to Schottwein diminished little by little, so much so that one day George, having gone to that part of the quarry where Tertschka was working, took the opportunity to snatch a few minutes by her side. For a little while the lovers forgot their woes in a passionate embrace, but almost at the same moment they heard the sound of rapid steps behind them. They started instantly apart and perceived the overseer, who, with an evil smile upon his lips and his face purple with rage, stood gazing at them.

"Ha! so I have caught you this time, you wretched creatures!" he hissed forth. "This is the way you obey my orders! And you think I do not see your little game! I know well that you were together last Sunday, but I wanted to surprise you in the act. You shall pay for this." As he spoke he seized George by the throat, and, with a savage shake, threw him with such force upon the ground that the dust and stones flew up around him.

"Take away your load of stones, you gallows-bird! then pack, and be off. If ever I catch you prowling about here again I will break every bone in your body!"

He kicked the poor fellow as he raised himself painfully, then following him to his cart, he drove him to the road with blows. Then he came back and glared at Tertschka with a ferocious glance of hatred. "As for you," he said, "we will settle our account by and by."

Muttering and growling to himself, he strode away.

Stunned and blinded by the shock, George had rejoined his comrades. He emptied his cart mechanically, and sitting down upon a stone, gazed before him with thoughts far away. Since the morning the day had become dull and the sky covered with clouds.

A biting autumn wind whistled in the tops of the pine trees. Suddenly the rain came down. But George never felt the icy drops which beat upon his face. Sparks danced before his eyes, and a shiver ran through his frame. Shame at the treatment he had undergone, mixed with the burning injustice which Tertschka, as well as himself, was enduring, brought the angry blood to his face. And now he was dismissed—separated from Tertschka—from that which was to him the most precious thing in all the world. The more he reflected the more his shame and rage increased. His timid and patient nature was stung to revolt, and he felt within him a new-born strength to struggle, to resist, to conquer any obstacles which should rise to separate him from his betrothed. Gradually his dejected countenance assumed a terrible expression, and his eyes shone with a strange lustre.

He rose and took his way towards the little hill where Tertschka worked. His companions eyed him curiously. He found Tertschka sitting on the ground in tears.

" Do not weep, Resi," he said. His voice was calm and gentle, but singularly grave.

She made no reply. He came to her side, and raised her head. Her sobs grew more violent.

" Do not weep," he repeated. " It was all for the best ; we now know what we have to do."

She looked straight before her.

" You will come with me when I go away ? "

She shook her head slowly.

" I shall try to obtain the post of crossing-keeper, which is given, I believe, to soldiers who have served during the war. You shall be my wife, and we will live in one of the little cottages beside the line. And if I fail in that," he added quickly, seeing that she made no sign of consent, and that her sobs redoubled—" if I cannot obtain this post we will work for years with all our strength, and economise as much as possible. But, Resi, speak—tell me that you consent ! Answer me ! "

" Alas ! " she moaned, " all that you say is Paradise, but you are not thinking of the overseer. He will never let me go."

" He cannot prevent you. You are no longer a child. He has no hold upon you, none. You are a worker like ourselves. You are free to come and go at your pleasure."

" Believe me, he will not let me go, and, above all, with you. I have never told you," she replied, after a pause, whilst a crimson flush of anger dyed her face, " but he killed my mother with his cruelty. I told him at the time what I thought of him. Ever since that day he has hated me like poison, and never loses an opportunity to revenge himself upon me."

George grew pale to the lips. He seemed as if he were choking.

" The scoundrel ! " he cried. " At any cost you must come with me, and we shall see if he will prevent you from going."

" Be careful," she cried in alarm. " He is quite capable of killing any being too feeble to defend itself."

" I do not fear him," said George, his small stature dilating. " He took me at a disadvantage before, but now let him come ! "

" Madonna ! " she moaned, wringing her hands in agony. " You must not fight ! I cannot bear it."

" No, no, it will not come to that," he replied, striving to appear calm. " First of all we will tell him our decision, and you will see that he will say nothing. Coward that he is, he will be forced to acknowledge that he has no hold upon you, and that you are free. Take courage, Resi," he added gravely. " Would you let me go away alone ? "

For answer she sprang towards him, and clung tightly round his neck.

" Now we will go and find him," he said, stroking her hair gently.

They went slowly towards the cabin, Tertschka in a tumult of alarm, George dignified and perfectly calm. When they reached the cabin, they found the overseer, knife in hand, seated before the table, peeling potatoes. He started on perceiving the two young people, but his surprise soon changed into a sort of frenzy.

" What do you want here ? " he cried, half rising, and gripping nervously the handle of his knife.

" You have dismissed me," replied George with a calm voice, " so I have come to get my things, and to tell you that Tertschka will go away with me."

The overseer made a movement as if about to spring upon them. Then, seeing George's determined attitude, he recoiled in alarm.

" I have nothing to reply to you," he said at last through his clenched teeth.

" That is not necessary. Tertschka is of age, consequently she is free to do as she pleases." The overseer burst into a hiss of fury.

" Take what belongs to you, Resi," George continued, taking down his own coat which hung on the wall, " and let us go."

The overseer gasped painfully for breath. A struggle was passing within him. He hardly knew what to do next. As he hesitated he threw a sidelong glance at Tertschka, who, unfortunately, could not control her agitation. As she walked towards her box he sprang upon her, and, grasping her by the shoulders, pushed her into the cellar, the door of which was half open, locked the door, and put the key in his pocket. "That is my answer," he bellowed with such fury that his whole body trembled. Then, gulping down his rage, he returned to his seat, and renewed his occupation.

This scene had passed so rapidly, and in a manner so unexpected, that George could do nothing to prevent it. Without any undue haste he buckled on his knapsack and approached the overseer slowly. "Let Tertschka out!" he said in a firm voice.

The overseer went on peeling his potatoes.

"Let Tertschka out!" repeated George again.

The overseer's hands began to shake. As George repeated his demand for the third time in a more imperative tone, he started up with clenched fists. "Be off," he shouted, "unless——"

"Unless what?" repeated George calmly. "You cannot frighten me with all your bluster. You ill-treated me when I was weak and defenceless. Now I defy you to your face!"

The overseer's countenance was terrible to look at. Hate and vengeance struggled on it with the basest cowardice. He gasped for breath, and his curved fingers seemed to clutch at something to rend to pieces.

"I advise you," said George, "to give up Tertschka, or else I shall use force."

In the midst of this scene several of the workmen had entered the cabin. Noon was approaching; perhaps they were also not unwilling to be witnesses of a scene which promised to be stormy. Their presence appeared to increase the irritation of the overseer. He felt that all their eyes were upon him, and to conceal his trepidation from those scrutinising glances he assumed an air of insolence.

"Just listen to the cur! He threatens me. Come, kick him out of the place for me."

The men looked hesitatingly at one another, but no one stirred.

"You see," George continued, "no one will touch me. I ask you for the last time to let Tertschka out, or I will use this hammer. Two blows, and the door will be smashed to atoms."

"You would break down the door, would you, you scoundrel? Be off, or I will send for the police."

"Send for them," cried George, his blood boiling with righteous indignation. "We will soon see who is in the right. You will have to explain why you have locked Tertschka up. Every one shall know that you have ill-treated her from childhood, that you have stolen from her the wages which she gained with so much labour. They shall also know how you oppress the feeble, and how you enrich yourself with the sweat and blood of the poor labourers confided to your charge." George stopped. The truth of his reproaches stung his adversary into frenzy. The overseer's face turned livid. With a roar like that of a wounded bull, with foaming mouth and glaring eyes, he sprang at his opponent with his knife. George, on the other hand, scarcely knowing what he did, had gripped his hammer; it flew aloft; a dull blow resounded through the room, and the overseer, struck full upon the chest, staggered and fell backwards on the ground.

For an instant a death-like silence reigned. George stood like David over the dead body of Goliath. "Resi! Resi!" he cried suddenly, as if returning to himself; and rushing to the door, he broke it open with one blow. "You are free, our tyrant is no more."

"My God!" she shrieked, as she rushed out and saw the body lying stretched upon the ground. "He is dead! Oh! George! George! what have you done? You will be dragged to prison as a murderer."

"So be it! Nay, I will render myself up to justice. I will answer for my conduct to the court. My comrades can bear witness that the overseer attacked me with a knife and that I struck in self-defence. Go," he added, turning to the men. "Go to the police and tell them that George Huber, the stone-breaker, has killed your overseer."

V

For four months George lay in the prison fortress of Wiener-Neustadt awaiting his trial. Then he and his witnesses, among whom was Tertschka, were brought before the court-martial. The following sentence was passed:

"George Huber, formerly a soldier in the 12th Regiment, having pleaded guilty of causing by a blow the death of the overseer at Semmering, is sentenced to a year's imprisonment. But taking into consideration the evidence of the witnesses, who swear that he only acted in self-defence, after the highest provocation, and his exemplary conduct whilst in the army, coupled with the personal testimony of those who know him, the Court reduces his sentence to the four months of imprisonment which he has already undergone in the fortress of Wiener-Neustadt since his arrest."

Two days after this George and Tertschka were sent for to the colonel's house. He regarded them for a moment in silence. Their sad story had touched him to the heart. Round these two poor creatures, tortured by the miseries of existence, shone the radiance of a love pure, deep, and sublime. He advised them to remain at Wiener-Neustadt, where he would procure them work, and a salary sufficient to supply their wants. He promised to do still more for them in the future, and he kept his word.

To-day, where the black rails wind beside the gleaming River Mour, in the midst of green pastures and forests of sweet-scented pine trees, where the castle of Ehrenhauser rears its lofty towers upon the hill which overlooks the village, there stands a pretty little cottage. Behind the house extends a field of vegetables and maize. Roses and great golden-petalled sunflowers bloom before the door. A hedge surrounds the whole, over which the sweet pea twines its delicate tendrils.

In this pretty cottage, whose gay exterior attracts the admiration of the passers-by, George and Tertschka dwell. Their work allows them ample leisure to cultivate their ground, to keep a goat and a brood of cackling fowls, and to bring up two chubby-cheeked, flaxen-haired children, who thrive amazingly behind the high hedge of sweet peas. In the evening they sit together before their cottage door, while the sunset dyes the sky with crimson flame, and their thoughts return to that well-remembered evening when first they saw each other upon the high summits of the Semmering, and to their past with all its suffering and its joys.

If these memories cast too sad a shadow on their minds they draw their laughing cherubs to their knees, and with the little, clinging arms around their necks, the silky hair against their cheeks, and the sweet innocent eyes regarding theirs, they forget, as if it were a dream, their past experience of the tears and sorrows which are the destined lot of every child of man.

LEOPOLD VON SACHER-MASOCH
1835–1895

THOU SHALT NOT KILL

COUNTESS MARA BAROVIC was the Circe, Omphale, and Semiramis of the mountainous part of Croatia.

Old and young (men, be it understood) were at her feet; and this despite the fact that she was regarded as plain-looking rather than pretty. Her ugliness, however, was the sort that strikes attention, attracts consideration, and excites interest. Moreover, she boasted a "past" that cast a halo about the present.

It was rumoured that one of her lovers had "accidentally" shot her husband while out hunting, and that this accident had occurred at a time when the Count had become "embarrassing."

Besides, she was original.

If it be true that woman is a work of art, as a celebrated poet has said, it must be borne in mind that in these days the agreeable and pleasing in art is no longer "the thing." Cruel, unadorned truth is preferred to draped loveliness, in love as well as in art.

The Countess belonged to the type demanded by the modern school. By her two most ardent admirers, Baron Kronenfels and Herr De Broda, she was termed respectively the iconoclast and the naturalist.

She mounted her horse like a hussar, was a dashing rider, and indulged a passionate fondness for hunting. One of her favourite pastimes was roaming field and forest in the picturesque costume of the Croatian peasant; and she could apply the horsewhip as dexterously and mercilessly to her creditors as to her refractory horses.

The fair lady was head over ears in debt. There was nothing she could longer call her own, not even the furniture in Château Granic, not even the false braid which adorned her well-poised little head.

The young aristocrats who danced attendance upon her ladyship explained the preference displayed by this Croatian Circe for the "wise men of the East"—as they called Kronenfels and De Broda—by the brilliant financial position of her two Jewish admirers.

Of the two, Baron Kronenfels's noble birth rested upon the more ancient foundation, and for that reason, perhaps, he enjoyed a certain priority in the fair lady's esteem. De Broda was a mere sapling in the forest of aristocracy, having been but recently ennobled. The unfeigned adoration he displayed for his armorial bearings made him the butt of endless practical jokes. His coat-of-arms glittered wherever it could find a resting-place. It shone upon the collar of his dog; it was emblazoned on his cigarettes, made especially for him at Laferme's.

Despite certain differences of taste, Kronenfels and De Broda were good friends, good comrades as well, for they were both officers in the Reserve. But how often does friendship stand its ground against the whispers of jealousy, especially when a woman's favour is the prize at stake? The relationship between the two grew strained and unnatural, and they were both secretly conscious that they were walking along a path where the least deviation from the centre would result in a catastrophe.

. . . .

The long-looked-for altercation took place one evening at the club. Wine had been flowing freely, the betting had been high. Countess Mara was the subject under discussion, and Baron Roukavina was telling an amusing story in that lady's eventful life.

She had not paid her taxes for years, was threatened with an execution, and had been moving heaven and earth to avert the impending disgrace. She had gone to Agram, from there to Buda-Pesth, importuning ministers, seeking favour with deputies, and had actually got so far as to ask an audience of the king. She had received hopeful promises everywhere, but the danger hung heavier over her head with the passing of every hour.

At this particular juncture Baron Meyerbach called on her, and offered to settle her troubles. Meyerbach was an intelligent fellow, with a good heart, and a purse with the proverbial open mouth; but Hungarian aristocracy could not receive him within its inner circle for the simple reason that he was a Jew.

"Have you so much influence?" asked the Countess. Her breath was almost taken away by the offer.

"Do not inquire too closely into my *modus operandi*, Countess," said the Baron. "It must be sufficient for you to know that my success is assured."

"And what do you ask in exchange for this service?"

"Simply this: that for the next two weeks you will take a walk with me every day for an hour in Vaitzen Street; that you will skate with me an hour in the park; and that each evening you will give me the privilege of escorting you to a different theatre."

"And is that all?"

"All."

The Countess yielded willingly to the Baron's terms. At the end of the fortnight she received a receipt in full for the payment of her taxes—thirty-two thousand florins—and Baron Meyerbach found Hungarian aristocracy ready to receive him with open arms even within its most inner of inner circles. The Countess had launched him.

The story closed in a burst of laughter, and the diplomat Meyerbach's health was drunk repeatedly and variously.

Of all the convivial party De Broda alone was silent. Finally, with Goethe's words in mind, he said in a low voice: "Everybody seeks money, and everybody clings to it."

Kronenfels flung his cards noisily on the table, looked savagely at De Broda, and said, with an ugly frown: "Do you imply by that that such a woman as Countess Mara Barovic would willingly let herself be blinded by money?"

De Broda shrugged his shoulders.

Springing from his seat, the Baron cried out scornfully: "You are a Jew."

For a moment participants and listeners seemed paralysed with astonishment; then De Broda, every nerve tingling with rage, hurled angrily back at his assailant: "You are another!"

A challenge to a duel was the result of the quarrel. Seconds were chosen on the spot, the weapons were to be pistols, and the oak forest near De Granic was to witness the affair early the following morning.

. . . .

De Broda had gone home. He was arranging his papers in order when Rabbi Solomon Zuckermandel walked into his sanctum.

"You are going to fight?" were the old man's first words.

"Yes."

"And with a Jew? No, Herr De Broda; you cannot, you dare not shoot a man! You will not do it."

"Pardon me, Rabbi Solomon, but my knowledge is somewhat deeper than yours in affairs of honour."

"Do you think so?" replied the old man, with an indulgent smile. "Ah, well, we shall see. You think we can wash our honour only in blood? My dear Herr De Broda, spotless honour needs no washing; and if it has a blemish, it cannot be effaced even by blood. The Baron called you a Jew. Is that an insult?"

"In the sense he attached to the word, yes."

"Not so. Neither in that sense nor in any other. Does the name of soldier become an insult because soldiers have deserted their flag? The Jews we call to mind when the word 'Jew' is used in reproach are those who have forsaken their standard. They are no longer Jews. Judaism is the fear of the Lord, love of liberty, love of the family and humanity. The honour of the Jew consists not in spilling blood, but in acting uprightly and doing good."

"You are right; but——"

"No, no. No 'buts.' When God in the midst of thunder and lightning gave the Tables of the Law to Moses on Mount Sinai, there were no 'buts'; He said: *'Thou shalt not kill!'* You are a Jew, Herr De Broda. In other words: Man, thou shalt not kill!"

The young fellow turned toward the window. The rabbi should not see his emotion. But the Jewish heart was touched, and the old man, who gave no thought to title and coat-of-arms, had conquered the aristocrat's pride and prejudice.

. . . .

Midnight had struck when Rabbi Solomon reached Kronenfels's quarters. The letter he handed the Baron from his adversary read as follows:

"DEAR SIR—You have insulted me grossly in calling me a Jew in the presence of a number of gentlemen, and have added to the insult, as it were, by making it at a time when Herr De Treitschke in Berlin has spoken of the Jews as the "schlamassl" [the plague of the Germans]. You are, however, an only son, the pride of your family, and I should like to avoid our meeting for to-morrow. You have often seen me hit the ace at a good range; and you know as well that I am no phrase-maker. I propose, therefore, that we shall both shoot in the air, and that we shall mutually exchange our word of honour not to speak of this arrangement. BRODA."

Kronenfels held the letter to the rabbi.

"What is to be done?" he asked, with a smile.

"Herr De Broda has proved himself a true Jew," responded

Zuckermandel gently. " Do not let him surpass you. Prove to him that you, too, are of a race which, boasting the most ancient civilisation, is above all others from the humanitarian standpoint."

Kronenfels wrote some hurried lines, which Rabbi Solomon conveyed to Herr De Broda before daybreak. The Baron's answer was couched in these words :

" DEAR SIR—I was about to address you when I received your note.

" I, too, should deeply regret having a mortal encounter with a young man upon whom so many hopes are placed.

" I accept your proposition.

" Moreover, between ourselves, be it said, we are Jews—in other words, descendants of ancestors whose house is more ancient than that of the Lichtensteins or Auerspergs, ancestors who have transmitted to us two qualities which Herr De Treitschke could scarcely possess, being as it were the offshoot of a somewhat recent civilisation : and these are, repugnance to shed blood, and the ' rachmonni '[1] of the Jewish heart. KRONENFELS."

The duel took place at six o'clock in the morning, the venerable oaks of De Granic forest casting an air of solemnity over the bloodless scene. The adversaries kept their word ; the pistols were discharged in the air ; and the witnesses declared that honourable satisfaction had been made. As De Broda and Kronenfels were shaking hands with hearty good-will, the brushwood parted, and old Rabbi Solomon slowly approached the young men. Raising his arms in benediction, he said, and the light of happiness beamed from his eyes : " Gentlemen, you are Jews ! "

[1] Mercifulness.